MW01137011

ENFORCE

Eagle Elite Book 1.5

by

Rachel Van Dyken

Enforce
by Rachel Van Dyken
www.rachelvandykenauthor.com

This is a work of fiction. Names, places, characters, and events are fictitious in every regard. Any similarities to actual events and persons, living or dead, are purely coincidental. Any trademarks, service marks, product names, or named features are assumed to be the property of their respective owners, and are used only for reference. There is no implied endorsement if any of these terms are used. Except for review purposes, the reproduction of this book in whole or part, electronically or mechanically, constitutes a copyright violation.

ENFORCE
Copyright © 2014 RACHEL VAN DYKEN
ISBN 13: 978-1505407778
ISBN: 150540777X
Cover Art Designed by P.S. Cover Design

To all of the Eagle Elite *fans who wanted to know* WHAT *in the world was going on in* Nixon's *head during* Elite...*this is for you!*

EAGLE ELITE SERIES

Elite
Evoke (free on WattPad)
Elect
Entice
Elicit
Enamor (included in *Elicit*)
Bang Bang
Enforce
Ember
Elude

Enchant (Prequel — free on WattPad)

CHAPTER ONE
The beginning of the very end

Nixon

I WATCHED AS THE parade of cars made their way through the black iron gates, as if somehow that barrier would protect them if the country went to war. Funny, they had no clue that the war — Lucifer himself — was already parading around inside, safe from the police, the feds, anyone who would be a threat.

Safe from everyone but me.

My eyes flickered to Phoenix on my right. He grinned as a new girl walked up to him and gave him a flirty wave.

I elbowed him hard in the ribs.

His grin turned sour as he glared at the girl and flipped her off.

Remember your place.

I'd said it once, twice, a million times to the guys, and they were still struggling with the idea that they weren't here to go to school, they weren't here to make friends. We weren't at peace. We were in a freaking war zone.

And Phoenix's family was our only key to redemption.

"That seems to be the last of them." Chase's cool gaze surveyed the main road that led into campus. It was easier on security to have one road in and one road out. Too bad life wasn't that convenient.

If someone didn't belong, it would take us minutes — scratch that — seconds to eliminate them, their family, all the while making it look like a very unfortunate accident.

"Wait." Tex squinted toward the iron gates. "I think there's one more car."

"The hell there is," I muttered. "I counted the cars. I've looked at the lists. We aren't missing anyone."

Chase yanked the list out of my hand and started reading through the names of all the freshman enrollees. His grin made me about lose my shit as he lifted his head and handed back the paper.

"I hear Wyoming's beautiful this time of year."

"What?" I jerked the list away and started greedily reading through the names.

One stood out.

Tracey Rooks, Female, 18, Casper, Wyoming.

"Great." I dropped the list onto the ground and smirked. "A girl who probably smells like cow shit. What's her background?"

Nobody answered.

I said it louder, this time grinding my teeth together.

Tex was the first to answer. "We couldn't really find any."

"Couldn't. Really. Find. Any," I repeated. "What the hell is that supposed to mean?"

"Look..." Tex shook his head. "...we have Sergio on it, but the girl doesn't really have a lot of information about her. Parents dead, Grandma dead, Grandpa her only living relative, and somehow her social as well as her birth certificate were both lost."

"Lost." I licked my lips. I told my head not to go there, told my heart to stay in my damn chest and stop hoping as images flooded my mind. Dark hair, dark eyes... *"Nixon, I'll save you."*

"Dude, you okay?" Chase elbowed me.

"Let's go welcome her to Eagle Elite."

Nobody moved.

"I said..." I started marching toward the girls' dorms. "...let's go welcome her."

"Why do I have a feeling this is a really bad idea?" Tex muttered under his breath.

"For once, Tex, keep your mouth shut and stay in the background, paste a shit-eating grin on your face, and let me and Chase deal with this. Do you think you can do that? Hmm?"

"Take a Xanax," Phoenix grumbled.

I sent a seething glare in his direction.

He mumbled a curse and walked off with Tex to wait by the tree while we continued the next few feet to the girls' dorms.

The car was a rental.

The grandpa was ancient.

The girl was... young.

And she had shit as belongings. Her suitcase was covered with stickers. Her grandpa handed her a small box, and I could have sworn I saw a tear escape her eye and roll down her smooth cheek.

"Hell no," I grumbled. "She'll be destroyed here."

"Won't last five minutes," Chase agreed.

"Tears." I wiped my face with my hands. "Tell me I'm not seeing tears."

"Girls don't cry here."

"They don't," I agreed.

"She isn't like them."

"No."

3

"We need Mo."

I laughed at that. "We need a miracle." With a curse, I quickly dialed the number for orientation and made arrangements for said *New Girl* to be moved to the third floor. Mo, my twin sister, was supposed to be on that same floor. I figured she needed all the help she could get. No way would little Wyoming survive the year with anyone else, not that I was happy about it. I mean, in hindsight that was probably my first mistake.

I'd officially invited her into my life — by way of my sister.

"New girl's here," I said loud enough for Tracey to turn around and gape. "So squeaky-clean and innocent. Like a little lamb. Right, Chase?" I tilted my head and offered her a smirk.

The old man reached in his jacket. It was a move I knew well. Another clue. He wasn't *what* he said he was. He wasn't *who* he said he was. As if noticing my calculating glare, he removed his hand and offered a forced smile. "A welcoming committee? This place sure is nice."

I had to respect his control. The way he protectively stood in front of Tracey as if he was the only thing standing in the way of my devouring her.

"Is there a problem?" He scratched his head, then rolled back his sleeves, revealing a small tattoo. One I'd seen as a child but couldn't place.

"Do I know you?" I blurted.

He laughed. "Know many farmers out in Wyoming?"

It was his tone that convinced me, the way his shook his head slightly, waiting for my challenge. It was the same look my uncle gave me when he wanted me to stop pushing.

It was the look that my dad had taught me when I was ten and had witnessed my first torture.

The girl was still staring at us. Easy target. I'd leave the old man alone; he reminded me too much of mine. And I didn't need that reminder. Not now.

I lifted my arms and stretched lazily.

The girl's eyes went wide as she stared at my body.

Chase hit me in the back.

I sauntered forward and tilted her chin toward me, closing her mouth in the process. "Much better." I licked my lips and fought the urge to kiss her. Yeah, I was losing my shit. "We'd hate for our charity case to choke on an insect on her first day." Her lips trembled as she looked from me to her Grandpa. I released her, before she could do anything, and walked past with Chase in tow.

I needed to talk to the girl at registration anyway. We disappeared behind the building, but I'd be back. I just needed the Grandpa to leave.

Within seconds, I peered around the building just as the rental car pulled away. And the girl was all mine. My heart thudded against my chest, and, for a second, I regretted what I was about to do.

But every possible outcome ended with either her death or her in danger. Weirdly, I didn't want someone like her at Eagle Elite. She didn't belong in my world.

She deserved a picket fence.

A husband.

A good college experience without classmates who'd rather see her commit suicide than survive the next four years.

They would destroy her.

And she would make it so damn easy to do so.

The only way was to beat them to it — to be the first, marking her as our target, our plaything.

Nobody messed with what was mine.

And in the end, nobody would mess with her. They'd allow me to entertain them with her innocence. I'd dangle her in front of them like a carrot, and at the end of the day, she'd be untouchable.

I sighed as she looked up at the building, gaping like someone who'd been homeschooled and never seen a skyscraper before.

She was too skinny.

I made a mental note to get her one of my access cards — she didn't need to know how much they cost — or that every single student at EE would kill to have one. Mo would take care of the rest.

She'd eat with us.

She'd want for nothing.

It was the least I could do after what I was about to make her endure.

Licking my lips, I approached her again, this time, damning myself to hell with each step I took. "Are you lost?"

"Nope." She grinned. Damn, it made her prettier. "Apparently I live in the United States." With a shrug, she tried and failed to lift her heavy suitcase and nearly toppled over onto her cute ass.

I muffled a laugh, knowing that Chase was doing the exact same thing. Being mean to her would be like kicking a puppy. But the world was ugly. I just hated that I would be her tutor in the ways of reality — her prince of darkness.

Hell, I would have done anything to be the hero.

"I'm Nixon." I stood directly in front of her, shifting my eyes from her poor-fitting clothes to her ugly shoes.

"Tracey, but everyone calls me Trace." She held out her hand.

I itched to touch it.

To touch her skin.

Instead, I scowled, shook her hand, then wiped that same hand on my jeans as if she was diseased.

"Rules."

"What?" She took a step back.

Chase moved past me, "He's right. As cute as you are, Farm Girl, someone needs to tell you the rules."

Her innocent gaze flickered between the two of us. "Can it be fast?"

Yeah, again, I almost lost my mind. Chase was probably ready to shit his pants. The last person who had talked back to him was Phoenix, and that had ended with a few broken bones and a trip to the dentist.

"You hear that, Chase?" I said, amused. "She likes it fast."

"Pity." Chase took a step closer, nearly touching her with his body. "I'd love to give it to her slow." His eyes raked her in as if she was the first girl he'd ever seen in his entire existence. Jealousy surged through me. What the hell? She wasn't his. Not that she was mine, but still. He was standing too close, too close.

"The rules." He stepped back. My heartbeat returned to normal, "No speaking to the Elect, unless you've been asked to speak to them." He circled around her, staring a little too long at her ass before he continued.

"Who are the--"

"—Nope. You've already broken a rule. I'm speaking, New Girl." Chase smirked. "Geez, Nixon, this one's going to be hard to break in."

"They always are," I said, lifting her chin with my hand. "But I think I'll enjoy *this one*." The first true thing I'd said. I would enjoy it too much. I'd enjoy her too much because she reminded me of someone I used to know. Someone who'd offered to save me when I was already past saving, someone who'd wiped my tears and cried as if they were her own.

Chase continued with the rules. Making me sicker as her face continued to fall.

Finally she asked, "Is that all?"

"No." Raw desire pulsed through me as I approached her, needing to touch her, needing to make sure she was real even though I knew I was acting like a complete and utter lunatic. Chase and I would have words later. He knew me better than I knew myself sometimes. I was going too far — pushing myself, pushing him.

My hand caressed her face then moved down her smooth neck to her shoulder. I moved my hand to her neck and then grazed her trembling lips with my thumb. I wanted to claim her, possess her, make her scream —not with fear, but with utter ecstasy. I had no idea who she was, but she made me want. And that was the problem.

For the first time in years.

I wanted.

I wasn't allowed to want.

I had to die to my own desires.

Because in the grand scheme of things? It wasn't about me. It was about blood, family, protection. Blood in, blood out.

Her eyes dilated. Furious that she'd reacted so easily, upset with myself for making my own body suffer, I snapped.

"You feel this? Memorize it now, because as of this moment, you can't touch us. We are untouchable. If you as much as sneeze in our direction, if you as much breathe the same air in my atmosphere, I will make your life hell. This touch, what you feel against your skin, will be the only time you feel another human being as powerful as me near you. So like I said... feel it, remember it, and maybe one day your brain will do you the supreme favor of forgetting what it felt like to have someone like me touching you. Then, and only then, will you be able to be happy with some mediocre boyfriend and pathetic life." Away from me. Away from it all. Safe.

A few more tears escaped down her cheek.

And I knew in that moment it was the beginning of the end.

My end.

My downfall.

My demise.

CHAPTER TWO
And the bad luck just keeps coming...

Nixon

BY THE TIME WE reached the guys on the opposite end of the lawn, I'd almost gotten my shaking under control. I looked like a damn drug addict in need of another hit.

"Hey, you cool, man?" Phoenix's eyes scanned me from head to toe, then narrowed as I stuffed my hands in my pockets and gave him a shrug.

"Course."

"New Girl's hot," Chase said, saving my ass. "And we all know Nixon's been as celibate as a priest these past few years so, yeah, he's probably having sexual withdrawals."

"Ass." I smacked him in the head, relief coursing through my body. "I don't have sexual withdrawals."

"She's innocent enough to draw your attention." Chase winked. "You always liked the pure ones. Hurry and get your dick under control before you embarrass yourself, man."

I glared.

"Pure." Phoenix snorted. "Not for long, especially at this school. She's going to get eaten alive."

"Right," I agreed then looked back toward the dorm.

Why the hell hadn't Mo answered any of my texts?

"Tex?" My phone was blank, no new messages, "Heard from Mo?"

He pulled out his phone and shook his head. "Nope, why?"

"Family stuff," I lied. "Look, I'm going to go see if she's in her room. Meet me back at the cave in a few, kay?"

"Sure."

Tex and Chase were already walking away from me, but Phoenix stood his ground, his piercing gaze making me want to punch him. What was his angle? We were already on shaky ground now that he knew we weren't just investigating every family — but that our focus was on his.

He said if it came to a fight, he'd pick our side.

The problem?

The minute he went against blood he was a dead man anyway.

I didn't envy his position. Being a part of a family that wouldn't protect him worth shit — but would kill him if he chose to do the right thing. His father was a piece of work. And was still refusing to meet with me.

"Are you sure everything's okay?" Phoenix asked, his tone light but his eyes still dark, like he'd lost all hope.

"Yup." I gave a firm nod. "I'll see you later, alright?"

"Yeah, yeah." He waved me off and went after the guys.

Once they were out of sight, I ran back toward the girls' dorms and took the elevator to Mo's floor. What room was she in again?

I sent Tex a quick message.

"United States, bro. Seriously? How'd you forget that?"

Cursing, I forced my phone into the back pocket of my jeans and walked to the end of the hall where Mo's room was. No wonder I'd thought to put Trace in that room — it was my twin's. Damn me to hell.

I knocked twice. Then pounded the door and yelled her name.

A few doors down the hall opened.

And then the giggling and whispering commenced.

There was a reason I hadn't hooked up with any of the girls at Elite. They were ridiculous, and I didn't have time for ridiculous.

Rolling my eyes, I tried the handle. It was unlocked. I let myself in and closed the door behind me. I'd wait for her. It's not like she would be hours. Classes hadn't started, and she wasn't allowed off campus unless she asked my permission, and it wasn't mealtime.

I went over to her bed and sat, enjoying the quiet around me. How long would it be like this, I wondered? How long would I be stuck in a world I didn't fit into? Eagle Elite wasn't my home; it wasn't what I wanted with my life. What I wanted was to run the business away from the watchful eyes of Elite. What I got was the life of a lie, the reputation of a sinner, and the inability to escape.

Girls started laughing from the hall. I heard a few shouts, and then someone tried the door.

It was a trick door, one had to both turn and push at the same time. If the girl on the opposite end didn't know that — then that meant she must be the new roommate.

Great, another girl I could scare shitless.

I waited.

The door didn't budge.

I heard huffing on the other end, and then the door went flying open. The girl fell to the ground in a heap directly in front of my feet.

I fought the urge to say *"I kind of like you this way."* Especially when those brown eyes slowly grazed up my body and scowled in my face. Hell yeah, it had been too long since I'd been with a girl...

Because for some strange, terrifying reason, I wanted to

slam the door behind her and push her against it.

Dip my fingers in her hair, tip my tongue into her mouth, dip my—

A few girls congregated at the door.

I offered my hand to help her up then remembered that I wasn't being the hero or the gentleman. Before our fingers brushed, I put on a leather glove and smirked. "Germs. You understand."

Scowling, she slapped my hand away and got to her feet on her own. Impressive. She was brave. Too bad I was going to break her — shatter that courage until there was nothing left.

A few girls started to giggle.

Cursing, I shouted, "Leave us!"

Doors slammed down the hall, blanketing us once again in silence. Damn it. When I'd asked orientation to put Trace on her floor, I hadn't meant in her room, in my sister's room.

Shit. They were going to pay for that.

Trace's lower lip trembled as her eyes closed. She shook as multiple doors slammed down the hall, and with each tremble of her body — I wanted. With each twitch of her lips — I was tempted.

Finally, the slamming stopped. I walked behind Trace and closed the door. She didn't budge.

I couldn't take it any longer. I had to be closer. My sanity was at stake. I swallowed and walked up behind her, my lips grazing the velvety softness of her ear. "You don't like rules, do you, New Girl?"

She shivered in response to my voice.

I almost touched her then.

Almost threw the entire act way.

Almost threw it all away.

But it would have been selfish of me to satisfy my own damn curiosity and needs, when she had no idea what was at stake, what she was risking by being at Elite.

I walked around her and smiled. "There is one final rule."

"What?" She tilted her chin into the air, earning my approval for faking confidence like a champ.

Licking my lips, I gave her a predatory glare and stalked toward New Girl. I pushed her body up against the door — exactly how I wanted her — trapped against the door, in my arms.

"You earn the right to use what we have." Actually that was only partially true, but I wanted her to be too terrified to question me. "The elevators are locked. The Elect have copies of the keycard. The pools, the weight rooms — everything you have access to, even your food, has a keycard."

I reached into my pocket and pulled out one of the extras that I'd made for Chase earlier that week. It wasn't the typical card we gave to new students, but it would do the job. Chances were, since Mo had put her under her own protection, it would just be a matter of time before she weaseled her way into our lunch hour. May as well invite her first — plus. I could watch her.

Not that I wanted to be creepy and stalk her.

It was from a business standpoint — nothing else. She needed to stay silent; she needed to appear to be our plaything.

And no chance in hell was I putting her with the rest of the student body.

"Say thank you." I was a jackass.

"For what?" Her eyes pooled with tears.

"Allowing you to eat, of course," I said in a smooth voice. Hating that her tears were making me want to hold her close — but mostly, hating that her tears reminded me of the girl who still haunted my dreams.

"What?"

"I'm not finished talking." I was pissed she wasn't afraid, that she reminded me of a past I couldn't forget — and a future I couldn't escape. "This key card gains you access into the elevator only once a week. It also gains you access into the cafeteria, twice a day. Not three times. We don't want you gaining weight." Another lie. I was going to freaking add protein powder to her food if she got too skinny, but I needed her insecure, so insecure that she'd rely on us for everything, so insecure that she wanted to leave Eagle Elite at break. "Use it wisely, and if you impress me with your ability to follow directions, I may just up your freedom. Until then..." I shrugged and cleared my throat. "...move aside."

She didn't budge.

I repeated myself — I never repeated myself.

Slamming my hand on the door beside her head, I leaned in, my lips almost brushing hers. Blood roared in my ears as my body scolded me for not taking what was right in front of me. It would be. So. Damn. Easy.

Too bad I wanted hard.

It was my life motto. If it wasn't hard — it wasn't worth having.

Unexpectedly, while I was in my daydream, her little hands pushed against my chest.

They were warm.

If I got shot that night, I'd still remember that one thing. Her hands were warm.

I liked it.

Too much.

And I hated being touched.

She pissed me off.

"Did you just touch me?"

"You threatened me!"

"I threaten everyone." I tried not to crack a smile at her huffy attitude.

"Then you're a bully."

I hadn't been called a bully since sixth grade. I opened my mouth to say something rude then snapped it shut. "So you wanted to touch me?"

Her face erupted in flames. Interesting.

"No." Her teeth clenched. "I want you to leave me the hell alone!"

"Say please." God, I could just devour her.

"Please?" she begged. What I wouldn't do to hear her say my name, to beg me over and over again.

She wasn't for me, I reminded myself. This wasn't a game. I blocked out the emotions, the warm feeling surging through my blood. "Hell. No." My lips did touch hers then, briefly, enough for me to memorize the texture of her mouth — enough for me to torture myself for the next five years of my life, if I lived that long.

I reached for the door and jerked it open.

Mo stood there, a cheerful look on her face, and then she looked behind me, and I could have sworn she was ready to reach for a gun.

I slammed the door again.

"I thought you were leaving." Smart-ass New Girl said.

"Change of plans," I muttered then went over to the window. Good, the games were still set up. Elite was all about extreme sports. Kids had been jumping out of their windows all day instead of taking the elevators. I'd never actually participated in welcome day or the games, but it was clearly a day of firsts.

"What are you going to do?" she shrieked. "Shimmy down the drain pipe?"

"Nixon! Open the damn door!" my sister shouted.

With a laugh, I stepped out onto the ledge.

New Girl shrieked.

It was cute that she was concerned, and here I'd thought she was going to push me.

She grabbed my shirt. "Are you insane?"

Yes. Very much so.

"Hands off," I yelled and then jumped into the air. I freefell for a total of three seconds before I hit the blown-up tarp.

"Nixon!" I heard her scream.

• Which was probably why, when I landed, my grin was huge. She cared. I was a total ass to her, and she cared.

That stupid warm feeling tried to spread through my body again. Without thinking, I blew her a kiss and jogged off.

Nearly running directly into Phoenix.

"Good show," he said in a hollow voice. "Did you take New Girl's virginity too, or was that not on the menu this afternoon?"

My hand clenched into a fist. He was baiting me.

"She bores me," I said in an even voice. "I was looking for Mo, and I had a keycard to give out."

Phoenix's eyebrows shot up. "And where did you put her? Red Cafeteria? The commons?" He shuddered.

"With us," I said evenly.

"So..." He fell into step beside me. "...you're bringing us a toy — how... nice."

"Don't play with her."

"Oh, I won't." He grinned. "I'd hate to take away your favorite bone. Besides, I don't do seconds."

With that, he walked off.

CHAPTER THREE
Who I really am: nothing.

Phoenix

WE ALL HAD JOBS to do. Mine? Make sure my dad didn't lose his shit for the billionth time — oh, and become his personal punching bag when he fancied it. The guys didn't know how bad things had gotten, and I sure as hell wasn't going to tell them the evil I experienced on a daily basis. The way I saw things — I, at least, was used to it. Used to the garbage, used to the hate, the pain, the rage — sometimes I felt like a sponge. My father was the water, and all he did was pour into me and squeeze.

Sighing, I knocked on his door again.

He was the dean, Nixon's way of keeping the De Lange boss close.

"What?" He jerked the door open; his eyes were pinpoints. Great, so he'd been using again.

"Pops..." I cracked my knuckles. "...the rounds are done. I need to get to class, but I wasn't sure if you wanted any help with—"

"Help?" he interrupted. "You're such a disappointment,

RACHEL VAN DYKEN

Phoenix. I groomed you to be strong. Now look at you," he sneered. "A pathetic made man for the Abandonato boss. You aren't even second in command — hell, you aren't even third. You're just a shit foot soldier."

"As opposed to you?" I rolled my eyes. "A boss to a scorned family in debt up to their eyeballs, selling God-knows-what to God-knows-who, and trying their damnedest to get away with murder? Really? I'm the loser in this scenario? Nixon's the most powerful man I know, and I'm his best friend. We just put up with you because killing you would be frowned upon."

My father's eyes narrowed before he spit in my face. "And I just put up with you because I like to torture you."

I wiped the spit from my cheek and turned to walk away.

"Wait," he called.

I froze, dread pooling in my stomach.

"We have a job."

"Job?" I refused to turn around, didn't want him to see the interest in my eyes. We'd been trying to re-fill the family coffers for decades, it seemed. Side jobs were the only way to make sure we could live the lifestyle we'd all been used to. Nixon sure as hell didn't pay me.

So I worked for Satan — my father — in order to own a new Corvette. Sue me. He had me by the balls, and he knew it. I'd kill him myself if I could make it look like an accident.

"Yeah, a few girls were brought in."

My knees knocked together.

"Virgins, but not for long…"

My stomach rolled.

"Just do the usual, and when you're finished, keep your favorite… as payment."

Was he for real? Bile rose in my throat. I choked it down and nodded firmly. "How much are you getting?"

"Half a mil," he said in a low voice. "Just make sure the girls are broken in. I'll text you the address."

"Right." I licked my lips and walked to the elevator, fingers shaking as I tried to hit *Lobby* twice before the button finally lit up.

The elevator doors opened and closed.

I leaned my forehead against the cool metal doors and fought tears as they tried to surface and roll down my cheeks. Men didn't cry. But I was no man. I'd stopped being a man and morphed into a monster.

Into my father.

Because I was going to go visit four innocent girls, ruin their lives, and drag them into hell with me — all for money. All for pride I'd never had. All for a father I'd never loved.

The doors opened.

Banners were everywhere in the registrar building, welcoming new students. Smiling faces mocked me as I walked slowly toward the main doors.

The last time I smiled — the last time it was real — was when Nixon said he'd be my best friend.

I hadn't smiled since.

My dad had made sure of that, because made men didn't cry. They also didn't smile. They showed no emotion because emotion was weakness.

Just like love.

It was why I couldn't be with girls — at least not in a normal way. I was violent with the way I took them. When girls talked about making love, when they gushed about romance, I usually ran in the other direction because it wasn't something I was capable of.

After all, a monster only knows what a monster sees.

And I was a monster.

Sex was violent.

Sex was murder.

Sex was necessary in order to put money in my father's pocket.

And one day… sex was going to destroy me.

CHAPTER FOUR
Girls, girls, girls

Chase

I HATED THE FIRST day of classes. We'd been doing this for four freaking years, and it was always the same. Scan the perimeter to make sure students are where they're supposed to be. Check in with Nixon at all times and make sure Phoenix and Tex keep their pants on.

Right.

Check, check, and double-check.

Grumbling, I made my way around the freshman dorms. The hairs on the back of my arms stood on end.

"Hey, Chase!" A few girls waved in my direction and giggled.

Ugh. Part of my cover? Being a whore. Right, it wasn't that much of a stretch for someone of my appetite, but it was getting old. I may have needed to make sure Tex and Phoenix didn't go roaming into restricted territory, but that didn't mean I didn't take advantage of the position I'd been given.

The girls were all the same. Damn, they even smelled the same. Nothing new, nothing exciting. I offered a lame wave back and winked as I rounded the corner of the dorms just in time to see Mo and Trace come barreling out the front door, grabbing at their skirts fluttering in the wind.

Wow, how pathetic was I? The most entertaining thing I'd seen all day, and it was the New Girl picking up her underwear off the concrete. Maybe I did need to get laid.

Rather than walk away and flip them off in the process, I hid behind a damn tree and watched.

Nixon was going to kill Mo; whatever the hell she was wearing, it sure wasn't a skirt. She'd been getting braver and braver, trying to catch Tex's attention and all that.

If she tried any harder, poor Tex was going to spontaneously combust. It was hard enough for him to keep his eyes inside his head whenever she walked by. Add heels and a short skirt to the mix, and the poor guy was ready to get high just to get rid of the constant state of arousal.

Trace ran in front of her suitcase and grabbed at another shirt, her face alight with life... something I hadn't seen in a while. A girl whose smile was actually real. A girl who smiled like she meant it, like she actually had something to smile about.

I sucked in a breath and held it. I held it while she stuffed her clothes back into the suitcase and looked in my direction.

I held her gaze, knowing she probably didn't see me, but not caring that I was drinking my fill of her. Dark brown hair swirled around her shoulders, her eyes were dark, but rather than them making her look plain, they made her look warm. Damn. I needed warm in my life.

She was like chocolate.

Sweet, innocent, full.

Speaking of walking around in a constant state of arousal. I shook my head and started walking in the other direction.

Warm girls? The ones with real smiles? They weren't exactly for me. They weren't for any of us. Because the thing about warmth? It reminded me of blood. When something was warm, it meant it was healthy, ripe for the picking. And, being who I was, I knew it wasn't only a matter of time before I sliced open the forbidden fruit and took my fill.

Leaving a corpse in my wake.

After making the rounds again, I ran back to my room and changed clothes. It was time for the welcome party.

One of these days I was going to take down that damn banner and replace it with one that said Welcome to Elite 666 or something just as appropriate, because that's what it was: hell.

The people here were possessed. Seriously. Imagine taking every single rich kid with a daddy-god complex and placing them — no, scratch that — *locking* them in a fifty mile radius. Oh, and giving them as much money as they want without a curfew. Right, it was like Sodom and Gomorrah up in here, and I hated every freaking minute of it.

Four years, and we still weren't any closer to figuring out what the De Langes were up to. We'd gone down every trail. Every single piece of information had been received and studied.

And still. Nothing.

It was wearing on Nixon.

It was wearing on all of us.

"Hey man," I called, when Nixon walked in looking like hell.

"I hate today." Nixon swore and grabbed the fifth off the counter and took a giant swig. "God created the earth in seven days, right? Rested on the last day?"

"Yeah." I squinted. What the hell was he babbling about?

"So…" Nixon took another swig. "…why did he create women again?"

I smirked. "You really need me to give you an anatomy lesson? And if the answer's yes? Number one, you're already drunk, and number two, pretty sure Tex would do a better job, you know, on account that he uses hand gestures."

Nixon gave me his own hand gesture.

I'd never seen him so... upset, and I'd seen him upset a lot. The kid was tortured half his life and still found a reason not to murder people in their sleep.

"So..." I sat down next to him and grabbed the bottle. "...what's up? Some chick turn you down?"

Nixon snorted. "Please. Like I've ever been turned down."

"Holy shit." I gaped.

Nixon looked away and rubbed his hands through his hair then slapped his face.

"Someone rejected you?"

"No." Nixon's jaw flexed.

"Yes." I grinned. Wow. Best day of my life. "Who was it? I won't tell Tex or Phoenix."

"The hell you won't." Nixon swiped the bottle from my hands. "And it was just a misunderstanding."

"Oh." I licked my lips, enjoying myself way more than I should. "So was it a language barrier? You spoke sweet Sicilian nothings into her ear, and she thought you were high?"

"Chase—"

"Or were you speaking English, and she just wasn't the crunchiest fry at the bottom of the box? Hmm?"

"She—" Nixon's mouth slammed shut. His teeth clenched together. "She's irritating, stupid, and not even pretty."

"Not even pretty?" I repeated. "So why do you care?"

One thing about Nixon? He was a freaking raccoon. Loved things that were shiny and pretty. His cars? All black and shiny. His guns? Shiny. He was a collector of all things pretty — almost OCD about it. We all had our quirks, so I didn't judge him for his.

Me? I loved women. LOVED them — all shapes and sizes. They all had something to offer, you know, as long as they weren't talking.

Tex, on the other hand, memorized body language. Never play poker with the guy because your chances are higher of getting hit by an asteroid than actually beating him. It was part of his ploy. Act stupid and nobody suspects anything. Sometimes it freaked Nixon out — how intelligent Tex was. He was like one of those child geniuses, not that Nixon wasn't. That guy was also terrifyingly smart.

And Phoenix.

Well Phoenix was the guy you wanted on your side when you killed people, because he enjoyed it so effing much that it was a bit terrifying. Watching Phoenix and Tex torture someone? Well, let's just say it brought a whole new meaning to the word *nightmare*.

Nixon groaned. "I'm just tired, didn't sleep well last night."

"Right, you're tired. That's why this chick didn't like you. Stupid bags under your eyes. Damn you, sleep!" I shook my fist and punched him in the arm. "Seriously though, get your shit together."

"When have you ever," Nixon spat, "and I do mean *ever* had to say that to me?"

"When we were ten," I said softly, "and her parents died and—"

"Fine." Nixon got up, his knees cracking. "You're right. It's time to get ready for the party. Screw her…"

"Because you kind of want to?" I offered jokingly.

Nixon rolled his eyes. "She means nothing."

"Keep telling yourself that."

"I have to," Nixon whispered. "I really do."

CHAPTER FIVE
And it just keeps getting better.

Nixon

EVERYTHING WAS IN PLACE. De Lange, the ass, couldn't be more thrilled about enrollment that year. But me? It made me nervous. Too many kids, too many background checks, too many possible loose ends. Mother of God, just shoot me now and get it over with. If I wasn't so tired from staying up until four a.m. doing said background checks, I'd probably be more amused at the fact that Mo had taken Trace as her new pet.

Like a cow.

Only cows weren't pets.

And Trace was like a goddess come to life. No make that a freaking ghost of a goddess come to make my life an absolute freaking hell.

I pasted a smile on my face like I always did and waited in the middle of the room as students started trickling in for the welcome party. The ones that waved were regular students. The ones that nodded? All in my pocket. Let's just say, I had more in my pocket than was probably legal at a private university, but this was the last year we had.

I had to get it right.

To not only clear my family's name... but to avenge her death. If I was being completely honest, it was more about her than me.

But I'd never tell my family that. I'd take it to my grave, just like she took all her innocence to hers.

My throat clogged up.

Damn it!

I closed my eyes and pinched the bridge of my nose. Not now. I couldn't show weakness. But all I could see were her giant brown eyes and wide smile. The same smile that had trusted me to make everything better when things seemed so dark.

My best friend.

Taken from me.

I'd been in the box that night... the night she died. My father had put me there on account that I'd shamed the family again by dropping my glass on the floor. It had slipped out of my hands, not my fault, but according to him, lazy, worthless, my fault. Even if I hadn't dropped that glass or been put in that box, it wasn't like I could have done anything. But in my mind... at least I could have tried, right? How stupid was that? I would have been what? Ten? Most likely I would have died too.

But at least, maybe, possibly, I would have died with some dignity, because I was convinced if I could have reached her fingertips, my last breath would have been her name — my last touch her skin. And I would have prayed for God to save her soul and take mine in its place. After all, when you're born into sin, you don't really have a lot to bargain for.

The room got progressively louder as more students filed in.

Chase approached, drink in hand, people congregated around, and I was so not feeling it. I just wanted the world to pause. For a minute. I needed a giant-ass timeout.

Time. Funny, people have no idea how much of it is wasted with their own insignificance. I wasted nothing.

Because in the end, she'd been given nothing. How was it fair for me to waste time I'd been given when she didn't have any at all?

I closed my eyes again and forced a smile when Chase smacked me on the back and threatened to cut off my balls if I didn't get it together.

He always saw through me.

Just like I always saw through his bullshit.

"Well, hot damn." Phoenix whistled next to me.

I jerked my head up, opening my eyes.

Trace walked in, wearing what I can only assume was something out of Mo's closetful of whores — not horrors. Whores.

"Damn it." I kept the mocking grin in place then stared her down. "Is she trying to get that much attention? Even after she cried in front of us?"

"Well," Chase's eyebrows rose a fraction. "She's getting it. She's getting all of it, and I can't say I blame any one of those guys for staring."

"Stare any harder, and I will personally remove your eyes from your face," I growled, "with a freaking fork."

"Whoa." Tex coughed. "Territorial much?"

"No..." I smirked. "...just... tired."

"Right." Chase and Tex shared a look. "Tired makes you look so sexually frustrated you're about five seconds away from humping the leg right off that chair."

"Tex..." I clenched my jaw until it popped. "...go irritate someone else before I shoot you in the damn toe."

"Wouldn't be the first time," he grumbled, walking off.

Chase put his hand on my shoulder. "Nixon, whatever you're going to do, just don't... okay?"

I shook his hand off and shrugged. "When you're the boss? That's when you can tell me what to do. Until then?

Screw off."

CHAPTER SIX

Why did she have to look so damn tempting?

Nixon

I TOOK OFF MY sunglasses and allowed myself the pleasure of slowly examining Trace from head to toe. Damn, I was going to strangle Mo for dangling her in front of me, and, by the look on her face, my sister knew exactly what she was doing.

Her gaze narrowed in, lips pressed together as if to say, *"Well? How did I do with her?"*

"Nice work." I nodded to Mo. "She looks like she actually belongs here."

Mo rolled her eyes. "She does belong here, you idiot." Her warm hands cupped my face as she air-kissed each cheek and stepped back. Our father had been weird about Mo showing me respect, even though we were the same age. I was the man; she was the woman. In his opinion, she would always be beneath him, and beneath me. Mo also knew it pissed me off when she faked that type of loyalty and love. Hell, I knew she cared, but that didn't make me feel any better when she gripped my hand and slid a note into it.

Well, shit.

"The way I see it..." I grinned, stuffing the note into my back pocket. "...she won a silly contest. The same contest we put on every year so that the poor underprivileged people of the world are able to join the high society. She..." I made a point of looking directly at her and leaning in, smirking so she could see all hostility, so she could freaking feel how badly I could hurt her—destroy her if I so wished. "...is just a number."

Trace's cheeks flushed red as she spat, "At least I'm not an ass."

I seriously had to fight to keep the shock from my face... and then it was nearly impossible not to laugh. Did she just call me an ass? In front of the Elect? Serious? It was funny as hell because she had no idea that in that moment there were most likely three guns trained on her, just waiting for her to make a false move. We didn't know anything about her yet — no background; therefore, she was a threat, and she'd just blatantly threatened me.

I licked my lips and approached her slowly allowing the vision of her flushed skin to burn into my memory. I lifted my hands. To do what? I wasn't sure, but the minute my fingers grazed her wrist the microphone gave some shrill feedback, making me step away.

"Is this on?" Thomas spoke into the microphone. "Attention, everyone."

Damn it. I forgot about my speech. I made my way toward the stage, my eyes slowly taking in the security around the perimeter. Hell, it would suck to get shot on the first day of school.

"Your student body president would like to welcome you all back to school!" Thomas clapped. Everyone else followed. A few girls tried to grab me but were quickly pushed away by security. No chance in hell would I let those senior skanks touch me.

People started chanting my name. Great, let Trace hear it,

let her know how much control I had, how I could ruin her life, break her neck, or protect her from such things by merely snapping my fingers or nodding my head.

My eyes met hers. All color had drained from her face as I started to speak. "I'd like to introduce someone. She's new here," Trace looked ready to pass out. "And I want everyone to give her a warm, Eagle Elite welcome! Please clap her hands for..." I paused, waiting to see if Trace would pass out or lift her eyebrow in a challenging glare. Ah, so it was going to be the glare. Nice. "...Dr. Tessa Stevens, our new history professor."

Trace visibly exhaled.

I smirked at her. Checkmate.

She matched my smirk with a smile of her own — the type of smile any man would sell his soul to gain just a glimpse of — and she's back in the game.

I waited for Dr. Stevens to wave and then addressed the crowd again. "Now, I know all of you are eager to start the welcome party." I winked at Trace and licked my lips.

She paled again. God, it was fun watching her every reaction. Swear, I could stand up there all day saying whatever shit came to mind, and I'd be happy... probably for the first time ever.

Mo wrapped a protective arm around Trace and tilted her head in a challenge.

Aw, Mo had to step in and ruin my nice-guy routine. Well, fine. Two could play that game. And now was as good of time as any to throw Trace to the wolves. At least here I could control what happened. Here she wouldn't be hurt, just... embarrassed, humbled. Yes, it was the perfect environment. And though my heart for some reason decided to thump against my chest in warning, I did it anyway.

I made the next move.

With a grimace, I scooted my pawn to her side of the board.

Chase had already moved behind Trace. No chance in hell he knew what I was doing, but the bastard was too smart by half. I nodded my head slightly and coughed into my right hand.

Chase knew the drill. Bring forth the prisoner and all that shit.

"I'm sure you've all noticed we have a new student. The winner of the annual Eagle Elite Lottery registered this morning." My smile widened to cheesy proportions. "Trace, why don't you come up here and say a few words?"

She mouthed *no* and dug her heels into the ground, but Chase already had ahold of her pretty tightly. Without effort, he scooted her toward the stage while Tex held a furious Mo. I tilted my head at her and offered a small smile while she managed to flip me off.

I blew her a kiss.

People clapped.

I held out my hand for Trace to take when she go to the stage. I wasn't that heartless to let her trip in those heels on the way up the stairs. I had plans for her, after all, and they didn't include that type of embarrassment.

Her eyes fell to my hand.

She hesitated.

I cleared my throat.

With shaking fingers, she gripped my hand and held on tight. And, I swear, in that moment I was transported back to my childhood.

"Nixon, Nixon!" She ran around and around in circles, driving me crazy before plopping down on the ground. "I think I scraped my knee."

"Are those tears?" I tried to sound disgusted when really my heart was breaking. I hated it when she cried.

"No." She crossed her arms. "Promise. I just got waters in my eyes."

"Waters in your eyes?" I repeated gruffly then held out my

hand. "How about I help you up, and we get that scrape cleaned up?"

Her giant brown eyes ate me up. So trusting, so... loving.
"Okay, Nixon... and you won't hurt me?"

"No." I gripped her pudgy little hand in mine and kissed it "I would never hurt you."

I released Trace's hand so quick I damn-near tripped, fell over backward, and collided with the back of the stage. Was that it? Was this one girl going to make me lose my mind? Maybe because she reminded me of her innocence, of what I'd lost. Of what I'd ruined by my inability to be old enough to avenge her death. Throat tightening, I quickly spoke into the microphone, "Trace Rooks, everyone."

I flexed my hand and released it, then stepped off the stage as people started clapping.

"She's going to throw up," Phoenix said next to me. We were on one side of the stage while Chase waited on the other.

"Think so?" I whispered.

"She's paler than a ghost. She looks like..." Phoenix shook his head. "Is that what you want? For us to humiliate her?"

"Yeah," I snapped. "It's what I want."

"Hmm, your new toy..."

"What about it?"

Trace waved from the stage. Good God, it was worse than I thought. Forget eating her alive. They were going to destroy her, rip her to shreds, and laugh while doing it.

"I can help..." Phoenix whispered.

What the hell were we talking about?

"Sure fine, whatever." I kept my gaze on Trace as she cleared her throat again and spoke confidently into the microphone.

"Trace Rooks. If that isn't a backcountry name, I don't know what is," she joked. "I come from a place where cows outnumber people, and the local bartender knows everyone by name. I guess you could say I'm completely out of my element, but I'm thankful nonetheless. I'm thankful for the opportunity to expand my education, and, even more so, I'm thankful that while I've been standing here, Nixon hasn't attempted to trip me or knock me off the stage. Guess there's hope for me yet. Moo."

"Holy shit, did she just moo?" I asked aloud.

Phoenix about died laughing.

My mouth dropped open slightly as I watched her wave at the crowd and gain approval from at least half of them.

Funny. I'd meant for them all to hate her then leave her alone.

And without knowing it? Trace had just painted a cow-sized target on her back…. because she'd proven she'd fight.

And what fun is torture if your prisoner doesn't at least kick back once or twice? I mean, that's the point.

You don't shoot the slowest animal if you're hunting for sport. You shoot the one that poses the biggest challenge.

And she'd just done that.

"Her funeral." Phoenix sighed. "Am I right?"

I tried to hide my expression as it fell on Trace. She slowly backed away from the stage and took Chase's hand.

What. The. Hell.

Without hesitation.

She gripped it in hers and then offered Chase, of all people, a smile. Chase, the same Chase that spent the better part of his morning assassinating an informant and ripping his fingernails off.

Really?

He whispered in her ear.

She colored.

And I freaking saw red.

"Tsk, tsk," Phoenix whispered to my right. "Doesn't little Chase know not to mess with the boss's favorite new thing?"

With that, he walked off. Leaving me pissed and

wondering what Chase had that I didn't, and why the hell it mattered in the first place.

CHAPTER SEVEN
Marking my territory — maybe

Chase

SHE WAS FREAKING MAGNIFICENT. My entire body went rigid with desire when her eyelashes fluttered across her high cheekbones. She waved to the crowd, and I had the sudden temptation to wrap my arms around her and protect her frail body from what I knew would come.

Not just Nixon.

But them.

The ugly.

The world.

Us.

The Elect.

Wow, just make a freaking list, why don't I? It was bad, and yeah, she'd just made it so much worse, but I had to admire her bravery. Hell, a lesser man would have pissed his pants. Instead she'd mooed.

Like a cow.

Yeah, we were in over our heads. Who knew the hardest part about senior year would be trying to keep the new girl alive?

"I knew you would be different," I whispered as I helped Trace off the stage. Her warm hand fit perfectly into mine. Possessiveness washed over me as I felt the heat of Nixon's gaze on both of us. When I looked up and met his eyes, I was suddenly thrilled we were in a crowd.

The man looked ready to pull a gun.

Cheerfully.

"Different?" She turned slightly, her eyes searching mine, asking more than just if she was different, but if she was safe. I knew that look. I couldn't find my voice at first.

Clearing my throat, I leaned in. "It's a compliment, Farm Girl." God, she smelled good. "Get used to it because you've just earned half the student body's respect."

"And the other half?" she asked slowly, her eyelashes distracting every logical bone in my body.

No harm in being honest with her, right?

"Follow the Elect and will stop at nothing to destroy you." I stopped her progress toward Mo and tilted her chin toward mine. Those lips were so innocent, so plump, I needed to taste them.

"And whose side are you on, Chase?" The lips moved, her breath fanned my face. Someone should have warned me girls from Wyoming were damn sirens.

I swallowed, tucking a piece of silky auburn hair behind her ear. "I always side with the pretty girls."

She hung her head.

As if expecting me to insult her after I just gave her an honest-to-God compliment. Damn Nixon, already ruining that confidence, and it looked so beautiful on her. It was a pity, destroying perfection. But it was something I wouldn't fight him on. He was good at what he did. He kept people safe.

He kept family alive.

And she wasn't our family, yet he was offering her that same kindness, which is more than he'd done for anyone —

ever.

With a sigh, I lifted her hand to my lips and pressed a soft kiss to her wrist, my lips lingering over her soft skin. When I released her fingers, it wasn't because I wanted to.

But because the minute I looked up, my eyes locked on Nixon.

And he was pissed.

Mo quickly pulled Trace into her grasp, and I left, making my way slowly toward my executioner. Why was this girl any different to him? Hell, why was she any different to me?

"Hey, Chase," Bianca grabbed at my hand, but I shooed her away, ignoring her pouting lips.

"Problem?" I asked once I reached Nixon.

His eyebrows shot up as if to say, *"Are you stupid?"*

"So?" I tilted my head.

"I feel like shooting something."

"Do you want me to find you a cat?" I offered seriously. "I mean, I'm pretty sure I can at least do you a squirrel…"

"Do me…" Nixon chewed his lower lip. "…a damn squirrel?" He laughed and then wrapped an arm around my body, pulling me in tight. "Sure Chase, just be sure to put your face on it before I pull the trigger."

"All this sexual tension isn't good for our relationships, bro," Tex said, hands held high in innocence as he walked toward us. "For real, it's super unhealthy."

"Weren't you just getting high like five minutes ago?" Nixon spat.

"Right." Tex rolled his eyes. "Oh, and by the way, the stuff isn't local. I checked it out." He tossed a lighter to Nixon. "Looks like someone's trying to traffic in the wrong area and all that shit."

I looked down at the lighter in Nixon's hand and winced. "Campisi."

"Tex—"

"Nope!" Tex held up his hands. "I'm out. You deal with

it, boss. There has to be some hot little number I can dip my hands into— Oh look, Mo!"

Nixon growled low in his throat while Tex waved us off and ran in her direction.

Phoenix chose that moment to step up. "Want me to deal with it?"

"Chase has this," Nixon said smoothly. "Don't you, Chase?"

I had shit, but sure, why not? I held out my hand and examined the lighter. "Do you think Campisi will ever stay put? Dear God, just leave Tex alone already."

"Ah..." Nixon released me and shrugged. "...no harm done. It's a scare tactic. I'll text you the instructions about the next shipment. I'm assuming he's selling pot. No money now that it's legalized, but he could be using it as a front. Find the dealer, kill him, and put a bow on his face when you mail him back to Sicily, yeah?"

"Yeah." I licked my lips. "You want him recognizable?"

"If I tortured him, he wouldn't be..." Nixon's voice shook. "...so you do it, but not until later tonight, alright? Go after the dance. Until then..."

"Until then?" I prompted.

"We have a girl to warn."

"You mean humiliate."

Nixon's hand damn-near punched a hole through my chest as he stopped me from walking around him. "Listen up. I don't know what kind of game you're playing, but you don't touch her, I don't touch her, none of us touch her. Got it?"

I whistled. "Phew."

"What?"

"Tex is right." I winked at Nixon and patted him on the back. "Sex. You should try it. May save someone's life someday."

"Are you suggesting I have sex to keep myself from shooting things?"

RACHEL VAN DYKEN

"Squirrels." I nodded. "I'm suggesting you have sex so you don't shoot the squirrels. Let them have their nuts, man."

Nixon closed his eyes, probably praying for patience. "Tell me you trust me to handle this the best way I see fit."

"I do." I nodded. "And the minute I see you losing your shit, I'm going to step in. That's my promise. And that's my job."

Nixon looked away, shoving his hands into his pockets. "And what makes you think I'm going to need you to step in?"

"That." I pointed at his face. "That look right there."

"What?" he snapped.

"It's attraction." I shrugged. "And it sure as hell isn't directed at me."

"You don't know what you're talking about." Nixon kept walking toward the girls as they sat around a table.

"Yeah I do," I whispered, letting him pass me.

Because it was the same damn look I'd been sporting all freaking day.

CHAPTER EIGHT

I love her… I hate myself, but I love her.

Tex

I PULLED MO ASIDE while the new girl sat at the table gawking at all the fancy decorations.

"Tex," she hissed, elbowing me in the stomach, "Not now. My roommate's right over there."

"But…" I slid my hand up her back. "…I'm right here."

She rolled her eyes.

I kissed her neck. "Skip the dance."

"No." She piled some food onto her plate and smirked. I knew her game; she knew mine. We flirted, we made out, and sometimes when she was feeling generous, she'd let me take off her shirt. But nothing had gone further, not since Nixon had discovered I was fascinated with his twin and thought his gun needed polishing.

But I couldn't stop thinking about her mouth, her smile — damn, just everything about that woman had me wanting to fall to my knees in worship. The stupid part? I wanted it to be her — Mo. I wanted her to be the one I finally came clean to about all the shit from my past. Recently, it had been building.

First finding my dad's pot getting distributed in the area. Second, seeing Nixon fully step into his part... as boss? Even while his dad lived? It made me wonder, it made me... want to have that kind of legacy. But I had nothing.

Nothing but Mo.

Which, honestly, I decided would be enough.

I didn't need to be boss.

I didn't need the responsibility of people looking to me for decisions.

I just wanted her.

"You're gorgeous," I whispered in her hair. "Tonight? When the girl who moos like a cow goes to bed..." I bit down on her lower lip and sucked. "...you're mine."

She pulled away, her eyes hazy. "What? Are you sneaking into my room?"

"Hell no." I smacked her ass. "You're sneaking into mine."

"Dream on, Tex."

"Oh I do, sweetheart. Believe you me." I licked my lips and closed my eyes, "I dream..."

"Go bother someone else."

"Tonight, Mo..." I winked. "...you'll be in my bed."

She shifted uneasily on her feet. "Sleeping with the enemy, hmm?"

It was like a bucket of ice water getting thrown over my entire body. Muscles rigid, I pulled back from her, forcing myself not to clam up. One simple taunting remark had me feeling like a kid again.

When I'd been unloved, unwanted, uncared for.

Hell, even now I belonged to no one.

And she'd reminded me — that I didn't even belong to her.

And probably never would.

"You're roomie's waiting," I said in a detached voice and walked off, wishing like hell I would have been born with a different name than Tex Campisi.

CHAPTER NINE
I should have walked away.

Nixon

THE DANCE WAS IN full swing by the time I weaved my way through the crowd. Mo and Trace were both sitting at a nearby table. I wasn't sure why I did it, my intention wasn't to stalk her like a lunatic, and I still wasn't sure what I was going to do with her.

It was a problem I'd never had.

Women.

Or a woman, to be exact, one that made me want to follow her anywhere, even though I knew that it was stupid, even though I knew my reaction didn't make sense. But it was like I couldn't help myself. I absolutely loathed her for it. I hated her for making me feel things that I hadn't felt in years. What right did she have? To walk into my life and make me want to be something better, something... good?

Frustrated, I cracked my knuckles and took a few deep breaths then made my way toward the table.

The crowds parted, people stared, like always, but my focus was on her and only her. I still wasn't sure what I was going to do. Kiss her? Taunt her?

Trace lifted the cup to her lips and took a sip. Almost instantly she started coughing and pounding her chest while my sister burst out laughing.

Tex was standing behind Mo, his hands massaging her shoulders. He met my gaze and winked. Yeah, I'd deal with that later.

Chase fell into step beside me. Great, probably to keep me from doing something stupid — and honestly I was thankful he was there, because that whole coughing fit had me gazing at her neck like a man freaking starved.

Phoenix pulled up a chair behind Tex.

Great, so everyone was there to witness it...

To witness my downfall, if you could call it that. When have I ever gone out of my way to talk to a girl?

"What? They don't have alcohol in Wyoming?" I'd had a good five-minute walk to their table, and that's what flew out of my mouth? Really? Chase and Tex shared a look while Phoenix chuckled behind his hand.

"Yes, but when you drink underage you get arrested, smart-ass." She set the glass down, refusing to look at me. She grabbed a chocolate-covered strawberry and twisted it between her fingers.

"There is no law here," I said, pulling out the chair on Trace's other side, pushing Mo out of the way, staking my claim. "And if there was a law, I'd be the sheriff, judge, and jury." I kept my voice even, hard, emotionless.

But all Trace did was arch one eyebrow and nod. "Good for you."

Then she did the strangest thing. She reached across the table and patted my arm, like a two year old who'd just learned how to get on his tricycle. I flinched, pulling my arm away, not because I hated it, but because I liked that feeling way too much, and I knew that she wasn't touching me out of affection. Hating that I wanted the reason behind her touch to be anything but what it was.

Damn it. I needed to put a stop to what I was feeling.

And end her desire to touch or speak to me.

Mo chuckled behind me. I kept my gaze on Trace, willing her to do something more, my heart begging her to see past the mask I was wearing and possibly challenge every damn word that left my lips.

Tex cleared his throat behind me. "May I have this dance?"

"Don't kill my brother, Trace." Mo laughed.

"I will try to control my urges." Trace saluted, and her gaze met mine again.

Chase grinned and plopped down on her left. "Oh, I wish you wouldn't."

"Leave!" I yelled, shocking myself and Chase.

He held up his hands and left the table, Phoenix laughing as he followed him toward the side of the dance floor. Losing my shit didn't even begin to describe the hellfire of emotions pounding through my chest. And all I kept wondering was *why?* Why her? Why now? Why the hell was I losing it?

"Why'd you do that?" Trace's head tilted, her brown hair falling softly across her shoulder.

"Because he shouldn't be flirting with you." I shrugged and plucked a strawberry off of her plate, needing something to do with my hands, considering they were awfully tempted to wrap around her hips and never let go.

She blushed from her chest all the way up to her cheeks, pissing me off all the more, because, in my mind, that meant she found his flirting... acceptable. And it wasn't. "He wasn't flirting."

"Yes, he was." I stole another strawberry.

"No..." She smacked my hand, sending the strawberry sailing to the floor. Holy shit. She just touched me twice in ten minutes. What part of the rules didn't she get? And why the hell wasn't I punishing her? "...he wasn't. He was just being nice. You should try it."

There went that damn blush again as she fidgeted with the hem of her skirt and glanced back up at me through heavy lashes.

"Sweetheart..." I inched toward her. "...I can be nice to you. Believe me. I can be so nice you won't know what hit you. But is that what you really want? For me to be nice?" I moved closer, making it so we were an inch away from kissing. I softly blew across her lips then licked my own.

Her breath hitched. She jerked her head away, still breathing heavy.

"Here." I held out the strawberry, daring her to take it, daring her to touch me for a third time, wondering if she was ballsy enough to do it.

The minute she reached for it, I pulled the fruit back and winked. "Tsk, tsk. Allow me."

I placed the strawberry against her lips, so damn jealous that the strawberry was getting the first taste that I couldn't suppress the moan escaping mine.

She leaned forward.

"Open," I commanded in a hoarse voice.

"No." She gritted her teeth, eyes dilating.

"Then no strawberry."

"I think I'll survive." She jerked away and stood, her entire body shaking. I reached for her wrist and tugged.

"Sit."

Slowly she collapsed back into the chair. My hand was still pressed against her wrist. The pulse on that girl was racing about as crazy as mine.

"I don't want to make your life hell. You know that, right? I don't want you to cry to sleep every night or curse me every morning. Know that you make your own choices. You create your own destiny. And baby, I have the keys. So either play by my rules or don't. The choice is yours." Worst speech in the history of threatening speeches, but as far as warning her away, it would do.

"Why does it matter anyways? Either way, I could never trust you."

I felt that statement in my gut like she'd just punched me over and over again. Because she did see through the mask, but what she saw wasn't worth saving, it wasn't worth trusting, and in my business, trust was more than love. It was everything. She may as well have taken my heart and twisted it until all the blood pooled to the floor.

"Trust is like love. It doesn't exist. It's a fairytale society feeds us in order to get us to conform. I don't expect you to trust me. I expect you to follow the rules. Rules keep you safe." There were only so many ways I could explain why it was important for her to stay away from the Elect but listen to us at the same time. If people saw the way I treated her, if they saw her as different, she was a target. So if she didn't trust me, if she refused to, then because of who I was, because of how I ran the school, I would have to destroy her. I would have to make her feel so little that she needed me.

And damn, I wanted to feel needed.

I knew what I was doing the minute the decision was made in my mind. I would embarrass her in front of everyone — set her apart, make her look weak and picked on — because if I did it, hopefully they wouldn't. If by hurting her I was protecting her, I'd do it, but at the same time, I felt angry that she was forcing my hand. Anger that she wouldn't just listen to me and do whatever I said.

"And if I don't?" she challenged like I knew she would.

I stood and dropped the strawberry on the plate. "Then you will be forcing my hand, and the last thing I want is to hear stories from my sister about how you cry yourself to sleep every damn night just because you couldn't follow a few simple guidelines."

Her nostrils flared. "Fine."

With a fake smirk, I straightened my tie. "I knew we'd

understand one another… eventually."

"I'm not agreeing with you. I just knew that would be the quickest way to get you to leave."

I fought to keep the bark of laughter in. That was more like it. The spark. The students would destroy her, break her, then make her suicidal. Damn, her spirit was beautiful, and it was going to get broken all because she was a pawn in a game she didn't even know she was participating in. It was my school, my job, my family. And she was standing in the way of me doing my job, in the way of me avenging her death — her parents' death.

Silently, I gathered my thoughts and then reached up and touched her cheek.

She shuddered against my palm, and again, it felt like the universe was giving me a choice to back off.

A choice I ignored. Again.

"Dance with me." It was a command, not a request.

She opened her mouth, probably to reprimand me again, so I tugged her toward the dance floor.

People gaped. After all, I rarely gave any girl attention, let alone a new student who was four years younger than me.

She started shaking the minute I tugged her into my arms.

When I looked into her eyes, I knew she knew. It was going to get worse before it got better.

We danced, and I imagined it wasn't because I was trying to make an example out of her — but because I truly wanted to dance with her.

I imagined a world where my family didn't exist, where it was only us dancing in college. It was a nice dream.

But I wasn't nice.

I'd never been nice.

And she was just about to find out how horrible of a person I could be, and this wasn't even the beginning of what I had planned for her.

The song ended, and I pushed her away, feeling the loss all the way down to my toes as she stumbled backward.

"What?" I yelled and then laughed, making sure I drew everyone's attention. It had to look realistic. "Are you insane?"

Trace shook her head then hugged her arms around her body.

"You think I would actually sleep with someone like you? What type of girl are you anyway? Do they do things different out on the farm?"

Her face turned bright red. Out of the corner of my eye, I saw Chase tense. Yeah, it was about to get so much worse.

"Oh, they must, huh?" I folded my arms across my chest. "Trust me, Farm Girl. I don't care how much makeup you put on or how expensive your clothes may be. I don't even give a rat's ass that half the student body likes you right now. You are charity. I wouldn't even screw you if you paid me. So, the answer is no. And next time you feel like showing up to one of my school's parties, at least have the decency to wear some new shoes."

Instead of sobbing, she lunged for me, but Tex was there in an instant, protecting me, not her. Though he'd probably think he was the hero, Tex knew exactly what I was doing. I could see it in his eyes. He was a coldhearted bastard, and he knew it needed to be done. Push her away so she doesn't distract me. Push her away so they taunt her. Push her away so she learns her lesson. And never comes back. She shook so hard in his arms that I thought she was going to pass out.

Mo flipped me off. I gave her a cool nod as if to say, *"Take care of it."*

Soon Chase joined Tex.

Trace was yelling for them to get away from her but neither of them budged. Even when students started throwing food at her — their way of welcoming her into the group, their way of saying, if they had to choose, it would always be me. Never her.

The minute it was impossible to shoot Trace without hitting both Chase and Tex, the students stopped and looked back at me.

They were waiting for their king to command.

I smirked and offered a shrug. "What? Isn't this a party? Where's the music?"

People laughed, and the music started again.

"So…" Phoenix said, falling into step beside me as I fought the urge to run after the girl I liked. "…that was… a bit out of character."

"It was necessary."

"Because?" Phoenix's eyebrows shot up. "I mean, don't get me wrong, I like angry foreplay as much as the next guy, but why the hell did you just push her away when it looked like it was harder than hitting one of the men with a hammer?"

I swallowed and popped my knuckles — damn nervous habit. "She was getting too close. We don't want her snooping around. If people see that a girl can make me soft, where does that leave us with the investigation?"

Phoenix cursed under his breath.

"Besides, she needs us, and the only way for her to realize how much is to see how ugly things can really get."

"You're testing her?"

"She's either for us or against us. Either way, she needs to know that even if we do offer her protection from the rest of the spoiled rich kids who go here, it isn't because we like her or because she's part of us. She will never be part of what we are. The message needs to be clear. We'll protect her when she finally comes crawling back, but everything comes at a cost."

"Nixon…" Phoenix patted me on the back. "…do you think that maybe you're over reacting? Damn, she's just a girl." His face shadowed briefly before he looked down. "She's beautiful, she's—"

"You touch her, I kill you," I spat. "And you're right,

she's just a girl, so find another one who can satisfy a man of your appetite."

It was a low blow. I'd never used his past against him, never discussed it, never made him feel as small as I *knew* he felt.

The shame that crossed his features was something I'd never seen on another human being. The horror, the sadness. And suddenly it was like I wasn't even staring at my best friend anymore but a complete stranger.

He nodded and stepped back, his jaw clenched. "Got it, boss."

He rarely called me *boss*. I was more friend than boss, more family than anything. After all, I'd promised him he'd be third in line, next to Chase.

Tex couldn't be, well, because he was Tex, and his history didn't allow it, but the De Langes? They needed it. Phoenix needed it.

"Phoenix—"

"See ya." He turned on his heel and walked off, shoulders hunched.

As I watched him make his way through the doors, I couldn't help but feel like I'd done something that I could never undo, and that the one action I'd just taken would seal our fate forever.

CHAPTER TEN
A dance and boots

Chase

HE SENT ME AWAY like a damn toddler.

What's worse? I listened to him. As if I had something to be ashamed of, as if I hadn't just been waiting for the chance to offer her a dance. What the hell kind of card was he playing?

With a sigh, I walked to the edge of the dance floor and watched while Nixon took her hand and smiled.

My fist clenched at my side. Nothing more fun than watching my cousin torture a girl that I could potentially like.

And when I say like — I mean it. She had brown eyes and dark hair. I hated to admit I was a sucker for both. She was sexy, innocent, untouchable, and I wanted her for myself, even if she was going to be a giant pain in the ass for the next few months.

He took her hand.

And led her onto the dance floor.

They were close. I was supposed to be doing a perimeter check, and all I could focus on was his hand on the small of her back. Since when did he make business so personal?

And then all hell broke loose.

I couldn't hear what he said. All I heard was shouting and then, "Trust me, Farm Girl. I don't care how much makeup you put on or how expensive your clothes may be. I don't even give a rat's ass that half the student body likes you right now. You are charity. I wouldn't even screw you if you paid me. So, the answer is no. And next time you feel like showing up to one of my school's parties, at least have the decency to wear some new shoes."

I froze.

We'd done a lot of shitty stuff to people. But honestly, in that moment, killing her would have been kinder. She reared back as if she'd just been slapped, and then Mo was instantly by her side.

"Tex—"

I didn't need to be told twice. In that moment, I made my choice, and it was her. Not Nixon. I didn't care that he was my boss, that he would probably kill me next time he saw me.

I just wanted to know she was okay.

I wanted to wipe her tears — I wanted to kiss them away. Nobody deserved that — physical wounds were a blessing compared to emotional scarring, and what he'd just done to her would be such a deep scar that the best shrinks would take years to stop the bleeding.

That's what shame was.

Shaming someone in front of others was our torture at Eagle Elite, and he'd just accomplished it beautifully.

"Get away from me!" Trace screamed when I walked to her side. I gripped her arm, not caring that she wanted to scratch my eyes out, only caring that she still had fight left in her.

The three of us walked in silence across campus.

When we reached the dorms, she began to shake. I didn't know what to do to fix it. She reached in her purse but couldn't seem to get her hands past the barrier of the half-opened zipper.

With a curse, I pulled out my card and swiped it across the access code for the elevator.

My hand naturally fell to her back as I gently pushed her in.

The elevator was big — but it may as well have been a shoebox. Every breath she took, every shudder that wracked her body destroyed my sanity.

I wanted to touch her.

Instead, I did the only thing I knew I could do that wouldn't flag me as being disloyal to blood.

I stood as close as possible. My hand hovered near her skin, feeling like it was damn-near singeing from the heat her body was giving off.

When we finally made it into their room, Mo started yelling.

"He's an ass! I know I shouldn't defend him, but if he would have known they were your grandma's shoes—"

I put my hand in the air. "I don't get it. What's so important about—"

"She's dead, you asshole!"

Yeah. I'd forgotten that.

Like a complete jackass.

Trace's face fell as more tears streamed across her plump lips.

And the pieces of the puzzle fell together. Yes, she was upset about what Nixon had done, but even when he shamed her in front of everyone it wasn't the fact that he'd embarrassed her — it was the fact that he'd unintentionally ripped her heart out and stomped on it.

By the looks of her clothes on the first day, she didn't have a lot of money or possessions, meaning only one thing. The shoes from her Grandma? Probably one of the only things she had of value.

With a curse, I stomped out of the room. Tex followed,

eerily quiet for a guy who normally talked his ass off.

"So…" Tex shoved his hands in his pockets once we were in the safety of the elevator. "…that was—"

"Shut the hell up," I barked and stormed out of the elevator so he wouldn't follow me.

Tex barked out a laugh and went in the opposite direction. With shaking hands, I dialed the number to the closest supplier.

"I need your most expensive boots from the new spring collection."

"I'd be happy to help you with your purchase, sir, but you need to know those specific boots are—"

"Get them for me. Now. I need them by six."

"Six?"

"In the morning," I said slowly. "Size nine."

"Of course, sir."

The line went dead.

But adrenaline continued to surge through my veins. I didn't know what else to do except sit outside the dorms and wait until the boots arrived.

So that's exactly what I did.

I sat in the shadows and waited. By the time five-thirty rolled around, I got another phone call, and the boots were delivered into my hands by one of my associates.

I wanted to put them at her door. I wanted to be the guy to apologize, and I wasn't doing it on Nixon's behalf. No, I was doing it for me.

Cursing the Mafia the entire way up to her floor, I clenched the boots in my hand and went to her room.

I'd written a note.

It was lame.

Who wrote notes? It was like I'd reverted to middle school, but I wanted to do something special, something extra. Hell, after that shitty day, I should have put a bottle of wine in one of the boots with a sedative.

I raised my hand to knock. Visions of Trace opening the door filled my head. She'd, of course, give me a hug, invite me in. Maybe it would be the start of our relationship. I'd slowly slink into her life and we'd... what? What exactly would happen?

She wasn't one of us. She didn't belong in our world.

I put my hand down and stared at the door.

Our future was over before it had even begun.

"Chase?" A female called out my name. "Is that you?"

I turned to the left where Molly, a past booty-call stood wearing nothing but a long tight t-shirt and a smile.

"Yeah." I looked away.

"You wanna come over for a bit?"

No. I didn't.

I wanted to knock on the door.

But instead of knocking, and potentially ruining a girl's life, a girl already on her road to ruination, I stepped back and shook my head.

"Maybe another time, Molly."

As my footsteps echoed across the floor, I wondered. One day, would I look back on this moment? And wish... I would have knocked?

CHAPTER ELEVEN
Sisters should be outlawed.

Nixon

Mo: *WTF*

The text came in at seven a.m., flashing across my screen. I was at our office on campus, though to the naked eye, it looked more like a bachelor pad with a full kitchen, bedroom, fresh clothes, and a crazy big-screen TV. Really it just looked like something a rich kid would have at a school he owned.

But it was a necessity for me. Because for the most part, I wasn't at home running things; I was at Eagle Elite, which meant I needed a place to sleep. Besides, it was so much easier accessing the system from campus than going home and hacking into it. De Lange didn't know about it — then again he wanted to stay in our good graces, so even if he did, I doubted he'd say a word.

I stared at my phone for a good five minutes then texted back Mo.

Me: *By WTF I can only assume you can't find your shoes?*

Mo: *Screw off. She's eating with us.*

Me: *Girls gotta eat.*

Mo: *Are you going soft, brother?*

Me: *Keep an eye on her — if she does anything suspicious, you know what to do.*

Mo: *I'm not killing her for being curious.*

Me: *I'm not asking you to. If she's curious in the wrong spot, I'll finish her off. Now go to class and try not to hike up your skirt. Tex is having a hard time concentrating.*

I got nothing in return but a smiley face. Between babysitting Trace and the rest of the gang, I felt like I hadn't slept in days. I was being pulled into the business more and more. Not only was I facing nothing but dead ends when it came to the murder all those years ago — the one that had destroyed the alliance between my family and the Alferos, but my main suspect, De Lange, hadn't made a false move in months.

They had no money, so maybe that was the problem. I made a note to do a deal with them, throw a bone, see if it tempted anyone enough to talk. I'd tried it before, but now that some of the associates were desperate, it couldn't hurt, right?

I quickly threw on my Elite uniform and walked out of the room. The door slid shut behind me.

The hallways were semi-empty; a few girls waved in my direction, but I ignored them like I always did. They weren't worth my time, unless they were on their backs, and even then I'd grown bored of it — of all of it.

"You look like hell." Tex caught up with me and slapped me on the back just as Chase intercepted us in the hall. His face said it all — guilt.

"How'd last night go?" I asked smoothly.

"A few scratches here and there." He tossed me his cell phone.

I scrolled through the pictures and nodded encouragingly. The face was recognizable but barely. Missing fingers, even a few missing toes.

"You let him keep his teeth."

Chase shrugged. "I was feeling generous."

"Funny, me too." Tex nodded. "Last night I was so generous I—"

"If this is about Mo, please refrain." I held up my hand.

Tex grinned, but his eyes flashed. Damn, I needed to watch my back with that guy. He was too smart by half, and it pissed me off that he let people believe otherwise. It even made me drop my guard around him, and, because of his past, I knew that was the last thing I should do, especially since I was boss now.

"Call your dad." I threw the phone back to Chase. "Tell him to throw De Lange a bone. I want to make a deal with them, a small deal. Give them some money and see if they use it for something."

"Got it." Chase sent off a quick text then groaned. "I freaking hate school."

Rolling my eyes, I slapped him on the back. "And you think I like it?"

"Class losers." Phoenix nodded to us from down the hall, "Let's not be tardy..."

"Right.' I snorted. "Because they could kick us out?"

"If only," Tex agreed. "If only."

My text alert went off on my cell phone. I was going to be late for class, and I'd very cheerfully told Professor Sanders that I'd take over his freshman poly-sci class.

It had been an asshole move. His mom had died, and I'd smiled — yup, freaking smiled — as I looked at the class list and saw Trace's name. What better way to spy on the girl who didn't belong than being her teacher? Damn, just thinking about bending her over a desk and — I shook my head. Not gonna happen. She was just another face, another girl.

Nothing special.

I stormed into the room and slammed the door. Most of the students were busy texting, flirting, going on with their lives like there wasn't a Mafia war taking place in that very school — like their lives weren't being protected every damn day because I made it so.

Irritated, I rolled my eyes and searched for Trace. The minute our gazes met, she averted hers and looked down at her desk. Red stained her cheeks. I grinned. Hell was coming for me, but wouldn't it be so nice to take a ride with her on the way there?

"You all know me, and if you don't, well then, ask someone next to you because I'm not repeating my name. Professor Sanders had a death in the family, and because I'm doing a business internship for him, he asked me to fill in. Many of you are seniors who have put off this class until the last year here. Welcome to Freshman Politics 101. This class is going to suck, it's hard as hell, and if you don't get a B, you basically flunk. But..."

I stepped around the desk and leaned against it, letting my words hang in the air as the class zeroed in. I had their focus, but not Trace's. She seemed hell-bent on not making any sort of contact with my face. My shoes, she was staring at my shoes.

"If you listen, do your homework, and keep your head out of your ass long enough to pay attention, you may just learn something."

Trace's eyes met mine — finally. And she smiled.

That was all it took for my hands to grip the desk so hard I was afraid I'd made permanent marks. Her damn smile.

"Trace," I barked out her name, a predatory smile forming across my lips at the way she straightened her skirt and stood next to her desk as was custom. At least Mo had told her to do that much."

"Yes?"

"Name all the presidents of the United States. You have three minutes."

The little girl smirked at me and started firing them off in rapid succession while the rest of the bright minds in the room gawked like she'd just solved world hunger wearing nothing but her underwear.

Wow! Bad, horrible thing to think about while trying to look authoritative. Trace's voice echoed around the class, until finally she finished.

She sat down as I purposefully made my way toward her desk, impressed she'd done it, but even more impressed that she'd done it so fast. The sound of my boots hitting the floor was the only echo in the room.

Trace's lips trembled as she lifted her eyes to meet mine.

I smiled.

I hadn't planned on smiling, or even walking by her desk. I'd planned on making fun of her, but I couldn't do it. I, Nixon Abandonato, chickened out, and instead said something so horribly stupid that I wanted to ram my face into the nearest wall. "Nice boots."

The class started whispering among themselves as I made my way back to the front of the class and crossed my arms over my chest. "First person who does exactly what New Girl just did earns an *A* for the day."

Hands shot up around the room. I called on several students over the course of the next hour — each of them tried and failed. Most of them messed up once they got past Hoover.

I dismissed class after giving them the homework that Professor Sanders had assigned and watched as students shuffled by. Trace tried to duck behind another student when I said loudly, "Are those Win's?"

She paused in the doorway then turned, her face grim. "Yes."

"Are they from my sister?" I knew they weren't, but I was hopeful, maybe too hopeful they were.

"No." Her nostrils flared, I bit back a grin.

"Did you buy them?"

"No." Cat and mouse was so fun when the mouse had an attitude. Damn, I wanted to trap her and never let her go.

"Who are they from?" I whispered.

She shrugged, looking hot as hell as she put her hands on her hips, driving me insane with the way her posture basically said, '*Look here.*'

"Mature." I snorted and looked away, pissed that my reaction was so violent, pissed that I wanted nothing more than to kiss that tempting mouth. "Can't we have a simple conversation? Who bought you the boots, Trace?"

"The boot fairy," she said through clenched teeth before stomping out of the classroom, nearly colliding with the door, but stomping nonetheless.

It was the first time a girl had turned her back on me.

On purpose.

I liked it.

Too much.

I stared at the door for a few minutes then let out a low chuckle. She wanted to play games? Fine, I'd bite... and I'd enjoy it.

CHAPTER TWELVE

Bite me, no really. Please?

Chase

"AH... LUNCH!" I ANNOUNCED, barging into the small room that only we guys and Mo were actually allowed to eat in. It had become custom after our second year at Elite to start separating ourselves from the student body. It gave them the view that we were untouchable, special, above them, which we were. Nixon had quickly ordered a new lunchroom built — for the specials. Sometimes we'd throw other students a bone and let them eat with us, but it was only to gain information. Most of them were so psyched they'd been invited we didn't even have to threaten them to keep their mouths shut about what happened.

"Stop yelling." Tex scowled from his regular seat. "Some of us didn't get much sleep last night."

I smirked. "You complaining about your nighttime activities, Tex?"

Nixon groaned from the head of the table. "Chase, we're about to eat. If you could just... not, that would be great."

I grinned as Tex chuckled and licked his lips in Nixon's direction, taunting him.

"Hey, Nixon," Tex piped up. "So last night I—"

"Phoenix..." Nixon interrupted what I was sure was going to be another barb about his twin sister. "...any word from your dad on the information he promised to grab us?"

Phoenix's hands froze on his water glass. His eyebrows pinched together in thought. "Uh, not yet. I'll ask again though. He's been busy with orientation."

"Well." Nixon leaned back in his chair, and it creaked under his weight. "If the old man's feeling a bit overwhelmed, we could always push him into an early retirement. Wouldn't want him getting burnt-out or anything."

Shit just got real.

Phoenix bit down on his lower lip, turning it completely white from the pressure of his teeth. "I said I'll talk to him. He likes his job, Nixon. Don't be a bastard."

Nixon shrugged. "Maybe I should check into how well he's doing his job... all things considered."

"Damn it," I muttered under my breath, shaking my head at Nixon. "Just leave it for once, man."

Nixon said nothing, his icy eyes piercing right through me, like always, while Phoenix brooded silently.

Phoenix hadn't been the same since the night of the dance. When I'd asked him what was going on, he'd simply shrugged and said it wasn't a big deal.

But it seemed like a big deal because suddenly Phoenix was... just off. I couldn't really put my finger on it, but something had shifted between him and Nixon, something epic, and maybe if I wasn't so obsessed with the new girl, I'd have time to figure out what the hell was going on, but I was a selfish bastard; therefore, I left it alone.

"So." Tex nodded encouragingly. "Good start to lunch. Good start. Hey, bright spot in our day — no gunfire!"

"Tex," I warned.

For one reason or another, Nixon was in one of his moods.

The door to the room clicked open. Mo strode in and took her usual seat just as the door opened again, revealing Trace.

I glanced at Nixon. His entire body went rigid.

Ah, the reason for said chipper mood.

Well, if he was going to be an ass... I managed to kick him under the table then held up my hand and waved Trace over.

Mo was busy elbowing Nixon. He was getting beat on all ends, but still no eye contact.

"Holy shit!" Phoenix slapped his hand on the table, scaring me to death. "Don't tell me those are from the new collection! What the hell, man! You been holding out on us?" He threw his fork at me and let out a bark of laughter. I'd just been telling him how hard it was to get the new collection of shoes, on account that they kept selling out after Kim Kardashian had worn them at an outing in LA.

I ignored Phoenix, like I always did, and stood to face Trace. It wasn't until I was standing and holding my arms out that I paused and had a *"What the hell am I doing* moment?" But my arms, they were out there flapping, damn-near making me look like a chicken. If she didn't return my hug, I was pretty sure Tex would piss his pants from laughter, and Nixon would think he'd won. Not that it was a competition.

At least not yet.

Trace bit her lip, causing lust to surge through my body, then stepped into my arms and pressed her head against my chest.

Heaven. I was in absolute heaven.

Meaning, Nixon was probably in hell. Take that, bastard. Maybe next time he'd be more welcoming — or maybe next time I'd still try to be first and beat him to the punch.

Trace pulled back, her deep brown eyes searching mine.

I opened my mouth to say something, but words died in

my throat when her warm lips pressed against my cheek. Holy. Mother.

"Thanks for the boots."

"Sweet. Imagine what she'd do if you bought her a car." This from Phoenix. The sound of silverware getting thrown was the soundtrack to our epic moment. Awesome.

I forced a smile even though it was apparent I was going to most likely get forked in the ass if I kept it up. "I'm sorry about—"

She lifted her hand in a noncommittal wave. "I've got boots. We're even."

Hardly. But I wasn't going to argue with her in front of everyone — in front of Nixon. Instead, I inclined my head and escorted her to her seat, like I was starring in some freaking *Pride and Prejudice* movie. I suppressed a groan when her fingertips brushed against my leg, and nearly collided with my own chair in an effort to keep myself from getting too overly excited.

"So, a restaurant? At a school? Really?" Trace directed her question to Mo, her eyes barely flickering to Nixon and back. It wouldn't have been noticeable, but apparently I was a stalker now, because I noticed. I noticed every damn movement of those long eyelashes.

"Nobody really knows about it," Mo said carefully. Her answer strategic, just like she'd been taught.

"We like our privacy," Nixon interrupted and snapped his fingers.

Our waiter appeared and leaned down, iPad in hand.

Nixon fired off his order in French.

Had I been free to groan out loud and gag, I would have. We only did that to impress the new students who we wanted to control and intimidate: order in different languages, confuse them, make them feel weak, vulnerable, stupid.

The rule of thumb was whatever Nixon, the boss, did, we had to follow. His plan was to go with the whole foreign thing? We obeyed. So the rest of us naturally ordered in French, leaving poor Trace staring gape-mouthed at everyone, as well as at the menu.

Way to go, Nixon. You've succeeded in shocking the hell out of her and making her feel about as dumb as a bag of rocks. Why was it necessary?

Trace whimpered a bit, her eyebrows furrowing.

Enough. I whispered to Mo in French, this time purposefully so Trace couldn't understand. Roughly translated, I also added, "Your jackass of a brother is trying to intimidate your new friend. Order her something that tastes good, and be sure to make it hot so that every time she blows across her food, it makes Nixon so painfully aroused he has to excuse himself. Homeboy's pissing me off."

Mo smiled warmly back at me, laughing, then ordered for Trace.

"French?" Trace's voice came out as a squeak. "How many languages do you guys speak?"

"Three." Tex held his water in salute. I about burst out laughing. Tex spoke way more than three, but that was his game, not to act too smart or people would ask questions.

"Two." Phoenix shrugged. Another lie. He spoke five. But whatever.

"Five." I sighed, jumping on the lie train, balls to the wall. I spoke six, so it really wasn't that much of a difference, and counting the language of love seemed cocky, albeit true.

Nixon cleared his throat.

"Tell her, man." I nudged him, curious to see if he would actually fess up or say something lame like, "'One, English, and as you can see, I suck at that too, but I can count to ten. So yeah, there's that.'"

Nixon cursed me in two different languages before mumbling the number "Ten" under his breath. I damn-near clapped. Look who wasn't a liar pants. The most dishonest out of all of us. Well done. Well bloody done. See, apparently I spoke British slang too — I'm freaking amazing.

"Ten?" Trace exclaimed, clearly impressed. "I can barely speak English."

"We know." Phoenix laughed.

Trace shot him a glare and threw her fork in his direction.

He ducked, causing it to hit Nixon's hand. Hmm... things just got way more interesting. She'd just inflicted pain on the boss.

"I like her." Phoenix nodded his approval.

"Yeah, well, I like kids. Doesn't mean I run around screwing everything I see in order to have one," Nixon spat.

And he'd been doing so well...

I managed to clear my throat and elbow Mo. She quickly started firing questions to Trace about class. How did she like Elite? Did it meet her expectations? And professors? Were they nice? Any favorites? Pick a major yet?

Our food was brought out a few minutes later, saving Trace from the dreaded *"What do you want to do with your life when you graduate?"* question.

She poked her meal with her fork. "I'm afraid to ask what this is."

"Heaven. It's heaven. It melts in your mouth and makes you scream with ecstasy. Girl, if you don't have an orgasm after experiencing that particular meal, then you're a hopeless case." Phoenix bit hungrily into his food and winked. Good to know someone had gotten laid and awoken on the happy side of the bed.

Trace's face went all red. Adorable. I could kiss her. Innocence looked good on her. I was fixated on the choice of ruining that innocence or just keeping it for myself. Decisions, decisions.

Mo nudged her. "Don't worry, Trace. Phoenix always talks like that. I think it's because he's never really had—"

Phoenix pointed his fork at Mo and glared. "Don't even finish that sentence."

Tex and I burst out laughing.

Nixon, Mr. *I have a baseball bat stuck up my ass*, refused to laugh. Damn, someone get me a feather or something. It was like the minute she walked in the room he was doing everything in his power to appear pissed off.

We finished eating in a tense silence. One where I watched Trace inhale her food and sneak looks at Nixon, while Nixon gave longing glares in Trace's direction... like he was pondering *screw or shoot*?

"So." Trace glanced at her cell and glanced around the table. "Who eats here next lunch hour?"

We all turned to Nixon. Yeah, that was his territory, his lie to tell, always was, always would be. He sucked in his lip ring and put his hands behind his head, leaning back on the legs of his chair.

Trace's eyes widened as she stared at his chest. Nixon was doing it on purpose, of course, kind of like the huge distraction before the kill. Where the male presents himself in such a fashion that the victim can only stare at the perfection and then — snap. Neck broken. Dead.

"Nobody..." he said slowly, pointedly.

"Huh?" Trace blinked. Get there faster, girl, before he pounces.

"Eats here," Nixon said, his tone clipped. "It's just us. Just this lunch hour."

"But..." Trace's eyebrows pinched together. "...then why am I here?"

"We like to slum it sometimes." Nixon grinned smugly. "Now run off before you're late."

Oh shit. Could he at least try not to be an ass?

Trace didn't move.

Thinking I needed to cut that tension with a giant-ass knife, I put my head in my hands and groaned. "I hate it when Mom and Dad fight."

Phoenix burst out laughing.

Nixon continued to stare at her like he was killing her with his mind.

With a curse, he pushed his chair back and stormed out of the room. The door slammed behind him.

Trace jumped in her seat at the loud sound of the door closing and asked, "Is he always like that?"

"Actually..." Tex leaned forward. "...no. I think you bring out the worst in him."

"Yay me," she said in a sarcastic tone.

"You're the first outsider who has ever eaten in here," Mo said. "He hands out keycards to control the cliques. To make sure fights don't break out between the kids from different countries at war and stuff. I just assumed he put you in one of the normal lunches."

"What do you mean?"

I offered my two cents in a way she'd understand. "He's not just in charge of the keycards. He's student body president. He makes sure that access is limited for each student. Take, for example, a kid from North Korea going to school here. You think they're going to get along with a South Korean? Or better yet, some ritzy American kid?"

"Um... no?" Her brown eyes were wide, questioning, as if she was afraid her answer wasn't correct.

Everyone laughed.

Phoenix shook his head. "That's a *hell no*, New Girl."

I uncrossed my arms and leaned forward, close enough to be able to smell her perfume or shampoo, whatever it was. I wanted more. "What if some sheik's kid goes to school here but he's from a different sect than some other kid? What if those same kids eat in the same lunchroom that serves pork?"

"Oh." She exhaled. "I guess that makes sense, but then doesn't that segregate everyone?"

Mo laughed. "Boots, it's college. We're segregated regardless, whether it be by major or class. This is just the way things are here. It keeps everyone safe. Keeps the fights down."

The table fell silent again.

Trace's eyes met mine. Oh damn, it was like telling Bambi that the father didn't die, just freaking ran off and abandoned his sorry ass.

"But if he hates me so much, why would he want me here?"

A clock chimed in the restaurant, causing everyone to push away from the table and stand. Thank God.

Trace's question remained unanswered. I hoped I could get away with it, but the look in her eyes was so wounded, so confused, that I felt another weak moment of pity.

She slowly walked out the door.

With a groan I chased after her and whispered in her ear, my lips brushing her skin. "Protection." And that was the truth. I just wished it wasn't such a horrible one.

"What?" She stopped walking and reached her hand up to her ear, touching where my lips had just been.

More where that came from. Much more.

"See ya!" I waved and walked down the hall. Needing to flee the situation before I ruined everything. Not just for her, but for the Elect.

CHAPTER THIRTEEN
Give me sex or give me death.

Nixon

AFTER LUNCH, WHERE I'D made an even bigger ass out of myself in front of everyone, Trace included, I went to my final class for the day.

"Yo." Tex bumped my fist when I reached the door. "Question. Would your father, sick bastard that he is, kill me if I asked to date your sister?" He coughed. "Officially?"

Talking about my father was right up there with getting kidnapped by Al Qaeda and starving in the desert.

"Officially?"

He shrugged. "You know, like, do things the right way." His eyes flickered between the doorway and mine. Shit, he was dead serious.

Groaning, I crossed my arms. "Tex, he's not even the head of the family anymore. I am. Asking him is like asking the dead. Just ask me."

"But..." Tex's eyes turned worried. "...he may not be dead yet, but he's still her father, and I want... I want to do it right, Nixon. The old way, where the guy asks the girl's father

73

for permission, not the brother, even though the brother is a bad ass."

"The brother may say no." I snorted.

"The brother can go to .hell. I want the father's permission. Can I ask?"

"Shit." I wiped my face with my hands. "At least let me talk to Mo first… see if she's even that far gone over your ugly mug that she'd risk going to our own father to ask permission to date a Campisi."

Tex's face twisted with rage as he backed me up against the wall, his nostrils flaring. "You know I hate that name."

"We all hate that name." I pushed his hand away "But it doesn't matter. In the end, it's what you are. You know it. I know it. Your biggest hurdle isn't going to be gaining my dad's approval to date her. It's going to be gaining his approval to mix bloodlines with the Cappo."

Tex looked down, shoving his hands in his pockets. "I'm not him, Nixon."

"No." My heart twisted a bit in my chest. I'd known Tex my whole life, known his past, known his baggage, and it killed me that he'd never truly fit in. It wrecked me that he'd never felt good enough, even with his own family. "But you're his son."

I pushed past him and went to my desk then sent Mo a text to meet me in her dorm after class.

The professor droned on and on about business ethics. I blocked it out, because I officially had no ethics, business or otherwise. Having ethics was like having morals: they didn't really do shit for me in the business I was in.

Damn Tex. I didn't want him talking to my father. Hell, I didn't even want to talk to my father. That meant I had to be in the same room with him, breathing the same air, and, well, I knew something that Mo and the Elect didn't even know.

This week was the week that I was going to end him.

I'd planned it.

Anthony knew.

The men knew.

Hell, my own father probably knew. But if that's what Tex needed in order to gain permission to be with Mo? I'd give it to him, not because I was a good guy, but because I knew that the future Tex had wasn't one where he ended up with my sister and a houseful of kids.

No, his future was about as set as mine.

Filled with blood.

And death.

By the time class ended, my mood was so dark I almost texted Mo again to see if we could meet later, but the minute I saw Trace walking slowly toward the dorm, I knew… I wanted to see her. Had to see her, because I was sick. Because for some reason I was obsessed with that dark hair of hers and her smile. It killed me because I'd never been so… curious.

I took a shortcut through campus and made my way up to their room. A picture of a cow with her face on it was taped to her door. Huh. Original. The girls in that dorm really needed to up their game if they wanted to intimidate her. I highly doubted something like that would make a tough girl like Trace cry.

Then again I would know.

I was the one causing the tears.

Shit.

I slid my all access card across the door and let myself in then paused. Mo's bed… I usually sat on her bed, but Trace's was so tempting that I found my legs carrying me to the opposite end of the room.

Everything was plain. From her white duvet to her bare walls. It was as if she didn't really have a life outside of going to school. Guilt gnawed because part of me wondered if the reason she 'hadn't put pictures on the walls was because she couldn't really afford anything.

I thought of her grandma's shoes.

And the boots Chase had given her.

My gut sank lower and lower as I plopped onto her bed and lay down, closing my eyes as I imagined her tossing and turning against the sheets.

Great. So now white duvets did it for me. I was getting so aroused it was pathetic. Her scent was on everything from her pillow to the damn air — I was saturated in her, and I wanted to stay that way for just a few seconds, because in those seconds, on her bed, I felt calm.

Just as I was about to close my eyes, the door burst open. With a huff, Trace threw her bag onto the floor, peeled the shirt from her body, and tossed it on top of the book bag.

Forget being aroused — I was gone, ready to rip the rest of the clothes from her body and slam her against the nearest wall and then take her on the desk. Then I'd run my tongue up and down her thighs until she was panting with--

Holy hell, she reached for her zipper. Should I cough? Make a noise? My body demanded I stay as silent as the grave, but then I started thinking about that stupid ethics class, morals, being a good human being...

Hell, just give me hell. I didn't want to be the angel. After all, I'd always been the opposite, so why change now?

Her face was adorable, like she was angry at the skirt for being on her body in the first place. I let out a chuckle — totally by accident.

Her hands froze. Trace glanced up, and her eyes went from shocked to horrified in seconds.

I stayed put and yawned. "Please, don't let me interrupt. Continue."

Eyes narrowing, she flipped me off. Damn if that wasn't an invitation. I laughed harder as she reached for the closest piece of clothing she had and threw it over her body.

I laughed even harder when I noticed it bore a picture of a unicorn, and it was inside out. Flustered much? Damn, I wanted to taste the blush from her neck. Steal it and keep it for myself.

"What do you want!" she snapped.

"Not sex, but thanks for the offer." Total lie. I'd take sex, lots and lots of sex. With her.

"I was not..." She took a few deep breaths and looked like she was counting to herself. "Why are you here?"

"Waiting for my sister. What else?" Truth, though to be honest, I could have waited outside, but then I would have missed out on the show. What a crime.

Her shoulders sagged with relief.

"What? You disappointed I didn't want an afternoon screw?"

"Not at all." She sat on Mo's bed. "Besides, if you needed one, all you'd have to do is knock on any door on this floor. Just be sure to use protection. I know how you are about germs."

"Only yours," I sang then offered up a teasing wink.

A pillow was launched in my face. I caught it mid-air and smiled.

"Can you at least wait for her outside?"

"Nope."

"Why?" Her teeth ground together, and her blush deepened.

I answered her as honestly as I could. "Because I like your bed. It's comfortable."

"It has my germs, and I swear to you, I drooled all over my pillow last night."

I hadn't taken the girl for a huffer, but she was doing a lot of that — huffing, looking away, crossing arms — it was adorable. "I only hate germs on people, not objects." I glanced at my watch like she didn't make me want to strip naked and slam my mouth against hers. I put my hands behind my head, closing my eyes against the images playing in overdrive.

"Why?" came her soft voice.

"Why what, Farm Girl?"

"Why don't you like people touching you? Is that *your* rule or an Elite thing?"

I hadn't expected that question. All the things she could have asked, and she'd asked that? Something so personal, something so... embarrassing and horrifying that I immediately clammed up and wanted to reach for my gun.

"You ask a lot of questions for someone so stupid."

I hadn't meant to snap, but she'd pried too much. And the awful part? She made me want to tell her, she made me want her pity, and I never wanted pity. I never wanted love or affection, but the way she said things— Damn, I craved it. I wanted to cave. I wanted to fall onto the floor and tell her my secrets. She made me want to trust, and I trusted no one.

"It is the only way to find out how to survive in this place." She sighed.

"You'll survive — if you follow the rules. I thought I told you that." I propped up on my elbow, thankful for the subject change. This I could talk about. "The system works, Trace. I know you think I'm an asshole, but if I was nice, they would eat you alive. Wouldn't you rather I do the tasting?" I eyed her up and down and smirked.

Her eyes flickered to my mouth. "Why can't everyone just be nice and get along?"

Ah and sing "Kumbaya" around the Christmas tree? Yeah, just another reminder she didn't belong in my world, and I sure as hell didn't belong in hers. Where ponies shit rainbows and guns shot flowers. "Maybe I will wait outside."

"You do that."

I walked to the door and paused, thinking that if I alluded to what I was trying to do by being mean, she'd get it. "Has anyone made fun of you today?"

"Is this a trick question?" she asked, jumping off Mo's

bed. "You make fun of me all the time!"

"Other than me." I shoved my hands in my pockets to keep from grabbing her by the shoulders. "Tell me the truth."

"N-no," she stuttered. "No one made fun of me today."

"I guess my point is made," I said softly.

"The hell it is." Another pillow found its way into the air, aiming for my face "You think you have that much power? To protect me from them? You think you're that much better? That what you do is better than what typical college kids could do to me?"

Did she just say *hell*? And why was I so turned on by it?

"Care to make a wager?"

"Fine!" And now she was poking me in the chest. The girl didn't stop, and if she poked one more time, she was going to have a hell of a problem on her hands, mainly me kissing the shit out of her. The poke, the simple touch, had my knees buckling.

"Please don't touch me."

She stopped.

I sighed and leaned in. "I'll stop bothering you... but when I win — when you can't take it anymore — when you are living in hell every single day, I want to hear it from your lips. Not Monroe's. Not Chase's. I want you to approach me. I want you to tell me..."

"Tell you what?" she whispered. Her mouth was so tempting... just a few more inches and I'd claim it.

"...that you need me." What the hell?

"When hell freezes over!" she snapped.

Well, apparently our moment was over. "Bring a parka because life's a bitch, and you just bought a first-class ticket, sweetheart."

I jerked open the door a bit too hard and left, sending Mo a text once I was safely on the elevator. I'd talk to her on the phone, but waiting in that room for ten more minutes would end in disaster because Trace wasn't one to just roll over and take things. No, she was a fighter, and it was so damn enticing I wasn't sure what to do with myself, how to handle her, or how I was going to survive the next semester without claiming her.

Mo texted back right away.

Mo: *Please tell me you didn't off my roomie. I like her!*

Me: *She's still breathing.*

Mo: *So what's up?*

I hesitated, my hand hovering over the text. I could tell her about Tex later. Right now, I just wanted to forget everything that Trace made me remember. Like simple caresses, smiles, love, trust.

Me: *Party tonight.*

At least if they partied, I could go talk to my father and let him know Tex wanted a meeting. Mo would be at the party, happy as a clam. I wouldn't have to see Trace's face again, and I could remind myself why I was boss, why I was protecting my family. The only way to remind myself? See what an ass my father was and get a good dose of reality.

Mo: *REALLY?*

Me: *Invite everyone. It will be at the usual. Free booze. I'll send Chase and Tex. Have fun.*

Mo: *I like Tex.*

Me: *Okay…*

Mo: *Do you think Dad would… approve?*

Me: *Dad isn't boss. I am. And I approve. Go get dressed, have fun. Will text later.*

Mo: *;)*

CHAPTER FOURTEEN

Don't mess with me... or do it and see what happens.

Chase

"AWW, PLEASE?" NICOLE'S FINGER ran up and down my arm as I set up for the party. "We'll be really quick."

Ha. Every guy's dream: *"Hey, let's go have sex real quick. I'll be fast. Let me just use you for your hot body."* Okay, so she didn't exactly say it like that, but still. Booty calls, she was known for them. And so was I.

With a sigh, I pushed her away. "I'm not really feeling it right now."

Her eyebrows arched. "You're not feeling *it*? Or *me*? What guy says no to sex?"

Ha. Good question. One who's in some deep shit and would probably find himself on the opposite end of Nixon's gun by spring semester.

"It's you," I said plainly. "You got fat."

She scowled. "Bullshit. You don't want sex? The great Chase Winter, player of the year, is saying no to me?"

"Well..." Phoenix came up behind her. "...you're kind of a slut. But hey, try the freshmen. They're always easy."

"Assholes," she muttered.

Phoenix grabbed her arm and pulled her against his body. "Say it again, and I cut out your tongue."

She gasped.

"Ah, fear." He nodded. "I respond better to fear than I do an invitation. Maybe next time you should give Chase that look when you offer your goods. Now run along and find a freshman to screw. He's too good for you, and you bore me."

Tears streamed down her face as she jerked away from him and ran out of the room.

"Harsh," I said, setting up the keg.

"Yeah, well."

Phoenix's face looked haggard, like he hadn't slept in days. I wondered if the nightmares were back but was afraid to ask because if they weren't back, then they would return just by me asking.

"Things cool, man?" I said nonchalantly.

His eyes flashed before cool indifference settled into place across his features. "Of course. Why wouldn't they be? We're seniors, almost done in this shit hole, and we get to get drunk tonight. Why wouldn't things be awesome?" His smile was forced, his hands shaking.

Shit. "You look tired." My way of telling him to go home.

"I'll sleep when I'm dead." His way of telling me to screw myself.

I held up my hands. "Just trying to be a friend."

"That's just what I need right now," he sneered. "More friends giving me shit about my life, making me feel—"

"Phoenix?"

"Never mind." The forced smile was back. "When's Nixon getting here?"

"He's not coming." I set the cups next to the keg and shrugged. "Had to go see his pops."

Phoenix's eyes narrowed. "And we weren't invited?"

"Nixon doesn't need a babysitter. Besides, when have you ever gone with him to see his father?"

"I haven't," Phoenix said in a low voice. "But Nixon promised he'd take me, just once, so I could learn the ropes better, see how things operated from the outside world..."

"Dude..." I shook my head. "...there's plenty of time for that. Don't worry."

Phoenix was quiet as I set up the rest of the drinks.

"Have you gone?"

"What?" My mind had journeyed into Trace-territory, meaning I'd forgotten Phoenix was still standing there.

He leaned across the keg, folding his arms. "Have you gone with him before? When they have their... meetings?"

I shrugged. "Yeah."

"And Tex?"

"I think so..." My eyes narrowed. "What's this about, Phoenix?"

"Nothing." He smirked, hitting his hand across the keg. "Nothing at all... damn. But it's already happening, isn't it?"

"What the hell are you talking about?"

"I'll never be good enough for your blood."

"Phoenix..." I rolled my eyes. "...stop being dramatic. That's not it at all. Nixon's just careful... I'm family, and Tex—"

"Is a freaking Campisi! An enemy! You've even invited the enemy into your own home! And what? A De Lange can't even step foot across the precious threshold?" He slammed his fist against the keg twice before stepping away. "Whatever. I'm out. I'll see you later tonight."

"Phoenix—"

He flipped me off and slammed the door behind him.

"What crawled up his ass and set up camp?" Tex said from behind me.

"No idea," I muttered. "But he's not acting like himself."

"If he's acting like an ass, he's acting like himself."

"No." I shook my head. "It's not that. He just seems… off."

Tex chuckled behind me. "Open your eyes, sunshine. Off is about as normal as we get. Now beer me. I want to forget about the fact that Nixon's asking his father if I can speak to him about Mo."

I snorted with laughter. "You don't need beer. You need shots."

"Please, like I want to get drunk before she gets here. I have plans… for her, for me."

"She, uh, bringing Trace?"

"Um, gee, I don't know, Chase. Do you want me to send her a note during the spelling test and ask her to circle yes or no?"

"Hilarious." I threw a cup at his face.

He grinned. "Chill, Romeo. It just so happens that Mo is bringing her cute little roommate. Why? You gonna hit that?"

"Yes, because I look forward to Nixon shooting me in the face. No. No hitting, but yeah, I may talk to her."

"Talk?" Tex burst out laughing. "Since when does Chase Winter talk to a girl without doing her later?"

"Since now." I pushed him away. "Now go be a pain in the ass elsewhere."

He held up his hands and laughed harder. "Got you all twisted up on the inside, doesn't she?"

"No." Yes.

"Cute. You finally fell. Too bad she isn't yours."

"She isn't his," I snapped.

"Not yet," Tex corrected. "Not yet."

CHAPTER FIFTEEN
The screams were my symphony.

Phoenix

I DRANK MORE THAN I usually did. Hell, it wasn't even the party that had brought out the animal. It was the last girl.

Out of four, the last one hadn't cried.

She'd just... stared at me, as if she pitied me, as if she hadn't been the one getting her dignity stripped while I had sex with her. Naturally, it was consensual. We drugged them with Molly so they didn't really care that they were getting used by yours truly.

But she hadn't responded to the drugs like the other girls. They'd been only too happy to spread their legs — I'd only puked twice that evening.

But the last girl. She'd looked at me as if she really saw me, as if she wanted to save me from myself, when I was the very one destroying her life. It didn't make sense. Then again, my life didn't make sense. Everyone was out partying, having the greatest time of their lives, and there I was... miserable and pissed because Nixon had thrown my past in my face.

The very past I was ashamed of. He may as well have

branded me and brought it to everyone's attention. I'd never be good enough.

Sure, Cowgirl was just fine.

But his best friend since childhood? Suddenly I wasn't.

I knew I needed to do something in order to prove myself, but I didn't know what I could possibly do that would make things better.

My mind flooded with images of that girl's face.

Nausea threatened.

And then Trace walked in the door with Mo.

I focused in on her.

She was pretty, innocent, the type of girl my father would love to sell to the highest bidder — but also extremely off-limits.

Why? Why was I getting jealous of a girl?

Why did it matter that Nixon was paying attention to her?

And why did it matter that she was causing the already-crumbling friendship with the guys to dissipate into powder?

It felt like something was coming, and unless I stopped it, I was going to be on the outside looking in.

Without thinking, I reached into my pocket and pulled out the tiny pill. I crushed between my fingers and dusted it into the cup I had and slowly waited.

I had to prove myself to him… again.

Prove my worth to all of them.

Or end up just like my father.

I would rather kill everyone in that damn school than have his future.

So I waited in the shadows, getting sicker by the minute, because my conscience had decided to come back full force.

She deserved the happy.

And I was going to give her the ugly.

I was going to force Nixon's hand.

It was selfish. Then again, I never promised I was

anything but selfish. It was all I had left... myself.

And the real shitty part?

When I looked in the mirror... the only things I saw was were his eyes, his hair, his features. And I hated myself more and more because of it.

CHAPTER SIXTEEN
I killed my father... and liked it.

Nixon

I PULLED UP TO the house, hands shaking, and looked at my screen on the phone. The party had just started.

The rest of the world was having fun while I had to go sit through a meeting with Satan himself.

Since I was going to be meeting my father, I'd called a meeting with the rest of the men. May as well update them on what was going on. Uncle Tony had thought it would be a good idea, and I needed an update on what they had on De Lange — another reason I was by myself. The last thing I needed was for Chase, Tex, or — God forbid — Phoenix to be there. The less they knew, the safer they were. Which basically meant if I died, they were screwed, but that's why we paid the men well. I wasn't really killable. Not now.

I opened the door to my Range Rover and shrugged out of my leather jacket. I always liked to approach meetings like I was going to war. Because that's what happened when you had two bosses in the same damn house. A war.

I was the new boss taking over from my dad, considering

he was too sick to do anything but cough and bark orders that made no sense to anyone but his own demented mind. But he still had the ring on his left hand.

I had nothing.

I checked both pistols and strapped them to my chest then made my way into the house. The door opened before I reached it.

Uncle Tony stepped out and lit a cigar. "He's in a mood tonight."

"He's always in a mood." I scowled.

"Nixon..." Tony flicked the cigar. "It's time."

My heart, what was left of it, froze in my chest. "We putting things on ice so soon?"

"He's demented." Tony scowled. "Talking crazy about wives switching husbands, kids that aren't his... He's even saying he doesn't recognize me as his brother. He's sick."

"The doctors—"

"To hell with the doctors. You're boss now. It's your call. I can only advise as to what would be the best option. But the men, they're ready, Nixon, and so are you."

Nodding, I stepped by him and made my way into the house. We had captains, foot soldiers, made men, and they all looked at me like I was their god, even though I was decades younger. I was the one calling the shots, lining their pockets, ruling their damn worlds.

"Boss." Vin shook my hand as I walked into the living room where I knew my father would be sitting on the couch.

The silence was deafening as I made my way toward his limp body. He coughed then started swearing in Sicilian, calling for my mother.

Tony was right.

Something needed to be done.

Hatred bubbled up inside of me when he stopped coughing and smirked in my direction. "You are not my son."

I rolled my eyes and pulled out my pistol.

The tension thickened. A storm was coming, brewing, twisting the air around my throat, making it impossible to breathe.

My father leaned forward, his smile mocking as his lucid blue eyes took me in. "You are nothing."

I smirked and tilted my head, returning his smile with a sour one of my own. "I am everything."

"I know why you are here." He looked away as if I didn't have a gun a few inches from his body. As if I didn't have my hand firmly on the trigger. "You will destroy this family. You will destroy everything I've built."

At that, I laughed.

Anthony tensed to my right.

"Old man, everything that's been built in the last four years is all me. What do you think they call me?"

His eyes narrowed as the room shifted.

One by one, the men slowly walked to my side, standing next to me, standing beside me, each of them standing at attention as if I was their god.

"Betrayal!" my dad shouted, falling into another coughing fit. "Anthony! Do something!"

The timer went off.

The end was near. For him, not for me. I'd always sworn I would kill him. I'd promised it to myself when I was a little boy, and I'd promised it to myself when I watched my mom die a little bit every day. I would kill him.

And I was finally getting my chance.

"Father…" My voice shook. "…may God extend the same mercy to you that you extended to my mother, to me, to the very men who have turned against you."

"You are nothing!" he shouted louder. "Do you hear me?"

I squeezed the trigger and whispered, "I'm everything. I'm the boss. *Sangue en — no fuori.*"

Time slowed as the pressure on my finger increased. One

single gunshot rang out as my dad cursed me to hell. Those were his final words to his only son.

And I didn't feel bad.

I felt nothing.

Even when the blood splattered all over my clothes.

When his limp body collapsed onto the ground, causing a mess to erupt around the living room.

I felt nothing.

And I had him to thank for it. He'd made me the way I was — heartless, a coldblooded killer — and in that moment, when I handed Anthony my gun and started wiping my hands on the towel Vin had thrown at me, I realized...

She didn't belong in this world, didn't belong with me.

I'd just killed my father.

In cold blood.

In order to officially step into the role he'd groomed me for from day one.

My future was staring back at me through cold, lifeless eyes. I was him, he was me, no matter how much I wanted to fight it.

I was the boss.

And I'd just sealed my fate for eternity.

"Salud!" Anthony shouted, pulling the ring from my father's cold hand and shoving it onto my finger. He kissed the family crest, and my heart hammered as each man did the same.

So this is what it was like — to be alive, but completely dead inside.

CHAPTER SEVENTEEN
The beginning of the fall into darkness

Chase

I SEARCHED GREEDILY FOR Trace. The party was already in full swing, and Mo had yet to show her pretty face, which meant Trace hadn't waltzed in and allowed me to sweep her off her feet.

Nixon wasn't going to be able to make it on account he had bloodstained hands — literally. I still couldn't believe he'd done it. Killed his father and then asked me about a damn party as if the stench of blood wasn't still fresh on his clothes. I'd answered as normal as possible, and with shaking hands, downed three shots in a row.

This wasn't supposed to be our life.

I remembered a time when I was little and I'd wanted to be an astronaut. How badass, right? To be able to see the world from above, to travel, to be something other than what was expected of me.

My dreams had been crushed the minute I'd confided in my father.

He'd laughed in my face and said that Abandonato men

did not become astronauts. *"Why..."* he'd asked *"...did I want to see the world when I was going to own it?"*

I'd had no idea what he'd meant at the time. Had I known I probably would have run away, but I wanted to impress my father. He was powerful, wealthy — everything I thought was important for a man to be.

And he didn't cry.

I cried.

Which made me weak.

But I knew that Nixon cried too. It had been the only thing that had kept me together when I heard my first gunshots.

When I saw my first kill.

When my father threw away my astronaut action figure and then set fire to the space magazine he'd found underneath my bed.

Little boys are meant to dream. They're meant to explore and discover their purpose.

My little trip down memory lane almost made me miss Mo's entrance. Trace was close behind, looking like she'd never once set foot in a party before.

Rather than approach, I observed while she weaved through the crowd, careful to keep her eyes averted like she was afraid to stare anyone directly in the face.

Phoenix elbowed me and pointed. "She's not going to last."

"She'll be fine."

He shrugged and grabbed another beer. By my count, he was well into his tenth drink, but I wasn't his mom or his dad, so for me to say something just seemed... stupid and totally out of character. I'd had my fair share of drunk moments.

"I'm going to kiss her," Phoenix stated boldly.

The hell he was. "No, you aren't."

"I am." Phoenix grinned and then hit his knee and laughed, spilling his drink over the cup. "Dude, you must have it bad if you're getting that pissed off over a kiss. Shit, it's not like I said I was going to screw her."

My fists clenched at my sides.

"Lighten up." He elbowed me. "It's a party."

I nodded and poured myself a drink. He was right. I was being an ass. I was acting like a lovesick idiot.

Trace turned and smiled in my direction.

My feet begged me to walk toward her.

Instead, when a girl stepped into my line of vision, a girl whose name I didn't even know... I kissed her aggressively across the mouth, tasting beer on her tongue, hating myself in that moment more than ever.

I needed to push Trace away.

Just like Nixon.

She was bad for us.

Bad for me.

Bad for my lifestyle.

And didn't belong in a world where guns were necessary. No, she belonged in space, with the astronauts, with the dreamers. And I wasn't going to take that away from her like my father had taken it away from me. She deserved more, and I needed to back off before it was impossible to give it to her.

The girl gripped the back of my head with her talons and moaned into my mouth. "Mmm, Chase."

"*Mmm,*" I wanted to say to stranger-whose-name-I-don't-know-who–kisses-like-shit. Instead, I threw her against the nearest wall and hurled my beer onto the ground. She wrapped her legs around me, and I allowed myself to get lost in the identity I'd created for myself at Elite, hoping like hell it would be enough to keep me far away from what I really wanted, and who I really was.

Hours later, after my little make-out session with... Bianca? Was that her name? She'd said it, but I hadn't exactly been paying attention, and who needed names to kiss anyway?

The party was coming to a close, and I noticed that Tex and Mo had all but secluded themselves in the corner, swallowing each other whole. Yeah, I snapped a picture of that and sent it to Nixon. Let him be the one to go head to head with Tex. I sure as hell didn't feel up to it.

When I couldn't find Trace, I panicked. Maybe she was at her dorm. When did I nominate myself her protector anyway? Cursing myself, I ran out of the house and nearly collided with Phoenix. I looked down and almost pulled my gun on him. "What the hell, Phoenix!"

His cold eyes met mine. "She's drunk. I'm taking her back to her dorm."

"Like hell you are! And her dorm isn't in that direction. What are you doing?" I pushed against him, and he stumbled slightly. Great. Still drunk. Freaking awesome.

Trace's eyes were unfocused as she looked at me then back at Phoenix.

"I'm doing her a favor, doing us a favor. Back off. You're already on Nixon's shit-list. I'm making everything better. You'll see."

He was right about that. Nixon was pissed I was getting too close to his territory, not that it would be a problem anymore. Liar.

Trace moved her hand, almost like she was trying to reach me. Shit. This was bad, and it was going to get worse.

"I'll take her," I mumbled, knowing exactly what Phoenix was doing. For the past few years we'd bullied and drugged both guys and girls that were pushing us too far. But they'd always deserved it. We'd never picked on the weak. We'd never, and I do mean never, made the innocent look as bad as Trace was about to look.

"You're going to do it? Really?"

"Just let me do it." I held out my arms. "And this comes straight from Nixon? He said to do this?"

Phoenix snorted. "You think I would actually do this on my own? Nixon wants to teach her one final lesson, and he can't make it, so we do the dirty work. Story of our lives, right?"

"But she didn't do anything wrong."

"Oh, but I think she did." Phoenix grinned. "She does... After all, she has you and Bossman fighting to keep your pants on, and she refuses to bend to our rules even after she's been warned. We can't have the rest of the campus thinking we've lost our touch. She makes us look weak. Nixon knows it, Tex knows it — hell, I'm wasted, and even I know it. We have to make an example out of the cowgirl."

In a twisted really dysfunctional way, he was right. I nodded my head and slowly made my way toward the guys dorm, cursing Nixon the entire time.

Had he finally snapped? Clearly, killing his father had done something to him, because we were about to make an innocent girl look like the devil. And look who was carrying her? Me.

I glanced up at the sky. It was a clear night. You could see thousands of stars, and I thought again about the astronaut-thing. Yeah, even dying in space would be better than taking the girl I liked into the guys' dorms and putting her in bed with the quarterback.

I was already reaching for her, already making the choice I knew would change the course of our lives forever. But I couldn't bring myself to let Phoenix do it. Something in his eyes told me that I couldn't trust him. They were empty — they'd been that way for a while, as if his soul no longer possessed his body but had long ago given up on him, leaving him damned for eternity.

"You're going to do it?" he snarled. "Really?"

"It's not like I haven't done it before," I whispered so Trace, if she was still conscious, wouldn't hear me. We'd done this prank more times than I could count, but it had always been to people who'd deserved it. Girls who'd whored themselves around and made fun of others... bullies. Basically, we took care of the bullies in the only way we knew how: take it too far and hope that when they woke up in someone else's bed without any recollection of what had happened, they change their ways or leave the school.

Trace screamed innocence.

So I was doing it — not because she was a slut.

But because I knew it was what was best. We needed her to leave school because things hadn't been the same since she'd arrived. Nixon was more pissed than ever, and he'd invited her into our group, into our lives.

"Just let me do it."

Her body fell into my arms, and I almost winced. She was so light, so soft. In another time, maybe another world, she'd be mine. I'd carry her to my dorm, take care of her, tell her that all guys weren't like that, they weren't like us. I'd tell her that one day a guy would earn her... not take what wasn't his to take.

"It's what Nixon wants," Phoenix said slowly. "He just doesn't know it. You know it's divided us too much already. When was the last time you went against him, Chase?"

I said nothing.

"That's what I thought. Deal with it in your way, or I'll deal with it in mine." Phoenix's eyes greedily took her in, and then he placed a kiss on her forehead. "It's a pity. She really is beautiful."

Not a chance in hell. I pulled her away, walked back to the SUV, and placed her in the front seat.

"Damn Mafia," I muttered, turning on the car.

"Wh-what?" Trace asked.

"Shh." I touched her cheek with the back of my hand and

noticed a blood stain on my wrist.

I jerked away.

But it was too late.

I was tainted. And I'd touched her.

And I was reminded again of how different our worlds were. Mine was bloody. Hers was pure.

"It will be okay, Trace," I whispered. "Tim won't hurt you, and in the end, you'll leave. It's better this way. You'll be safe. And everything..." My voice shook. "...everything will go back to normal."

By the time I made it to Tim's room, I was full-on sick. He opened his door and looked down. "For real?" The girls loved him because his Asian looks pegged him as an exotic, yet he still had the whole football-body thing going for him. He worshipped the Elect— Then again, we had so much shit on his family it wasn't even funny. Homebody had signed his life in blood. He'd never be rid of us, and he knew it.

"Make it look real." I placed her on the bed. "Nixon wants to make an example out of her."

"Ah, so that's what Phoenix's text was about. He said she needed to be naked so..."

"Hell no!" I spat, damn-near punching him in the jaw. "It's a setup, a simple lesson in who runs things. You actually touch her, and I'll remove every finger on your right hand and sew them on backward. Feel me?"

Tim paled and nodded his head slowly. "So what? I just take some pictures of her lying here and stuff?"

My eyes narrowed. "Wait. Nixon hasn't texted you to follow up?" Something felt wrong about it, but the last thing I wanted to do was argue with the boss, especially after he'd just shot someone in the head.

Tim's text alert went off. "Never mind. I got instructions."

So Nixon had set it up.

Bastard.

I hated him.

I wanted to kill him myself.

Then again, I was just as bad. I may not have made the order, but I'd carried out the command like a bitch. An innocent girl was going to wake up in the quarterback's bed, rumors would spread, she'd be called a slut, and she'd come running back to the Elect for protection. And everyone would see that this world was one of our own creation, and it was out of the goodness of our hearts we let them live in it.

Tim sighed. "Just for tonight?"

"Yeah, come back around six thirty, alright?"

"Cool." He licked his lips. "I'll go stay down the hall. Text me the story I'm supposed to stick with before you leave in the morning, alright?"

"Great." I nodded and moved out of the way as he left me alone in the room.

I'd never stayed before.

I usually gave Tim instructions, paid him well, considering he was technically on football scholarship, and went on my merry way.

But that's the thing about the Mafia running a university. We had everyone in our pocket, including the quarterback who just happened to have been paid by the Abandonatos to win football games and do every damn thing we said.

Tonight. This night. I stayed.

Because leaving her there by herself made me feel like shit. I set her on the bed just as my phone rang. It was Nixon.

And I was too pissed at him to answer.

So I let it go to voicemail and tucked it back in my pocket.

How the hell did a person get so pretty? And why did it matter that her skin looked like velvet? Or that her lips were so red I wanted to taste them? Yeah, pretty sure kissing a girl while she was unconscious was frowned upon. Then again, so was undressing her.

Hating myself, I gently tugged off her clothes, leaving her

in nothing but her bra and underwear and stared.

Like a complete stalker, lunatic, insane person.

My phone rang again.

I kept staring.

She moaned in her sleep.

And for the first time in years, I wanted to be different. If I had been born into a different family, lived a different life, I would have had a girl like that — a girl like her. One who was so damn innocent that when she saw French cuisine, her eyes got big.

A girl who probably didn't know the difference between a merlot and a cab. I wanted a girl who got excited when she saw things for the first time, a girl unjaded.

I wanted Trace.

For no other reason than she wasn't like anyone I'd ever known — and I'd only known her a few days.

Which again should prove the point.

I leaned down and kissed her cheek. "Pretty girl..." I closed my eyes. "...I'm so sorry, but you can't stay here. You can't be in our world. You'll either die or wish you were dead. You're already in too deep, and you don't even know it." I kissed her again, lingering so close that I could smell her shampoo.

Cursing, I looked over at the clock. It was past midnight.

I took off my shoes, jumped onto the bed with her, and pulled her into my arms. She may be unconscious, but I wanted her to feel safe — secure, even if she wasn't aware of it. Maybe it was because it made me feel better.

I held her all night, and when Tim knocked on the door early in the morning, I told him the story to stick with, ran outside, and puked.

It wasn't minutes later when I got a phone call from Phoenix. "You did good."

So why did it feel like I'd just sold my soul to the devil? My reflection stared back at me through the mirror in the room. How many times did a person have before they lost their soul for good? Before they turned to the other side?

I had a sinking feeling I was already there. And the one reason — the one person who could pull me from it — was going to hate me forever.

I found Phoenix in the main lobby. Without saying a word, I sat down next to him and closed my eyes.

The sound of laughter woke me out of my sleep. Phoenix stood, I followed, and soon the door to the hall burst open. Trace barreled through it, tears streaming down her cheeks. A coward would look away. A coward would avert his eyes in shame.

I was no coward.

So I met her gaze as if I knew exactly what I was doing — as if she deserved their ridicule.

She launched herself at Phoenix. He flinched as she pounded his chest, and something flashed across his face. Regret? I wasn't sure, but he wasn't fighting her back, almost like he wanted her to beat him to death.

Too early to deal with his masochistic tendencies, I blocked her next hit and stood in front of him. "Let it go, Trace."

"You son of a bitch!" Tears collided with her lips. "Why would you do that to me?"

Because I was weak.

Because in the Mafia we don't ask questions.

Because she was dangerous.

Take your pick.

"Maybe don't drink so much next time." Phoenix smirked.

I released Trace as guys filtered out into the lobby yelling "Whore!"

She ran out the door, and I just stood there.

The entire football team bullied her.

And I'd helped it happen.

She was crying.

And I stood there.

I deserved nothing from her — not even a smile. I deserved death, and it was about time I let go of the fantasy that I would have anything but that in my future.

"Let's get ready for class." Phoenix slapped me on the back. "It's done. Nixon texted this morning and said he didn't want to talk about it, so do us both a favor and just leave it, Chase. He's been through enough, yeah?"

"Yeah," I croaked. Like I wanted to relive what had just happened? Hell no. "You're right."

"Course I am." Phoenix's eyes flashed with sadness before he shook his head and smiled. "Now if only the English teacher would think the same thing. Been trying to get in her pants all week."

And that was it.

No more talk of Trace.

No more talk of Nixon.

Just us, pretending like we were normal college students.

What a joke.

CHAPTER EIGHTEEN
Feeding the monster

Nixon

MY CELL WENT OFF way too early for my liking. It was Mo. She'd want to know what our father had said.

Hell, if the bastard could speak it would probably be something like, *"My daughter will never date a man with Campisi blood."* Or something along those lines. So when she texted me with a question mark I answered.

You have his blessing.

Which was a lie.

Because my father was currently keeping court with Satan, compliments of yours truly.

I sighed as another text alert went off.

Mo: *Um, do you have any more keycards?*

Me: *I always have keycards. Why?*

Mo: *Trace isn't comfortable eating with us anymore.*

I damn-near threw the phone against the wall. Not comfortable? After having given her everything?

Me: *Fine. Whatever. I'll give her a red card if my presence pisses her off that much. It's better that way.*

Mo: *The Red Cafeteria???*

Me: *If she eats in the commons, she'll get poisoned.*

Mo: *Right. Thanks.*

The door to the room opened. I'd stayed on campus last night on account that every time I'd tried to close my eyes I'd seen my dad's face. I'd seen the betrayal, and I'd tasted blood on my lips.

"Hey..." Chase's gaze didn't meet mine. "...so rough night, it seems?" He popped his knuckles and collapsed onto the couch.

I tossed the phone onto the table, and it made a loud clattering noise. "Yeah, not every day a son kills his father."

"Not every son would have the balls to do it, Nixon." Chase looked like shit. Dark circles made his eyes look tired, and there was no spark, no life, just... death.

"The party that bad?"

He barked out a laugh. "Right. Act like you don't know. Classic move. What you don't know won't be on your conscience, right?"

"What the hell are you talking about?" I shook my head. "It's too early for you to bitch to me. Can we do this after class? Or how about never? I need to find a red card for Trace."

Chase's face hardened. "So it's going to be like that?"

"She made it like that," I spat. "So stop defending her."

"Fine." Chase shot up from the chair and stomped toward the door. "I thought you liked her."

"What does her eating with us have to do with me liking her? And why the hell does it matter? She and I won't ever happen. She's a distraction, a problem, something I need to deal with. We have bigger shit going down than the new girl. De Lange stopped cooperating."

Chase banged his head against the door, not turning around. "Seriously?"

"Yeah," I croaked. "He has no money and is refusing to

answer any more questions. Said he wants to get paid first for the information he knows, which is shit, by the way. Just another dead end. I can't find who killed the Alfero heir which means..."

Chase swore. "It means Frank Alfero is going to make his way out of hiding. He only gave us until this year, Nixon. Hell, we're lucky he hasn't already come after us."

I shook my head and stretched. "We're more powerful than him, but we don't want him as an enemy either."

"Too late for that, I'd say. Should we set up a meeting?"

"Nah, he wants to talk to us. He'll find us."

"Right." Chase laughed humorlessly. "So on top of keeping security for the entire campus, keeping new girl out of our business, and making sure Tex doesn't take Mo to Vegas, what? Now we're on the lookout for Alfero associates?"

I slumped back down into my chair. "Looks like it."

"Well, shit. No offense, Nixon, and I mean this in the nicest way possible, but the older bosses are scary as hell, and Frank... he never got over it."

"Would you?" I asked quietly, my mind going back to the little girl, my best friend, the one who'd lost her parents and held my hand when I cried. "Would you get over it? If you loved someone that much?"

Chase hesitated, turning only slightly to face me. "No. I wouldn't get over it. If I loved someone that deeply, and they were taken from me, I'd start an all-out war to get them back to avenge what happened."

"So, we keep a lookout... you see any Alfero men, you call me or Tex."

"Not Phoenix?" Chase opened the door a crack.

"He's De Lange. We can't exactly trust him right now, not until we're sure his father is willing to keep cooperating, not until we have that family exactly where we need them. They're about ready to crumble, and we need to be the ones to pick up the pieces. We need to control it or risk another war."

"Awesome. So we have the De Langes, who hate us by the way, and the Alferos, who for four years have been using your face as target practice and — wait! Who's on our team?"

I let out a laugh even though it wasn't funny. "Um, Nicolasi?"

"Hates you." Chase joined in laughter.

"Campisi?"

"Hates everyone and blames your family for Tex's so-called abduction, and if you say the feds love you, I'm giving you the finger."

"We give them money. They do love us," I pointed out.

"Whatever. We have no friends."

"We have each other," I said softly. "It's just us, Chase. Remember that."

"I do." Chase sighed. "When things get hard, I do."

My walk to class was shit, on account that I couldn't stop thinking about the impending doom looming over our family. To make matters worse, I still had to teach class, a class Trace would be in.

I forced myself not to stare at her when I walked in the door and started firing off directions to the freshman. "Today we're going to work in teams." I started handing out sheets of paper. "I know many of you are familiar with *Settlers of Catan*. It's a board game where you are in charge of your own country, and you sell and trade with other countries. It's more complicated than that, but today I want you to form your own countries. Each of you has something someone else needs, whether it be oil, wheat, or even land. You will barter with team members in order to build your own country. Come up with a flag and a team motto. You have the rest of the class period."

Well, I wasn't going to be getting any Teacher-of-the-Year

awards after that stellar speech, like I cared. My mouth felt funny, my damn hands were sweaty, and I could have sworn Trace was staring at me, even though I hadn't actually looked down enough to notice.

Once the papers were handed out, I went back to the front of the room, finally trusting myself enough to look up.

Naturally, because God hated me, and I'd just committed a sin against one of the ten commandments — on purpose.

Trace's hand shot up.

"Yes, Farm Girl?"

She rolled her eyes. "Aren't the teams assigned?"

People around her snickered.

Idiots. "Nope, you work with groups. So pick a group and work with them."

"Any group?" Her eyes fell as a blush stained her cheeks.

"Any group," I snapped, needing the conversation to end so I could go back to torturing myself with thoughts of what her kiss would taste like.

Nodding, she stood and walked over to a group. I almost winced. Bad choice, but hey, her funeral. I only caught the last part of it, but I could have sworn Trace had just been called a whore.

My fault, considering I'd been an ass to her, but she needed to learn to be tough.

Trace's shoulders slumped in defeat as she marched toward the back of the room. The group laughed and high-fived one another. When she turned around again, I averted my eyes. They revealed too much — like pity.

I quickly grabbed the closest book and cracked it open. Her perfume hit me first. It was sweet, tempting.

"What can I do for you, Trace?" I kept my eyes firmly on the page of the book. They just so happened to focus on *breast*. What in the ever-loving hell was I reading? It was helping about as much as if Trace were taking off her shirt and tossing it in my face.

"The groups won't take me," she whispered, her voice containing a slight quiver.

Well, shit.

"Then I guess you fail." Blood roared in my ears. What the hell kind of perfume was she wearing? Was that stuff even legal? It didn't just float into the air; it swirled around me, making me damn-near choke with ecstasy.

She let out a little gasp. "It's not my fault."

"Ah, there's the excuse I was looking for." I snapped the book closed and glanced up. Time for the talk. "This is the real world, Trace. You can't just tattle on the mean kids in class. Nobody wants you to be in their group? Be in the group anyway. Make them notice you. Make them pay attention. Now, run along."

The hurt in her eyes was like a punch to the gut, and then she did the strangest thing. She straightened her shoulders, took a deep breath, and turned on her heel. She stomped the entire way to the first group who had rejected her. With her paper fisted in her hand, she pulled out a seat with the group and started speaking.

Every member gaped at her then slowly nodded their heads.

"Well, I'll be damned," I muttered, my respect for her growing by leaps and bounds. Which I really didn't need. I was already attracted to her Bambi eyes and gorgeous legs. I didn't need to fall in love with her personality too. Or her fierceness.

Shit. I just said love.

I looked back down at the book.

Sexual Encounters.

I really needed to look at book titles before I picked them up, especially considering I was already ten seconds away from bending my student over my desk. Now that was a fun mental picture I could do without.

By the time class finished, I'd already imagined a

hundred different ways to keep Trace behind, but she was already storming out of the room the minute I chose what excuse to use.

Irritated, I followed her. Plus, I had to give her the new keycard since my presence offended her so much. I still wasn't sure why Trace was backing off. I should be thrilled; instead I was completely offended, even though I was the one pushing her away. Maybe part of me wished that in those moments where I was being the least humane, she'd see past the mask and save me from my own darkness, recognizing that it wasn't me but the person I had to be in order to protect those I loved.

"Sister," I said, stopping next to both girls.

Mo flinched. "Lucifer."

Slowly, Trace turned around to face me. Her lips were red as if she'd just chewed the crap out of them. They were swollen, and I wanted to touch them. Damn, she made me want, so I pushed her away in a desperate attempt to fight what I knew was inevitable.

"Please tell Farm Girl to stop looking at us," I said in my coldest voice.

Trace averted her eyes, immediately making me feel like shit.

Students started walking slower around us, swarming was more like it, waiting for me to put her in her place again. I needed to get out before I was forced to be the ass I didn't want to be.

I slid the card into Mo's hand and shrugged.

"Thanks for... this," Monroe said.

"I'm doing it for you. Not for her," I lied. "Wouldn't want anyone uncomfortable."

Trace flinched as if I'd just hit her. I almost lifted my hand to caress that cheek, almost pulled her in for a hug and confessed my idiocy. Instead, I slowly backed away and left it.

Why was it that every time I walked away from that girl, I knew in my gut it was the wrong choice?

CHAPTER NINETEEN
Red Cafeteria? May as well put her in hell.

Chase

CLASSES SUCKED. MY DAY sucked. Tex was sucking face with Mo — oh, and Phoenix was nowhere to be seen.

Suck. Suck. Suck.

I could really use alcohol or something to take my mind off all the drama swirling around me. The girl I'd made out with last night even cornered me in the hallway. When I tried to sidestep her, she freaking launched herself at me, face first. Thankfully, I'd seen the attack before it happened, moved aside the crazy, and allowed her to face-plant into the wall. She cursed at me, but I was untouchable, so I merely tilted my head to the side and said, "Do I know you?"

"We kissed!"

"Must not have been that memorable then," I said smoothly. "Shouldn't you get to class?"

Seething, she gave me the finger and marched down the hall. So what if I watched her ass sway and then finally yelled after her, "Ah, Bianca! I remember."

"Go to hell, Chase!" she yelled back amidst the laughter

from other students.

Laughing, I walked off and nearly collided with the girl I'd been trying to avoid all day. Trace was staring at the door to the cafeteria like it was entry into a foreign country.

I cleared my throat and said, "Need help?"

With a sigh, she took her lower lip between her teeth and muttered, "You could say that."

"Here." I held out my hand. She slapped the card into my palm. I pocketed it and directed her toward the correct hallway.

The Red Room. May as well be hell to a girl like her. We called it that because it just dripped with pyschos and hatred. It wasn't the normal cafeteria, which was good, but to me it was just as bad. It was filled with kids that were lower on the totem pole than the Elect but not normal like the other kids.

"Is this hell?" she asked in a small voice.

"Not exactly." I offered a sad smile. "But it's best to be seen and not heard in here. You get it?"

I slid the card across the pad and waited for the red light, thus *The Red Room* title, to flash. "Good luck, Trace. And, for the record, it will get better."

"Right." Her chin trembled as she grabbed the card from my fingers and slowly walked into the dimly lit restaurant.

I had to force myself not to follow her. So many questions ran through my head, like why the hell she would be eating there when she could eat with us.

I couldn't help but think it was my fault. I'd helped do Nixon's bidding, and part of his punishment was probably making her eat with people I knew frowned upon killing any sort of animal for food.

The door closed, and I managed to force myself to walk toward my usual lunchroom and take a seat next to Nixon.

Trace's seat remained empty. Mo said nothing, but she did check her cell every few seconds. What? Did she think they were going to kill Trace in there? She'd be fine.

Phoenix's seat was empty too, which wasn't much of a surprise. He'd been acting sketchy and was probably still pissed Nixon was somewhat cutting him out.

"So..." Nixon spread his hands across the table. "...security's gonna get tighter these next few days."

Mo's head snapped up. "Tighter than it already is?"

"Yeah." He nodded. "No going outside the gates of Elite. That's an order."

"The hell it is!" Mo yelled., "Screw you, Nixon! Who died and made you God?"

It was on the tip of my tongue to say *"Your dad,"* but I refrained. Tex and I shared a look while Nixon gave his twin a cold stare. "I'm keeping you safe. It's not because I want to control you, Mo. It's because I don't want to plan your funeral. Get it?"

"Funeral?" Her eyes narrowed. "Why the hell would things be that bad? When have they ever been that bad?"

The answer was never. We all knew it. Something was shifting. Nixon was boss, and it wasn't going to go over well when Alfero, the second most powerful family in the US came knocking on our door. Not with the death of Nixon's father so fresh, not with the men itching for answers as to who had really killed Alfero's daughter all those years ago.

It sure as hell wasn't us. But we couldn't prove it. All evidence had led to the Abandonatos getting jealous.

And the only person who may have had more answers had just been shot in the head by his one and only son.

Yeah, we were in deep shit.

"Mo..." I cleared my throat. "...just do what he says, alright? We can control security on campus, but outside? It's more difficult."

"Not to mention it's a bitch getting shot at." Tex chuckled. "Aw, Mo, don't pull that face. You know I'm kidding. Nothing's going to happen to us."

Nixon met my gaze.

We shared the same look.

Because we both understood Tex shouldn't make promises that all of us knew he wouldn't be able to keep.

There would be a body count — and we'd be included in it, maybe not tomorrow or the next day, but it would be soon. War between the families had been brewing for too long. The hatred was too great. And the only people capable of bringing them together were Nixon and Frank Alfero, the freaking Capulets and Montagues. Great.

"Look at it this way, sweetheart." Tex pulled Mo in for a hug. "You can shop online all you want."

Mo scowled. "What about Trace?"

Nixon let out a growl. "What about her?"

"She's my roommate. Will you protect her too? Say the worst happens and a family gets in the school... will you protect my roommate? Or is this a selfish thing? Only blood?"

I opened my mouth, but Nixon silenced me with his hand. "We protect blood first, but you have my word... no harm will come to Trace, not if I can help it."

What the hell? Since when have we cared about a commoner? Since when have we cared about the very girl that Nixon was putting through absolute hell? The girl was probably eating a soy burger right now because of Nixon, and suddenly he goes all Mother Teresa on her? It made no sense. Then again, nothing was making sense anymore.

My feelings for her.

His feelings for her.

The fact that we were both drawn to the wrong thing.

And the fact that one of us was going to eventually crack.

CHAPTER TWENTY
Granola bars are peace offerings. Check.

Nixon

I FELT GUILTY ALL through lunch about giving Trace the red card. She wouldn't see it as the kindness it was. Eating in the commons would destroy her. At least, in the Red Cafeteria she wouldn't have to worry about people bullying her. Then again, I couldn't make promises because I couldn't predict a damn thing the girl did.

Once lunch ended, I tried to escape my sister's pensive gaze. Tried and failed. She grabbed my arm and twisted.

"Satan." She seethed.

"Mo, can we argue later? When I'm not so stressed out I want to shoot things?"

She released my arm and grinned then held out a granola bar.

"Um, thanks, but I just ate?"

"Not you, you ass." She rolled her eyes. "Trace just texted me. She didn't eat. She's hungry. She isn't like your usual girl who pretends to eat lettuce only to throw it up later. Girl's going to pass out if she doesn't get food."

"And you're telling me this why?"

"Because you like her."

I looked away. "Damn twin."

"Ha, you love me, and, regardless of what's been going down between you and her and even Chase..." She shook her head. "...I like her. She's my roommate, she has no friends, and every single odd has been stacked against her. Yet she wakes up every day with a smile on her face and tries to encourage me, of all people. She makes me want to be better, and the sad thing? I think you know it. I think you're so damn scared of your own feelings that you're using family shit to force your hand. This is the real world. You're an adult. So here."

I took the granola bar and stared at it like it was some weird foreign object.

"Peace offering." Mo slapped me on the back. "If you wait by the lab, she'll be walking by in a few minutes."

"Are you matchmaking?"

"Course not." Mo winked. "Oh, and PS, think I could bring Tex by the house when I talk to Dad?"

"Talk to Dad?" I repeated. "Why the hell would you want to do that?"

Her face fell. "Well, I thought he gave us his blessing."

"He's not well, Mo. He's... dying." Wow great lie. "It might be best for you to wait."

"But what about the family dinner?"

"Let me get back to you, okay?" I forced a cheesy grin and kissed her on the forehead. "And thanks for the granola bar."

"Yeah well, when you're being an ass, I'm the only one you'll listen to."

"I listen to Chase."

"Ha, Chase likes your girl, so I think those days are long gone."

My gut twisted. She was so right it was scary. "I'll see ya, sis."

"Later, loser."

Ten minutes later, and I still felt like the loser she'd called me. I was leaning against the wall, waiting for a girl to walk by. Right. My world had officially crashed and burned. What the hell was I doing?

Trace was staring at the ground, slowly making her way down the hall, her face pale and tired.

Slowly that face lifted. She met my stare with ice, like she wasn't sure if she wanted to punch me in the face or just set my pants on fire.

"There were rumors you didn't get lunch." Yeah, that was the best I could do.

Her eyebrows arched. "Rumors, huh? Well, alert the authorities. Oh wait, I forgot. You're what? The judge, jury, and—"

"Stop." I said it so low my voice cracked. With a sigh, I walked toward her until she had nowhere to go but against the wall, exactly where I wanted her. She tried to sidestep me, but I moved in the way, our faces nearly colliding. "I'm speaking to you."

"And I'm leaving," she hissed.

"Just…" I scratched my head and tried to conjure up any sort of game. Normally, girls just threw themselves at me. The ones who were afraid didn't need nice words or smiles. They just wanted the power behind my name. I was at a complete loss. The thought made me smile. Hell, it made me want to break down in chaotic laughter. I was afraid of nothing — but her. I was afraid of her.

Trace's mouth dropped open. She took a step toward me, probably not even realizing that she'd lifted her hands as if she wanted to cup my face.

Slowly, I reached behind her and gently pushed her into the alcove, pinning her against the wall, willing my eyes to stare at her brown depths rather than her plump lips. I wanted to taste them so bad I hated me for it. I hated her, and I hated that life had given me someone like her at the worst possible time.

"Eat," I urged softly.

Her mouth snapped open, tempting me further, so I did the next best thing. Rather than kissing her, I shoved the granola bar in her mouth.

Yeah, I was a regular lady killer.

Her stomach growled loud enough for me to hear.

I smirked. "See? I knew you were hungry." Right. Like music to every girl's ears.

She moaned a little.

I died a little more.

"Of course I was hungry, you ass! I was in the Red Cafeteria! I half-expected to be eaten myself in that place, and they don't serve meat. NO MEAT, Nixon! Some cow gets to live another day because the people in there eat tofu! Do you even know what that stuff is made out of?"

Shocked, I could only stare at her open-mouthed. Then her little finger poked me in the chest, causing blood to surge in all the wrong places. Holy shit, was she reprimanding me? And why the hell was it so damn hot?

"And let me tell you something else. I did not sleep with Tim! Well, I may have slept, but I definitely didn't touch his— And, and... I—"

My eyebrows rose. I had no idea what she was talking about, and why the hell would I care about our lame-ass quarterback, but this side of her? The one with spunk? Yeah, I freaking craved it, so I licked my lips and leaned forward. "Oh, do continue. I love getting reprimanded. You gonna spank me later too?" Dear God, please say yes.

Her nostrils flared, and, just on cue, her stomach growled again. She closed her eyes as if trying to disappear altogether.

"Good Lord, woman! Just eat the damn granola bar and say thank you!"

Her eyes narrowed. "Where were you last night?"

The smile froze on my face. Oh, you know, committing murder — no big, though the stains gonna be a bitch to get out of my favorite henley. "I gotta run."

"Wait." She grabbed my arm.

It was enough to make me pause, to make me want to stay firmly planted in front of her. Hell, it was enough for me to want to ask her for a hug and never let go. When had I become that person? The type that was so starved for human affection that I was basically ready to push myself into the arms of a girl who deserved so much better than what I had to give.

Unable to control the tremble in my arm, I jerked away. "Please." I closed my eyes so I wouldn't see the hurt on her face. "Don't touch me."

I walked away before I blurted out everything.

Killing my father.

Hating my best friend for the same reason I hated myself.

War between families.

Life.

I wanted a friend.

For the first time in my life, I wanted a friend who was a girl.

A girl like Trace.

The memory rushed forward. Unable to stop the pain as it swirled in my chest, I let myself remember a similar girl, a girl who was so much like Trace.

"Don't be sad!" Bella shouted.

I plugged my ears.

Her little lip jutted out. I unplugged my ears and sighed. "What are you gonna do about it, huh?"

"Wanna play Barbies?"

"No." I folded my arms across my chest. "Boys don't play Barbies."

"You have a G.I. Joe."

"*It's not a Barbie.*"

She let out a giggle. "*Um, yes it is. Mommy said so.*"

I looked away from her because I knew the truth. She wouldn't get to talk to her mommy ever again, and I felt like it was my fault, like I could have stopped it even though I was too young to do anything but eavesdrop on conversations between the adults.

"*I'll always be your friend. You know that, right?*"

"*Yes, Nixon.*" *She nodded firmly.* "*I know that. You're my best friend. Now, let's play Barbies before Mommy comes home.*"

But she didn't come home.

And I never saw my friend ever again.

CHAPTER TWENTY-ONE

Waiting for the light. Taking hers in order to fill my dark.

Tex

I GROANED AND FLIPPED over onto my stomach. The nightmare was getting worse. Swear, it felt like the fires of hell were licking at my heels. The only time I ever saw my father's face was in my nightmares — and I hoped to God it stayed that way.

With a curse, I got up from bed and went over to the window. Campus was quiet. I'd stayed in our special Elect dorm that night while Nixon went back to the house to get more bloodstains out of the carpet — no, for real. He'd had to replace the whole damn thing once he shot his father. The stains had apparently dripped down the hall, thus the need to get the blood out.

Mo came up behind me, wrapping her arms around my middle, leaning her chin against my back. "What's wrong?"

So many damn things I couldn't even keep the pain straight.

I couldn't give the princess the future she deserved, and the very fact that my father's blood ran through my veins made me want to vomit.

"Run away with me," I challenged, refusing to turn around and see her pity-filled eyes.

Instead, I focused on the moon, wondering if he was staring at the same one, wondering if one day he was going to come after me and rip everything I held dear right out of my hands.

Mo laughed, her lips curling around my skin in a kiss. "Alright, where would we go?"

"Anywhere but here." I sighed. "And I think it's safe to say Sicily's out."

She reached around me and pulled my face down to her lips. "Tex," Her lips were warm, tender. "It's college. Stop being so dramatic."

"Who says I'm being dramatic?" I frowned.

"It's three a.m., you're staring out your window after a great night full of mind-blowing sex, and you still don't look happy. Is..." Her eyebrows knit together. "...is it me?"

"Hell no," I growled, pulling her into my arms. "Don't ever let me hear you say that again."

She nodded but didn't look convinced.

So I kissed her — hard.

And when she didn't respond right away, I lifted the shirt from her body and tossed it onto the ground. Naked from the waist up, just the way I liked her.

"Mo, look at me."

Her eyes blinked open.

"The problem in this scenario will never be you. Mo Abandonato is always the solution, never the problem."

She wrapped her arms around my neck as I lifted her into the bed and hovered over her. "And Tex Campisi, what is he?"

The problem. Always was and always would be — the damn problem.

"Horny," I answered. "And right now... the only solution... is you. Get it?"

She rolled her eyes and let out a laugh while I pulled the mask firmly back over my face.

I was Tex, funny, happy-go-lucky Tex.

But deep down inside? Vito Campisi was just dying to get out. I figured the more I starved that part of my soul — the more it dissipated.

I had no way of knowing.

That I was dead wrong.

No way of knowing that the fire never really got put out, not when you left the coals, thinking they wouldn't simmer back into a burn.

"Tex." Mo let out a little moan as I jerked the shorts from her waist and buried myself deep within her.

It was a metaphor for my life: the deeper you go, the further you fall. Right?

"Love... you."

"Love you too." Our foreheads touched, and in that moment, my world was perfect again.

CHAPTER TWENTY-TWO
Turning point

Chase

THE DAYS GOT HARDER... as in, we still couldn't get De Lange to cooperate, and we'd already caught two of Alfero's men on campus. We'd sent them back with giant-ass bruises — trying to send a message — but who knew if it had been received.

Nixon and I had started calling meetings on campus, something we'd never had to do before. Even Phoenix was irritated that it had taken so much of our time away from our social lives. But newsflash! We didn't get that opportunity, especially now that Nixon was officially the boss. His life was over, and by association, so were ours.

Tex had spent every free moment with Mo in order to relieve his so-called tension at being the black sheep of the Abandonato drama.

And Phoenix had spent his days drinking — a lot. He'd been kicked out of class twice for showing up completely wasted. It was out of character, even for him, but Nixon had told me not to touch it. So I didn't.

And me? Well... I'd tried not to stalk the new girl.

Nixon was in the same boat. Between the two of us, the girl probably had more bodyguards than the president. Nixon was always asking the security about her schedule. Was she happy? Was she eating? Did she fall and scrape her knee? I would be irritated if I wasn't so damn concerned myself.

What the hell was it about that girl that had both of us losing our minds? Maybe it was her spirit, or maybe our lives were just pathetic enough that all it had taken was kindness from an outsider to make us feel human again.

"Class," Nixon growled, glancing at his cell. He looked horrible, like he hadn't slept in days. Then again, if I'd killed my father in cold blood I probably wouldn't be dreaming of unicorns either.

Tex and Phoenix left to go to the opposite end of campus, while Nixon and I walked down the hall of the business building. People freaking parted like the Red Sea when we walked, irritating to say the least. I just wanted normal, not that I'd ever experienced it. But I imagined it would be awesome, like getting ice cream without having to worry about someone pointing a gun at my head, or walking to class and actually being the one to get tripped and bullied, rather than the other way around.

I let out a pathetic sigh when Nixon stopped dead in his tracks. I knew that look. It was the one he gave people before he killed them.

"Nixon?"

"Slut, slut, slut!" The chanting grew louder as we turned the corner. Close to a hundred students were standing around a girl on the floor. There were broken egg shells by people's feet, along with condoms and what looked like ice water. I shook my head in disgust, ready to tell them to give the girl some space and do the usual *"Let the Elect deal with the trash"* speech.

And then I saw dark brown hair.

Wide, innocent brown eyes blinked against the water

124

streaming down her perfect face. I was about ready to go all Rocky on everyone, when Nixon gave a slight shake of his head and stepped forward.

"You are nothing. Do you understand?" an evil bitch said in a hateful tone. "You don't belong here. Say it."

Trace gave her head a slight shake.

The psycho pulled Trace's hair harder, causing a shriek to erupt from her lips. "Say it!"

"I—" She shook her head and then lifted her chin. "—I belong here."

Half the group burst out laughing, while the other half gasped in outrage, making me want to roll my eyes and pull out my gun.

"Leave her alone." Nixon stepped forward.

The girl holding Trace's hair snorted. "And who do you think—" She jerked away from Trace the minute she saw it was Nixon and then paled. "I did it for you, Nixon, for you! She can't dismiss you like that. She can't—"

"Stop speaking." Nixon pushed her into me and sneered. "Take care of this, will you?"

The girl freaking trembled in my hands, and I had to admit I liked that she was afraid, because it was about to get a hell of a lot worse.

All around me people waited.

I grabbed the girl's arm and practically dragged her down the hall. The rest of the students followed because, hey, who doesn't like a free show? Hell, it wasn't like I was going to hurt the girl. I didn't hit girls. That wasn't my specialty. I would never hit a girl unless I had no choice, my life or hers.

"So..." I gently pushed her away. "...what's your name?"

"B-Brit." She wrapped her arms around her stomach.

"How old are you, Brit?"

"Twenty."

"Major?" I sighed, shoving my hands in my pockets while it went deathly silent around me.

Her blue eyes flickered with uncertainty; she tucked a piece of red hair behind her shoulder. "Business."

"Father's name?"

People whistled.

She pressed her lips together.

"Father's name? Don't make me ask again, Brit."

"Arnold."

"Ah..." I snapped my fingers. "Ben Arnold, Democrat. Was elected into the House of Representatives a few years back. Loves to golf, has a dog named... Henry and a goldfish named Stu. Cheated on his wife of twenty years with a stripper and was caught embezzling money from the State of Iowa but wasn't penalized or taken to prison. Good ol' Ben." I chuckled. "Loves his little girl. I mean, he really does. After all, that was his plea, *"Don't do this to my family."* I sighed. "It's just too bad."

"Wh-what?" Brit gasped, tears streaming down her face. "What do you mean?"

"Prison... is not for the faint of heart." I sighed. "Do you understand what I'm saying to you?"

Brit shook her head.

I pulled out my cell and dangled it in front of her face. "One phone call from me and your father will be behind bars so fast you won't even get to say goodbye. One phone call, Brit, and I suck every possible future from your pathetic life. You'll be lucky to be working as a prostitute once I'm finished with you. Because let's face it, even prostitutes need to have some class, am I right?"

People around me started whispering.

"So here's what's going to happen..." I cleared my throat and approached her until she could feel the heat from my body. "You talk to Trace again? I make that phone call. You talk about her, and I hear about it from one of your ugly friends? I make the phone call. Daddy goes to prison, all the family money gets taken, and, just because I love making people suffer that much, I tell the freaking world about your mother's little... problem. Got me?"

Her lips trembled as tears cascaded down her puffy cheeks.

"Great." I smiled and turned. "Anyone else want to tempt fate today, or are we good?"

Nobody spoke.

"Awesome. Then go back to class, make good choices, don't do drugs, and— Go Eagles!"

I sent Nixon a quick text to let him know the situation had been dealt with, though I was kind of irritated at him. He'd been the hero while I'd had to take care of the dirty work. It was what I did, but for the first time... ever, I wanted to be Nixon. I wanted to be the guy who took care of business, not the second-in-command. What I did was important — I knew that, he knew that. Hell, everyone knew that. But I wanted more than importance. I wanted the girl too, and I was finally starting to see I wasn't going to get her, not if Nixon wanted her, not if Nixon as much as desired her. Because I was second. Not first. Always second. And, above all else, I listened to my boss. Blood before girls, blood before life, blood before death. I was in it until I passed into the afterlife. It just sucked that while I wallowed in self-pity, Nixon was holding the girl of our dreams and wiping her tears.

CHAPTER TWENTY-THREE

I would kill them all for hurting her — if I could get away with it.

Nixon

"ARE YOU HURT?" I leaned down and touched her face, but she slapped my hand away.

Cursing, I tried to pick her up, but she still shied away from me. The hell with that. I was taking her out of this shithole even if she held a freaking gun to my head.

"Shit." I examined her face. "This wasn't supposed to happen. I didn't..." I chewed my lower lip until I felt searing pain from biting down too hard. What could I say? I didn't know they would take it this far? Because I had. I'd known. I wasn't stupid. I'd known it was a possibility, and I'd let it happen.

I held out my hand to help her up.

She eyed it like it was the plague.

I couldn't blame her.

Reluctantly, she took it, and I used the opportunity to pull her into my arms and carry her down the hall.

She gasped, and then the fight left her as she leaned her wet head against my chest.

And suddenly everything clicked into place.

It felt so right, having her in my arms, protecting her. I was half tempted to growl *"mine,"* as professors watched us walk down the hall. I'd deal with them later, what the hell? A girl gets bullied that bad, and they'd just watched, sipping their coffee like it had been a normal occurrence. Assholes.

Trace's hand pressed against my chest.

My breath hitched. I fought to keep the moan in. Touch from girls had always been something I loathed because it always seemed like there was a selfish reason behind it. They wanted to be screwed, they wanted to say they'd been with me, or they wanted my money. It was never what was behind the mask of Nixon Abandonato, but what I could offer them.

Touch had been made worse when I was little.

My father used to beat me within an inch of my life, making me shy away from any sort of human contact. Could you blame me for not wanting to show weakness? It just seemed better to hate touch — to hate pity, to hate everything — than show that it was actually a huge chink in my armor. The longer her hand stayed there, the warmer I felt, as if the heat from her palm was cracking through the ice, reaching into my chest and massaging my heart back to life.

Thump, thump, thump. It picked up speed, like it had been starved for years and was finally getting fed.

My entire body relaxed as I led her into our room, the one we had meetings in, the one I'd been sleeping in. It was our dorm, but it was private, nestled away from everyone else. Hell, it even had a special card that only we four had access to. Even the dean had to ask permission to get in.

I tapped my red Eagle card against the door, it slid open. I walked in, but didn't put her down. Not yet. She struggled a bit in my arms, but I held her firm.

I imagined what it was like seeing our place for the first

time. It looked a hell of a lot like a bachelor pad: PlayStation controllers were still on the couch, the flat screen had ESPN blaring at a piercing volume, and we had a full bar in the corner.

Trace glanced up at my face. I tried to keep myself from smiling at her awestricken expression.

When we reached the bathroom, I glanced down, first at her eyes then her full lips. "You need to clean up."

"Because I'm a whore?" Her voice was hoarse from crying.

Trace's expression was priceless as if she was more irritated at being called a whore than offended. "No, I think we both know you're not a whore. You need to clean up because you smell like egg and sugar water."

Her brow furrowed.

With a sigh, I plopped her in the middle of the bathroom. "Get in."

When she didn't move, I started pulling off her clothes.

"What the hell, Nixon! You can't just strip me—"

"I can, and I will. Now step out of your skirt like a good girl." I already had the zipper down and was fighting temptation, fighting the urge to go slower.

She huffed but stepped out of the skirt while I went over and started the bath water. When I turned back around, I nodded for her to lift her arms up. When she did, I tugged the tank top and tossed it to the floor. I glanced back up and froze. She was clad in only her underwear, a sexy-as-hell bra, and her knee-highs. I wasn't a prude. I'd had many schoolgirl fantasies, and every damn one faded in comparison to what was standing in front of me.

She quickly wrapped her arms around her chest, looked away, and then launched herself against me sobbing. "I miss cows!"

Sexually tense moment officially gone.

I burst out laughing, unable to help it. Clearly, when she

was hungry, this was how she dealt with trauma. "Sweetheart, I'm sure they miss you too. Now do you think you can manage the rest?"

"The rest?" She blinked at me through thick lashes, her hands still on my chest. It felt so damn good. She closed her eyes and sighed.

I cupped her face. "Open your eyes, Trace."

When she opened them, she was staring directly at my lips, leaning forward. It would be easy to kiss her — too easy. And for some reason I'd found my morals and decided it would be wrong to take advantage in her current state — no matter how right it may feel. *Wrong. Wrong. Wrong.* Yeah, chant that a few times.

"Do you need me to help you take off the rest of your clothes, or can you make it from here to the tub without killing yourself?" I whispered.

"No, um, I can do it."

I was still chanting the word *wrong* when I leaned forward and breathed in her neck, allowing her scent to wash over me, tickle my senses, tempt me beyond redemption. "You sure? I wouldn't want anything to happen to—"

A fist came out of nowhere, hitting me in the arm. Chuckling, I stepped back. "Towels are in the cupboard under the sink. We have everything you need next to the tub. Just... don't drown, okay?"

"Why would I drown?"

How the hell was I supposed to know? But it could happen! And I was suddenly aware of every single disaster that could strike in that damn bathroom. "Just..." I slammed my fist against the counter, upset at myself for being so weak. "...just, don't make me worry, okay? I hate worrying." Because that didn't make me sound like a complete nursing-home escapee.

"Fine." She nodded. "I'll try really hard to keep myself from mermaiding it, deal?"

If I looked at her again, I was going to lose all control. Already too close, I nodded and slammed the door behind me then leaned against it, allowing my body to cool. Not working. So not working. With a curse, I peeled my dampened t-shirt from my body and stared at it. I was just about to lift it to my nose and smell it... Right. Smell the egg from Trace's body — I knew it sounded insane — when yelling commenced from the other side of the door. Naturally, I went into Superman-mode, jerking it open and screaming, "What happened?"

Trace was standing in the middle of the bathtub.

Completely.

Naked.

Without clothes.

Without shame.

Absolutely, I would sell my soul a million times over if I could just have stared for five more minutes. Beautifully naked.

Her eyes locked with mine, and slowly her cheeks turned red as I allowed my eyes the great honor of staring at her breasts.

Mother of God. I was going to go down in flames for wanting her that much.

I took a step toward her and then another. My fingers clenched at my sides. Just one kiss, harmless really, in the grand scheme of things.

"Nixon! Are you in here? Is she okay?" Chase's voice sounded from behind me.

Panicking, I backed up and slammed the door as he rounded the corner.

"Dude." Chase slapped my back. "Why is your shirt off?"

"Uh..." I scratched my head. "It was wet."

"And you're staring at the door like you want to hump it because... it's going to magically grow lady-parts, or what?"

"Shut up." I pushed him away and scowled.

"Dude, it's fine. Remember Tex and his weird fascination

with Mrs. Butterworth?"

"He was ten." I gritted my teeth. "And she's fine, by the way."

"Mrs. Butterworth?" He grinned.

"Trace."

"Ah, the hotter of the two. Good to know." He plopped down on the couch. "And everything's taken care of. I did a little bit of threatening, there were tears, a few hiccups, the usual."

"Hiccups?"

"They came after the tears — more of a gasp, *Chase, no!* type of hiccup, which is a hell of a lot better than a black eye, if you ask me."

"Like that girl would have punched you."

"Girls are like cats, completely unpredictable and scary as hell when cornered."

"Been attacked by a cat recently?"

"Whatever. They're creepy. Stop getting off the subject. How's our girl?"

I growled.

"Just checking to see if you've marked your territory, which apparently you have." His jaw flexed. "Anyway, you should grab her some clothes."

"And while I do that, go grab her a new uniform."

"Already called one in."

"Really?" My eyes narrowed. "How do you know her size?"

"I'm a manwhore. I know sizes." Chase smirked. "I'll go grab the goods. Try to keep it in your pants."

I rolled my eyes and ran into the bedroom to grab some clothes. I wasn't really sure what her size was, but Mo had left a few clothes from her last shopping expedition here on campus, just in case she needed them, whatever that meant. I found a pair of jeans, a sweater, and some lingerie, thinking it would have to do, and went to knock on the bathroom door just as it swung open, revealing Trace in nothing but a damn towel.

She collapsed against my body.

My fingers dug into her shoulders, and her nose smooshed against my chest. My breathing was erratic as blood pounded through my body at an epic speed, demanding I tug the towel and push her against the closest object that would hold both our weight and a hell of a lot of movement.

"You need something?" I whispered into her ear. My lips grazed its' wetness. My knees damn-near buckled at the touch.

"I need..." Her voice cracked. "...um, I need something to wear."

"Hmm..." I gently pushed her away and glanced at her towel. "Are you sure about that?"

She quickly looked down.

"I'll find you something. Give me a few minutes." I tucked the clothes under my arm and went back into the room and exchanged the sweater— What the hell was I thinking? I switched out the bra size too and returned.

"So..." Suddenly nervous, I scratched my head. "...I, um, I guessed on the sizes, and I honestly didn't want to offend you by guessing too big or guessing too small, which is why it took me five years to pick something out. So don't get pissed if I was wrong, okay?"

She let out a little laugh. "Okay, I promise I won't get mad." She took the clothes and went back into the bathroom.

Nervous, I waited in the main living area, my eyes watching the TV but not really soaking everything in. My ears were perked, ready for any noise emerging from the bathroom that would give me an excuse to run to her rescue again.

Soon, the door opened, and Trace walked out.

"Better?" Needing something to do with my hands, I reached for my water and took a sip.

"Squeaky clean." She sighed. "And I'm happy to announce that no drowning took place in your bathroom."

I smirked.

She cleared her throat, making the silence more awkward. "Well, thanks for... everything. I'll just go back to—"

"You aren't going anywhere until classes are dismissed. You still have two hours to burn. So make yourself at home." I pointed to the couch.

"But..." She held up her crap uniform. "I need to get these cleaned and..."

I swore, stood, and grabbed the uniform. I took aim and tossed it in the trash. "Done."

"What? You have a magical trashcan that cleans clothes?"

"Nope. You can't wear those again. They're ruined, and there are rules here. You can't just wear a ruined uniform."

"I hate the stupid rules!" She stomped over to the trashcan and tried pulling the clothes from it. "This uniform is all I have!"

Cursing, I pried the clothes away and returned them to where they belonged — in the trash — and dragged her to the couch. "Sit."

"But—"

"Sit," I commanded. "You thirsty?"

"No."

"Hungry?"

Her stomach growled loudly. She closed her eyes, refusing to answer me.

"That's what I thought."

Why was it so hard for her to accept help? Was it because I'd been so horrible? I needed her to trust me, and, well, the only way I could think of to make her feel better was to cook for her. It was what my ma would have done. So I threw a hamburger patty into the microwave, hit defrost, and went to work baking some fries. It was a staple in our kitchen. For some reason, it made me feel normal, less Italian, when I had a hamburger and fries. The guys always knew it was a bad day if I was at Mc Donald's. Not that I'd been there in weeks, considering we were on high security.

When the food was done, I put everything on a plate and walked back into the room, holding it out to her.

Tears pooled in Trace's eyes as she took the plate and whispered, "Thank you."

"You need to eat more." I cursed.

Just then, the doors opened. Chase strolled in with a garment bag, followed by Mo, Tex, and Phoenix.

"Are you okay?" Mo ran to Trace's side and hugged her.

Trace had just taken a huge-ass bite out of the burger, so she nodded and then coughed.

"I made her half a cow," I explained. "I'm sure she's in meat lover's heaven right now."

"Aw, you killed a cow for her?" Mo sighed and gave me a wink.

Annoying twin sister. Yeah, yeah, first a granola bar, now a cow. Laugh it up, Mo.

"Good God, people, he put frozen meat in the microwave and pressed defrost," Chase muttered. "Is this all you needed, fearless leader?" He held out the garment bag.

I nodded, ignoring his sour mood. What the hell was his problem? Chase's eyes fell to Trace then back to me. Right. She was the problem. Or better, it was me being with her that was the problem. "Right sizes?"

"Yup."

"Good," I said in a cold voice. "Just put the bag over there, and we'll take it over once classes are out."

I said *we* on purpose so Chase would know I wasn't backing off. I wasn't going away. He glared but did what he was told — because Chase always did what he was told, which made me feel slightly guilty. He may like Trace, but I liked her too, way more than I should, and I wasn't going to let him sneak in and steal away the one girl who made me want to feel again. The one girl who, for some reason, had snuck into my heart and refused to leave.

Phoenix leaned against the counter, his stare pensive, and directly set on Trace, like he was waiting for her to call him out or something, which was crazy. Then again, Phoenix had been acting bat-shit crazy for the past few days. I knew I needed to talk with him, but part of me felt guilty because I'd been the one to snap at him at the party.

Tex squished himself between Mo and Trace and put his arm back on the couch. "So, what are we doing this weekend?"

"We..." She placed her hand on his knee. "...are doing nothing. *I'm* going to be a good friend and hang out with my roommate who was brutally assaulted by the stupid assholes who go to our school."

Tex pouted. "Nixon, can't you just order a hit on the ones who started it so I can have some alone-time with your sister?"

Trace laughed. "Order a hit? You guys talk like he's Mafia or something."

The room fell silent, and then everyone laughed nervously — it was awkward as hell.

The rest of the hour went by fast between Mo and Tex arguing over what to do with Trace, Phoenix staring a hole through the wall, and Chase trying to sit as close as humanly possible to Trace. I was ready to lose my mind.

"Guys! Just go hang out. I was going to go to the store anyways," Trace finally said above the noise.

"No!" We all responded in unison. Right. Like that didn't look totally suspicious.

Her eyes narrowed. "Is the store dangerous or something?"

Mo shrugged. "No, it's just not smart. I mean, you shouldn't leave campus by yourself. Besides, you need a car. You don't have a car."

"I'll take a cab."

Mo faked a horrified look. "A cab?"

Tex burst out laughing. "Do those still exist?"

"So..." Chase asked, thrusting his hands in his pockets. "What will it be, Nixon?"

All eyes fell to me.

Because that's what I did.

I made decisions. And I'd been the one who'd told everyone we couldn't go out — we had to hunker down on campus. I eyed Trace briefly before answering. "I guess we're all going shopping." It was the least I could do.

"But—" Monroe started, but I glared, telling her with my eyes to stop.

"We'll take security." I shrugged it off like it wasn't a big deal to go marching out into the wild while Alfero men were on the hunt.

"But last time—"

"I said..." I hated being challenged. "...we'll take security."

There hadn't been a last time; we all knew that. Well, not Trace. It was just Mo's way of trying to argue the point.

She was afraid.

And I hated that I'd caused the fear, but she was my sister and I would protect her at all costs. We could take security, and if we stayed close enough to campus, it would be fine. Besides, who would kill a newly minted mob boss in cold blood?

The answer?

Frank Alfero, that's who.

I just had to be smarter than the old man or die.

The things I would do for a girl I hardly knew — a girl I wanted to know a hell of a lot more.

CHAPTER TWENTY-FOUR
The explosion

Phoenix

THE LAST TIME I'D brought my father crap news he'd pulled a gun on me. This time I was more prepared. Nixon said he wasn't cooperating, and I was going to force him.

I knocked on the door to his office. Nothing.

I knocked again.

Finally, he jerked the door open. "What the hell do you want?"

"And hello to you too." I pushed and tried to get in, but he held it firm.

"I'm busy."

"The hell you are." I pushed harder, he stumbled back, and that was when I saw how busy he really was.

With two girls.

Two of the ones I'd broken in the week before.

I almost vomited right there. What type of person kept underage girls in his office, the office of a university, then screwed them during coffee break? And what type of person did it make me, that I'd been first, my own father second.

Shit, I hated myself.

I hated him.

I hated everything.

Hands shaking, I reached for the cigarette pack on his desk, I hadn't ever been much of a smoker, but I needed something to do and puking was out of the question, along with shooting him between the eyes.

"Should you be playing with the merchandise?" I asked.

"Deal fell through." He shrugged. "Thought it a waste to let them go."

A waste?

"What do you mean the deal fell through?"

"Guy backed out," my dad sneered. "We didn't get the money, and it's your fault. He said they were too pure, so clearly you didn't do a good-enough job making them dirty for him. Which reminds me, Nixon owes me money."

"Nixon owes you shit. You talk, he pays, that's the deal."

"Yeah, well, what if I'm done talking?"

"Then he shoots you."

My dad rolled his eyes and barked out a laugh. "Can't kill a boss without signing your own death sentence."

I hated that he was right.

"Wanna join?" My father's eyes were challenging me to say no. "I have two... only used one. The other's still good."

He pulled out a knife and ran it down the first girl's cheek. She was brunette, maybe seventeen, high as an effing kite, and apparently, under the impression the knife was a lollipop, she opened her mouth. He touched the blade to her lips.

"Stop," I growled.

"What?" My father shrugged. "She won't feel a thing." Glaring at me, he shoved the knife past her lips. Blood spurted from her mouth, and I lost my shit.

I lunged at him, slamming him against the wall. His punch collided with the left side of my body — a kidney blow, nice. I kneed him in the balls just as he landed another deadly blow to my ribs.

When he fell to the floor, I looked at the mess around me — the mess I'd helped create. It was only natural I cleaned it up.

The girl was sobbing as blood continued to come out of her mouth.

And I was numb.

Completely numb.

Because, in that moment, I couldn't see her as a person anymore, only an object. If I had seen her as a person, I would have had an honest-to-God mental breakdown. I threw a towel in her face and dropped a few hundreds onto the floor then sauntered out of the room, head high.

It wasn't until I was making my way across the campus that the shaking started.

And it wasn't until I saw the SUVs parked out in front of the girls' dorms that images of every single face came back full-force.

They'd ranged in ages, shapes, sizes — it hadn't mattered. The number was in the hundreds. Nobody had forced my hand.

That was all on me.

I wanted to die.

But I wanted to prove myself more than that... if it was the last thing I did. I would prove myself to Nixon.

I would come out on top.

Because I... was all I had left.

CHAPTER TWENTY-FIVE
And so it begins…

Chase

"SHOPPING…" I SIGHED AND slammed the door shut. "Really Nixon?"

"Deal with it." He rolled his eyes. "Oh, and mind riding with Phoenix?"

I glared. "So it's going to be like that?"

"What?" He shrugged.

"You gonna hold her hand on skate night too? Maybe give her your sweater or something?"

Nixon rolled his eyes. "Whatever, man. I'm protecting her, not trying to get in her pants."

"That's a lie." Phoenix snorted, walking up to us, a cigarette in his mouth.

Since when did he start smoking again?

"You want in her pants so bad you aren't even paying attention to shit going on around us."

Nixon's eyes narrowed. "You got something to say, Phoenix? Say it."

"Fine." Phoenix threw the cigarette onto the ground and

stepped on it. "It's time we left Elite. We don't belong here anymore..." His eyes were haunted. "We just need out — I need out."

"Newsflash." I rolled my eyes at his dramatics. "We don't get a freaking out."

Phoenix rubbed his face with his hands. Damn, the guy looked like hell. "My father isn't cooperating with me anymore... he thinks I've grown weak. He's—"

Nixon held up his hand. "Has he..." He swallowed and looked away. "...hurt anyone?"

Phoenix rubbed his hands together. "He always hurts people."

"Look man..." Nixon sighed. "...stay on campus from now on, or go to my house. Don't put up with that shit."

"Screw you!" Phoenix yelled. "A real man would put up with it. A real man would get the job done! I'm getting the freaking job done, Nixon! Alright? What else do you want from me? Or do you even know? Are you too focused in on all that brown hair?"

"This has nothing to do with her!" Nixon roared. "Don't make it about her. She's a stranger, Phoenix, not part of our world."

"Good to hear you finally say it." Phoenix shook his head. "She isn't a part of our world. In the end you choose us, not her. We are family. She's nothing, Nixon. Nothing." Shaking, he pulled out another cigarette. "Whatever. I'm out. Have fun catering to Cowgirl."

He stomped off, leaving me in stunned disbelief.

Nixon stared at the ground then barked, "Tex!"

"What up?" Tex pressed *End* on his cell and glanced between the two of us. "Shit. Who died?"

"Ride with us. Chase, I need you in the other car doing—"

"Yeah, yeah." I waved him off. "Doing what I do best. Guarding the boss."

"Chase—"

"Leave it..." I held up my hand. "...and let me do my job, which is to protect your fine ass."

"He called your ass *fine*." Tex nodded. "Just sayin', if he's staring at your ass, that means he's been looking at mine, and, by my calculations, that means Chase's favorite appendage has been getting zero play." Tex pointed his finger at me. "Get laid before I punch you in that handsome face."

"The last chick that said that to me earned a black eye."

"Did you just call me a chick?!" Tex roared.

"Ladies..." Nixon clapped his hands. "...go to the cars and remember, you see an Alfero, we're out."

I saluted Nixon and went over to the other Escalade just as Trace and Mo walked out of the dorm. She was still wearing the clothes Nixon had given her. Smile bright, she looked questioningly at one of our guys as he followed her to the car. Her jaw dropped when she appeared shocked that we had four Escalades waiting at the curb.

Yeah, it was a bit excessive, but Nixon didn't want to take any chances.

Sighing, I grabbed my semi-automatic and placed it across my lap just as Phoenix came back and jumped in the car.

"Changed your mind?" I asked.

"Whatever." He pulled out his pistol and was as silent as the grave while Vin followed the SUV in front of us.

"If things are bad..." I cleared my throat. "...you can talk to me, Phoenix. You know that, right?"

"Bullshit," Phoenix spat. "You'll run to Nixon. I'm fine. I've dealt with my father's shit before, alright? It will blow over. I just need... I need to get out of Elite. I need to start my life, you know? My life with Nixon, with the Family. Too much bad blood with my own. I just want out."

"You'll get it, man," I said encouragingly. "Look at it this way. Tex's family is way worse than yours, and Nixon's letting him sleep with his sister."

Phoenix's face cracked a smile. "You're right." He nodded and held out his fist. "Thanks."

"Anytime. I'll always be your friend. You know that, right? Regardless of what goes down, Phoenix. You'll always be a part of us, a part of the Elect. We stick together, bond over blood, yeah?"

He nodded, his face going pale. "Yeah, bond over blood."

We sat in silence the rest of the way to the store.

CHAPTER TWENTY-SIX
The necklace

Nixon

TRACE WAS PRETTY QUIET. Then again, I would be too if I'd just gotten in a car with me. I still wasn't sure where we stood. I'd gone from bully to protector all within the course of a day, and I knew that the trust between us was shaky.

I also knew that I had to start small.

Thus the shopping trip.

Paranoid, I glanced at the SUV behind us. Chase flipped me the bird out the window. Awesome to know he was still irritated with me. He usually always rode with me, but I needed him as my lookout. He was one hell of an aim, and I wanted to make sure I kept Trace safe. And Mo? Shit. When had it shifted to protecting Trace above my own sister? Something was seriously wrong with that thought, and I felt like shit because of it.

I twisted in my seat. The car was too hot. I was going to sweat to death. But Trace looked cold, and for some reason I felt like being nice, even though I was still pissed. All I wanted to do was drive back to the school and pull off the fingernails of every single one of the students who dared touch what was mine.

I liked to start with fingers.

For some reason, when you threatened someone with a knife, they hesitated. When you put said knife on a finger and started slowly moving it from right to left, they apologized.

And then pissed their pants.

I wanted them to do more than piss their pants.

So maybe I'd go for the cement.

Or the brass knuckles.

I gripped the steering wheel and imagined punching some of those bastards over and over and over again. My knuckles turned white. I wasn't paying much attention to Trace, just answering questions.

"Are we almost there?" She adjusted her sweater.

My eyes greedily fell to the expanse of flesh just above her breasts. Insanity poured through every inch of my body — and then a necklace fell out of her shirt.

I'd voted for something else to fall out.

But I wasn't in a position to be picky.

Trying to concentrate on both the road and the necklace as it swayed back and forth, I answered, "Yup, in like ten— Holy shit!" I slammed on the brakes, nearly causing us to get in an accident. "What the hell, Trace?" Did she realize what she had on? What that meant to me? To my enemies? To Phoenix? She may as well have a big giant red X on her face. It had to be a joke. A sick joke. Phoenix had probably placed it under her door and said it was from me to make me shit my pants.

Or maybe Chase. He'd been pissed at me anyway — I wouldn't put anything past him.

Shit. Shit. Shit. Forget sweating. I was going to murder whichever one of them had pulled that stunt.

"Where the hell did you get that?" I stopped at a red light and tried to grab the necklace.

She smacked my hand away.

"Stop." I gritted my teeth as I examined the back of it. *Alfero*. As if I'd just gotten burnt, I jerked back, my heart slamming against my chest. Without realizing it, I'd started cursing in Sicilian.

"It's not worth cursing over." Trace shrugged. "It's just a necklace."

And I'm the bloody pope. Oh right, no big deal, not worth cursing over. Wait, how'd she know I was cursing?

"You understood me?"

Trace's eyes narrowed, and then she looked back at the road. Her jaw went slack, her eyes closed, and then she was yanking at her seatbelt like it was choking her.

"Crap," Mo muttered. "I think she's having a panic attack."

Trace started pulling at the seatbelt harder. We were going at least fifty, and I couldn't take the chance that she would open the door and jump out. I'd knock her out before I let her kill herself.

"Damn it!" I gripped her hand over the seatbelt. "We're in the middle of traffic. You're staying here. I don't care if you think your freaking heart is going to explode. We can't be vulnerable, and right now, we are." Especially considering it was entirely possible I wasn't the only one who had seen that necklace.

Shit. I looked in the rearview mirror, half-expecting an Alfero SUV to be tailing me, guns blazing.

Luckily, I saw nothing except for Chase in the other SUV.

For the next ten minutes, my cursing got so creative that even I had to give myself credit for making up words I'm pretty sure hadn't existed until that very moment.

When we pulled up to the store, I snapped. "Leave. Both of you. I'll deal with this."

Trace tensed next to me, her hand still on the seatbelt, and mine still covering it.

I needed to concentrate on something — anything but her smooth skin. She could be the enemy. She could have been planted there to distract me. Hell, anything was possible at that point. I wasn't sure if I should pull a gun on her or calmly ask what the hell she was doing with that necklace. A necklace that basically said I couldn't have her, and that even if I did, I never deserved her in the first place. Not that I liked her. Or wanted to kiss her — my eyes fell to her lips. Damn it!

Popping my knuckles, I closed my eyes for a brief minute before asking, "What's your last name?"

"Rooks," she said slowly. "Why, what's yours?" Well good. At least she still had her sense of humor. She'd need that — if she lived to make it to the grocery store. I lowered my hand to the side door where I kept another gun. It sucked.

My life sucked.

A girl that reminded me of one I'd lost.

And I may be ending her life in a few minutes.

A life wasted.

Another life wasted.

Too much blood on my hands.

I shifted the safety off. "I'm asking questions. You're giving answers. You understand?" I tried to give her my most threatening glare, pissed at her for lying, pissed at myself for not realizing she could be out to get my entire family. Revenge was a bitch. "Now, I can ask nicely. Or I can use force. What is your last name?" My finger was on the trigger. I'd never wanted someone to lie to me so badly. I wanted her to say I was crazy. I wanted her to laugh it off.

Nausea overwhelmed me. I didn't want to kill her.

But I would.

To protect Mo, to protect my family. It wasn't just blood in, blood out for the Sicilians. It was blood in — no way out, except death.

"Rooks!" Tears pooled in Trace's brown eyes. "It's all I know!"

I carefully pulled my hand away from the gun and reached across to unbuckle her seatbelt. She was telling the truth. Her eyes were scared. She was damn-near shaking the car she was trembling so much.

I grabbed the necklace and turned it over. "Damn it!"

Alfero. I hadn't been wrong. The worst part? It had their family crest on it. Not that she would know that.

And I wasn't about to tell her what it meant to have a picture of an owl as part of the design.

"What?" Trace whispered. "Look, Nixon..." She tried to pull away from me. "...this was a bad idea. Take me back to the dorms. I don't need the security detail like you guys do. I'll just come back in a cab or something. Plus, you're freaking me out. I'll just find my own way home."

Home.

She was home.

She just didn't know it.

Because a necklace like that? Didn't get into the wrong hands. Which meant only one thing.

She was one of *them*.

And she was in my SUV... under my protection. Did Frank know? Was it a setup from the beginning? How could I be so blind! And WHO the hell did she belong to?

"The hell you will," I mumbled, dropping the necklace against her chest and reaching for her hand. "Let's just, let's just get this over with, okay?"

With a grunt, I pulled the same gun that not minutes before was going to be pointed at her head and stuffed it in its holster on my hip.

"Uh..." She pointed. "...why are you packing a gun?"

Yeah. Wasn't ready to explain that one. Because it would probably sound exactly like a bad Mafia movie. "Because it's part of the rules."

"Of the school?" she blurted, sounding cute as hell.

I fought the urge to smile. Damn, it was too easy around

her. "No." My smile felt forced, sad. "My family. Now, let's go."

She stormed off. I trailed after her, letting her have her tantrum while looking for any suspicious characters.

Once I checked in with Mo, I went in search of Trace. She was mumbling to herself and tossing stuff into her cart like she wasn't going to eat ever again.

"Almost done?"

She screamed.

Shit.

Her eyes went wide as saucers. I turned and shook my head. "I scared her. Nothing's wrong." My associates nodded and walked off.

"Who are you?" she whispered.

I leaned in, almost plastering myself against her as I breathed in her scent. "I could ask you the same thing." Her eyes beckoned me, as if she was asking me some sort of hidden question that she was too afraid to voice out loud. I could get lost in those eyes. They were the same as... hers. Adrenaline surged through my body. Was it possible?

Her breathing turned ragged.

Yeah, I was probably scaring the shit out of her.

"Brown. Interesting."

"They're plain," she whispered.

"They are beautiful. Don't let anyone tell you any different, Bella." I used the nickname I used to call my childhood friend — the little girl who used to chase me around the house and call me names. The little girl whose name I never even knew because when I was little, I'd decided in my heart that she deserved a beautiful name — to equal her beauty. So I'd called her Bella... beautiful.

She didn't flinch.

And the hope that had once blazed inside me slowly died. It wasn't her. She was lost to me. Never to be found.

CHAPTER TWENTY-SEVEN
The light bulb of cash

Nixon

"GLAD TO SEE YOU'RE buying enough food so you don't starve in between classes." I smirked. It irritated me that Trace didn't want to eat with us anymore — that she was so offended by my presence that she'd rather eat fake meat.

I'd never been that guy.

The one girls ran from.

Well, actually, that wasn't entirely true. But still... I hated that she didn't want anything to do with me almost as much as the fact that she seemed to be scared shitless to be in my presence. Not that I was doing anything to alleviate that phobia.

"It's your fault I have to buy food," she said through clenched teeth, tossing packages onto the conveyer belt like she wanted them to explode and get all over me.

"What do you mean?" I licked my lips and gave the cashier a polite smile.

"My keycard, you asshole!" Trace threw her hands into the air, and a bag of corn went flying by my head, nearly taking me out. Was it wrong to want to hide my gun and any sharp object from her?

I rolled my eyes at her dramatic outburst. "Stop being difficult. You have two keycards." The one I'd given her the first day of school, and then one that Mo had begged me for a few days back.

"Huh?" She squinted her eyes. "Are you high?" A bag of potato chips went sailing past my ear, grazing it with a crunching sound. "Phoenix stole my card the night you made him set me up! The same night you were off-campus doing who knows what! I only have the red card that you gave me the other day!"

I swayed on my feet. It was rare to take me by surprise — but suddenly I was sick.

"What the hell are you talking about?"

"In the hall!" She continued tossing food onto the belt, not caring that I was ready to strangle Phoenix. "You said it was the best you could do and—"

Her lips were moving. In theory I knew she was talking, but it was falling on deaf ears, because nothing was adding up. At all. I never let anything get by me. Set her up? Was she talking about Tim? How the hell was it my problem that she got drunk and—

Damn it!

They wouldn't.

Would they?

Behind my back?

The more she explained the sicker I felt. "Bastard. I'll deal with it. Do you still need all this food then? If you're going to be eating with us now?"

"Yes." Her eyes darted to the floor.

I knew that look.

I wore that look as a kid, when my dad tortured me, when he tortured Mo. It was fear.

And I'd been the one to cause it.

Had she been starving this whole time?

"That will be one hundred dollars and seventy-two cents." The checker interrupted my thoughts.

Trace slowly pulled out a wad of dollar bills that would probably take an eternity to count out. Why didn't she just use a credit card? Were they that backwoods? They didn't even have credit cards?

The bills fell to the floor.

Trace reached for them and then paused.

"Something wrong?" The line was building up behind us, and I wasn't in the mood to be gawked at. People knew who I was, or at least they assumed. It's not like I wasn't ever in the news. Or gossiped about.

I owned this city.

They knew me.

They all freaking knew me.

"Uh, no, yeah, umm…" Trace slapped the wad of cash into my hand. Confused, I looked down.

"Shit," I hissed then tried to hide my trembling hands as I stuffed the thousand-dollar bills into my pocket.

I swiped my card, typed in my key, then pulled out my phone and dialed Tony.

He wasn't pleased I'd just used my bankcard at a store so close to the school. I wasn't supposed to be out and about. I was supposed to be doing my job. "How easy would it be to track you right now, Nixon? Do you want to die?"

Hell, sometimes he acted like my father. I called him a dip-shit and hung up. I probably could have handled it better, but my nerves were shot.

I signaled for my men to follow us out, giving us security just in case some brilliant hacker was lying in wait to shoot me in the head, or worse, shoot Trace.

They helped us to the car and then went back into the store to clear the area and destroy any evidence on camera.

"Um, are we safe here?" Trace asked, making sure her

door was locked.

Monroe had already gotten back in. "Of course, why wouldn't we be?"

"Oh you know..." Trace gulped. ".. because of that." She pointed to a few men as they tucked guns into their jackets and walked into the store.

"Are we witnessing a murder?"

I almost laughed. Almost. I looked in the rearview mirror and saw everyone shift uncomfortably.

"You guys need to go. We have some more shopping to do and it—"

"Yeah." Mo glared into the rearview mirror. "I can imagine how it's going to be." With a huff, she and Tex exited the car. "See ya later, Trace!"

The doors slammed. I pulled out the money and examined it. The money, the necklace, no credit card — it was too much. All of it.

"Ha ha, you can't catch me!" She ran around the corner and squealed with laughter.

"Stupid girls! You can't even run fast!" I chased after her and tackled her against the carpeted floor.

"Hey! Stop!" She started punching me in the chest. "I'm a girl, so you can't punch me!"

"I'll punch you if I want to punch you!" I fired back.

A tear made its way down the side of her face.

Uh-oh. Ma was going to kill me. "Hey, no, don't cry. Please don't cry. I'm sorry."

She sniffled. "You mean it?"

I hated tears.

"Yeah." I nodded.

The hair on the left side of her face fell back, revealing a small scar underneath her ear. It looked kind of like a heart. I smiled, liking the idea that I was the only one that would be close enough to see it. For now.

Slowly, I looked over at Trace.

She was buckling her seatbelt and then pulled her hair over her right shoulder, revealing her bare neck and the skin just below her ear.

I wasn't sure if I wanted to cry or scream.

Her.

I pounded the steering wheel with my hand and swore. "It's going to be a long afternoon."

"Why?"

"Because we are freaking living our own Romeo and Juliet." Because I used to be in love with her. Because when my dad put me in the box — I'd dreamt of her, and only her. Of her smile, of that little heart-shaped scar, and of the life I could have had, if she wouldn't have died, right along with her parents.

I'd blamed myself for her death, her disappearance.

And now, God had given her back to me, only to take her away again. Angels didn't date demons.

I was fallen.

And she was still in heaven where she belonged. I swore I'd keep it that way — this time I wouldn't fail. This time. I would save her. Even if it meant dying to do it.

"Alright, new bag, right?"

"Yeah, oh, and I need to pay you for the groceries too. I feel so stupid. I had no idea I had big bills, or that they even existed, or that Grandpa..." Her voice trailed off as her eyebrows knit together in confusion.

I didn't want to be the bearer of badness, but her grandpa just so happened to be using money that was most likely marked by the feds. Ass.

"Those bills went out of circulation in the fifties. You know that, right?" I asked, prodding a bit to see if she knew any information. I was an expert at reading people, but her expression was blank like a canvas.

She shrugged and reached for the radio control. "Sorry, I'll figure out a way to cash them out so I can pay you."

"You don't understand." I laughed to keep from yelling. "I would never accept your money. Ever."

"What? Why?"

"It's no good to me!" I snapped. "Just drop it." Damn blood money is what it was! I would never take from an Alfero; just thinking about it had me pissed off all over again. Frank was going to be livid. If there was one thing I knew, he was going to find me — and soon.

But maybe I could find him first, twist the tale, make it so that I was not the object of disdain. He was.

When we pulled up to a stop sign, I sent a quick emergency text to Chase; we needed to meet as soon as possible.

Because shit was about to get real — fast.

Trace was quiet the rest of the way to the mall, and all I could think of was how I was going to tell this innocent girl that the life she'd always known was one giant lie.

Violence? Blood? Organized crime? That was her heritage.

She was the one, the girl with the scar, the girl I dreamed about. I was sitting a few inches from her and the pathetic part? I wasn't the hero. In my dreams, I'd always rescued her, I'd found her parents' murderer, and I'd redeemed my soul.

The minute I saw that necklace, hope had died in my chest.

This wasn't the stuff of dreams. It was the stuff of nightmares.

CHAPTER TWENTY-EIGHT
Frozen yogurt turns me on.

Nixon

WE WALKED IN SILENCE through the front doors of the mall. Trace looked behind her and chewed her bottom lip. I tried to see the world through her eyes.

Ten guys followed us.

All of them were dressed in dark colors and expensive-looking suits. I liked it when my men looked good, not like typical gangsters, but actual men. People around us stared curiously, but for the most part, they probably just assumed I was a celebrity or something. Which, in a weird, twisted way, I was the number-one celebrity in Chicago.

Seriously, it even said it under my mug shot.

Which the feds kindly destroyed after my family gave them the information they needed on the corruption that was De Lange.

Then again, that was years ago.

And if there was anything certain in this life, it was that the feds had a very short-term memory. They were like a real-live version of Dory from *Finding Nemo.*

"Do they have a second-hand store or something here?" Trace asked, her eyes worried as she took in the stores around us.

"Hell, no. Second-hand store? Are you—" He cursed and shook his head. "Second-hand? A freaking used clothing store?" Was she insane?

"Okay, you can stop repeating it already," she snapped, trying to jerk her hand free from mine. Yeah, not happening.

"Girls like you don't shop there."

Immediately she glanced down at the ground as if too embarrassed to make eye contact with me "Um, what about a Ross? Or Wal-Mart or something?" Confused I could only stare at her in hopes of trying to understand why she'd be so upset about me taking her shopping.

Her damn lower lip even started trembling. I released her hand and cupped her chin. "Trace, did you not hear anything I just said?"

Tears pooled in her eyes. She tried to jerk free from me again.

I wrapped my arms around her body and sighed into her hair, allowing myself one selfish moment where we really were just normal college kids out shopping, and I was the guy who wanted to kiss her lips, caress her face.

"You are... impossible."

She slumped in my arms, so the hug must have been a good call, which was a relief, considering I wasn't sure if she still hated me.

One of my guys was staring at me like I'd completely lost my shit. Then again, the last time we'd had a pow-wow, I'd been cleaning my father's blood off my hands. So yeah, he was probably a bit stunned. "Mason, don't follow so close, alright?"

"Of course, sir," he mumbled, stepping back and motioning for the rest of the men to do the same.

"Sir?" Trace's muffled voice sounded against my shirt.

"It's a respect thing."

"You're like twenty." She pulled back, eyes narrowing.

I felt myself tense before flashing a smile. "Right. Twenty." I looked away so she wouldn't see the truth, wouldn't pry. "Age doesn't really matter in my world."

"Your world?"

I stopped in front of the store I was looking for.

"Prada?" Her words were dripping with disbelief. "Are you insane?"

I smirked and pulled her toward the store; her heels dug into the ground. Awesome. So now she hated both me and shopping? Finally, she relented, nearly colliding into my back as I wrapped my arm around her shoulders and led her into the store.

Her eyes widened, and her mouth dropped open. I suddenly wanted to give her the world — not just a damn backpack. If her expression would always be that pure, that... excited? Over something so easily given? All she had to do was ask, and I'd give it to her. I wouldn't even think about it.

"May I help you?" A skinny woman in a black suit smiled in our direction. Her gaze flickered across Trace like she was a bug beneath her shoe and landed on me. Ah, a cougar. Fantastic.

"Messenger bags, do you guys carry messenger bags?" I asked, my eyes trying to find something that would work for Trace. "Something classy."

The woman beamed. "Right this way."

Five bags. But Trace didn't look super excited about any of the ones the saleslady had brought to us. She examined each bag slowly, like it needed to pass some sort of inspection or test.

I finally lost my patience. "Trace, pick a bag."

Nodding, she glanced up at me then behind me, and her eyes lit up like a Christmas tree before turning back to the row of pricey objects in front of her.

I turned and saw the object of her affection right away. It was set high away from the rest of the products in the store, and it was in one of those specially lit shelves.

"This one." I grabbed the blue bag and handed it to the woman.

A muscle twitched in her jaw. "This is a special edition—"

"For a special girl." I put a possessive arm around Trace. "Then it's perfect."

Shaking her head, the woman walked to the counter and rang up the purchase. "That will be one-thousand-seventy-five dollars and eighty-nine cents."

Trace coughed.

I fought the laugh bubbling in my chest and handed over my AmEx. Pretty sure Anthony was going to wonder why the hell I was dropping money at Prada on a school day.

"Can I see some ID, Mr.—"

The card dropped out of her hands. Shaking, she licked her lips and shook her head. "Never mind."

"What?" I leaned forward. I could almost smell the fear rolling off of her. "You don't need my ID?"

"No, Mr. Abandonato. Th-this — this will be fine." With trembling fingers, she handed over the receipt and the bag. "Is there anything else I can get for you?"

I flashed a smile. Good, let her be afraid. She knew I could crush not just her, but her entire store, career, family, life — take your pick. Sometimes it was good to throw your weight around; other times, people just needed to see your name. See, I really was a celebrity in Chicago, just not the good kind. And definitely not the kind you wanted roaming around in your stores if you had a fear of guns. "No, I think we've had enough. Thank you for your... help."

The woman nodded, her face paling further while she pinched the bridge of her nose. You'd think I'd pulled a gun on her or said "boo" for as much as she was freaking out.

"What the hell, Nixon? You like the godfather or

something?" Trace laughed out loud and elbowed me. She'd meant it as a joke, when actually it was a reality — maybe not mine, more like Tex's, but whatever. That was an entirely different story I really didn't want to think about — that wasn't going to be a happy ending.

"So, frozen yogurt?" I changed the subject.

"Why?"

I shrugged. "Because I'm hungry?" And because I didn't want our normal afternoon to be ruined by the Mafia or guns or shooting. I just wanted to go on a date with her. Though I hadn't established it as a date, I had held her hand, twice. Yeah, I was in deep shit if I was already justifying things in my head. She was an Alfero, for shit's sake. She was my Juliet, the one girl I wasn't allowed to have.

And the one I wanted most.

She sighed. "Fine, but this isn't a date, and it isn't babysitting detail. You know I can take care of myself, right? You can just take me back to the dorms. I've got a paper to write anyways and…"

I grabbed her hand, silencing her as we made our way past the crowds.

"It isn't safe, Trace," I said once we were out of the largest of the crowds. "Just trust me, okay?"

"Then why are we getting frozen yogurt?"

I shook my head and smiled. Did the girl ever cease from asking so many damn questions? Couldn't I just feed her? Like a normal person? For once in my life? Then again, I couldn't actually come out and say, "I feel better when you eat because it's like I'm making up for all the times you couldn't." And well, when she was little she'd loved ice cream. I just figured frozen yogurt would be a close second.

My men waited outside while we walked into the small store.

"Okay, what do I do?" She held out the cup and frowned, staring at the machines like they were spaceships.

"Uh..." I scratched my head. Was she trying to be funny? "You eat it?"

"The cup?"

"No, not the cup." I barked out a laugh. "You're kidding right? You've never had self-serve?"

She swallowed and looked down at her hands. They gave a slight shake like she was nervous. "Look, just forget it."

The cup was shoved back into my face, but I gripped her wrist and flipped her around so that her back was against my stomach. Damn, but it wasn't helping things. As it was, my pants were so tight I was ready to bust free. Just having her pressed against me, and my mind went wild with possibilities.

"Read the flavors," I ordered in a hoarse voice as her ass pushed against me. Holy damn, I was going to lose it.

"Out loud?" she snapped.

"Hmm, I think I may like that." I chuckled, my lips itching to nibble down that neck of hers.

"New York Cheesecake, Blueberry, Chocolate Chip, Vanilla, Chocolate, Cake Batter..."

"Why do they sound better coming from your lips, do you think?" I whispered in her ear.

She froze. Hell, I wasn't even sure she was breathing. The air around us tensed.

I needed to move before I stripped her naked then licked the frozen yogurt from every crevice in her body. "Want a sample?" I reached for a pink spoon and held it out.

She closed her eyes and nodded.

"Open."

Her lips parted.

I slowly slid the pink spoon through, not even remembering what flavor I'd given her. "You like?"

She looked drunk with pleasure. Damn, was the frozen yogurt that good? I was so beyond tempted — I simply acted, my head dipping closer to hers and then finally my lips grazing her mouth, my tongue sneaking a taste of the frozen yogurt before pulling back.

Holy shit. I'd just kissed her. Holy shit. Talk about kissing the enemy. Frank was going to shoot my face off. "Sorry, I thought I saw some frozen yogurt. My mistake." I laughed it off when really my heart was pounding so hard I thought I was going to have an attack and pass out on the floor. One simple kiss had done that. Huh.

"Liar," she said breathlessly, pushing past me. "So what, do I just pull on one of these thingies?"

"Well, I prefer the word stroke but—"

Her face erupted with a blush. She jerked her hand away and added some frozen yogurt to her cup — though it was a bit shaky. She managed to get as much frozen yogurt on the ground as she did in the container. Then again, I wasn't exactly practicing fine-motor skills either. Pretty sure my tongue hanging from my mouth and my arousal gave outsiders the impression I got off by watching people eat frozen food.

I quickly grabbed my own helping and followed her to the toppings area. "Wow, didn't take you for the gummy-worm-type of girl."

"Huh?"

I pointed to her cup "Uh, yeah, I love... worms.

I had to damn-near pinch myself to keep from laughing out loud. I was doing that lot with her, having to remember not to laugh, forcing myself to stay stern when really all I wanted to do was laugh my ass off then kiss her senseless.

"Ready?" the bored teenager at the till asked.

"Yup." Trace placed the yogurt on the scale like I did mine. "Twelve dollars and nineteen cents."

Shit. I forgot I had no cash. Reluctantly, I handed over my black card. Anthony was going to piss himself — again.

The kid glanced at the card and then did a double-take. Ah yeah, he was going to have one of those reactions.

We started to walk out, but he spoke up. "Um, I know

this sounds really dumb, but can I have your autograph?"

I froze, rarely did I write my signature on anything. This kid had hero worship in the worst way. He knew what I was known for, probably because his dad or a friend had an obsession with the Chicago Mafia. And the sad part? He'd probably glamorized it with what he'd seen on TV, not even realizing how deranged my life was.

"Sure thing..." I calmed myself down then signed my name on a napkin. "What's your name?"

"John." Freaking stars exploded in the kid's eyes.

I wrote down his name and also included a threat. Tell no one. That's all it said, but John would probably do the exact opposite. "We have an understanding, John? Nobody knows we were here?"

John's eyes widened as he looked at the napkin then back up at me. I leaned over the counter. "I need to hear you say it, *John.*"

"You weren't here." John stumbled over his words. "I swear."

"And where did you see us?"

"On the street. You, uh, you were going for a run."

"I do like running." I winked and smacked the guy's shoulder. "Thanks again, *John.*"

"N-no problem, Mr. Abandonato."

All signs of Trace's smile were gone as we made our way to the car — replaced by curiosity.

Damn, but I wished it would have been fear.

At least then she would walk away, or allow me to.

Instead, she looked... accepting.

I wasn't sure if I was elated or not.

CHAPTER TWENTY-NINE
We own the world.

Nixon

"ONE MORE STOP." I took the next exit and sighed as we pulled up to the bank. Just something else we owned next to car dealerships, garbage companies — hell, sometimes it just felt like we owned the freaking world. I'm sure it looked that way too when you typed our name into a search engine.

Anthony was going to flip his shit, but I figured the best way to let him know about the dire situation was to wave her in front of him like a bull. I could text him, but seeing her in the flesh, yeah, it was going to be one hell of a day. Besides, she couldn't just walk around with that type of cash.

So what if we had GPS trackers in every card we made?

So what if I was using it as an excuse to make sure she was never out of my sight?

"The bank?" Trace looked up at the spiky modern building.

"Yup."

"Why?"

I let out a laugh, "Asks the girl who's carrying around

thousand-dollar bills. I take it you don't have an account?"

She hung her head, shoulders hunching. Damn it, sometimes she was so fierce it knocked me on my ass; other times, like a beaten puppy.

"Well, let's go then." I jumped out of the car and grabbed her hand, leading her toward the glass four-story building.

"Nixon, where'd the rest of the suits go?"

I didn't answer because there were enough lies for the day, couldn't really say *"Well, they're all downstairs drinking coffee and watching you on the big screen while cleaning their guns."* The bank was another hangout for lots of the men; nobody would dare attack me there. It was a freaking fortress, not to mention it had some of the best security in Chicago.

We walked right past all the desks where people were answering phones and working and went into the elevator.

She let out a little gasp as it descended into hell. Ha, kidding — just Anthony's main office, but it sure felt like hell sometimes.

The doors opened, the smell of fresh-brewed coffee burned my nostrils as I dragged Trace down the hall.

"Hey, Priscilla, where's Anthony?" I asked, almost hoping I could just do everything myself without Anthony seeing Trace first.

She didn't look up. "Oh, you know, sharpening kn—" Her mouth shut she glanced up and offered her hand to Trace. "I'm sorry, and you are?"

"Trace. Trace Rooks."

Priscilla nodded slowly, her eyes narrowing in on the necklace that just so happened to have turned to show the glaring Alfero family crest. "Rooks, you say?"

"Yup."

"Doesn't sound like—"

"Pris, we need to open an account." I leveled her with a glare.

Her smile didn't reach her eyes. Yeah, bitch was trying to

put two and two together. I made a mental note to take care of that later. Make sure she didn't talk to any of the men; that's how rumors spread, and that's how heads rolled — literally.

"Of course you do. I'll just let Anthony know you are here."

I shook my head. "No need. I'll let myself in."

"Enter at your own risk, Nixon."

"Come on." I tugged Trace's hand and went down the stairs through the hall of bosses — men who served us or were actually bosses of our family. I purposefully didn't look at the newest picture — the one of my father. Hell, if I had it my way, it wouldn't have gotten the honor of a spot on the wall. But respect was everything, and it was my job to show the men that yes, even though I'd killed him, we still respected blood — unless we were double-crossed; then we just killed them.

I pressed my thumb against the magnetic strip. The door opened. "Anthony?"

"In here."

I walked into the wide office and grimaced. All the windows were open looking out onto the pond. To Trace, it would look like a penthouse.

"We need to open an account." I hoped he'd keep the questions to a minimum and just work his magic on the computer.

"We?" Anthony turned around.

My uncle turned, leveling me with a curious stare before setting his cold blue eyes on Trace. He looked just like me; then again, Chase and I could be brothers for how similar we looked. When we were little, people thought we were twins, rather than Mo and I.

I cleared my throat. "Technically, she needs to open an account. I would have gone to one of the other branches, but lucky girl has thousand-dollar bills."

Anthony's eyes widened briefly before he turned to

Trace. "What did you do? Rob a bank?" He cracked a smile. Awesome, so now the man had jokes when I was ready to lose my freaking mind with all the information I had stored.

She returned his smile with an innocent one of her own, making me immediately want to rush her out of the room. This was a bad idea, all of it, but there was no backing out now. Leaving would show Anthony she was worth something; staying was already doing enough damage. Hell, I'd just purposefully dropped her into my world; she would never escape, not now, not ever.

"I didn't know they were big bills. My grandpa gave me some money before I was dropped off at school, and there was a fiasco with my uniform and bags and..."

"Fiasco?" Anthony's brows lifted. "This I have to hear."

"Anthony—" I tried to interrupt but was dismissed. Right. In public I was always dismissed because people would ask questions if I was the guy ordering around the man who was old enough to be my father.

"Make yourself useful, Nixon, and grab yourself a drink," Anthony barked.

I muttered a curse and walked over to the bar, purposefully clanging the glasses as I made myself a drink.

"So, you were saying?" Anthony's smooth voice was like nails on a chalkboard to me.

"I, uh... the people at school kind of drenched me in sugar water and raw eggs. My messenger bag suffered a very slow, sticky death."

"The worst kind I'm sure," Anthony agreed. Damn, I forgot how nice the man could be when he was curious... you know what they say about curiosity. Couldn't he just make the account, do the background check that I'm already one–hundred-percent sure is going to come back positive and let us leave?

"Absolutely," Trace agreed. "I guess technically, it's my fault since I rejected that one's rules on the first day." I pointed at Nixon who narrowed his eyes. "But he did save me from social suicide. Not that I was already high on the popularity totem pole anyways... but yeah. Long story short, we went shopping. I busted out my money. Nixon almost had a stroke. Men in suits entered the grocery store with guns. Pretty sure I'm going to see that on the evening news, and... now we're here."

"Alright. Sounds like a normal day in the life of Nixon. Welcome to the family..." Shit, shit, shit. I leaned against the bar, my fingers digging into the granite countertop. Trace had no way of knowing what Anthony was really saying... it was more of an invitation to hell. By welcoming her in, he was saying she had no out. Only she didn't know that; she probably assumed Anthony was teasing her about our relationship, when really, that should be the least of her worries at this point.

"Oh, no, no, no, no." She let out a nervous laugh. "No, it's not like... that."

"I've known Nixon for a long time, and I can tell you one thing for sure. It is very much... like that."

Hell, we were going to have words later. I cursed and turned around, leveling him with a glare.

"Now, an account... Do you have your social security number?" Anthony completely ignored me.

Trace tucked some hair behind her ear and shrugged. "Grandpa said it was lost in the move." She was so damn innocent. Hadn't she thought to ask her Grandpa how the hell he'd registered her for school without a social security number?

"The move?" Anthony repeated, walking around his desk and hitting a few keys on his computer. "Where did you move from?"

"Chicago."

I had just taken a huge sip of my drink. The word *Chicago* startled me enough to spit its contents out onto the floor. What the hell was my problem? I knew who she was, but just hearing her confirm my suspicions, damn but it made my heart hammer in my chest, made me want to collapse into a sobbing mess at her feet. Bella, my Bella, the little girl I would have died to save, was standing right in front of me, and instead of saving her? I was throwing her back in with the wolves. Me, being the alpha... "Sorry, Uncle Tony."

Tony shook his head in annoyance but said nothing. "So, you're from Chicago. Why did you move? Your parents come with you?"

Trace's eyebrows knit together in confusion. Shit, either she had no idea or she'd suppressed all horrible memories of her childhood, not that I could blame her.

I walked over to where she stood and grabbed her hand, giving it a little squeeze.

"My grandparents thought the city was too violent, I guess? I don't know. My parents were killed in an accident when I was six so..."

"An accident?" Anthony repeated, while my heart damn-near ripped from my chest and threw itself onto the floor.

It was hard to breathe, hard to think.

"My sincere apologies for your loss."

She shrugged. "I don't remember much." Thank God.

"Probably for the best," Anthony said pointedly, giving me a look I couldn't decipher but probably meant we'd have words later.

"Um, what does this have to do with opening a bank account? I'm sorry, I'm not trying to be rude. I'm just really exhausted."

"Shopping does that to you," I said jokingly.

Anthony laughed. "I'd say Nixon does that as well..."

"Very funny." I shook my head and then nodded toward his computer, my way of saying *"Alright, jackass. You've questioned her enough. Get to typing."*

"Very well. Miss Rooks, was it?" He coughed into his

hand.

She nodded, still clenching my hand.

"I'll work some magic and open your account without your social security number. I'll add the address of the school you attend. Do you have a phone number where I can reach you?"

She gave him her phone number. I mentally stored it, just in case I wanted to text her, or call, or make sure she hadn't gotten stolen by the Alfero bastards.

"And the cash?" Tony held out his hand.

I reached into my back pocket and handed it to him, knowing that pretty soon the bills would be traced back to Alfero or another crime family, again confirming our suspicions. Bills like that were always marked, which made me wonder. Why the hell would Frank give her bills that would put a giant red X on her forehead? Did he want her to be discovered? Or was he just turning senile?

Anthony counted out ten grand and put it through the machine. Once the paperwork was signed, he gave Trace one of our temporary cards that had the GPS device in it. She quickly put it in her purse, and all the tension left my body. At least I knew I could keep her safe. At least I would know where she was at all times.

"We good?" I asked, folding some of the paperwork and stuffing it into my pocket.

Anthony nodded. "For now."

"Alright." I grabbed Trace's hand again. "See you Sunday, Uncle Tony."

"You too, Boss. Don't forget the time, or your pops is gonna throw a fit."

"Yeah, yeah." I waved him off and forced myself to look happy, when really, I knew Tony was just testing me to find out how much Trace knew about our family.

Luckily, she just grinned like a fool. Sunday dinner. How nice!

Right. With my dead father, that should be interesting, and considering I didn't make a habit of conjuring up demons, pretty sure his seat was going to be empty. Then again, I sat at the head of the table now.

I fought the groan rising up from my chest and managed to get her out of the building without turning on my heel and pointing a gun at Tony's head for daring to challenge me like that in front of her. Blood roaring, I almost didn't hear Trace's question.

"Why are people afraid of you?" she finally asked after the silent car ride all the way back to school.

We pulled up to the dorm. The radio played softly in the background, but I was anything but relaxed. "Aren't you afraid of me?"

She gulped. "Sometimes."

That hurt, and I had no one to blame but myself. I reached across the console and gripped her hand, "You know I would never let anyone hurt you, right?"

"See!" she yelled. "That's what I'm talking about! A few days ago you were telling me I was basically the cockroach beneath your shoe! And now you're taking me shopping? I'm sorry. It doesn't add up." Her eyes filled with tears before she looked down at our clenched hands.

"Yeah, well, life rarely does." I swore then groaned. I felt too old and tired — so damn tired of this shit. "Look, I was just warning you, that's all. And just because I'm being nice to you doesn't change the fact that you have to follow the rules if you want to survive here."

"Thanks. Got that memo loud and clear once I was drenched with sugar water and drugged." Trace rolled her brown eyes.

"Damn it, then why not just do what I say?"

She shrugged her shoulders. "I don't like being bossed around."

"No shit," I smirked, watching the soft rise and fall of her chest as she breathed. Hell, something was wrong with me if I was watching her breathe and liking it. "But sometimes it's for your own safety. Can't you see that? Maybe the world isn't as shiny and fun as you once thought. People are mean. Humanity is a cruel joke, Trace. I'm just trying to prevent them from getting the last laugh."

She sighed, turning to face me, and a curtain of brown hair fell across her face. "So, why do they listen? Why do you get to make the rules?"

I froze as the moonlight hit her cheek, casting a glow across her lips. With a sigh, I cupped her face. "I wish that wasn't the case. I wish I didn't have to make rules... or enforce them."

"Then don't." Her hand pressed against my chest. I wasn't sure if she was stopping me or encouraging me.

It felt good — her touch. Especially now that I knew the girl from my past and present were one in the same. "Sometimes we aren't given choices. We just are."

"What does that even mean?"

Slowly, I opened my eyes and removed her hand from my chest, "It means that you should have listened to me on the first day of school. Don't touch the Elect. Don't breathe the same air as the Elect, and don't..." I cursed. "...just don't."

"Why?" Her lower lip trembled. I wanted nothing more than to take that lip between my teeth and then kiss that mouth for hours. I wanted to comfort her, but I was stuck between needing to protect her from everything. I'd failed once, I wouldn't fail again, and it wasn't going to be on my head if she was brought back into her world. I would fix it. I had to fix it.

"Because you are up to your eyeballs in shit, and you don't even know it. And once you know... what everything's about... the choice will be taken from you too. Hell, what am I saying? The choice was gone the minute your gramps dropped you off." I'd said too much.

"Choice?" She rolled her eyes. "You're pretty serious and cryptic to boot. You know that, right? What are you? Some kind of famous celebrity? A politician's son? The president's dirty little secret?"

I smiled. Right. I wished I was a dirty little secret. That would make things so much easier than admitting I shot people for a living and ruled the world with an iron fist.

"Hmm, that dirty little secret thing sure rings a bell. Don't worry your pretty little head over anything, alright? Go do your homework and relax."

With a huff, she grabbed her bag and opened the door. "Thanks for… everything."

"My pleasure. Now go get some work done. I'll send Chase over in a few."

"Chase? Why?" She placed her free hand on her hip.

Damn, the girl had no idea how inviting her every single movement was. To a man like me? It was like getting to see perfection up close, every second, but each time I wanted to touch, a wall was thrust in place, making it so I could look, but that's all. To do more would be like inviting her in, and that would be a death sentence, one I wasn't sure she would ever forgive me for.

I shrugged. "So no one bothers you, why else?"

"Why don't you check on me yourself? Why send a minion?" Her eyes narrowed.

I had to admit to being pretty damn pumped. She'd just referenced Chase, sex-god Chase, as a minion.

I barked out a laugh and made a mental note to tell Tex. "A minion, huh?" I bit down on my lip and then sucked the metallic ring into my mouth. "If I came and checked on you, I'd definitely be bothering you."

"Annoying the hell out of me is more like it," she shot back.

"Bye, Farm Girl."

Yeah, fighting with her was turning me on way more

than it should. The longer I stayed the more danger she was in. I could send Chase. I *would* send Chase.

"Thanks for that." The girl flipped me the bird!

I responded in the only way I knew that would make her laugh. I mooed and drove off.

CHAPTER THIRTY
Sexy dreams and babysitting duty. Shoot me now.

Chase

I DREAMT OF HER, not in a creepy way where I was taking advantage of her, and she was loving it and then somehow she morphed into the picture of my last ex-girlfriend, and then a cow showed up and watched— No, nothing like that. I just dreamt of her smile, which to me, was just as scary.

I didn't dream of girls' smiles.

I dreamt of other things... other body parts, other... images. I couldn't get her out of my head, maybe because I was worried about how long she and Nixon had been gone.

Wiping my face with my hands, I let out a few curses and decided to run to the closest Starbucks. I needed to get out.

My text alert went off.

Nixon: *I need you to watch Trace.*

I snorted, and texted back.

Chase: *You do realize how creepy that sounds?*

Nixon: *She's an Alfero.*

Holy shit! I damn-near dropped my phone onto the ground. My heart was beating so loud and fast I was afraid I was going to have a heart attack. I didn't even know what to text back, how to respond. I knew Nixon would be losing his mind. After all, she had been his best friend when they were little. Next to me and the guys, he'd kind of taken to protecting her. After her parents died, and he'd thought she died too, it seemed like he was never the same.

Chase: *Do you know for sure?*
Nixon: *Short of drawing her blood...*
I let out a growl.
Chase: *You hurt her I shoot you.*
Nixon: *I would never hurt her.*

Too late for that, but whatever. Great, so I was crushing on his childhood best friend, long-lost soul mate, and the greatest enemy of our family. Could my day get any better?

Nixon: *Just go to her dorm, make sure she does her homework, and let me know when she's done. I have a bone to pick with you, but I'm guessing it's more of a bone to pick with Phoenix.*
Chase: *Phoenix?*
Nixon: *Finding her in Tim's bed? Know anything about that?*

Shit. That couldn't be told in a text message. With a curse, I dialed his number. He picked up on the first ring.

"Wow, must be bad if you're actually gracing me with your voice, cousin."

"Screw off." I rolled my eyes. "And I'm just as guilty as Phoenix. He said he got a text from you to do the usual to Trace, what we do to new kids who we want to leave, so rather than have him all up in her business I took her and—"

"Please tell me you didn't set her up. Please tell me that she really was acting out like a drunk college student and accidently found herself in the quarterback's bed."

"Nixon." My eyebrows furrowed. "Dude, you told us to. Or you told Phoenix."

Nixon started yelling so loud I had to pull the phone from my ear. When he finally calmed down, he wasn't even speaking in complete sentences; a mixture of Italian and

English rolled off his tongue in waves. "What the hell is wrong with you?"

"A lot of things," I muttered, "Look, I had no reason not to believe him, and it's not like we haven't done that before. You know just as much as I do she doesn't belong in our world."

"Doesn't mean we have to destroy every shred of dignity she has in order to keep her out of it, Chase."

"Nixon—"

"No... your punishment is to babysit. No complaining, and I swear to all that is holy, if you touch her — even by accident — I'm cutting off your hands."

"What if she falls?"

"Then you sure as hell better hope she lands on a tree branch instead of your arms. I mean it, Chase. This isn't over. I'll deal with Phoenix later tonight. Just head over to her dorm, play nice, and try not to talk her out of her clothes."

"Yeah." I bit down on my lower lip. "Nixon, I honestly didn't know. I'm sorry, man. You know I'd never intentionally hurt her."

He sighed heavily on the other end. "Sometimes, I wish you would... I wish you were the type of guy who'd just stay away, but that's not in your nature. You aren't that guy. You like her."

It was a statement not a question.

"So do you."

More silence.

"Just..." He cursed again. "...play nice and text me when she's done."

"Right."

He hung up, and I stared at the wall of my dorm for a good three minutes before I finally made my way over to the girls. How the hell was I supposed to act normal when I knew that Nixon was... number one: losing his shit, and number two: struggling with his feelings big time. And number three?

I'm feeling the exact same way.

I knocked on the door.

Trace opened it, her big brown eyes widening a fraction of an inch before a blush stained her cheeks. Damn, was it wrong to be hopeful that I had that effect on her? Because she sure as hell had a similar effect on me.

Her rich brown hair swept beneath her shoulders effortlessly, her full lips curved into a shy smile, and I wondered how many guys had touched those lips. Had Nixon? Bastard. I'd kill him with my bare hands. I was just about to say something when Mo yelled my name.

"Hey, Mo," I called back and winked at Trace. "Hey, Trace."

She crossed her arms. "Nixon send you?"

"Yup."

"You staying?"

"Yup."

"You gonna say anything but yup?"

I placed my hands on the doorframe and leaned forward. If I went any further, I'd be kissing her. "I'm not much of a talker. I'm more of an action sort of guy."

"Bet you are." She nodded, her grin spreading like I wasn't dead-serious about taking her against the closest wall. "Please come in. Make yourself at home in our lovely prison."

"It's not prison." Monroe rolled her eyes. "Nixon just wants to make sure you're safe, and although I could probably kick a couple asses on our floor, we'd be screwed if the football team decided to pull a prank on us."

Yeah, good one, Mo. More like guns and knives, but sure we'll go ahead and say we're terrified of the tiny football team and their small man-parts.

"And why would they pull a prank on us?" Trace asked, interrupting the silent battle between me and Mo.

"You're the shiny new thing. Who wouldn't want to play with you?" I shrugged. "I know if I had the chance to—"

"I think it's safe to say I know where that sentence was going to end." She held up her hand.

"Oh yeah?" I plopped down on her bed and put my hands behind my head. "And how's that?"

"With my shiny new boots up your ass." She smiled sweetly.

"Damn." I already needed to adjust myself after being in her presence less than five minutes. That had to be a record. Damn Nixon.

"What?" She pulled out her notebook.

I sighed. "Nixon's a lucky bastard."

"Huh? Why?" The girl was either clueless or stupid.

Then again, I'd never met a girl who was so unaware of the effect she had on the male species. It was like she had no idea she was gorgeous. No flipping clue that, by just looking at her, I was ready to lose my mind. And it wasn't just that. She was one of those people who made you... feel. Yeah, I *felt* when I was around her, and, like an emotionally starved lunatic, I kept crawling back for more, because in our business it was rare to feel — anything. Maybe that's why Nixon was attracted. Maybe his attraction was all physical, whereas mine? It felt different, because she was different. Hell yes, I wanted her, but I also just wanted to sit by her and soak in her goodness. Maybe in doing that, the bad days would stop being so bad.

I shook the thoughts from my head and grinned. "I was never good at keeping my hands to myself though."

Mo came alive at that. "Chase, don't. It's like a death wish, just... don't."

Yeah, got that message loud and clear.

"You won't always be around, Mo," I snapped.

"No, but if you touch what belongs to the devil, he'll probably damn your soul, just saying. And if you want a part of the business when you graduate, you need to be on your best behavior."

I cursed. She was right.

"Right. So that was a weird conversation. I'm just going to work on my paper." Trace turned her back on us, which was good since I was mouthing the word *bitch* to Mo while she flipped me the bird and rolled her eyes.

Trace quietly worked on her homework while I closed my eyes, not really sleeping, but needing to give them a rest since every single movement she made caused them to strain in her direction.

See? I was losing my mind.

It had almost been three hours. I sent a quick text to Nixon to let him know it was safe to visit now that she was probably almost done with homework. Finally, I succumbed to a catnap only to have a textbook land near the family jewels, almost castrating me.

"Shit! What did you do that for?"

"Fun. It was fun. And I'm finished, so you can go. I have done all my homework in peace because of you."

She walked to the door and opened it. She pointed to the not-so-empty hall, while keeping her stare on me.

I laughed and didn't budge. Nixon had his hand up to knock and a confused look on his face.

Trace stomped her foot. "Chase! I mean it. You don't have to stay—"

"He's just doing what I told him to," Nixon said from the door. "You done with your paper?"

She sent me a glare, and then her eyes widened as if a light bulb had turned on in that pretty head of hers.

Soon, clothes were flying, and I was staring at her ass pointing into the air as she rummaged through the small closet. Psychotic break? Because of Nixon? Wouldn't be the first time.

"Mo, your friend has officially lost it," I whispered under my breath.

"Trace." Nixon walked up behind her and placed his

hands on her hips.

Damn him.

"Trace."

I flinched as his lips grazed her ear. When I looked at Mo, she merely shrugged as if to say *"Told ya so."*

"What are you doing?" he asked, his body shielding her from my stare.

She hung her head. "Looking for hidden cameras."

"What kind of guy do you take me for?" He flipped her around and braced her shoulders.

"The kind that carries guns and sends his friends to babysit me at my own dorm. The kind that knows the minute I'm done with my paper and magically appears at my door. That kind."

Nixon burst out laughing. "Wow, sometimes you are just too much." He reached into his back pocket.

She backed away as if she was afraid he was going to pull a gun on her. I had to admit the thought bore merit. What would a little Alfero do? Would it trigger something? Hell, she had Frank's blood running through her veins. That son of a bitch was scary on a good day. I couldn't imagine what he was like on a bad day.

"Ever seen one of these?" Nixon flashed her his cell. "Chase texted me ten minutes ago and said you were close to being done."

"He was sleeping. He—"

"Is a light sleeper and was under strict instructions to tell me when you finished."

"Why?" She crossed her arms. "So you could send in the next shift? Who's it gonna be this time? Tex? Phoenix?"

The name *Phoenix* had Nixon's entire body tensing. Ah, I knew that stance well. Phoenix was going to have to dig his own grave, which meant I was guilty by association and was going to most likely get the shit beat out of me later that evening. Awesome.

"You done?"

"Yes, but—"

"Thanks, Chase. See ya later." Nixon pulled her out of the room so fast I didn't even have time to say goodbye. The door slammed after them, blanketing me and Mo in silence.

"So…" She crossed her arms. "…spill."

"Spill?" I chuckled. "Aw, cute. You wanna gossip. I can make popcorn. PS, are all things big in Texas because I heard that when you and Tex—"

She threw a pillow in my face then, honest-to-God, pulled out one of her knives and flashed it in front of me.

I groaned. The girl was a knife throwing lunatic and a hell of a lot better than most men I knew. "Fine, put the knife down."

Grinning, she shoved the weapon back under her pillow and leaned back against the wall., Her naked feet hung over the bed. "Do you know what's going on?"

"Well…" I mimicked her movements, leaning my head against the opposite wall. "…your roommate's a legend."

"Legend?"

"Yeah… she's an Alfero."

Mo's eyes widened. "Shut up."

"I will not." I sent her a mock glare. "Pretty sure that means she's the granddaughter to Mr. Frank Alfero… you know, the one that makes grown man shit their pants? That Frank."

"He's retired."

"Ha!" I barked out a laugh. "He's very much active. A boss never retires, you know that, Mo. To retire means you get a bullet to the head and dipped in holy water."

"So…" She let out a sigh. "…does she know who she is?"

"Doubtful, I mean, she'd have to be the best actress on the planet. Have you seen that girl blush? You can't just force a reaction like that." I licked my lips, wishing I was licking hers.

"Well… sucks to be you."

"Huh?"

"You like her, Nixon likes her. You do realize that in this little scenario there is no way in hell you're coming out on top."

"Aw, Mo, that's okay. I don't need to be on top all the time. I can let the girl do some work..."

She rolled her eyes. "Disgusting. You're my cousin. Be mature. And you know it's true... now that he has her back."

"He's changed... she's changed," I defended. "And she's a big girl. If she wants him, fine, but that doesn't mean I'm not going to put up a fight. He's the worst type of person for her."

"What?" Mo snorted. "And you're the best?"

"I'm not boss." I shrugged. "I don't have a bounty on my head. I'm more normal than Nixon will ever be. So yeah, I am the best, and I can still take care of her."

Mo frowned and glanced out the window. "You should tell Tex and Phoenix."

"Not my job." I rolled off the bed and stood. "Nixon will deal with it. For now, I'm going to go back to my dorm, sleep off the scent of that gorgeous girl, and pray Nixon wakes up disfigured from lack of sex."

"Wow, such a good friend." Mo laughed.

"The best." I held open my arms.

With an eye roll, she pushed off the bed and launched herself into them.

"Love you, Mo."

"Love you too, Chase."

CHAPTER THIRTY-ONE

I'd kill the whole football team. The idea gets more enticing by the minute.

Nixon

"WHERE ARE WE GOING? And why are we in a hurry?" Trace stumbled against me as I swiped my card across the elevator and shoved her in.

"Nixon, what the—"

I slammed her body against the closest wall. My mouth devoured hers like I only had twenty-four hours to life. I lifted her into the air, dipped my tongue into her mouth, and just took. Swear, that's all I was doing: taking, sucking, and taking some more. She tasted so damn good, and I was so pissed, so done with pretending that she didn't matter, that I didn't care. Especially after what Tim had told me. Phoenix had set the whole thing up. Bastard.

I kissed her harder.

She let out a moan. My lip ring rubbed against her bottom lip, causing such a hot friction that I groaned, my mouth resting against her neck.

Trace reached for me.

I flinched and backed away, not because I hated her touch — quite the opposite — and pretty sure it was frowned upon to strip her naked in an elevator. "Please, no touching."

"Nixon, you can't just—"

"Yes, I can." I folded my arms across my chest and leaned against the wall. "And I did." I pushed the elevator button again, causing it to jolt down to the lobby.

My body was buzzing with awareness at her proximity — a few feet and I could have her again. I popped my knuckles to keep from grabbing her.

"So is that how this works then, Nixon? You take, but you can't receive?" Trace taunted.

Ah, little girl, play with fire. See who burns hotter.

I bit down on my lip and stalked toward her just as the doors opened. "Funny. I didn't think I was taking."

"Oh yeah?" Her eyebrows shot up.

"Yeah." I grabbed her hand. "I was giving."

She stuck out her tongue, tempting the hell out of me, making me want to throw her against the closest object and rip every article of clothing from her body. I'd never had such a violent attraction to a girl. Ever. She made me forget myself, and maybe that was a good thing. Because the person I was? Not so great.

"Do it again. See what happens," I threatened, begging her to tease me one more time. If she did, I wouldn't hesitate to turn her over my knee. In fact, I'd enjoy it way too much.

She must have sensed my desperation, or maybe my eyes were terrifying in the way they pierced through her clothing like I wanted to devour her. Whatever it was, she backed off and was pretty silent as we made our way across campus.

"I didn't know..." I cursed. "...about what Phoenix did."

"I thought you told him to do that, because of our little challenge earlier about you not offering me protection and stuff."

I stopped and pulled her against me. "Do you really think I'm that much of an ass that I would really drug you, set you up to look like the school slut, and then take away your keycard so you were up a creek with no paddle?"

She shrugged. "You said you wouldn't protect me anymore, that—"

"Shit. Girls are so dense sometimes." I ran my hands through my hair in absolute frustration. "I was upset, Trace! You're so damn argumentative, and you never listen! I was trying to scare you for a few days. I wasn't going to throw you to the freaking wolves!"

"Oh." She frowned.

I grabbed her hand. I needed to be touching her, needed to feel her pulse beat against her wrist. Damn, so now I was counting her heartbeats? Making sure they weren't normal for an eighteen year old?

"Where are we going?" Her voice was trusting.

I bathed in it, rolled around and freaking basked in that trust. If she would just give me a little of her trust, she'd never regret it for as long as she lived. I'd make sure of it.

"You'll see."

We picked up pace when we got behind the sports complex, near the back side of the fence where a few trees had been planted in order to make the place look more like a park, rather a prison. Fences had ways of making you feel trapped, so we'd added lots of greenery to convince the students they were here by choice, which, for some of them, they were.

I released her hand and stopped in the middle of the grass. It was quiet. Good. We would need quiet. With a sigh, I lifted my fingers to my lips and whistled.

The football team emerged from the shadows as a few lights turned on. Tim slowly made his way into the middle of the group, shaking like a leaf. Oh, fear. The smell of it was always the same.

Pathetic.

Trace gasped.

I glanced at the direction she was looking. Phoenix and Tex were watching from the sidelines. I imagined it was Phoenix that had her a bit freaked. With a nod, I took off my leather jacket and held it out. Tex slowly walked up to us, winked at Trace, then took my jacket.

"Tim," I said in a commanding voice. "Do you know why you're here?"

Tim nodded, his eyes flickering to Trace's and then back to mine. Dude was going to give himself a stroke with all that head-bobbing.

"Words, Tim. I need to hear you say it." My voice shook with authority as I clenched my fists. Blood soared into my knuckles, my body awakening, readying itself for the inevitable fight.

"Yes."

"Yes, what?"

"Yes, sir." Tim's voice was strained.

"Tim, did you or didn't you have sex with this girl?" I pointed at Trace, hating that I was putting her on the spot but needing to establish her as protected.

"No."

"No... what? I'm losing patience, Tim."

"No, sir. I did not have sex with Tracey Rooks."

"Interesting." I made my move, walking slowly toward him, making a show of cracking my knuckles. "And who told you to spread the lie about Tracey?"

Tim said nothing.

"You hear that, everyone?" I turned around and lifted my hands into the air. My muscles tensed. "His answer is silence. Well, at least he's not a rat. Right, Tim?"

Tim didn't say anything, he just stood there. Head held high.

With a laugh I reared back and landed a right hook to his jaw. He stumbled to the side. Blood poured from his lip. My ring had caught some of the skin, tearing it enough that he was going to need stitches from just one hit.

"How long will this take, Tim?"

The bastard smiled.

So I punched him again. He fell forward, and I used the momentum to knee him in the nose. He fell to the ground. Pathetic. I wasn't even sweating. "Still silent, Tim? More?" I asked, tilting my head to the side.

He said nothing, so I rained a few more punches to his face and two to his stomach. Each blow was like letting off steam at the fact that he'd been near her, in bed, and helped make her look like a whore in front of everyone. From this day forward, people would be taking their own lives in their hands if they as much as looked at her.

"Phoenix!" Tim finally cried out. "One of your own told me to! He said you would be pleased."

"He said I would be pleased?" I repeated with a laugh. "Tim, do I look pleased?"

"No." He shook from his place on the ground, covering his head like a coward.

"No, what?" I snapped.

"No, sir. Sorry, sir. It won't happen again. It won't—"

"Damn right, it won't happen again. Now get off your sorry ass and apologize to Trace."

Tim slowly got to his feet and stumbled toward Trace. His left eye was beginning to swell, and blood was smeared on his face. "I'm sorry for any trouble I may have caused you, Trace."

I walked up behind him. I gripped him by the shoulders and tossed him into the crowd of players. "Clean him up."

"One more thing," I said loudly.

Everyone froze in place.

My eyes fell to my best friend, a man I'd trusted with my very life. "Phoenix... come here. Now."

His face paled. "Yes, sir."

"Why?"

"Because you never—"

I didn't let him finish; the sound of his voice pissed me off too much. I sucker-punched him in the face, feeling the bone in his jaw crack on impact.

A resounding hush fell over the crowd. It was rare for the Elect to fight in public, and I'd never made an example out of one of my own. Until now, I'd never had to.

"What should your punishment be?" I circled him. "I leave for the night to take care of family business — a business you have interest in — and when I'm gone, you betray me by ordering your own hit on the new girl?"

"She was disrespecting you!" Phoenix yelled, his eyes desperate.

Damn, but I knew that look. It was betrayal pure and simple. It was greed. It was madness. He'd finally snapped. And it was my fault. I'd pushed him, and now I was going to sever all ties, making him fall deeper into the rabbit hole. But he'd forced my hand.

And I had to protect her.

At all costs.

I had to protect her.

I leaned down. "So you thought to disrespect me, is that it? You thought disrespect equaled more disrespect?"

Phoenix said nothing. His eyes went from fear to hatred.

"Since when has it ever been okay to drug an innocent girl? Hmm, Phoenix?"

He was silent and then, "Chase took her."

"He also told me everything tonight and will be carrying out his punishment over the next year."

Silence.

"What? Nothing to say?" I roared.

Phoenix shook his head; utter defeat marked his features. It was about to get a hell of a lot worse. "No, sir. I'm sorry, sir."

"You will be," I mumbled. "You're out, Phoenix. Broken. You're a cafone."

"What?" Phoenix surged to his feet. "You can't do that to me! My father will—"

"Son." De Lange walked up to us.

Yes. I'd made a deal with the devil. His son was out, no longer under my protection, meaning, if they didn't cooperate as a family, they would all die. It was the final straw.

"It's already been discussed. Just let it go."

"What?" Phoenix roared. "I gave everything to you! To your family! You promised!"

He lunged for me, but he was sloppy. I easily stepped out of the way.

"You son of a bitch! I'll kill you!"

De Lange came up to Phoenix and whispered what I'm sure was the mother of all threats in his ear.

"This isn't over, Nixon. You can't just break away from this — from us! You're making a huge mistake. I hope you realize what you're doing."

"I do," I said with confidence. "And I hope you enjoy working in fast food. Because it's the only place that will hire you if you as much as breathe in her direction again."

Phoenix spat at the ground and jerked away from his dad. He disappeared into the shadows of the night.

De Lange, the dean to be exact, stood there helpless. "Are you going to... tell—?"

"No." I cut him off. "This is between us, *was* between us. Just keep him away, and it won't go any further."

That is, if he continued to play by my rules, my game, my school.

"Thank you, sir." The way he said it was so mocking that I almost ran after him and landed a blow to his kidneys.

Instead I nodded, and De Lange walked away.

Let him hate me.

Let them both hate me.

Maybe by pushing them they'd finally mess up, and I'd find out who'd really killed Trace's parents, because it sure as hell wasn't my dead father... and if I didn't find out soon... Frank was coming.

Everything was coming to a head, and I was powerless to stop it. All I could do was pull the strings, cut some loose, and pray that it all made sense in the end. Pray that it was enough.

"What the hell kind of school is this?" Trace muttered from behind me.

It was Tex who answered. "I thought you'd have known by now. It's his."

"Says who?"

"The American dollar, a couple billion of them to be exact... well, that and the Abandonato family."

"So the last name Abandonato covers a multitude of sins. Is that it?"

Tex swore.

I waited for his answer.

"The last name Abandonato either covers the sin or gets you killed. Either way, the outcome is the same, I guess."

"And what's that?"

"You're never free."

My stomach twisted. I hated the truth of that statement almost as much as I hated the fact that Tex was spilling our dirty secrets.

"Of what?"

Tex didn't answer. Instead he glanced up at me. He knew he'd said all he could say.

"You okay?"

"Do I have to say *yes sir* too?" She said in a shaky voice, it was hard to read her, but it seemed like she was trying to lighten up the situation. I could love a girl like that... a girl who could laugh in the face of violence, in the face of the man creating it, the man willing it into existence.

Tex burst out laughing. "She's all yours, man." With a

whistle he shoved his hands in his pockets and walked off, leaving us staring at one another.

Me, wanting to pull her in my arms, and she, probably ready to fight me off if I as much as sneezed.

"You okay?" she asked, her voice small.

Hell, how did I get so lucky to have the girl who'd just witnessed me beat the shit out of a few people ask if I was okay?

I nodded, fighting the emotion swirling in my chest. "I'm good." Blood was caked around my knuckles. They were starting to get sore now that the adrenaline was done pumping through my system. With a curse, I handed her my jacket then pulled off my long-sleeved henley and wiped the blood from my hands. It wasn't lost on me that this was my job lately — wiping blood from my hands -- never to be cleansed from the darkness that seemed to stain my skin.

When I was finished, I grabbed the jacket and put it back on.

"So…" Trace rocked back on her heels. "…I'm not sure if I'm supposed to say *thank you* or *what the hell were you thinking?*"

I shrugged, going for the simple answer. "They had it coming. Tim should never have listened to Phoenix, and Phoenix should have stayed the hell away from you. He had rules, and he didn't follow them."

"There we go with the whole rules thing again," she mumbled.

"Rules make the world go round." I laughed and put my arm around her. "The rumors should die down now, okay?"

"Yeah, but aren't people going to talk about this? And why was the dean so chill? I mean, he's like twice your age."

I knew she'd have questions. I just wasn't ready to give her any answers— Hell, would I ever be ready?

"We have an understanding."

"Right." She nodded. "What type of understanding? He

follows your rules or you shoot him in the face?"

I couldn't help but burst out laughing. Who says that? "Wow, thanks, I needed that. Is that what they do on TV? Shoot people in the face?"

"Yes, well... no. I guess — I don't know." She sighed, her shoulders hunching a bit. "What are you? Some sort of gangster or something?"

Ah, so close, sweetheart. "Sure." My fingers moved to the back of her neck, playing with the hair that had fallen loose from her ponytail. "Let's go with that. I'm a gangster."

"Have you ever killed anyone?"

"Have you?" I fired back, trying to deflect the question on account that I was pretty sure telling her I'd lost count wasn't the most romantic thing to be discussing, when all I wanted to do was kiss her again. That conversation wouldn't end well.

I moved my hand to her neck, cupping it with my hand.

"It's not fair," she said breathlessly.

"What?" We stopped walking, and all I could focus was on her lips as they moved.

"That you can touch me, but I can't touch you." She sighed and stepped away from me.

Was she bothered that I freely touched her? Was it because of what she'd just seen me do with my hands? Rejection slammed into me. "Would you rather I not touch you?"

"No!" she blurted, her cheeks puffing red. As if realizing what she'd just done, she covered her face with her hands.

I let out a chuckle and pulled her against my chest.

"I just don't understand. What's so different? I mean we're touching now, but..."

"I'm in control of it." I let out a breath and tilted her chin toward me. "I know it sounds crazy. I just... I don't like it when people touch me without permission. Ever since I was a kid, after—" I swallowed, fighting with telling her or just leaving it. My past was so heavy, my burden constant. It would be wrong to give it to her. Hell, it was wrong to share it with anyone, but she made me want to. She made me want to close my eyes and believe in dreams again, forget the nightmares and sleep peacefully. For once in my life, she made me think it was actually a possibility. "Anyway, it doesn't matter. It's just this thing I have."

"Like the rules?" she whispered, her breath hot on my chest.

"Yeah, like the rules." My thumb grazed her lower lip. Damn, I wanted to kiss her so bad. "You're beautiful, you know."

She let out an awkward laugh and tried to pull away.

"Don't," I murmured against her cheek as my lips brushed her ear. "Don't pull away from me, please."

"Okay." Her voice shook.

I couldn't take it anymore. My lips found her neck — and drank. I licked the bone above her shoulder. The warmth of her skin sizzled against my tongue.

"So sensitive," I murmured, moving up her neck, my tongue swirling in a figure eight beneath her ear. "So damn sensitive. Your skin's so soft right here."

She shivered as my mouth met her jaw, biting just a little before kissing again. My hands dug into her hair, nearly causing it to pull all the way out of the ponytail. I tugged her closer.

"Nixon." Her voice was barely a whisper. "What are you doing?"

My lips touched hers, brief enough to tease me, never enough to fulfill. "I wish I knew."

"You can't just..." She swallowed, her eyes darting between my lips and my eyes. "...you can't just go around kissing people you hate."

"Who said I hate you?" I released her head and stepped back.

"Well, you weren't exactly shaking my hand and shouting my name a few days ago."

Damn, she had to go there. I eyed her up and down, my entire body heating with desire. "So you want me to shout your name? Is that what this is about?"

Laughing, she pushed me away.

Ha, good call, because I was about to ruin her on the football field.

"Stop being such a guy. I'm serious."

"Oh, believe me…" I ran my hand along her collarbone and down her shoulder. My fingers danced along the front two buttons of her shirt. All I needed to do was slip, and I could have that same shirt on the grass in seconds. Hell, if I breathed wrong, I could undo the buttons that were so loosely put together. "…I'm dead serious."

She stepped away and nervously tucked a piece of hair behind her head. "So gangster, you gonna tell me why you've taken personal interest in running this school?"

Yeah, totally had Rihanna's, "Run This Town" pop in my head at the worst possible moment.

I fell into step beside her. "I like things to be fair."

"Wow, then you're at the wrong school for that," she joked, elbowing me in the side like I didn't just beat the shit out of two people.

"You know what I mean. I do what I can when I can. Besides, it's kind of one of my jobs to keep the peace around here, keep the secrets, keep everyone happy. It's exhausting actually." And there it was. The honest-to-God truth.

She squinted up at me through long lashes. "I have a hard time imagining anyone making you do anything."

I let out a bitter laugh. "Then clearly you haven't met my dad." And she never would. Thank God.

She stopped walking and tugged my hand into hers. "What do you mean? Is he… is he bad?"

I sighed. "Well, he's no Mickey Mouse or Santa Claus, if

that's what you're asking." I bit my lip to keep from saying *"Oh, and I killed him when you were getting setup with the quarterback. Surprise!"* Instead, I let out a grunt and grabbed her hand. "Doesn't matter. Anyways, I was going to ask you earlier, but then I got distracted by all your drug money..."

She rolled her eyes.

"Does the name Alfero mean anything to you?" My body froze, waiting for her answer.

"Alfero?" Trace repeated. "Hmm... as in Alfredo without the *D*?"

"Yes. As in the food." My eyes flickered down toward her chest. "It's on the back of your necklace."

"So?"

"So..." I nodded my head., "...you know it's okay for you to tell me. I won't say anything. I mean, I know I'm an Abandonato, but it's not like, you know, I'll set Jimmy on your or anything."

She burst out laughing. "Are you high?"

My eyes narrowed. Was she deflecting or just proving again her innocence? "No."

"Wow, then you have to know I have no idea what you're talking about."

"You don't?" Stunned, I could only stare like some crazy person, while she continued to frown.

"Nope."

"Good." I sighed and kicked the ground to keep from jumping into the air and clicking my heels together, not that I'd ever been guilty of doing such a thing, but then again, I was doing a hell of a lot of weird stuff around her. Nothing surprised me anymore. Nothing. "That's, wow... that's really, really good."

"I think you must have lost more blood than you realize in that fight." She nudged me. More perfume floated from her skin into my face.

"At least I can say I'd freaking bleed for you, if that's

what it took."

"Took?"

I stopped and reached out to touch her chin. I tilted her face toward mine. "To keep you safe."

"So you'd die for me?" She joked, but her face was lit with emotion, like my answer was life-altering. It was.

"Don't you get it?"

My breathing became erratic as I leaned close enough to kiss her again. "I'd give my life for yours."

"Why? You don't even know me."

Oh, but I did. I knew everything. All there was to know. And I wanted so badly to tell her in that moment, confess my sins, ask for forgiveness, freaking get on my knees and beg. When have I ever begged? When had a girl ever mattered? But she'd always mattered, my little Bella, the one who'd held my hand and caught my tears. Damn, but she'd been my sunshine in a life full of rain.

I closed my eyes, so she couldn't see the pain — the truth. "You have no idea what I know, and believe me when I say your life is worth a hell of a lot more than mine. And yes, after tonight, you better believe I know you better than anyone, even better than you know yourself. I hope to God it stays that way, Trace."

Trace opened her mouth just as a few black SUVs pulled up. And then the black Mercedes. The one Frank was known for. It had his crest on the side — the bastard was cocky like that.

Well, shit was about to hit the fan a lot sooner than I thought.

"Trace, go inside," I barked.

"But..."

I gripped her arm and squeezed. "Trace, I need you to listen to me right now. You take this." I handed her my black keycard. "You don't walk. You run until your legs burn. You run into the building, you run into the elevator, you run down the damn hall, and you lock your door until I come and get you. Do you understand?"

Her eyes were wide with fear. She nodded once as I gripped my hand over hers and slid the keycard into it. "Run."

She ran like hell toward the dorms.

When she reached the building, she turned just as Frank emerged from the car. A few of his men blocked what would have been the perfect view for her to see his face. They started making their way toward her.

I reached for my gun. I'd pick off every last one if I had to.

Instead, Trace closed the door behind her. Good girl.

Seconds ticked by in slow motion as the men turned from the dorm and made their way toward me. I rolled my eyes and crossed my arms. They could intimidate all they wanted.

But hurting me?

That was like signing their own death certificates.

So when they circled, I laughed.

That is, until Frank Alfero stepped into the circle with a .45 and pointed it at my head. "Son, we need to talk."

"Clearly." I rolled my eyes. "You wanna do this here? Out in the open? Where everyone can see and hear?"

"I knew I recognized you." He ignored my question, scratching his temple with the barrel then pointing it back at me. His white beard was trimmed short to his face, his brown eyes wide with anger. "I knew it the minute you opened your damn mouth."

"So you knew who I was..." I nodded. "And you still let your granddaughter stay here? Are you insane?"

"It's secure."

"It's Abandonato territory." I spat. "And last I heard, you wanted my head. So your granddaughter? Flirting with the enemy? Not the wisest move, old man. As of right now..." I checked my Rolex. "...I'm guessing Tony has every last shred of information on her. Damn, I bet I even know what her bra size is. If you were sending her here to dangle her like a carrot, then well done." I clapped twice. "But know this... she's not my enemy. She will never be my enemy, and I'll protect her until the last drop of blood leaves my body, even if it means I have to protect her from her own grandfather. Now get out of my sight before I truly give you a reason to shoot me."

The men around him whispered.

Frank held up his hand. "Fine, this isn't over."

"No..." I shook my head. "...but you better believe I'm going to be the one to end it. Now get your ass back in that car, and don't you dare show your face until you've talked to Trace and told her the truth — not your version, but the actual truth — then you and I? We can talk. Then we can have this conversation. Then we can do this the right way."

Frank's eyes twinkled for a brief second before he lowered the gun. "I always liked you better than your father."

"Get that a lot." I cursed. "Now get the hell off my property."

He chuckled and called off the dogs.

While I waited for my heart rate to return to normal.

When the cars pulled out, I quickly dialed Trace's number. I just needed to hear her voice. I didn't think I'd have trouble finding my own. When she said hello, so breathless and sexy, I lost all train of thought. Just breathed into the receiver then freaking hung up like I was in middle school and had never had any experience calling a girl before.

Laughing, I shook my head and sent a quick text to Chase.

Nixon: *Frank has landed.*

Chase: *Cool, he bring anything from Wyoming? Cows? Guns? He shoot you?*

Nixon: *No cows, he did have a gun pointed at me. I yelled at him.*

Chase: *I'm sure that went over real well.*

Nixon: *Just let Tex know.*

Chase: *And Phoenix?*

Nixon: *Out. He's a cafone.*

Chase: *Shit.*

Nixon: *Just get it done, I'm going to go check on her.*

I quickly shoved the phone in my pocket and made my way up to Trace's dorm. Damn, I'd been there, what? Three times in one day? Talk was going to start — not that I cared. I just hoped she wouldn't.

I knocked on the door and waited.

My phone rang just as the door opened. I quickly checked it.

Phoenix. Bastard.

And then Trace was in my arms.

Actually, she was plastered against my chest, all arms and legs wrapped like tentacles around my body.

Hell, I needed to scare her more often if this was the response I was going to get. Imagine what would happen if I faked my own death? Morbid thought.

Slowly, I returned her embrace and held on tight, setting my chin on her head.

Mo's eyes danced with excitement. Right. Looks like her twin found he had a heart. Hilarious.

Trace let out a little yelp and smacked me on the chest. "You scared the crap out of me."

I grinned. "You sure do run fast, Farm Girl. They teach you that in Wyoming?" I winked and walked around her to hug Mo, whispering in her ear. "I'm fine. It's fine. Don't worry." She immediately relaxed.

"Something's very wrong with you." Trace slammed the door and crossed her arms.

"Don't I know it," Mo muttered. "And what the hell, Nixon? You can't just go scaring my roommate like that. I thought she was going to have a heart attack and tell her grandpa she was witness to your murder."

"Believe me, her grandpa would not have come to my

rescue." I snorted. Hell, the man had a gun pointed to my temple less than five minutes ago. Safe to say if I was the last man on earth and his only hope for survival, he'd still pull the trigger with a grin on his face.

"Hey!" Trace pointed. "You don't even know him! He's a good guy." Right, and I'm Santa Claus.

"Did I say he was bad?" I held up my hands. "I just said he wouldn't come to my rescue."

"If I asked him to he would," she argued, nodding her head as if to say *"And that's final."*

I laughed. "Your innocence is both aggravating and shocking."

She clenched her fists.

Damn, she was beautiful when she was upset. I lived for her reactions almost as much as I thirsted for her touch.

"We should watch a movie," I said, lying across Trace's bed and tucking my hands behind my head.

"She doesn't want to," Mo whined.

"Who were those guys?" Trace asked.

I ignored her question, hoping she'd forget she asked it. "She saw me beat the crap out of two dudes tonight. She should watch something funny."

Mo nodded. "A chick flick and maybe some chocolate?"

"Hello!" Trace waved her hands in the air. "I'm right here."

I waved back, smirking at her irritation.

"Nixon," Trace hissed. "Who were those guys, and why did I have to run?"

"Guys from work." I shrugged. The type of work that people don't come home from. "They just had a few questions about what went down tonight. I just didn't want you to stay if things got weird, and the less people that they know who know about what happened, the better."

Her eyes narrowed, I could tell her brain was working a mile a minute, but I knew her thoughts wouldn't go in the direction of the Mafia or her freaking grandpa being one of its leaders.

"Fine. We'll watch the stupid movie," she grumbled.

"Excellent."

Mo tossed me the DVD. I put it in the computer then stretched out again on the bed.

Trace grabbed a pillow and smacked me in the head.

"What the hell was that for?"

"It slipped." She shrugged innocently, her eyes taunting. She had no idea how close my control was to snapping.

Two seconds, and I could have my sister out the door on her ass.

One second later, I could have Trace pressed up against that same door.

Half-a-second — the time it would take to remove her shirt, ripping buttons, and dip my tongue into that delicious mouth. Yeah, Trace. Hit me again and see what happens. I freaking dare you.

"Slipped, my ass..." I croaked.

"Children!" Mo sang. "Behave, or I'm not going to give you snacks."

"She started it—"

"Nixon Anthony—"

Trace laughed and pinched me in the arm. "She totally middle-named you just now."

"Trace..." Mo warned her eyes giving me a warning. I couldn't sit this close to her, touch her, tease her — and not taste her. My body wasn't allowing it.

Trace blushed and sat as far away as she could. Damn, it was like we were both in different countries.

Within minutes, Tex and Chase arrived. Tex sat by Mo, and Chase took one look at the middle spot on the bed and claimed it. Bastard.

Swear if his leg got any closer to hers, I was going to accidently cut his femoral artery and apologize in the eulogy.

Okay fine. So I was being dramatic.

But still.

I even sent him a warning text.

My phone quickly vibrated with his reply.

Chase: *Finders keepers.*

I responded with a graphic picture of the last guy I beat the shit out of, causing him to laugh his ass off. Not really what I was going for.

Trace soon started nodding off, so I took the opportunity to pull her closer to me. Her breathing turned heavy as her head dipped onto my chest.

Chase rolled his eyes in annoyance.

Round one: Nixon.

She opened her eyes a few hours later — catching me staring at her. To be fair, I was just getting ready to leave when she woke up. It wasn't like I'd been staring at her while she slept.

Not that I hadn't thought about it.

"Are you trying to give me nightmares?" she whispered in a grumpy voice, her fingers gripping my arm.

"No." I swallowed twice before I was finally able to get the hoarseness from my throat.

Brown silky hair fell across her cheek, and I wanted to push it out of the way and then kiss that grumpy mouth. Without thinking, I flipped her around and spooned her.

The amount of times I'd ever done that with a girl?

Zero.

But now it was one.

And I liked it.

Way too much.

She wiggled back against me.

Shit, I was going to die.

My body responded immediately. I could feel my own blood roaring in my ears as every nerve ending demanded I take her.

I let out a low groan. "So not helping, Trace."

"Oh."

I brushed her hair aside and kissed her exposed neck as my right hand dipped beneath her shirt. Mo and Chase were right there. It wasn't like I could try anything. I just wanted to be close. I wanted her skin pressed against mine, even if it was in complete innocence.

My fingers rested against her stomach.

"Nixon—"

"Please..." I whispered against her ear. "...I just want to touch you."

She nodded and soon sleep overcame both of us.

It was the best night I remember ever having.

CHAPTER THIRTY-TWO

Coming in second isn't winning. Newsflash! It means you're a loser.

Chase

I SPENT THE WEEKEND pissed off about everything. Every time Nixon asked me what had crawled up my ass and died, I was tempted to throw my gun at his face and charge him full speed.

Because he knew exactly what was bothering me and was either too chicken shit to admit it or was just waiting for things to blow over.

I wasn't that type of guy — the guy that just ignores the giant-assed elephant in the world and continues to whistle and twiddle my thumbs, while the entire world is crashing around me.

It was Sunday.

I should be doing homework, God knows I was going to fall behind again if I didn't, and the one thing I knew about my job was that if Nixon needed me to do his bidding, and I had to skip class, I was going to fail.

Which sucked.

I didn't want to fail school, because I already felt like I'd somehow failed life by not living up to the expectations of my father... and not winning the one girl who had managed to turn my head.

"You look like hell." Tex whistled when he came into the room.

I continued tossing the basketball into the air and rolled my eyes.

"Seriously, you need to let off some steam?"

"No." I tossed the basketball again and caught it with my fingertips. "Just... anxious."

"Wanna know what I do when I'm anxious?"

"Don't you mean who you do?"

Tex smirked. "Don't knock it till you try it."

"Thanks, I'll pass."

"Shit." He slumped onto the couch next to me and pushed his reddish brown hair away from his forehead. "You really are in a dark place if screwing some random chick's brains out doesn't appeal."

"Is that how you see me?" I caught the ball and turned. "Am I really that guy?"

Tex's eyes narrowed. "So I'm assuming by actually putting the question out there you want me to be serious and not my normal one-liner self." He sighed and cleared his throat. "Look man, your actions don't have to define you, but yeah, you are that guy. You're the one that sleeps with girls and gives them a high five once you're finished, then forgets what they look like the next day and actually hits on the same one less than twenty-four hours later." Cursing, he jerked the ball from my hands. "Does it have to be that way? No. But that's been your cover for the past four years, and, honest moment, you've kind of gotten lost in it. I get it though. It's hard to compartmentalize with the type of life we live. You go from shooting someone between the eyes to flirting with some random chick during biology class — and it's all been for this one thing that's finally coming to us full circle. I mean, we've been busting our asses for four years, and Alfero's granddaughter just shows up at our school?" He gave his head a hard shake. "Something isn't adding up, and Nixon sure as hell isn't giving us any hints as to what's going on, but something bad's coming. I can feel it."

I leaned back against the couch, my head pounding with all the information he'd just thrown at me. "You think we'll have to fight the Alferos, don't you?"

"I think," Tex's eyebrows shot up. "…that if the girl you like is lounging around right now doing homework, you should find an excuse to see her."

"Ha." I snorted. "Hilarious, and what? Find my heart outside my body once Nixon discovers I've double-crossed him?"

"They aren't married."

"Doesn't matter. He's staked his claim."

"But he's boss." Tex nodded. "Remember that man. He doesn't have the same freedom we do. He doesn't get to choose who he loves. Now, who he shoots? That he can choose."

"Which is exactly why my ass stays planted right here."

"Fine. Don't listen to Dr. Love."

"Please don't call yourself that."

"I'll see ya later. Mo wants to hang out."

"And by hang out you mean—"

"Hold hands at skate night. What do you think I mean?" Tex threw the ball at my head.

My arms shot up just in time to block it.

"Stop moping."

"Yeah." I cleared my throat. "I'll do that."

But I didn't.

Not two hours later.

Not five.

And not that evening when Nixon asked me to run a perimeter check and make sure Phoenix wasn't causing any trouble.

At midnight, I found myself outside her dorm room, just staring up at her window like some misplaced Romeo.

She was staring out the window.

I wondered what consumed her thoughts. Nixon? Her grandfather? Life at Elite? I wondered if I ever crossed her mind — or if I ever would.

CHAPTER THIRTY-THREE
Lovesick Mafia boss, party of one. Your table's
ready... hell.

Nixon

MY EYES GREEDILY SCANNED the classroom as I waited for Trace to walk in. From every angle I was screwed, and not the type of screwed where I know I can actually sweet-talk my way out of the situation, but so screwed that I was okay with it.

Since when had I ever been okay with being trapped? Small spaces? Not my thing. Boxes? Torture? Not so much — reminded me too much of being a kid, of being beat. But with Trace? Damn, I was like a lab rat, just begging to go into my prison so I could repeat the same shitty process over and over again. I was classically conditioned to want her — and it was all her fault. From her ability to treat me like a complete ass most of the time, to the way she challenged everything that came out of my mouth, only to get me to become dangerously obsessed with everything that came out of hers.

I leaned against the desk as the class started walking in. They were used to me subbing by now, and I was more than happy to do it. Which again proved the whole trapped theory. I wanted to see her, and I was willing to do anything — arrange my entire schedule and slice the professor's tires so he'd had to take a sick day once he got back from the funeral. Really. Anything. To be in her presence. To make sure she was safe. Because I didn't trust my men, and I sure as hell didn't trust Chase, not after watching him — watch her.

He was addicted, just like me.

But I wasn't into sharing.

Not like that.

And he didn't know the history I had with Trace. Our history had destroyed me, it had created me, molded me into the person I was today. All I'd ever told him had been the basics, but I knew he'd assumed it was more than I'd let on.

"You drool," I whispered the minute Trace walked by me toward her desk.

Her entire body froze. And then, slowly, she turned and shot daggers in my direction. God, I'd go through hell if she'd just glare at me like that every second of every day.

Trace raised her hand.

I crossed my arms, waiting for her to flip me off or at least make a face.

Instead, she just rolled her eyes and shuffled to her seat.

I loved being under her skin, almost as much as I loved touching her skin, feeling the barely restrained desire bubbling beneath the surface. I wanted her so bad that every time I kissed her, my body was slammed with such a heady desire to push her against the wall, most of the time, I had to step away. Losing control wasn't something I was comfortable with — no matter how tempting she may be.

Once everyone was seated, I took attendance and turned down the lights. "Movie day."

Cheers erupted around the room. Hell, we were in bad shape if these were the future leaders of the free world.

Trace shifted in her seat and pulled out a notebook, not

even noticing that I'd walked around the back of the class and sat down behind her.

Tucking her dark brown hair behind her ears, she leaned back in her chair and sighed.

"Hey," I whispered, my tongue dancing along the edge of her ear.

"Crap!" Her desk moved a few inches to the left before she turned around and glared. "Are you trying to kill me?"

If she only knew how she was killing me, ripping me to shreds, peeling back all of the armor I'd placed so strategically over the past few years. If she only knew.

I offered an easy smile and began toying with the edge of her shirt, rubbing the thin cotton material between my fingers. "Not at all. Remember? I'm the one who keeps you safe. I'm the one that would die for you and all that? Why? Want me to prove my loyalty?" Sign me up. I'd prove it in a heartbeat.

"I'm trying to watch the movie," Trace stuttered, her voice wavering before clearing her throat and looking down at the desk.

"No, you're not." I sighed and leaned back against the crappy chair. Damn, her eyes were beautiful. They almost looked black in the darkness.

"Yes. I am." She gritted her teeth, and damn if the girl didn't turn around and try to focus on the lamest movie ever created. It was cute, her determination to ignore me. What was even cuter? The fact that she thought she was able to lie about the way she felt, when her body sang to me every chance it got.

Like it was singing now.

I yawned, my arms reaching out on either side of her body before very slowly pulling her flush against the back of her chair. Exactly where I wanted her. Where I could feast on everything she had to offer. On my time. After all, teachers have the final say in class. Right? Her skin was so soft, my hands kneaded around her neck, and then dipped into her hair. The silky tendrils floated between my fingertips, wrapping themselves around and around until I dizzied from lust.

It wasn't enough.

I lifted her hair to my face and inhaled.

Body on fire, I tried to adjust myself as best I could in the seat without falling out of it and glanced casually around the room. Nobody was paying attention. Then again, we were far enough back that all it would take was one student to turn around, and we'd be screwed. The idea should have made me stop; instead it made me desperate for more as the air buzzed with tension.

With deliberate slowness, I moved my right hand underneath her shirt, the pads of my fingers grazing the sensitive skin just above her hip before slowly moving upwards toward her bra.

Trace froze. Her entire body was on fire. I could feel its heat through my palm. Her breathing hitched as she gripped the sides of the desk and leaned back, giving me better access.

My left hand joined my right, and I was exactly where I wanted to be, playing with the fastener of her bra and imagining bending her over the very desk she was sitting in. Pretty sure that wouldn't be put in the Eagle Elite yearbook.

Then again, what a freaking gorgeous picture — Trace underneath me. I shuddered and moved my hands under her bra strap, grazing the tips of her breasts. She jumped a foot and let out a little moan.

"Hmm. I took you for more of a comfortable-type of girl. Is this lace?" My lips grazed her ear again. The temptation was too much, I licked along the edge of her earlobe and then sucked before adding, "It's sexy." As. Hell. My teeth tugged again as my hands moved against her hips, pulling her body tighter against the desk. Damn inconvenient to have two objects between us. I grunted in frustration. Why the hell had I thought this was a good idea? How was I supposed to hide all evidence of what was going on? I was nearly exploding from want, and I still had to go stand in front of the entire class.

I dipped my thumb into the top of her skirt and then pushed my hand down just as Trace let out another moan — this one embarrassingly louder than the first.

A guy from the front row turned around just in time for me to peel my hands from Trace's body and send him a glare from the pit of hell.

It helped that the same guy who'd turned around may have seen me throw a knife at Chase's face last semester.

Paling, the guy nodded once and then, stiff as a board, returned his attention to the movie.

The rest of class I kept my hands to myself.

Not because I wanted to or because I suddenly found the ability to practice self-control. No, it was because I had been about five seconds away from throwing everyone out of the classroom and locking the door behind them, trapping Trace with me and keeping her until I had my... fill. And I was pretty sure I wouldn't be satisfied with just a few minutes.

The more time I spent with her, the harder it was to walk away, and, in the end, that was exactly what I intended on doing. My life wasn't hers, and I was going to keep her out of the line of fire if I had anything to say about it.

When class ended, I made my way back to the professor's desk and waited for Trace to walk by. When she did, I reached out and grabbed her just as she was about to make her escape. "Where do you think you're going?"

"To class?" She didn't turn around, just nervously grabbed at the necklace around her neck.

"Come here," I ordered gruffly, unable to soften my voice even if I wanted to.

"I didn't hear *please*." Her voice was teasing, taunting.

Didn't the little girl know it was dangerous to tempt the lion? I'd devour her on the spot.

I took a few steps toward her and very quietly pushed the

door closed in front of her, then whispered against the mop of brown hair, "Please."

I stepped back and waited while she turned around. Her face was drawn tight, angry.

"Sit," I commanded, pointing to a nearby chair.

She dropped her bag to the floor and crossed her arms, her eyebrows shooting up.

"Please." I smirked.

"Fine." She went over to the desk and leaned against it. Her skirt hiked up, flashing me a view of her muscular thighs. My eyes followed the line of her long legs.

"I need you to do me a favor."

"I won't have sex with you. I'm not that kind of girl." Trace said it in such a bored tone I almost did a double-take. Why the hell did she have to say *sex*? Especially standing there in what every sane guy would explain as the perfect schoolgirl fantasy? Short uniform, long legs. I tried not to growl in irritation.

One. Two. Three. Four. I regained my calm and answered, "I deserved that."

"And more." She grinned.

"Care to punish me?" If she said yes. All bets were off.

"I'm leaving." She rolled her eyes and pushed away from the desk.

"Wait." I reached out and gently touched her arm. "I just… I wanted to warn you. Be careful, okay?"

She nodded.

"I'll see you at lunch?" I didn't want her to think that's all I was after — her body. I wanted so much more. I wanted things a guy like me wasn't allowed to want. When you wanted something as bad as I wanted Trace, people saw it as a weakness. A chink in my armor. They'd eventually use her against me, and I'd be lost, because I'd do anything to keep her safe. I'd die, in order for her to live.

"Yup, remember? I've got your keycard." She flashed me

ENFORCE

a smile.

"Keep it." I shrugged then looked down at the necklace she'd been toying with. Shit. Phoenix could not see that necklace. "Another favor?"

"Wow, you're just full of requests this morning, aren't you?"

What was she doing? Trying to see how desperate she could make me? Had she any idea the effect she had on me? Did she even know one simple word would seal her fate? I wouldn't hesitate to rip that tiny skirt directly from her body if she as much as nodded in my direction. And that wasn't me. Not my style. But I wasn't exactly thinking clearly after the movie foreplay. I licked my lips. "Oh, I can think of some more favors. How bad do you want an *A*?"

"Not bad enough to see you naked," she retorted.

I laughed softly and tilted her chin toward me, examining her too honest eyes and full lips. "Don't wear expensive jewelry during the school day. I would hate to see you lose something important to you." I nodded at her necklace. "Please? That's something even my money can't replace."

Trace's eyes widened as if she didn't know how to respond to me.

One kiss. I could handle one kiss, and then I was going to explode. I quickly brushed my lips across hers and whispered, "Have a good day, Trace."

She started to speak, but I pressed my fingertips against her mouth. "Don't ruin it by saying something. Now. Go to class."

Nostrils flaring, Trace jerked away from me and grabbed her stuff. She pulled open the door to the classroom with a flourish and stomped out into the hall.

"Good show," a voice said from the professor's adjoining office.

Shit. I froze then slowly turned.

"Chase?"

"You trying to get yourself killed or are you really just playing with her? Didn't you know? It's rude for the predator to play with its food before it kills it."

I slammed my hand down on the desk. "It's not like that, and you know it."

"Then what is it like?" Chase snarled. "Hmm? What the hell has you so wound up, Nixon? She'll make you weak."

"This isn't about weakness." My eyes narrowed in on Chase. "It's about her, isn't it?"

"You'll be the death of Trace," he defended, placing his gun on the table and pulling out a knife then tossing it into the air. "You'll kill her."

"And you won't?"

"Nixon..." Chase leaned against the desk. "The professor was supposed to be gone a day, max. Upon his return last night, you caused him to get into an accident so you could take over his class. So you could toy with her emotions. Again. So you could get what you want and damn the consequences. Again."

"You can't speak to me like that," I snapped.

"I sure as hell can!" Chase tossed the knife onto the desk, and it clamored against the pencils. "I'm the only one with balls enough to tell the boss when he's made a mistake, and that's what you're doing, Nixon. Frank won't like it. That's his granddaughter. You think he's just going to give her to you? You think he's going to let you play house?"

"I don't want to play house."

"Too late," Chase whispered, picking up the gun from the desk. "You aren't a sure thing, Nixon. You could be dead tomorrow."

"I could be dead in the next five minutes with the way you're waving that gun around." I ran my fingers through my hair.

"You're losing your edge," Chase pointed out. "And you're all this family has."

"What exactly are you saying?" I knew what he was saying, but I needed to hear it. I needed to be reminded.

"I'll take care of her."

"Chase—"

"Nixon," Chase yelled. "You. Will. Kill. Her. Do you understand what I'm saying? We don't know what Phoenix is up to. He knows you like Trace, and Frank looks like he's about one slip away from pulling the trigger on you. Let me."

"Giving you this job..." I closed my eyes. "By doing this, by protecting her, choosing her... I divide us."

"Nixon," Chase walked up to me and placed his hand on my arm. "It's been slowly happening for a while. I can't help it. Just like you can't help it. But I can do a better job, at least admit that."

"Fine." I jerked away from him. "Give me some time with her, just a little... more. More time."

"I give you more time, and Frank pulls that trigger." Chase groaned.

"The let him pull it, damn it!" I yelled, pushing all of the books off the desk and then kicking it.

"You're not yourself."

"No shit!" I spat.

"I'm your best friend. When the time's right, assign me to Trace-duty. I'll do what you can't..."

"And what's that?"

"Protect you first... love her second."

"I—"

"You're the boss. You live," Chase answered. "Period."

I nodded and walked out of the room, sick to my stomach because I knew before Chase had even said anything I wouldn't be the death of Trace. Not if I could help it.

But she just may be the death of something else.

Chase and my friendship.

And I had a sinking feeling I'd just sealed our fate.

CHAPTER THIRTY-FOUR
The darkness kept me sane... until now.

Phoenix

I WAS ALONE.

My father wanted nothing to do with me considering I'd failed him in sticking close to the Abandonato family, and I'd officially been cut off. Freaking cut off financially. All because I'd done the right thing in trying to control my own fate. Some fate. I really was going to end up working at McDonald's — if they'd have me.

Pissed off, I'd spent the weekend drinking, and when that hadn't worked to numb the pain, I'd finally come up with a plan. I'd use his weakness against him as a way to get back into his good graces.

"Crap!" Trace yelped as her necklace caught on her hair. She twisted around in a circle while other students shuffled by.

Damn, I hated her. Because she was the reason he wanted nothing to do with me. An innocent girl with brown hair, a girl who, by all means, shouldn't even be at that shitty school.

What was it about her that made him go all protective?

Why was she different?

Why did she have both Nixon and Chase panting?

She was pretty.

But that's where it ended. I'd stopped looking at women as objects of desire, only a means to an end. Damn, I couldn't even touch a girl without being repulsed at my own fingertips grazing her skin.

The necklace she was battling clattered to the floor.

"Allow me," I whispered, reaching down and picking up the necklace. Light from the window flashed against the metal.

Alfero.

One word.

I steeled my expression and managed to mumble, "Pretty."

"Thanks." She held out her hand, her chest rising and falling as if she'd just run a marathon.

"What? I can't be nice?" I smiled and flipped the necklace over. It was Alfero alright. It even had the family crest. Well, son of a bitch. He was protecting the enemy. How... cute. "Hmm, pretty cool. Family heirloom or something?"

"I guess." She shrugged, her nostrils flaring as if she was upset I was touching her shit.

I nodded and plopped the cool metal object into her hands.

She took a step back as if I was going to hit her or something.

"I don't bite, you know."

"No, you just drug girls." Her eyes were cold when they met mine, and they reminded me again why Nixon was the winner in this scenario and I, the loser. I hated the look she gave me because it was the one I would give myself. Hell, it was the look I gave myself every damn day.

My stomach clenched as I held up my hands in front of me. "I guess I deserved that, but are you really going to side with the same guy who last week embarrassed you in front of the entire student body?"

She took a step back and shrugged. "He apologized."

"Nixon Abandonato apologized to a farm girl from Wyoming?" I sneered, irritated that he was always going to be the good guy... and me? Well, I was the exact opposite. Had this girl any idea what we actually did for a living — what we were capable of? She wouldn't be running into his arms. She'd be running away from them. I wasn't the only monster in this story — he was just as bad. Yeah I did horrible things, but so did he. So did all of them. Why the hell was I taking the fall?

She nodded confidently, like Nixon freaking hung the moon and the stars. The sickening feeling got worse... like I was the bad guy, when all I'd ever done my entire life was try to be good. And look where it got me.

Screwed.

On the outside looking in.

No friends.

No family.

A nobody.

"Hmm." I crossed my arms. "Now, why does that sound suspicious?"

"What, that he'd be nice to me?" Her head snapped up.

"No. That he'd apologize to a nobody." I was being an ass, but she had to see how odd it looked. A man like Nixon apologized to no one. Hell, he didn't even apologize to me, and I mattered a lot more than her. An Alfero.

"A nobody?" Her nostrils flared. "At least today when I eat lunch, I'll be sitting with the Elect. Where will you be?"

Pain sliced through my chest at her truthful statement. "Don't you worry your pretty little head where I'll be... but good to know whose side you're on. It makes what I have to do so much easier."

I would ruin her.

Gladly.

Because in the end she didn't belong in our lives. He

would see it, eventually, and then I'd be accepted back into the fold where I belonged, the only place I'd ever belonged.

It was her fault I'd been kicked out.

She was an Alfero, she was the enemy, and Nixon needed to see that. My stomach clenched. I didn't want to hurt her. God knows I'd done my fair share of terrifying the female sex, but all I felt was anger when I looked at her. All I saw was rage. She was just another object, another female trying to exert power over me.

Just like the women my father had chosen over me.

Like the women I'd raped in hopes he'd finally approve of me.

She was just like them.

A jezebel.

Evil.

Corrupt.

My vision blurred with hatred. I smirked, offering her a salute, and walked off in the other direction, clenching my fists to keep from barreling them into a wall.

She'd pay.

They'd all pay.

CHAPTER THIRTY-FIVE
Mysterious phone calls

Nixon

LUNCH WASN'T A PLEASANT experience. Phoenix's chair may as well have been a homing beacon for every damn set of eyes in the room. Trace kept glancing at it, while Chase gave me stern stares from beneath his hooded gaze, and Tex and Mo just looked sad.

Then again, I was sad. I just didn't want to admit it.

What Phoenix had done was wrong, yes, but he was still Phoenix. We'd been best friends since the first grade. I hated that a girl had been the one thing to separate us, almost as much as I hated that the same girl was coming between me and Chase.

How the hell was I going to stop it?

I made a mental note to send him a text. At least I could have him do a few jobs on the side while I decided what to do. One of the associates was acting... off, and he was closer to Phoenix than any of us. If I could throw Phoenix a bone, maybe he'd let the whole Trace thing go. Maybe he'd help get his father to cooperate.

Damn, there were a lot of maybes in there.

Trace's cell phone rang, piercing the silence.

She glanced down at the screen and smiled.

"*Grandpa.*" She mouthed to Mo then got up and walked around the table for privacy.

Both Chase and Tex shook their heads. Yeah, it was weird thinking of Frank going soft... even if it was his granddaughter.

"Fine." She sighed into the phone. "Are you okay? Has something happened? Are the cows out?"

"*Cows?*" Chase mouthed to me.

I shook my head.

"Seriously?" Tex chuckled. "Cows. Can you imagine Frank with cows?"

"Shh!" Mo hit him in the chest and flashed a smile at Trace.

Trace just kept talking like we all had no idea who was on the other end. Ha, Funny, considering he'd just pointed a gun at my face not too long ago.

"Life insurance? Shouldn't that have been taken care of a while ago?" she asked.

My ears immediately perked up.

More silence and then, "Grandpa, are you sure you're okay? You never go into the city, and aren't there some branches in Cheyenne?"

Shit on a stick. He was here to stay.

Trace scratched her head. "Sure, um, yeah—"

She ended the call and stared at the phone.

I sighed, rose from my chair and walked up behind her. "Everything alright?"

"Grandpa's acting weird," she mumbled, still staring at the phone in her hands.

I tried not to tense, but it was damn-near impossible. "What did he say?"

"Something about Grandma's life insurance and stuff. I

don't know. Shouldn't he have taken care of that months ago?" Her eyebrows scrunched together.

I offered a shrug. As far as excuses went, that wasn't a bad one. "Who knows, Trace? Sometimes it takes a while to get death certificates and stuff. You just never know."

She nodded. "He's, um, he's flying into Chicago tomorrow."

"When?" My jaw twitched. The bastard was already here, but whatever.

"I don't know. He said he'd see me at seven."

"Shit," I mumbled. That didn't give us a lot of time. It didn't give me a lot of time with her. Time I needed to explain things before it all went to hell. Time to tell her how I felt... Time... I hated that word.

Trace's brows knit together in confusion. "Huh? Why is that bad? He's my grandpa. He's—"

"I know. I just..." My grin was forced. "I had plans. I wanted to take you out." I could practically feel Chase's eyes burning a hole through me. I flipped him off behind my back.

Trace smiled. "Well, you can take me out tonight."

"Did you just ask me out?" I grinned.

"Uhh..." Her mouth dropped open.

"Intelligent as well as beautiful. Whatever am I going to do with you?" I reached for her face and rolled my thumb across her lower lip. "Fine, Trace. I'll go out with you. How about six tonight? Sound good?"

"No, no, not good, wait—"

I walked off to my seat before she could change her mind. Tex chuckled.

"Sorry," Chase said, once Trace reached the pulled-out seat. "Nixon can be a little..."

"A lot." She nodded. "He can be a lot. A lot of the times."

Chase threw his head back and laughed. "Yes, yes he can."

Monroe threw a napkin at his face, or at least tried to.

"Hey, watch it. He may be the devil, but he's my brother."

"I'm right here," I said in a loud and irritating voice.

Chase ignored me. "So, he's my cousin, which gives me familial rights."

"What?" Trace's voice shrieked.

Shocked, I just stared at her while Chase shrugged. "I thought you knew."

"What, through mind reading?" She threw her hands up into the air. "Unbelievable. Are all of you related?"

"Oh God, I hope not." Tex winked at Monroe.

I kicked him under the table.

"Nixon said you met my dad." Chase took a swig of water.

"Anthony?" She blinked a few times as if trying to put two and two together.

She leaned in, close enough to kiss the bastard, and I could tell he was enjoying it way too much.

Chase cleared his throat. "Uh, could you not stare like that? I'm not as used to it as Nixon."

"What do you mean you're not as used to it?" She puppeted.

Chase shrugged. "Simple, I'm not the man-whore of the group. Women don't gawk at me as much when he's around. I mean, come on. Look at him. He's trouble with a capital *T*."

I rolled my eyes. Right, I was the man-whore? I may get more stares, but it had everything to do with the fact that none of the girls could claim to have slept with me, while at least a third of them had slept with Chase — twice. "If you weren't my cousin I'd think you were hitting on me."

"If I wasn't your cousin, I just might." Chase winked and blew me a kiss.

"And too far." Trace threw her hands into the air and covered her face. Her innocence never failed to entertain me. "You are trouble though. Hmm…"

"What?" I grinned, meeting her gaze. "Tell me."

She bit her lip, something I could tell she did often when she was nervous and didn't like answering my direct question. "No, no, it's not…"

The table fell silent.

"Tell us." Tex started clapping his hands and chanting. Idiot.

Trace giggled. "Fine, it's just, Nixon reminds me of that Taylor Swift song, "Trouble? You guys heard it?" She laughed as we all shook our heads in unison. "Yeah, well, if I didn't know any better, I'd think Nixon had dated her, dumped her, and she'd written a song about him."

She kept laughing.

The rest of us stopped, including Mo.

You could have heard a pin drop in the lunchroom.

Trace's eyes widened. "Shut up. No way! Did you date Taylor Swift?"

Hell no. The last thing I needed was that type of publicity. I laughed and pointed at Chase, who, in turn, opened his mouth to say something and then pointed at Tex.

Tex turned around and pointed at Phoenix's empty chair. "Damn. I have nobody to blame."

"What? You all dated her?" She crossed her arms.

"What happens in the Elect stays in the Elect." Chase held up his hand for a high five.

"This isn't Vegas." Trace eyed us suspiciously.

"Drugs, gangs, sex, money, and guns? You sure about that?" I winked.

The bell from the clock-tower chimed. Trace slowly rose from her seat and started making her way toward the door.

I bolted out of my seat and followed. "Where do you think you're going?"

"Class?" Her voice squeaked.

"Hmm…" I tightened my arms around her body, resting my chin on her head. All I wanted was her touch, a reminder that I wasn't crazy for wanting her. Maybe I was just a glutton for punishment, a masochist. Because I knew it wouldn't end well, and we would end. That I was sure of.

"How about you skip?"

"I can't just skip class!" She tensed beneath me.

I released her body long enough to twist her around to face me, my fingers dancing along her chin. "But you kind of want to, don't you?"

"No." She looked down at her shoes. Damn, I hated — hated — that I still made her that uncomfortable.

"Fine." I sighed and stepped back. "But don't forget about tonight. No faking illness or saying you have homework, okay?" Because then I'd be forced to knock down her door and carry her over my shoulder.

She was still staring at the floor when she offered a small smile and nod.

"Okay, off you go." I stepped around her and walked the few feet to the door. The minute she walked by, I slapped her butt. It was just too tempting.

She let out a little squeak, and I burst out laughing. Yeah, I could live every day with a woman who was that innocent.

"You're going to hurt her, you know." Chase's voice damn-near had me colliding with the wall.

"Don't sneak up on me. It's weird. Creepy too."

Chase snorted and moved to stand right next to me, his eyes trained on Trace as she walked down the hall. "Let her go now... before the shit hits the fan."

"Let her go," I repeated. "So you can swoop in?"

"Well to be fair..." he shrugged. "I'd wait at least twenty-four hours."

"How thoughtful."

"Yeah, well..." Chase didn't hide his shameless grin. "...that's what the ladies say."

"Stay away."

"Make me."

"Girls..." Tex stepped between us. "...since when have

we ever fought over a chick? Since when has that same chick been our sworn enemy? This is some weird shit, and if you two don't figure it out, then we're all screwed. So tuck your panties back in and toss your bras into the fire. I don't want to have to bury two of my best friends just because they don't see the bullet aimed for their hearts the minute Frank learns that his precious granddaughter isn't just flirting with the enemy... but sleeping with him."

"I'm not—"

Tex held up his hand. "But you will, won't you?"

Chase growled.

"Get to class," I barked. "And stay out of my love life."

"Ah, so now it's love?" Chase moved toward me. We stood chest to chest. "You can't even let the girl touch you without wincing, and it's love? Really?"

"Wow, it's like I didn't just make a pretty epic speech." Tex cursed and pushed both of us away. "We have bigger shit to deal with."

"He's right." I sighed.

"Course I am." Tex rolled his eyes. "Voice of reason. Never thought that particular title would attach itself to my name, but I kind of like it."

Chase and I shared a look of irritation, but not with each other, with Tex, because he was right, damn him, and for once it was Chase and I... who weren't thinking with logic.

But something else far more dangerous.

Emotion.

CHAPTER THIRTY-SIX

Oh look, Tex was right. Shit, meet fan.

Nixon

"READY?" I HELD OUT MY hand to Trace. She looked beautiful in a short black dress. My eyes went lower. And Chase's boots. Right, so it was like he was on a date with us. Fantastic. Bastard. I was going to burn those boots one day.

The entire day had gone so freaking slow I thought time had actually stopped just to torment me. As it was, I had gotten to Trace's dorm fifteen minutes early, only to find myself checking my watch and then tapping the glass, thinking it wasn't working.

I hadn't been on a date since...

Well honestly, I'd never been on a date, not that I was going to tell Trace that. There wasn't really room for dating in my life. There had been room for one-night stands, promises never made, secrets never shared, but I'd never had an honest-to-God relationship, which is probably why I was ready to start pacing in front of my car.

When she finally appeared, I damn-near swallowed my tongue whole. How could a girl that beautiful truly not know it?

Trace took my hand. "Yup."

"Still hate me?" I asked once we were safely in the bulletproof Range Rover.

"Still not telling me who you are?" came her snarky reply, making me want to pull over and kiss her senseless.

"And off we go!" I laughed to cover up for my insane need to dip my tongue into her mouth. "So, you may have noticed we don't have security tonight."

She nodded and tilted her head toward me, twisting her hands in her lap like she was nervous I was going to bite.

Perhaps I would.

"Why?"

"Other than the fact I'm packing?" I said in a rare moment of honesty.

She was silent.

Good job, Nixon. Scare the shit out of the girl you want to date. Good move. Five minutes in, and she was probably looking for an exit out of the moving vehicle.

"Chill." I pulled through the open security gate. "It was a joke."

"So you aren't packing?" She gulped.

"Not technically," I said slowly.

"Right." She turned on the AC and closed her eyes. "So where are we going? I'm guessing it's safe, since we're not having to worry about security?"

"Absolutely."

"Cool."

"Want to know where?" I couldn't pull back the smile that had forced its way onto my face.

She let out a little laugh. "You want to tell me, don't you?"

"So bad." I leaned over the steering wheel and fought the urge to laugh like a kid. I was excited — more than excited she'd said yes — and I had planned the best date in the history of dates, guns included.

"Surprise me."

"I get too excited when it comes to surprises," I grumbled. Probably because I had a shit childhood, and the one and only time my dad said *surprise* to me was when he opened the box he used to trap me in, only to throw in my teddy bear so I'd stop crying. "Okay, I'm going to try, but you can't talk to me, or else I'm going to blurt everything and ruin it, okay?"

"Not talk to you? Whatever will I do?"

I felt my blood heat as I eyed her up and down. "I've got a few ideas of other things you could do with your mouth—"

"And I'm pretty sure if I searched hard enough, I could find a gun and shoot off your man-parts, so say that again. I dare you."

I gulped, too aroused for words. Damn, just imaging her pointing a gun at me had me ready to strip her naked. How sick was that? "Silence, it is."

"That's what I thought."

"Damn." I shook my head. "Well played."

"I know." She smirked and gave me another glance out of the corner of her eye. It was like she didn't want me to know she was staring. I almost flexed my bicep but decided against it.

A thick silence descended in the car. Between her staring at my face and me trying not to look at her legs in that short skirt, I was ready to lose my mind.

"Almost there." Losing the battle, I reached over and placed my hand on her thigh. She had tights on, making it so I couldn't feel her skin, but damn did I feel the heat against my palm. Touching her sent me into overdrive. It was already the best date of my life, and we hadn't even done anything yet.

She let out a little gasp.

"Okay?" I pulled down the familiar dirt road. "Close your eyes."

RACHEL VAN DYKEN

She looked around us then closed them. "Are you going to kill me?"

"No." I let out a bark of laughter. Please. Like I'd kill her on my own property. That would be just lazy on my part.

She seemed to relax.

"I didn't bring my silencer." I just had to say it, didn't I? The guys would have laughed their asses off. Trace? Not so much. She stiffened under my touch and tried to jerk away, but I held on for dear life.

"Trace, calm down. This is supposed to be fun, remember?"

"Yeah," she said breathlessly.

I turned off the car and made my way around to her door, carefully unbuckling the seatbelt before lifting her into my arms.

She sighed, her breath tickling my neck, and in that moment, life stood still. Things were perfect. Life was as it should be.

The girl I'd sworn to protect as a boy.

Was finally in my arms as a man.

I didn't want to let her go, but knew I had to. I couldn't just hold her the entire date — as much as I wanted to.

Finally, I set her on her feet. "Open your eyes."

"Are those—"

"Cows." I laughed, staring out at the large pasture. "Yes, real live cows. I hear they even moo from time to time. And this..." I pointed behind us. "...is our picnic under the stars."

"With the cows," she added, her voice filled with wonder.

"With the cows. Though I've heard a few goats live out here too. Don't want to leave out any farm creatures and take a chance on offending them."

"Right." Her lower lip trembled.

Sighing, I pulled her into my arms and held her. I kissed her head twice, wanting a third, fourth, fifth, sixth, seventh—

Hell, honest moment? I wanted all of them. Every. Single. One.

"I know you miss it. I know you miss your grandpa." It still pissed me off to think that he'd thrown her to the wolves — literally. "But being at Elite it's where you belong." With me, always with me. "As much as you miss all of this "You're home. Right here." In my arms. Like it should have been a long time ago. I'd be damned if I was ever letting her go.

"Hungry?" I released her.

"Starved." She walked over to the back of the Range Rover. "Nope, you sit right here." I opened the trunk, picked her up, and sat her on the ledge so her feet dangled off. "There now. Stay put while I get this all ready."

I pulled the blankets from the back and started laying them on top of one another. The grass was semi-wet from the rain the night before. Four blankets later, and I was confident the wetness wouldn't seep through. I grabbed the containers of lasagna and spaghetti and placed them on the blanket along with the paper plates.

When everything looked good, I lit a cylinder candle, put it inside the lantern, and set it in the middle of the picnic.

I glanced at Trace and held out my hand. "Your dinner awaits."

She jumped off the back of the SUV and gripped my hand, then took a seat on the blanket. "Thank you."

We sat in silence while I poured her a cup of sparkling cider and handed it to her.

Since I'd never been on a date, I wasn't sure if I would offend her by piling her plate as high as mine. Then again, she was Italian, even if she didn't know it, and one thing about Italians? We eat. We eat a lot. Food cures the soul and all that. So I piled the food onto her plate and handed it to her, hoping I wouldn't get slapped for assuming she could eat her body weight in pasta.

With a giggle, she took the plate and stabbed her fork into the still-steaming food. She brought it to her lips and let out the sexiest moan known to humanity.

"Shit." The fork fell out of my hand and landed on the lasagna, causing it to drip onto the blanket. "Sorry, it's just..." I looked away and took a long gulp of the cider, wishing like hell it had alcohol. "Ah, slippery fork and all."

"Right, because of the rain." She rolled her eyes and took a bite of spaghetti. What I wouldn't do to be that freaking fork. She winked and let out another perfectly timed moan. Just as I took another sip of cider.

I started choking to death.

"Are you okay?" She leaned over and patted my back, her damn dress showing me something black, something lacy, something that needed to be removed immediately.

I nodded and took her cider. I drank half of it before placing it back on the blanket. "Yeah..." My voice sounded like I'd just finished smoking two packs. "...I just... was... choking."

"Right." Her eyes narrowed mischievously.

My face went hot all over.

Great, so now I blushed? I was that guy?

"Who made the food?" she asked after a few more bites.

"I did."

Laughing, she pushed me with her free hand and took another bite.

"You don't believe me?" I asked, a bit insulted. "You think I'd lie about something as important as food?"

She dropped her fork and held her hands in the air in mock surrender. "Sorry, Nixon. Yes, I believe you, and if you ever get tired of running around in your little gang, you could become a world-renowned chef."

"My little gang," I repeated. Memories of my childhood came crashing to the forefront of my mind. "You sound like Ma."

"How?" Trace tucked her legs underneath her.

"She used to call us guys her little gang." I pushed some

food around my plate, losing my appetite as a vision of her lifeless eyes flashed before me. "Not so much anymore."

Trace pointed at the food. "Did she teach you how to cook?"

"Oh yeah, my father hated it." I leaned down on my side and smiled. "I spent all my early years in the kitchen, holding onto my mom's skirts and testing all her food. She cooked a lot."

Trace's eyes widened before she looked out into the pasture, her face unreadable.

"What?" Nixon urged.

"Nothing." She gave her head a shake. "Or, well... It's just — I don't remember much from when I was little. Grandpa said everything was too traumatizing with my parents dying and all, but I remember being in a kitchen with this little boy and getting in a food fight."

I chuckled because I'd been that little boy, and she'd called me stupid. "What happened?"

"I think he got mad because the cook let me have a taste of the cookie dough first. Anyway, all I remember is that he threw dough at me, and I threw it back at him. We fought, and I think he tripped and hit the side of his head on the counter. I'm sure it left a scar."

"Wow, you were a terrible child." I nodded my head, happy that she'd remembered part of the story even if she hadn't remembered me. It was a good memory. "I'm impressed."

I scooted as close to her as I could without scaring her.

When she glanced up, she jolted then grabbed my hand.

"Do you remember anything else about your parents?" I asked softly, prodding, hoping, wishing. It would be so much easier if she actually knew the truth or discovered it on her own. What would happen if I told her? Would she have a psychotic break? Even believe me? And why did I have to be the one to tell her? Damn Frank. "Or would you rather not talk about it?"

"I don't really know how I feel about it." She shrugged, hugging her arms to her body then scooting closer to me. "I mean, the memories are so scattered."

"Like a movie you can't remember?" I asked, thinking about my own traumatic past. Some of the images were just like that, pictures that seemed fake, except I was in them.

"Something like that. I see pieces…"

"Tell me one…" I leaned over and kissed her cheek. "…if you don't mind."

"Alright, um… I remember things being really loud when I was little. We always had people over, lots and lots of people. I remember the dough thing… and a really pretty woman."

Holy shit. This was it. Come on Trace, put the puzzle together. "I like pretty women."

"Very funny." She squeezed my hand. "I don't know why I always remember her. I know it wasn't my mom, because I've seen pictures and remember her face a bit."

"What did this pretty woman look like, hmm?" I moved my hand from hers and started massaging her neck. My entire body was taut with frustration to finish the story for her, to fill in the pieces that were needed in order to write our ending.

She clenched her teeth. "She… she had really blue eyes. Like yours."

My hand stopped moving as anticipation wracked my body.

"And she had a really pretty laugh. It sounded like…"

"Church bells," I finished, unable to help myself.

She jerked away. "What?"

Shit. I dropped my head. Too soon. I knew it was too soon. "I read minds. Why, what were you going to say?"

Trace's eyes pierced right through me, making the guilt all the worse. Because I knew the answers to her questions but was unable to give them to her. Better she not know than I tell her and put her life in danger. It already was the more time she spent with me.

I stood and held out my hand. "Dance with me."

"In front of the cows?" her voice squeaked.

"Uh, yeah." I glanced between her and the cows. "I don't think they'll mind. Why, what kind of dancing were you thinking of doing? Were you hoping to embarrass the cows and get them to moo?"

Narrowing her eyes, she swatted me with her hand then stood.

"Come on." I tugged her body against mine so there was no space between us. I couldn't use words with her. After all, words were never safe, and they were easily twisted.

But showing her? I could do that. Even if it meant I had to stay silent the rest of my existence, I'd show her by my actions.

That to me?

She was everything.

CHAPTER THIRTY-SEVEN
Cops and Cows. Yay, an orgy. Or not.

Nixon

"NIXON." TRACE PULLED AWAY, her dark brown eyes frightened, unsure. I was an expert at reading people, and she looked scared shitless. "Are you leading me on?"

Not what I expected her to say. Shocked, I gripped her shoulders, needing to hold on to something so she wouldn't run from me, run from us. "What?"

"L-leading me on." She looked down at those damn boots. "I mean, are you doing all this so you can just — I don't know — throw me to the wolves later?"

"You don't trust very easily do you?" I asked, nearly wincing because, no shit, she didn't trust easily. I'd basically threatened her within the first five seconds of meeting her. I wouldn't trust me, and the sick part? She really shouldn't trust me. Not if she knew who she really was. The truth? If she knew her own family's history, she'd be holding a gun to my head, not hugging me.

She shook her head.

"I don't blame you." I sighed and pulled her back into

my arms where I could keep her close, keep her safe. "And no, I'm not leading you on. I've told you before. I want to protect you. In the beginning, you were just another new kid that I needed to show the ropes to, but now…"

"Now?" she repeated in a hopeful voice.

"Now you're the girl who… moos?" I offered with a chuckle.

She squirmed in my arms.

"You're…" I stopped our dance and glanced into the dark depths of her eyes. "You're beautiful. In a way, I've been searching my whole life for you."

Truth. I'd been searching my life for this girl, thinking her dead. My heart had never felt so broken yet complete at the same time.

"Wow, easy on the corny movie lines." She laughed.

I didn't join in because it was real. My feelings for her were real. More than she could possibly know.

"I'm serious," I whispered. "I just wish you would rem—"

I crushed my mouth against hers to keep from saying anything else that I knew would get me shot at. With a growl, I picked her up and wrapped her legs around my body then laid her down against the blanket.

I hovered over her, unsure if I should kiss her more or try to restrain myself.

With a curse, I started to pull away, but in that moment, Trace reached up and wrapped her hands around my neck, bringing her mouth against mine.

With a sigh I leaned my forehead against hers.

What the hell was I doing?

Seriously.

And did I care?

My teeth grazed her lower lip as I ran my fingers through her silky brown hair. "You have no idea…" I blew across her wet lips and moved my hands to her neck, pulling her closer. "…how much I want you."

Her breathing picked up as I crushed my mouth to hers again, tasting every part of her and craving more. I expected her to freak out; instead, she deepened the kiss.

And I was freaking lost in a mess of my own making.

A beautiful mess with a girl who loved cows and had the most beautiful brown eyes I'd ever had the pleasure of seeing.

My tongue pressed against hers, tangling, beckoning her to dive deeper into the void I was lost in.

Trace matched my every kiss, my every move, like we'd been made for one another.

Her hands moved to the loops of my jeans. She tugged me closer to her, until there was nothing but friction. My jeans against her tights — the only things that separated us, and they sure as hell weren't going to stop me now. Damn it, but Tex had been right. She was going to be sleeping with the enemy, and I didn't even feel guilty. Because for the first time in forever, I felt — she made me feel — everything. I wasn't afraid of touch.

I craved it like a drug.

So when the heat of her thighs burned through my jeans, I held on for dear life, kissing her harder, moving my hands so that I could grip her hips. I settled between her thighs, letting out a moan as she squeezed around my body.

I cursed as she damn-near bit my lower lip off with her aggression. When her tongue found my lip ring, I just about died on the spot, then flipped her around so that she was straddling my body. Gravity caused her to fall against me in such an erotic way that I swear I saw black.

I lifted her up and ground her against me.

Trace's lips caressed mine, softer this time.

I knew we were at a crossroads. Take it further — or call it a night. My body said to take it further. Everything else said I needed to take things slow…

But I'd been waiting for her for too long.

And she wanted it as much as I did.

I pushed my conscience away, at least what was left of it, and stared at her, willing her to tell me no, needing her to say it for me to actually stop.

Rather than say no, her mouth quirked into a smile, and she lifted her arms.

Shit.

I pulled the jacket from her body and stared at the nearly see-through dress and black lacey bra underneath it, making a mental note to thank my evil twin for most likely helping Trace plan that outfit.

For a minute, I just stared.

Why?

Because I could.

Because she was mine, damn it.

I closed my eyes and whispered, "It was always supposed to be like this. Always."

"Like what?" she asked.

"Like this." My fingertips skimmed her breasts and moved down across her hips until they finally settled on the small of her back. "Like this," I repeated as my hand touched her face and traced the outline of her lips with my fingertips. "And like this…" My hand moved from her lips to her chest.

Her heart was racing.

"I—" Swallowing down a curse, I tried again. "—I have to kiss you. I have to have you — all of you." I wasn't sure she understood what I was asking her, what I was demanding from her. Not just her body but her soul, her everything. No going back. I'd have to die to give her up.

Her eyes hooded, and with a nod she reached for me.

I tugged her down onto the blanket and kissed her neck. She arched against me, her body ready for the taking.

A siren sounded in the distance.

I ignored it. Damn cops. What use was having them in your pocket if they bothered the hell out of you when you were trying to kiss?

"Stay," I mumbled as Trace tensed beneath me. "They won't see us."

"Okay." She gently pushed my head back and kissed my neck.

Damn, I let out a growl and chuckled as I pulled her harder against my body. Her thighs clenched around my waist. My hands moved to her dress, slowly inching it up so I could peel it from her body.

The sirens got closer. And then I heard a car door slam.

My hands froze as footsteps neared us.

"Shit." I rolled my eyes and gently pushed Trace away as I stood. Either that cop was going to get a bullet to his body, or I was going to have a nice long chat with the police chief — guns included.

I pulled Trace to her feet. Her dress fell against her legs just as the cop rounded the corner, his flashlight pointed at my face.

"This here is private property," the cop stated in an authoritative voice. Apparently he didn't recognize me. Pity for him.

"I know," I replied coolly.

"Then what the hell are you kids doing out here?"

I threw my head back and laughed. Kids? Wow, it was like he was begging for me to call his superior and fire his ass.

"I know the owner," I said, my smile still in place. "I'm sure he won't mind."

"Won't mind?" the cop repeated. "Son, do you have any idea who the hell's property this is? I can guarantee you he'll mind! In fact, if he finds out you kids are out here this late at night, even I can't protect you from that son of a — "

The flashlight fell on my face and stayed there. Ah, so now he looks.

I squinted and put a hand in front of my eyes and chuckled. "Go on, *that son of a...* what?"

"Uh... gun. Son of a gun. Sorry, Mr. Abandonato, I didn't

realize..."

"That's okay." I stuffed my hands into my jean pockets. "You didn't realize. Right?"

"My badge number is—"

Shit, that's the last thing I needed. For Trace to actually know that the cops worked for me, not the city. "That won't be necessary. I'm not going to report you. You were just doing your job. Though it's a damn shame it had to be at this very moment."

The officer's eyes flickered to Trace as he lifted the flashlight to her face. "Damn shame, sir."

She rolled her eyes and moved closer to me.

"So..." He nodded his head awkwardly. "...I'll just be on my way. Say hi to your old man for me, will ya? He still having trouble with—?"

"Thank you." I shook the cop's hand and ushered him back to the patrol car. "Have a good night."

He nodded, face still pale, and got into his car, this time with the sirens off.

I turned around and grinned. "Well, that didn't go as planned."

"Oh really?" Trace crossed her arms. "And how was it supposed to go?"

I crooked my finger. She stumbled into my arms, our mouths met, and my tongue licked her lower lip. "Hmm..." My hands dug into my hair. "...like this..." I smiled when she let out a small moan. "...and a bit like this..." I slid my hands down to her ass and lifted her against me. "...and a lot like this." My tongue swirled into her mouth, dancing against her wetness.

My phone started buzzing in my pocket.

Worst timing ever.

The guys knew not to call me right now, which meant it was bad news, bad enough that they'd risk me shooting them for interrupting the best night of my life.

"Shit, I um…" I glanced at my cell. It was Chase. "I have to take this. Hold on."

"Remember that fan we talked about? And shit hitting it?" Chase chuckled into the cell. "Game over."

"What?" I barked.

"You planning on meeting with Frank tonight? Because I just got word that two of his armed cars are on their way to your fun little picnic."

"No. That's impossible. Not until tomorrow." I quieted my voice. "Trace was supposed to meet with him tomorrow. It seemed like he was busy tonight and—"

"Busy spying on your sorry ass." Chase sighed. "Just get back to campus. It could be nothing but—"

"Yeah, but." I sighed and cursed into the phone then switched to Italian.

"You think he would hurt her?"

"You think he won't?" Chase countered.

"Lock down. We'll be there in five minutes. Make sure security at the gate knows, and Chase?"

"Yes, pumpkin?"

"You were right."

"About?"

"Me being a danger to her."

"Yeah well… being right doesn't feel so hot right now. Stay safe."

"Will do."

CHAPTER THIRTY-EIGHT
You want me to do what?!

Nixon

"WE HAVE TO GO," I barked.

"What the heck? No *please* this time?" Trace teased, lazily picking up her jacket off the ground.

"Not this time." I dumped everything onto the blanket and quickly stuffed it in the back. "It's more of an order, as in, get your ass in the car before I do it for you."

"Wh-what?" Trace's face went ashen white.

Shit.

"Get. In. The. Damn. Car. Now!" I snapped. My palms started to sweat as I jerked the door open and got in.

Shit.

Sometimes cops were such idiots. Thanks, genius, for just telling everyone within the good ol' US of A my exact location. Really solid, guy. I should send him a cake or something.

I had two guns with me.

One shotgun under the back seat.

And my trusty old Colt 1911 under my own seat.

"Shit," I mumbled again. If they trapped us, if we didn't

make it back to campus...

It wasn't just the Alferos who could be after us, but every other freaking assassin who had a hit out on me or one of my family members. I had enemies — a lot of them. And a lot of them wanted me dead. Most of the time I had protection with me, so this was about to get loads more interesting.

I put the SUV in drive and sped toward campus.

Trace looked out the window, silent, probably confused, pissed. I reached across the console and grabbed her hand.

"Hey..." I squeezed and maintained a calm voice. "...I'm sorry about..." I released her hand and hit the steering wheel. Why couldn't anything be normal? I'd wanted to be a normal guy for her. Take her on a normal date. Have a normal make-out session where visions of guns and blood didn't dance through my head. "Damn, I'm just sorry I freaked out. But we needed to get out of there." Yeah, that wasn't vague as hell.

"But it's your property," she argued in a shaky voice.

"Which the cop had no problem explaining to his other little friends who were out patrolling tonight." Little friends who worked for other families, who carried out tasks for my enemies, and who would stop at nothing to shoot at me if I was alone.

"Whatever," Trace grumbled, biting her lip and crossing her arms. "I don't even know why that matters. Why would you care? It's not as if they were going to come watch us make out too!"

Her blush was freaking adorable.

I burst out laughing. "I wasn't worried about them, Trace." I couldn't care less if I stripped naked in front of strangers — as long as she was in my arms. I seriously had no shame. I was a Mafia boss. Embarrassment wasn't an emotion I practiced.

"I don't understand."

"Protecting," I said honestly. "I promised to protect you, right?"

She finally looked at me and nodded.

"So trust me. What I'm doing right now? This is me trying my damnedest to protect you. Okay?"

"Yelling at me and ordering me around is protecting me?"

Well, when she put it that way, I sounded like some grouchy old bastard.

"I said..." I pinched the bridge of my nose. "...I said I was sorry. You're right. I shouldn't have been so rude, but we needed to get out of there, like fast."

She was silent again.

Irritated, I clenched the wheel with both hands and finally started to see some of the city lights. Good, no tails — yet.

I turned the corner and then looked in the rearview mirror again.

Well, damn it all to hell.

Trace moved in her seat to look. I slammed her back against the seat with my arm. "Don't look."

"Nixon," Her lower lip quivered. "What aren't you telling me?"

Oh you know... just about everything.

I took a hard right, trying to lose the tail. "Nothing you need to know... yet."

Hell. They were still following us.

"Um, Nixon. Nixon... the car behind us? They have guns. Nixon, they have guns."

No shit. They also had a few semi-automatic weapons, but to name every piece of ammunition they had just seemed pointless.

"Shit." I reached for my gun. "Trace, I need you to lay low. Can you do that? Just lean down in your seat. Alright, sweetheart?" I was starting to sweat. She leaned down in her seat as I took another right and then pointed the gun out the window and started shooting.

The guy behind me shot directly for my hand, missing me and hitting the window, thank God.

I brought my arm back in and stole a glance to my right. "Trace, how are ya holding up? Talk to me, Trace," I said in a smooth and calculated voice. I wasn't afraid for me — but for her.

"I'm... fantastic," she said through clenched teeth. The SUV hit a bump, and she let out a scream. The car behind us was trying to run us off the road.

"Are they trying to kill us?" she shouted.

Hell yes. "Possibly. I'm guessing they just want to see who I'm with and why I'd go to such lengths to hide you." Because she was everything — the key to my salvation. They key to my soul. They weren't touching her. I'd die before I let anything happen.

My mind was going a hundred miles a minute. We weren't far from campus. It may come to a gunfight. I'd lose. It was just me. The guys wouldn't get there in time, which meant I'd have to pull into an open lot and tell her to run while I held them off.

Five minutes, maybe six.

And I'd be dead.

She'd have to make good time. I hoped to God she was a runner, if it came to that — it's the only thing that would keep her alive.

The car behind me swerved. They must have had an idiot driving. I smiled in triumph.

"Why are you smiling?" Trace's voice was bordering on hysteria.

My smile grew. One mile to the school. "Because we're almost to campus. They know we're on our way and no chance in hell are those guys coming within a hundred feet of the place. We're almost there, sweetheart." We may just make it through after all.

The car jolted again. My poor Range Rover was going to

be scratched to hell.

Trace let out another scream.

I kind of liked it.

As in, if we were in a totally different situation and she was screaming — you know because I was making her scream, I could come to really like that sound coming out of her mouth.

"Oh my gosh. Oh my gosh!" Her eyes squeezed shut, and then she shouted. "I'm going to die a virgin!"

"What?" I roared. Holy shit. She was a virgin? I'd guessed, but hearing her say it out loud? I should have been horrified — instead I was amused, pleased as hell, feeling a bit prideful that it would be me. Nobody else would touch her for that first time. She didn't want to die a virgin? Hell, I'd help with that. Sign me up.

"I'm going to die a virgin!" she repeated, her voice rising higher and higher. "I'm going to die without ever going overseas! I've never even been naked in front of a man before."

I shifted uncomfortably in my seat.

"Oh my gosh! I'm never going to have kids! What if I want kids! What if—"

"Trace," I interrupted.

"Nixon!" She smacked me in the arm. "You have to promise me that if we live through this — and that's a giant if, considering we're literally trapped between two death machines — you have to take my virginity. Take it!"

"Trace, I don't think this is the time to—"

"Promise!"

"Trace—"

"Promise me, damn it!"

Never in my life have I made a promise so fast — scratch that, it was a freaking vow. I'd take her virginity, and when I was done, I was going to take her overseas. Then I was going to possess her over and over again until she forgot all about guns and car chases.

"Crap, crap, crap!" She covered her face and started rocking back and forth.

I pulled the car up to security and gave the guard a quick rundown of what happened while Trace's face turned about thirty different shades of red.

She was silent the entire drive through campus.

With an amused sigh, I pulled her hands away from her face. She held on to herself with the cutest death grip ever.

"Trace," I whispered, my lips so close to hers I could almost taste her, "Are you okay?"

She whimpered and then shivered. "No, I'm not okay! We could have died! Who were those people? Why did they have guns? Is it like this all the time when you're out and about in public? What the hell, Nixon! I need answers."

And I needed her to change the subject. "As well as a volunteer." My eyebrows shot up in amusement.

"Come again."

I burst out laughing at her confused look. "Yes."

"Yes, what?"

"My answer." I winked. "Just name the time and place. I'll be there." With freaking bells on. "It would be an honor." She had no idea how serious I was. So she'd never been with a man before? Never let them look upon her naked perfection? Good. Because no man would ever see her — no man but me. "I mean, I would love to be the one guy going into uncharted territory and…"

"Shut up! Just shut up!" She covered her face again and moaned. "Oh my hell, I'm so embarrassed."

Pity, because I was so turned on I couldn't think straight.

"Hey," I nudged her. "That was a real bonding experience back there." I gently pulled each finger from her face and kissed the inside of her wrist. "And don't worry, we'll wait until you're ready…" Or until I die from want. I may die first…

"You'll be waiting a long time." That's what I was afraid

of.

"It's not like you didn't," I teased.

Her eyes narrowed as she let out a little gasp. I took the opportunity with enthusiasm, crushing my mouth against hers with all the aggression that had built up over the past fifteen minutes.

I used my lips to convince her it was me — I was hers. It was a punishment. Hell. Getting to only kiss her, instead of taking her up on that promise right then and there? Could only be described as hell.

I reached around her body, tugging it closer to mine, as close as it would get with the console between us. It would be so easy to lift her into my arms, to toss her in the back seat, to convince her that this was what she wanted — even though I knew it wasn't what she deserved. My body screamed in frustration as her tongue swirled with mine.

Her taste was my heaven.

"Now is good too..." She surprised me by saying as she tugged my hair with her hands.

Hell yes.

I lifted her, slowly. Hell, I was a Mafia boss. The straight and narrow? Moral compass? Yeah, not in my vocabulary.

I was going to wreck her for anyone else.

And then my worst nightmare came true.

At first the knocking was distant, and then it became louder. I pulled back and stared Frank Alfero down.

His eyes narrowed.

He opened his jacket and pointed at his gun.

And I knew in that moment, whatever fantasy I had created for me and Trace, whatever future I may have built up — was about to come crashing down at my feet.

Funny, I always thought I'd die before I experienced heartbreak.

And there I was... twenty-one years old, and feeling like my heart had just been ripped from my chest.

He would take her from me.
And this time — I wouldn't survive it.

CHAPTER THIRTY-NINE
The big guns

Chase

I SENT NIXON A text, warning him that Frank was waiting outside the dorms. Clearly he was otherwise occupied, if the steam taking up the front windshield was any indicator.

"Ten bucks says he gets shot in the ass," Tex piped up next to me.

We were about fifteen feet away from them in the bushes. We didn't need binoculars and were close enough to hear words or gunshots — if it came to that.

Frank knocked on the window.

Tex started to chuckle.

The door opened.

Trace stepped out, her face flush with pleasure. I gripped my gun so tight in my hand I could have sworn I almost broke it in half.

"Down boy. She's not yours until she's not his anymore, got it?" Tex whispered, elbowing me in the ribs.

"No, but thanks for the pep talk."

Tex grunted.

RACHEL VAN DYKEN

Trace stepped awkwardly into her Grandpa's stiff arms. "Hey, Gramps, you're early."

He returned her hug, his eyes glued to Nixon. "You."

"Aw, shit." I pointed my gun at Frank and waited.

Tex flashed me a grin. "It's better than watching a movie. Look, Nixon's not even shaking. Damn, I'd be shaking. Frank's scary when he's pissed off. Ever notice that weird vein that travels down his temple? Swear, it's like its own entity."

I shot him a glare and focused in the scope.

"Me," Nixon said in a cold voice. "Great to finally meet you, Mr. Rooks."

"I didn't catch your name." Frank crossed his arms refusing Nixon's hand.

"Now that's rude," Tex huffed. "Refusing to shake the boss's hand? Frank knows the rules."

"Yeah, but Trace doesn't," I argued, eying them through the scope. "And Frank looks less mobster — more killer — Grandfather right now."

"Really? I could have sworn you knew it already." Nixon moved until he was almost chest to chest with Frank. When Trace tried to break them apart, they both reached for her at the same time, gently coaxing her out of the way. It was a man's game.

"I'm old." Franks laugh was hollow. "Tell me again. What's your name... son?"

Nixon's jaw flexed. I could tell he was about two seconds away from punching the guy in the face. "Nixon Abandonato. But most people around here just call me sir."

"You're too young to be a sir," he seethed.

"Aw, hell. No handshake, and now he's insulting him," Tex muttered under his breath.

And the Alferos wonder why they have guns aimed at their precious little heads.

"And you're too old to be protecting your granddaughter."

256

"Good one, Nixon." Tex sighed. "Insult for insult — it's like watching children argue about whose dad's bigger."

"I've been protecting her my entire life." Frank poked Nixon in the chest, but Nixon didn't budge. "And last I checked, I don't take orders from a mere child."

I exhaled. "Is it weird watching Frank's face turn that purple while he pokes Nixon?"

"Poke the bear, poke the bear!" Tex chanted.

"Maybe it's time to let someone else protect her," Nixon said, his voice wavering a bit.

If I didn't know him so well, I'd think he was feeling guilty at what he'd thrown innocent little Trace into.

She raised her hand. "Um, just FYI, I'm standing right here, and I have no idea why you guys are being such idiotic men right now, but I really want to go inside. I mean, I did almost just die back there."

Frank's nostrils flared. He reeled back and punched Nixon in the face.

"Ha ha, classic." Tex raised his hand for a high five while I kept the gun steady on Frank's forehead.

Trace groaned into her hands. "Grandpa, he saved me. He—"

"He…" Frank pointed at Nixon. Blood was gushing from his nose. "…is bad news, Tracey! I don't want you seeing that boy anymore!"

"Boy?" I repeated under my breath. "Alfero has a death wish."

"Don't we all?" Tex yawned.

"No!" Trace yelled. "Why are you being like this? Grandpa, I miss you. I haven't seen you in weeks, and you just punched my boyfriend in the face! Are you insane?"

"Did she just say boyfriend?" I hissed, moving the red light to Nixon's forehead rather than Frank's.

"Easy tiger," Tex warned.

"Boyfriend!" Frank wound up his arm to punch Nixon

again.

"Do it. Hit him," I growled.

Trace stepped between them just in time. I cursed under my breath.

Frank dropped his hand. "Trace?"

"I like him." She leaned back into Nixon's frame, sighing when the bastard put his arms around her.

Come on. Frank just hit him already.

"He even beat up a guy that bullied me. He's good. And I was going to tell you all about him over dinner tomorrow. Actually, I was going to invite him, but now that you've punched him in the face—"

"Trace." Nixon's voice was raspy. "It's fine. You should spend some time alone with your grandpa tomorrow. Don't go to class. Take a day off. Really, it's probably best that you do, all things considering. You had a rough night."

She turned in his arms and stared at him.

Nixon was immobile, like a statue. Shit. He was pissed and trying to push her away. I freaking knew he would hurt her — knew this would happen!

"Why are you doing this? Come with us tomorrow. It will be—"

"It will be best if you do as your grandfather says," Nixon finished and licked his bloodstained lips. "It was... interesting meeting you again, Mr. Rooks. Be sure to keep an eye out for the shadows tomorrow evening. They've been lurking."

"Hell." I sighed, pulling the gun away. "At least he did his civil duty and warned Frank about the De Langes not cooperating..."

"He should have left her alone." Tex moved to stand. "It would have been kinder than what's about to happen."

"Frank won't let Nixon have her," I agreed.

"Nope."

"He won't let me have her either?" It was more of a

question.

"You're not the son of the boss he claims killed his son... so who knows what he'll let you do. But my advice? Leave it, Chase. Only heartache there. It sucks wanting something you can't ever have. You tell yourself that having just a taste is enough to satisfy, but it never is... it never is, man." He tucked his gun back in his pants, his face haunted.

I knew he was talking about Mo, and his own past. Tex didn't often let people in, probably because being in meant you saw the scariness that was his legacy. The darkness that never let up.

"Anyway..." Tex shrugged. "...Nixon's gonna wanna meet."

Nixon jumped into his SUV just as Frank pulled Trace in for a hug. Things were just about to get really bad. My stomach plummeted as Trace wiped a tear from her eye and made her way into the dorms.

I may not have caused that tear.

But it was still my fault by association.

I put away the scope and gun.

"Let's go." Tex slapped me on the back.

We walked in silence all the way to the waiting Mercedes.

As expected, Nixon was waiting for us at his house.

"Aw, Rocky, get in a fight?" Tex teased while Nixon wiped the blood from his chin and flipped us off.

"Tell me you guys were there to at least cover my sorry ass."

"Chase was covering." Tex pointed at me.

"Ah." Nixon met my gaze. "And were you covering me or Frank?"

"Depends." I sneered. "Did you make her cry and get her

to call you her boyfriend all within the span of like five minutes?"

"Be a bitch later." Nixon rolled his eyes and winced as he wiped beneath his nose. "We have shit to wade through."

"My favorite thing." Tex pulled out a chair. "Shit wading."

Nixon placed his gun on the table and leaned back in his chair. "He's gonna tell her."

"How do you figure?" I toyed with the wine glass Tex had set in front of me and waited for the liquid to follow.

"He wants a meeting." Nixon threw the bloody rag onto the table and held up his glass to Tex. "At least, that's what the note said that he shoved into my pocket after he hit me in the face."

"Got you good too." I pointed with a smirk. "Think you'll need stitches?"

"The note?" Tex held out his hand.

Nixon slid it across the table.

Tex picked it up while I poured myself a glass of wine and waited.

"Well, that sounds like a good time." He handed me the note.

It didn't say much, just a time and location. "We'll need our men to come with us." I set the note down and took a large gulp of wine. "Lots of them, just in case."

"Yeah." Nixon licked his lips and stared into his glass. "I'll make the call… you guys should go to bed, actually." His eyes found mine.

Damn it.

"You wanna run one more patrol by—"

"Yeah, yeah." I waved him off. "I'll just chug the rest of this wine then drive over to campus and stare at your girlfriend's window. Kill me now."

"Don't run into any squirrels, sunshine." Tex laughed.

I shook my head and stood. "You know, you shouldn't

let me window shop. Just makes me want to max out the credit card, Nixon."

"Max it out, see if I don't cut out your liver."

"I think he's gotten more graphic with age, Chase? Any thoughts? Added commentary?"

"Nah," I grabbed my gun. "I think I'm done for tonight."

Nixon glared in my direction. I didn't blame him. I was being an ass. He was asking me to do my job, the job I'd always done.

Except now? Now it was personal.

Because of her.

Because of him.

Because of everything.

CHAPTER FORTY
Midnight texts

Nixon

I STARED UP AT my bedroom ceiling. Everything was going to go down tomorrow. Trace would finally know the truth.

That I was a murderer.

And her grandpa wasn't far behind me.

On one hand, I wanted her to know so desperately that it hurt. On the other hand? Her knowing meant her possibly hating me, meant me possibly having to push her away, which meant hurting her.

Damn, I couldn't tell which way was up or down.

My text alert went off.

Trace, my Bella: *You gonna tell me what happened tonight?*

Oh you know two mob bosses going at it, normal stuff.

Me: *Sure, u offered me your body — I'm free if u r?*

Trace, my Bella: *U r an ass and that's not what I'm talking about.*

Me: *I'm an ass? That's not what you were saying when we were kissing. Want me to come over?* ☺

It was a bad idea, being with her, spending time with her.

But what the hell? I'd been engaging in said bad ideas since I'd known she existed. What was one more night before she knew the real me was covered in blood and death?

Trace, my Bella: *Bring popcorn* ☺

By the time I made it to Trace's dorm, snacks in hand, Chase was outside waiting, doing the job I'd told him to do. He took one look at me and scowled.

"You've got to be shitting me."

"Skittles?" I offered, holding up the bag full of groceries.

"At least take me with you." He scowled. "I've been doing this damn perimeter check for over an hour, and I'm starving." He swiped at the Skittles while I tugged the bag away.

"Fine." I offered him a tense smile. "Think of it as a peace offering. You come hang out with us. Keep your hands off of her, and I'll let you have candy."

"Wow, thanks Dad. You're looking out."

"Don't want you to get cavities."

"I'm a sweet bitch. It happens."

Two girls walked by just as the words left Chase's mouth. One tripped, the other damn-near swooned into the wall.

"Think you could turn down the charm?"

Chase rolled his eyes and punched the buttons to the elevator. We both walked in. "Nervous it might work on your girl?"

"Hell no."

"Lies. I bleed charm."

"Ah, is that what they say?"

"Yup, seriously. I shoot, I torture, I kill, and in the end, they still love me. What can a guy do?" He shrugged and offered a cheerful smile that made me want to smack him in the face.

"What movies you bring?" Chase asked as we walked.

"Ugh," I scratched my head. "I grabbed stuff from Tex's stash." I held out the movies.

Chase read the titles aloud. *"The Godfather?* Really? *Scarface... Tommy Boy..."* Cursing, he kept reading through them. "You took her to see cows for your first date, and what? For your second you want to make sure you never have sex again?"

I reached for the movies.

"Well, well, well." The elevator stopped as Chase held up the movie. "What have we here? Looks like Tex is a closet romantic."

"I'll believe it when I don't see people shit themselves while he tortures them with that little kit of his."

"The Notebook." Chase sighed. "This gets guys laid."

"I thought you didn't want me to get laid."

"Hence me handing her the movie, jackass."

I pushed him against the wall as the elevator doors opened.

He laughed and shrugged out of my arms.

We made our way down the hall, much too fast for the groupies hanging out their doors in anticipation that we'd stop and give them the time of day. I swiped my all-access card against the girls' room and pushed the door open.

"Do you have access cards to every room or something?" Trace put down her eReader and jumped off her bed.

"Of course." I winked.

She rolled her eyes. "I don't see popcorn?"

"About that." I scratched my head. "Chase was bored so..."

"The party is here!" Chase shouted from the doorway, loaded with the groceries I'd brought over. "Move over, Nixon. It's chick-flick time, and I've got the goods."

"Is he high?" She crossed her arms and leaned in to examine his eyes.

"No," we said in unison.

"I'm my normal awesome self. I've had two Red Bulls though, so my bad for the loudness. Damn, I was bored. You saved my life." Chase winked and set the groceries on the shared desk in the dorm.

Trace stared at him a bit too long for my comfort. I slammed the door shut in order to get her to stop staring at his ass.

"So..." Trace started unpacking the groceries. "...what movie did you guys bring?"

Chase chuckled. "Well, funny that you ask that."

"Chase," I warned, knowing damn well he'd spill.

"Nixon here was pouting about your ruined date, and I thought to myself, *Wow, what would make him feel better? What would inspire him to be more romantic?* I mean, cows, man? Really?"

"It was romantic," Trace defended, walking straight into my arms.

My smile may have been a bit cocky.

"Cows. Cows are romantic?" Chase shook his head. "I think not. And in my opinion, or that of my dear mother's, Nicholas Sparks is the shit. Therefore, we're going to watch... drumroll, please."

Trace and I just stared while Chase bounced his hands against the desk. *"The Notebook!"*

"Shoot me now." I cursed under my breath.

Trace smiled. "Hey, it's a good movie."

Chase smirked at me. "Say it, dude. Say it."

"Say what?" Trace asked.

"V-vampire?" I guessed, taking a scene from *Twilight*. If that combined with *The Notebook* didn't have her in my arms by sunrise, nothing would. I put Chase into a headlock and cursed. "Fine, you were right to choose Nicholas Sparks. Good job. Too bad you can't use any of that romance on finding your own girl."

Chase pulled away and shrugged. "I've already found my girl."

My eyes narrowed. Too far. He was always pushing too

far and often, way too damn often.

Chase stalked toward Trace and put his arm around her. "You see. I have it worked out perfectly. The minute you screw up — and let's be honest, you're like a time bomb — I'm swooping in for the kill."

"Romantic." Trace picked Chase's arm off of her shoulder and stepped away.

I gave him an icy glare. "Not in this lifetime, dude."

"You never know," Chase fired back.

I was ready to throw a punch in his direction.

Chase's chest heaved.

Holy shit, were we really going to throw down in her dorm room? Next to *The Notebook?*

"Okay, too much testosterone!" Trace stepped between us. "Let's just watch the movie, alright?"

Chase snapped out of his funk and smiled. "Sure, let me just get the chips and dip out. Oh yeah, and popcorn. I also got some licorice and Skittles."

"Skittles?" she repeated.

"He wants you to taste the rainbow." I groaned. "It's one of his lines, and then he puts the Skittles in his mouth and kisses you. It's a very tired line that he can't seem to let go of, huh, Chase?"

"Bastard," Chase joked and went about putting our snacks together.

I lay down on the bed and held out my hand to Trace.

She cuddled next to me. Her eyes were drooping by the time Chase had all the snacks ready.

"It's okay," I whispered into her ear. "You can sleep. I know it was a rough night."

"But…" Her eyes didn't open. She did, however, yawn. "We were supposed to talk about tonight and why you have guns and… Skittles."

"Skittles?" I chuckled. "What, you trying to taste *my* rainbow?"

"I love rainbows." She smiled.

With a sigh, I tucked her hair behind her ear and whispered, "I've always loved you."

"You too," she said back.

I froze. Did she realize what had just left her lips? I wasn't sure if she did, because then she started mumbling about Skittles again.

Chase was too busy setting up the movie to notice. So I moved in and kissed her neck.

"I'm glad you're safe, Trace. Now sleep."

She fell asleep before the music even started to play.

"Good work," Chase whispered. "She'd rather sleep than make out with you."

"She wouldn't make out with me anyway. You're here."

"Awesome. You're blaming me for your inability to have any sort of game. Good call, Nixon, good call."

"Ugh." I held out my hands. "Does this mean we're stuck watching *The Notebook* together?"

Chase barked out a laugh. "Think so. After all, she's safer with us here, both of us, and you know it."

"Yeah." I swallowed the bitterness. "I do."

"For what it's worth..." Chase's voice wavered. "...I wouldn't do that to you."

"What?"

"Sweep in for the kill, charm her pants off, kiss her without permission... I talk a lot, you know that, and you know I like her... but I would never betray you just because a girl's hot."

"She's more than hot, Chase."

"Yeah." He popped a Skittle in his mouth. "That's the problem, isn't it?"

We both fell silent as the music in the movie started.

"You cry, and I tell Tex." I warned.

Chase flipped me off. "Whatever, I've got tear ducts of steel."

And that's how we spent the evening. Chase and I, watching a sappy love story while I held the girl of our dreams in my arms, knowing damn well that he wished he could switch positions, knowing damn well, it would be better for her if he did.

When the movie was over, I set Trace's alarm for her and ushered a sleepy Chase out the door. We had a big day ahead of us. A day where I wasn't sure Trace would ever look at me with those trusting eyes again.

We made our way through the dark parking lot.

Chase paused and looked up at the dorm. "You think she's going to be pissed?"

"Yeah." I croaked. "Wouldn't you be?"

"Depends." Chase shrugged.

"On what?"

"If I felt like I was being used... like a game piece."

"It's not like that."

Chase nodded his head. "Then make sure she knows it."

CHAPTER FORTY-ONE
And the walls came a-tumbling... hard.

Chase

NIXON KEPT CHECKING HIS text messages like a damn teen. Finally, probably because I didn't hold back my scowl, he put his phone away.

"She's freaked."

"Can you blame her?" I grunted. "She has no idea what she's walking into, not one clue."

"Hell," Tex piped up. "That's what she's walking into."

"Helpful." I smacked Tex and kept on driving. I'd never been on the Alfero estate — that was all Nixon. His creepy childhood had included many visits here. He said I'd been, but for the life of me, I couldn't remember.

The large iron gates opened, revealing a massive brick and white mansion with a circular driveway.

I pulled the car in, my heart hammering in my chest.

"No going back now," Tex whispered under his breath.

The minute I put the SUV into park, at least ten men shuffled out of the front door, guns already trained on us. Fantastic. Luckily, we had at least five cars following us with men of our own. It wouldn't be an easy battle, but it would be a hell of a bloody war.

Nixon cursed and got out of the car. "Call them off. We're not here to fight."

The guy in charge stepped forward. "Frank doesn't want any trouble."

"And he thinks we do?" Nixon countered. "Where is he?"

The man nodded to the men who slowly lowered their weapons. "He's bringing the girl. They should be here in a few minutes."

"Tracey." I gave him a cold stare. "She has a name."

The man narrowed his eyes.

I knew it was hard for the older guys, the ones who had been in the business so long they'd almost forgotten what the real world looked like. They saw Nixon and I with our tatted-up arms and what they no doubt assumed was a bad attitude and assumed we had nothing but disrespect for the old ways, when really we were the ones fighting to keep things calm within the families.

"Follow me." The man nodded as we all walked up the stairs into the mansion. White marble flooring greeted us. A chandelier hung in the middle of the entryway, and a nice man with a patch on his eye started patting us down, Tex first.

Which naturally earned him a punch to the jaw. He staggered back, swearing in Italian. Tex grunted and lifted his shoulders to Nixon. "What? He was getting too friendly."

Nixon rolled his eyes and addressed the guy in charge. "Look we have guns, our men have guns, you have guns — let's not pretend any different."

"Fine." He gritted his teeth. "We'll be meeting in the family room."

He motioned for us to follow him, but Nixon stayed put, his boots planted against the marble like it would take an act of God to move him.

"You coming?" I called back.

"Nah," He wiped his face with his hands. "It's probably best I wait right here for Trace."

Actually, that was the worst idea I'd ever heard in my entire life. One look at him, and she was going to get the shock of her life, all before he was able to even defend himself.

Well shit. With a curse I went to stand by him. I may want Trace more than anything, but I wasn't going to let him take the fall on his own.

The front door opened, my breath hitched, and in walked my father. He looked every inch the made man from his black Italian suit, shiny leather shoes, and his dark sunglasses. The man screamed Mafia while Nixon and I just screamed hellions.

"Nixon." Anthony nodded in his direction then turned his cool gaze to me. "Son."

I bristled. Couldn't help it. I had no reason to hate my father. He'd sheltered me my whole life, fed me, kept me warm, but there was no love between us, only competition. Maybe that was it. When he looked at Nixon, he saw more of a son than when he looked at me. It was a reminder that I was, again, second best, not as good — never have been, never will be.

Anthony moved to stand beside us just as the front door opened a second time.

I heard Frank's voice.

And then Trace appeared, her eyes wide with fear her, mouth open in amazement.

Her gaze was at the ceiling and then it flickered to Nixon, Anthony, and finally, myself.

My stomach clenched into a tight ball as her face went from fear to absolute betrayal. I'd done that. I'd stolen that smile, that innocence, but just standing there, I had taken away a part of her I would never be able to give back.

"Ready?" Nixon asked, his voice gruff as he eyed Frank up and down like he was Satan.

"Yes," Frank snapped, ushering Tracey into the living

room, just out of our reach. There really was no going back. At all.

Nixon and I sat on the couch opposite Trace. Her face was pale, her lips drawn back into a tight expression. Her normally sunny disposition was replaced with something so heartbreaking it hurt to look directly at her.

Our men circled around us, guns trained on Frank's men, while they kept their guns firmly pointed at us. It really was like a horrible Mafia movie and not realistic at all, but there was so much bad blood between us that the trust that should exist? The healthy respect between bosses? Was long gone, severed, and destroyed by needless death and sacrifice.

"You broke the rules," Frank said, leaning back against the black leather couch.

Nixon smirked. "What? You think I actually knew right away?"

"You grew up with her!" Frank yelled.

Wow. Three seconds in, and he was already needing anger management.

"She was six!" Nixon all but shouted.

"You may as well have pulled that trigger. Your father..."

"Is dead." Nixon smirked. "Cold and lifeless, lying right next to my mother."

"What?" Trace shrieked. Ah hell, really, Nixon? Great timing, no really, epic. "You said that—"

"Monroe doesn't know, Trace." Nixon's eyes softened for a brief second. "He'd been sick a while. It's..."

"None of her damn business." My father spat, glaring at Trace like she was already tainted beyond redemption. I'd never seen such hatred in my father's eyes, and then as soon as it appeared, it disappeared, covered with a mask of indifference.

"Gentleman." I cleared my throat. "Back to the reason for meeting."

Frank bristled. "As I was saying…" He wrapped his arm around Trace and squeezed. "The poor girl lost her parents at six. That's still old enough to recognize people. You should have known Nixon."

"I told you the minute I did," Nixon defended himself. "And it wasn't like I could have done anything!"

"You took her outside school property."

Oh, for the love of God, of course he did! What was he supposed to do?

"Before I knew." Nixon sighed heavily. "I didn't even guess until I saw the damn necklace with *Alfero* on it."

"Then you should have stayed away."

It was like playing ping pong. Nixon would say something then Frank, then Nixon, both of them right in their own ways, yet still wrong in the way that mattered most, which was Trace's safety.

"Careful," My father spoke up. "You may be within your rights to call him out, but he's still the boss. Has been for some time. So tread carefully, old man."

Frank cleared his throat. "Excuse me, Mr. Abandonato." He spat out the words like they were venom. "But the minute her cover was blown — the very second — you should have locked her in her damn room."

Nixon tensed next to me, his fingers flexing against his thigh. "She's just a teenager, Frank. What did you want me to do? Blow everyone's cover? Ruin everything? And for what? Precaution? We've been in this for four damn years." His eyes fell to my father. "Some of us longer. How was I supposed to know you'd drop her directly into the fight? Your own granddaughter? We were doing just fine until you did this to us!"

"And you still have no proof!" Frank shouted.

"We're close!" Nixon fired back. "We just need more time."

"Time doesn't give Trace her parents back," Frank said

softly. "Time doesn't heal a broken heart, and time will not fix the fact that you have successfully helped expose my innocent granddaughter to our world. I only meant to appease my dying wife, while at the same time allowing Trace to be used as bait, only if necessary, and what do you do? You claim her for your own! An Abandonato!"

And there it was. The elephant in the room. Nixon had taken something that wasn't his to take — her alliance, her allegiance, her love. Something only Frank could be familiar with, considering his son and daughter–in-law's story.

"All I can say is I'm sorry. I didn't know. But would you rather have me leave her helpless? Admit it. She would have known something was up if I'd locked her in her room, and honestly, we weren't even sure she was exposed until last night when we almost..." Nixon swallowed. "...got killed."

"Until it was almost too late!" Frank nodded his head. "So what are you going to do now? How do you hope to make amends?"

"Easy. We'll let things die down, and we have to work faster to infiltrate the De Lange family."

Fran nodded his head, clearly liking that answer. "She must be protected."

"We've been protecting her," I said through clenched teeth, glaring at Frank.

"And she almost died," Frank repeated. "Last night. Isn't that right? Or wait, were you too busy sticking your tongue down my granddaughter's throat."

In an instant Nixon had his gun out and pointed at Frank. Well shit, and things had been going so well.

"Disrespect your granddaughter in front of my men and yours one more time, and I will end you."

I smirked, couldn't help it. Served him right for saying anything negative about the girl we'd all die to protect — his own blood!

Frank scowled. "I would never do such a thing. I love

her. I put her into hiding. Fifteen years of work gone just because of you!"

Nixon put his gun down and cursed. "She wasn't supposed to get in to the school."

A tenderness crossed Frank's features. "Her grandma was the culprit. She told me on her deathbed it was time for Trace to know the truth. I thought I could give my wife her dying wish, and at the same time appease my granddaughter. Allow her to experience the luxury she should have grown up with. The life that had been stolen from her. Like I said, I did not think she would be recognized and figured even if she were, we could use her to pull out the De Lange family."

Nixon looked between Frank and Trace. "Using your own granddaughter? I think we're done here."

"I think so." Frank rose from his seat. Nixon and Frank embraced one another and kissed each cheek before saying *"Blood in — No out"* in Italian.

I stole a glance at Trace. Damn she looked horrible. Tears pooled in her eyes. I wanted to hold her and never let go, but most of all, I just wanted to tell her how sorry I was that she was caught between hell and hell, two rough spots she'd never be free from.

I wanted to tell her I'd tried not to love her.

I'd tried to protect her.

Tried to push her away.

But in the end, you can't stop destiny, you can only put it on pause for a while.

I mouthed *"Sorry"* to her and kept my head bowed as we shuffled out of the room.

"One more thing," Frank called from behind us.

In a flash, he pulled out his gun and shot at Nixon's feet.

Nixon didn't move. He just stared at the ground then back up at Frank with cool indifference. "Noted." Nixon nodded like the old bastard hadn't just fired a round dangerously close to his big toe. We followed him outside.

My father whispered something to Nixon before getting in his car and leaving. I walked to the Range Rover and started it.

Tex was silent.

Nixon was silent.

I was silent.

Yeah, it was a bad day. We all felt like shit, because we were all responsible for ruining someone's life.

Being born into the Mafia, you know what your destiny is. You know what's expected of you. You live, you kill, you eventually die with honor. But being thrust into it like Trace? There's no chance in hell for you to get used to the idea that every day could be your last.

Every moment, every breath, every experience — taken from you because of some beef with another family.

"Shit." Nixon hit the dash with his hand while I put on my seatbelt.

We drove away from of the estate, eighties music playing in the background.

"So," Tex cleared his throat. "she's stuck now."

"She's in deep." Nixon whispered. "She's going to hate us, all of us."

"Not true," I argued. "We can still fix it. We just have to give her time to digest the information."

"And how long do you think that's gonna take? Hmm?" Nixon spat. "Oh by the way, Trace, your parents were murdered by some psycho from the De Lange family who made it look like it was my father, the lover scorned in the little triangle that was pissed off at their happiness. Or how about this? Your parents died because of greed? Because of money? They died for no reason, and it's my fault. My father's fault, my family's fault, because if we can't pin it on the De Langes, if we have no evidence by the time the year's up, Alfero's going to stick to his promise."

I swallowed the dryness in my throat and croaked, "Wipe

out the entire Abandonato line."

Nixon cursed again. "It's his right. You know it is."

"You can't just kill a boss," Tex pointed out. "Even if you have the right to."

"Frank can." I sighed.

"Frank will," Nixon agreed.

"Well, look on the bright side!" Tex clapped his hands twice. "At least I'll live. I'm Campisi."

"Tex," We groaned in unison.

"I'll take my chances with Frank over your father any day," I whispered under my breath.

"You and me both," Tex muttered.

"So what now?" I asked, hoping Nixon would have some sort of game plan that included us stealing Trace away and putting her into hiding.

"Drive back to campus... I'll take the SUV. I need to think." Nixon tapped his fingers against the console and sighed. "I need to figure out what happens next."

"In the Mafia?" Tex chuckled from the back seat. "Blood, you can always count on lots of blood."

CHAPTER FORTY-TWO
Apologies in pink

Nixon

I STARED AT MY phone for a good ten minutes once the guys left me alone with my thoughts.

I sat in my car with the AC on full blast, just letting the cold air hit me as I stared at my phone, at her number. Calling her would probably be a mistake. Texting her? It was the same thing, wasn't it? But I couldn't help myself. My fingers hovered over the screen. Finally, I typed the only thing I knew I could say, given the situation.

Me: *I'm sorry.*

Within seconds, she responded.

Trace, my Bella: *Can you come back? Need to talk...*

Well, that was better than getting cussed out.

Me: *Sure give me a minute to find a bulletproof vest. U do realize I was shot at last time I was in that house?*

My phone rang while I was waiting for her answer. It was Trace.

"Trace—"

"Please, Nixon. Please."

Pain drilled its way through my chest, piercing my heart with what felt like a million needles.

I sighed long and hard, ending my exhale with a curse. "Give me an hour."

"Thank you."

"Oh, and Trace?"

"Yeah?"

"Do me a favor. Tell your grandpa you invited me so that they don't shoot me on sight. You don't want innocent blood on your hands."

"Are you?" she whispered.

"What?" I was almost afraid of what she was asking, what I would tell, what it would reveal.

"Innocent?"

"No." My voice shook. "Not since the day I was born, not since the first day my dad raised a hand to me, not since the first time I watched my mom huddle in the corner, and definitely not since the first time you let me kiss you. No, Trace. I'm anything but innocent."

The line went completely silent.

I cleared my throat. "Do you still want me to come?"

"Yes."

"See you soon, Trace."

This time, driving to her house, it wasn't apprehension that had me sweating, but excitement. She wanted to see me, which meant she wasn't as angry as I thought she'd be. What the hell had Frank told her?

Before I'd even put the car in park, a few men filed out of the house and waited at the bottom of the stairs. Great, now it was my turn to have a welcoming committee.

Things sure had done a one-eighty since Trace's arrival at Elite. I had a sudden flashback of her tears, her smile, her glare, and her trembling body when I touched her. I wiped my face in irritation and slowly got out of the car. I walked toward the stairs, fully expecting her to reject me just like I'd rejected her that very first day...

"Farm Girl," I said. Beautiful... I thought.

"Dirty..." I hissed.

Pure... I'd focused in on her clear brown eyes, so pure that it hurt to look at her...

My legs were heavy, weighed down by responsibility, but still moving, pressing forward because of hope.

A hope I'd never known existed.

A hope I'd never known I needed.

All in a girl I'd thought was dead.

A girl I'd been fighting for — my entire life.

When the door opened, I saw her, and my world felt right again, everything came into focus. This wasn't about the Mafia; it wasn't about bad blood; it was about her and the meaning she had in this universe, in my life. I made a vow right then and there I would fight to the death for her, even if it meant in the end I wasn't the victor.

Our eyes met, and I offered a smile, one that would reassure her that her crazy grandpa wasn't going to shoot me.

Frank held her tight, his gaze shooting laser beams through my body, setting it on fire.

I tried not to look intimidated, and it wasn't like I was fearful of him. I was more afraid of what he wanted me to do than what he would do to me.

Our conversation on the phone hadn't lasted long. I'd immediately called him after Trace had hung up the phone, not trusting her to tell him that I was arriving and not trusting myself not to pull a gun on him if he tried pulling one on me first.

I'd told him I was coming over, and that if he tried to stop me, I would simply ram my Range Rover through the front door and wave around my semi-automatic until he led me to Trace and assured me of her safety.

He'd laughed.

The old bastard had laughed.

And said in a low voice, "Of course you'll visit... you need to say goodbye, after all."

"Goodbye?" I repeated.

"I'm calling in a favor, Nixon." His voice sounded tired, so strained I felt a twinge of pity in my gut. "Boss to boss, leave her alone. I cannot lose my granddaughter... I've lost too much. Do me this favor, Nixon, and I'll stand down. Just leave her."

He may was well have asked me to cut out my own heart and offer it to the Alferos as a sacrifice.

Leaving her alone was basically the same thing.

But I agreed.

Why?

Because he was right.

I hated him for it.

But he was right. She deserved a chance at normal. The more attention I paid to her, the darker I painted the target on her back. If she was viewed as being special to me, important, then my enemies would stop at nothing to destroy her.

And Frank was right. Their family had suffered enough.

But so had I.

Trace tilted her head in my direction. I forced another smile, allowing myself to memorize every single detail about her face from the curve of her lips to the cadence of her breathing.

Would those memories be enough to satisfy me at night?

No.

But they had to be. Because she would be safe. And I needed her safe, at all costs.

I lifted my hands into the air as one of Frank's men patted me down. He pulled one of my guns from the back of my pants, a knife from my boot, and a set of brass knuckles from my pocket. I thought Trace's eyes were going to bug out of her head, I wanted to laugh but knew it would probably just prolong the process, and I really *really* need that girl in my arms.

Frank released her.

And Trace launched herself in my direction. I barely had enough time to brace myself before her body met mine.

This was what I was giving up.

My head lifted, my eyes slowly meeting Frank's steel gaze. The bastard better keep her safe, or it was his head.

Because this... I inhaled... this was what I was saying goodbye to.

I couldn't take it...

We hugged for possibly a few seconds before I let out a hiss and pushed her away. Funny, how a few weeks ago her touch damn-near destroyed me. Now? It was a drug that I craved on a daily basis, one I would never again be able to experience.

Ha, I thought I'd felt true pain before.

I'd felt nothing.

Trace reached for my hand, but I pulled it away and shook my head slowly. This wasn't the time or place, and we had an audience.

The sound of stiletto heels hitting marble interrupted the stare-off between me and Frank. A lady cleared her throat. A pretty woman with straight black hair smiled at Trace. "Lunch is ready."

Frank turned around and followed her into another room. I did the same, as Trace trailed behind me. If I wasn't invited, he'd make it known by the bullet-sized hole in my forehead.

The medieval-looking dining room was just as I remembered. A long, wood table was in the middle of the room. Dark wallpaper lined the walls, and a few bronze chandeliers hung in the middle, casting a glow on the cold pastas and bruschetta that were ready for consumption.

I'd always been terrified of that room as a kid... it had just seemed too dark and a lot haunted. I was too little to know that ghosts didn't exist, and all too aware of how darkness could consume you from the inside out.

My glass was filled with red wine.

Thank God.

Trace looked at hers with narrowed eyes then glanced at me with a pleading look. She reached for my leg. Damn, but her touch brought me way too much comfort. Wasn't I the one in the wrong? Shouldn't I be comforting her? Kissing her? Telling her that I was sorry?

It was backward.

So freaking backward.

I was the reason she was hurting, yet she still reached out, which just goes to prove how amazing the girl was, and how unworthy I would always be.

Lunch was silent. So silent I wanted to laugh at the ridiculousness. Since when were Italians silent during mealtime? Tex would have swallowed his damn tongue over that.

Loud chewing was our soundtrack, well, that and Frank's sudden outbursts of cursing, thanks to his inability to do anything except stare at every movement Trace made in my direction.

"Grandpa, may I be excused?" Trace asked politely, finally breaking the tense silence.

He nodded his head as she reached for me. "I need to talk with you."

I glanced at Frank.

He cleared his throat and said under his breath, "Remember the terms, Nixon."

"How could I forget?" I sneered and grabbed her hand to keep myself from jumping across the table and smacking the old man in his wrinkled face.

CHAPTER FORTY-THREE
Goodbyes are for chumps.

Nixon

"Good God, I forgot how pink this room was." I laughed and looked around the bright pink monstrosity that used to be Trace's room. Pink stuffed animals lined the walls along with wallpaper that had pictures of ponies and castles. I pushed the animals off the bed and lay down. How many times had I done this as a kid? When I'd been afraid of my father. When my ma had told me to go hide during one of their meetings. Trace's bed had been like a safe place for me, and now?

Now it seemed to be the exact opposite. Temptation, lust, everything I wasn't supposed to feel for her — I did. How sick was it that the very thing I was protecting her from... in the end... was me? I was the most dangerous of all, because once I grabbed ahold of something, I didn't release it. And I was holding Trace — no, I was freaking latching on to her. Suffocating her, bent on ruining her, just so I could have her all to myself.

I hated that Chase had been right.

Almost as much as I hated that for the first time in

years… I was wrong.

I needed to make the cut, but that's the thing about Trace. Cutting her out of my life? To protect her? Would be like stabbing myself in the heart. It wouldn't be a mortal wound. It would destroy all that was still good within me, bleed me dry; it would end my existence. But for her? I'd do it a thousand times, a million times. I'd die every day… over and over again, repeating the process until she was safe.

"I must have really liked pink." Trace laughed.

"You hated it." I put my arms behind my head and sighed. "In fact, I distinctly remember your mom putting you in a pink dress, and you taking it off in front of the entire dinner party." I left out the part where I'd been beaten for staring.

"Please tell me you weren't—"

"I was nine!" I laughed and rolled my eyes. "Trust me. I was horrified. I thought girls had cooties. I closed my eyes and pointed, though."

Trace blushed a pretty pink and crossed her arms then sat down next to me on the bed. "Rude. You should have saved me."

The air was thick with tension. Oh, how right she was. Did she even know how many sleepless nights I'd had since her arrival at Elite? I'd been worse than a damn stalker. I had freaking turned on her location services on her phone just in case I lost her. Embarrassing, to say the least, when I wasn't just texting in class, but checking the blue dot to make sure she was still on campus. Hell, I would go to the bathroom with her if I could.

With a sigh, I reached for her hand. "I was always saving you. Even when you didn't know I was there, I was saving you."

"Did you ever visit Wyoming?" Her voice was small, as if she was embarrassed to be asking the question. Her hand moved across my chest, and then her head lay across me. The smell of her shampoo was hypnotic. I breathed in my fill and sighed.

"Trace, you're putting me in a hard spot. I can't tell you everything, because it will just make you sad. I can't be completely honest, and it kills me. It makes me want to scream, but I have responsibilities — not just to you — to my family, to your grandpa..." I cursed, feeling totally trapped. How did I convey to her the danger she was in? The danger her family was in? "Everything is pretty screwed up right now. I didn't know you were going to find out this way. Believe me, if I had known, I would have..." My mind whirled with the possibilities, tightening as the pressure of her kiss flooded my mind.

"What?"

I licked my lips and let my mind go there. I let my imagination take me to the place where I was making love to the most beautiful girl in the world. Touching her body, bringing her pleasure, hearing her scream out my name as I made her mine. "...I would have kissed you harder. I would have fought for you more. I don't know. I would have stolen you away, taken your virtue, made myself so permanently etched on your person that every time you took a breath it was my scent that was permeating the air."

Trace's breath hitched.

My fingers danced along her wrist, stopping at her pulse then sliding up to cup her face.

"I never visited Wyoming. My father wouldn't let me, and at that time, I wasn't in charge of anything, so I couldn't bully my way into it."

"When you came to be in charge, you were eighteen?" she pried, probably unable to help it. The girl was too damn curious. Curiosity got you killed in my work. Just another reason for me to lock her up away from me, away from the family, in Chase's arms. Holy shit. I was going to shoot the guy if he as much as sneezed within three feet of her.

I cleared my throat. "Yup. Father wasn't doing well. He wasn't able to make good decisions. He developed pneumonia and was never the same after that. Always out of breath and whatnot. So I took over some of the operations, and then more and more, until I was running everything while he stayed at home and drank whiskey."

Trace winced.

"At any rate, that's done with now." My hand clenched on her arm then released. I still remembered pulling the trigger, was haunted by it even though he was an absolute monster...

"You are nothing!" Father spat, "Anthony, get him out of my sight."

"No," I said in a cold tone. "He doesn't answer to you."

"And he answers to you?" Father threw his head back and laughed then began coughing so hard he nearly fell out of his seat. "I needed a good laugh today."

"Funny." I reached into my pocket and pulled out the Glock. "So did I."

"Nixon..." Father's eyes narrowed. "What the hell are you doing?"

"My job," I spat. "You should know. You groomed me. You made me what I am. You created me... you did this." The gun shook as I held it out and pointed at his head. "Any last words?"

Father didn't flinch, simply looked around the room as the three men with us hung their heads, turned around, and left.

"So..." He nodded. "...this is it then."

"It is." I bit down hard on my lip... requiring the distraction of the pain to remind me that I needed to do what I was doing. "So?"

Father stood, shaky on his knees, and tumbled toward me, his knife high and raised. He sliced across my lower lip, cutting me deep, before falling onto his knees with a curse.

"And the purpose of that?" I wiped my mouth with the back of my hand.

"To prove a point, son." Father didn't turn; instead, he hung

his head as if he was praying. "You will always be marked by me, always controlled. When you look in the mirror at that pretty face, I want you to see that mark on your lip, that mark on your face, and remember. You're. Just. Like. Me."

I moved behind him and held the gun to his head as he lifted his hands into the air. "May God have mercy on your soul."

I pulled the trigger, and he fell to a heap in front of me.

The wound wasn't fatal, but it had caused a divide between us that was bigger than before — wider, bigger. The trust that should have been present was replaced with rage, hatred, anger.

A week later I got my lip pierced. Not to be disrespectful, as Chase always teased, but because it covered what he had done. What he was still doing, charring me from the inside out. When I looked in the mirror, I saw him. Because of that scar, I saw him.

"I'm sorry, Trace," I whispered, bringing myself back to the present as I ran my fingers through her silky hair. I was apologizing for what I couldn't say. For what I was about to do. Killing her would be a kindness. I knew firsthand what the pain of a broken heart felt like when she'd been ripped from me the first time. I didn't wish that type of pain on my worst enemy.

"For what?"

"Not telling you the truth. I knew the day we went shopping, and then, when you took out all that money? Damn, I knew for sure then. I had Anthony do a background check on you. Apparently, Tracey Rooks doesn't exist. So I went through all the Traceys in our school, and there you were — Tracey Alfero, eighteen years old, granddaughter of the second most powerful Mafia boss in all of Chicago. The same Mafia boss that still blames us for his son's death."

"You forget. Technically I have De Lange blood in me, too," she muttered.

"Right. Which means I really should have killed Phoenix." I itched to end that bastard's life. I scowled and pulled myself away from Trace, getting to my feet. "He can't ever find out who you are. If he does... Trace, he's dangerous, seriously."

She had no idea how dangerous. I'd been watching him closely. He wasn't eating, or sleeping, and all he did was drink. He was losing his touch with reality, and every single time he glanced in Trace's direction, it was with utter hatred.

"We've been keeping tabs on him. He's lost his freaking mind. He's next in line after his father dies, and his father's more insane than he is. I have no doubt that family is into some shady business."

Trace sighed, tilting her head to the side as she twisted a piece of hair around her fingers. "Do I want to know what *shady business* is?"

No. She didn't. And I wasn't about to tell her all the gory details, so I skimmed over the truth. "Probably the sex trade, cocaine, money laundering — typical things you'd see on TV, but definitely not what this family is about, that's for sure."

Her eyebrows pinched together. "What do you do?"

"A little of this and a little of that." I fought laughter as I watched her eyes narrow. "Nothing too illegal. We aren't desperate for money, unlike some people." I shuddered to think of the De Langes, the deals they'd made with other families in order to continue living the lifestyle they've been used to.

"I'm sorry..." Her chest heaved, and tears glimmered in her eyes. "...for leaving you. I'm so damn sorry, Nixon. I remember. I saw a picture of us when we were little and... I left you! I promised I would keep you safe, and I left you!"

She fell into full on sobs and hugged herself. Heart. Broken. She may as well have reached into my chest, pulled out my still beating black heart, and told me it was beautiful, clean, pure. The love I had for her... the love she had for me? I couldn't fathom it, never in my life had I experienced such a pure emotion. I didn't deserve it or her.

"Trace, sweetheart." I reached for her and lifted her onto

my lap so her legs were straddling me "Those were pretty big promises coming from a six-year-old. There was no way you could have protected me or Monroe from him."

Her lower lip trembled. "But I promised—"

"And I promised I'd find the people who killed your parents. So I guess we both failed, Trace."

"You'll find them," she said through her tears. "You won't give up?"

"No." I kissed her cheek and then her lips, my tongue smoothly moving over her mouth, licking up the salt, tasting, and craving so much that I wanted nothing more than to lock the door and throw her against it. She had no idea how much self-control I was practicing by being able to even nibble on her. It was an appetizer, and I freaking wanted the main course.

"I just... Trace, I have to keep order between all the families here. The three families have been just fine for the past ninety years. If something happens... if the balance is thrown off, or, God forbid, if any of the originals hear about the happenings with Phoenix..." Shit, if Nicolasis? Or Campisis knew? We were screwed.

"Believe me, you do not want any of the Sicilians traveling to the states."

"They won't." Her mouth found mine.

I groaned when her tongue tentatively flicked my lip ring.

"Phoenix hasn't done anything yet, and when — if — he does... you'll be there."

I closed my eyes for patience, to cool my lust. The thought of Phoenix anywhere near her undid me. "Yes, but so will you."

"By your side," she confirmed. My heart damn-near broke all over again. Because no, no, sweetheart, you won't be by my side. But you'll be safe. I vow, you'll be safe.

I refused to lie to her face in that moment. There would

be enough lies to last a lifetime in the next few weeks. Instead, I found her lips and claimed them both. When she gasped, I tasted her tongue. I sucked. Every movement my lips made across hers, I imagined myself marking her, making sure she knew she was mine. No one else's.

Desperate, I was desperate to show her that she was my life, that even if I did something horrible to her, it would be at the cost of my own heart and soul. Her arms snaked around my neck. My fingers danced along her collarbone then slipped down her sides and slowly pulled up her shirt. One look. One touch. I told myself it was okay, because in the end? I would probably end up dead. And I wanted her. Nobody else, for the rest of my existence. My fingers came into contact with her bra. One pull. And I could rip it off her. Another pull, and her clothes would be gone. Five minutes. We'd both be naked, and I'd make her mine. I'd brand her.

And she'd remember.

Even when she was eighty, and I was dead or gone.

She'd remember that she never belonged to anyone but me.

"Damn." I growled, a war raging inside me.

"What?" She kissed my neck. Girls did not kiss my neck. They wanted to be screwed, but they didn't want anything more. But Trace? She made kissing my neck damn-near more erotic than sex itself.

"Your grandpa's going to shoot me if he finds out I'm doing this right now... I promised..." I sucked down on my lip ring and pulled back, cursing myself for losing such complete control.

Her hands drew circles around my bare stomach. Damn, when had she lifted my shirt? Like I cared. Like it mattered. I closed my eyes and groaned as her hands continued torturing me. "I need you to remember something, Trace."

"What?"

I kissed her softly then braced her face gently within my

hands. "When I make a promise, I keep it. Regardless of whom it hurts, even if it means it hurts me or someone I care about the most. Sometimes... sometimes in life we're asked to sacrifice something for the greater good."

"Okay, you're making me nervous. Can't we just make out?" Her smile was wide, perfect, loving. I adored her. I didn't just love her. I adored her. Everything about her. She was too precious. Too precious to screw in her childhood bed. Too precious to mar with my darkness. Too precious for a man like me to even touch.

I wish I could have said something in that moment. I almost did. I almost asked her to run away with me. I had enough money for us to live more than comfortably. I had houses everywhere. But eventually. We'd be found. And we'd be dead. Maybe by then we'd have kids. Having that held over my head? Over hers? I imagined a life without the Mafia. A life where Trace and I had a house in the suburbs. A life where her belly was swollen with my children. Children I would love until my dying day. Damn, why couldn't my father have been an accountant?

I tried to smile. "I love you, Trace. I always have. Just remember that, okay? Hold on to it. No matter what I say or what I do... and trust me, I'll do some terrible things. Just know. I love you. With every fiber of my being." I would beg. I would get on my knees. She had to believe — the love I felt for her was otherworldly. And I'd love her until my dying day. Even if it meant I'd spend my life suffering for her happiness.

Tears clouded her vision as she kissed me hard across the mouth then whispered, "I love you too."

That was it.

All I needed.

Goodbye, sweetheart. Goodbye... my treasure.

"I have to go." I rose from the bed.

"Don't!" Trace yelled.

Laughing, I lay back down on top of her and kissed her

mouth. "Trace... your grandfather's not a patient man. Let's not give him a heart attack."

"Seeing us make out would not give him a heart attack," she argued. "You taking me up on my whole virginity offer? Yeah, that would do it."

Holy shit. How the hell was I going to stay calm, knowing someone else was going to be doing the honors? Anytime I even thought about a guy touching her I wanted to pull my gun out and end his life. Damn, I'd do it with such a cheerful smile... Shit, shit, shit.

"Please. Just please don't ever. Trace, you have to promise — shit — you have to promise that no matter what happens, you wait, okay? You wait until it's with someone you love."

Someone like me.

Which meant hopefully... she would wait.

Not for me, since it was too dangerous now. But for someone... someone who would take care of her. A vision of Chase flashed through my mind. I almost puked. That's what the truth did to you. It made you want to throw up breakfast. If anyone in this scenario was free to disappear? It was him. Not me. Him. And he could... he did... he— It wasn't friendship he felt for her.

Her smile widened.

And my heart broke for, oh, I don't know, the fiftieth time in the last ten minutes? She thought I was talking about us.

"I promise."

I felt my eyes well with tears. When was the last time I'd cried? And now within two days I'd been so damn emotional I was getting ready to cry over a girl. But it wasn't just any girl. I nodded once and sighed when she pulled my face to hers, kissing me across the mouth. Our lips collided, sliding against each other. The friction of my lip ring against her mouth sent jolts of electricity down my body, making it harder to walk away. I slid my tongue into her mouth. One last taste. One last drink.

A knock sounded. I jerked away from her so fast I nearly collided with the floor. Instead, I stood and nodded for her to open the door.

Frank stood, arms crossed, and glared at me. "It's time to say goodbye."

In more ways than one. Huh, old man?

Trace rolled her eyes at him. It was too damn comical to see someone like Frank brought to his knees by a girl.

And then she latched on to my arm, and I was done for. So yeah, with her every breath she brought the scary Mafia to their knees. That was a secret I was taking to my grave, along with her kisses. We walked in silence to the front door. "I'll see you at school tomorrow, Nixon."

I locked eyes with Frank. He shook his head. Damn Mafia.

I kissed her softly, earning a hiss of disapproval from Frank but not caring in the least. He was making me give up everything, and he was right to ask it. I collected my two guns, four knives, and brass knuckles from the waiting security, and pulled Trace in for another hug. "Remember what I said, Trace. Remember."

When the door slammed behind me, I was in a trance, numb from head to toe. I got into the Range Rover and called Chase.

"What?" He groaned into the phone. A girl's laughter echoed behind him.

"You busy?"

"I'm in bed… with… er…"

I rolled my eyes. "You forgot her name?"

"Did you need something?" Chase snapped.

"Trace."

"Is she okay? What happened? Where are you?"

I licked my lips and looked back at the house. The

princess was going back to her tower. The dragon, back to his lair. Now it was time for the white knight to ride his horse through the iron gates.

"She's going to need you."

"Are you saying—"

"I'm out." I clenched my brass knuckles in my other hand, needing to ruin something.

"As in... you don't love her, or as in you can't?" Chase whispered.

"As in... Frank's orders go. I'm going to do what he says. I'm going to stay away, which means you have to stay close."

"You know what you're asking me to do, Nixon."

"Yeah. Unfortunately I do."

I sighed heavily into the phone.

"You make me do this, and all bets are off, Nixon."

I swore into the phone. "You don't think I know that? But there's no other way, Chase! Damn it! Don't make this harder than it already is!"

"Fine." He sighed. "For what it's worth. I respect you. I could never, I mean... I—"

"I gotta go," I croaked then pressed *End* on the cell phone. I stared down at it in surprise as something wet dropped onto the screen.

A tear.

I'd spent my life being a hard ass. The last time I'd cried, I was a little kid. The first time I'd shed tears in my adult life.

Tracey.

For her.

CHAPTER FORTY-FOUR
Well hello, bad news!

Chase

I THINK THERE COMES a point in every man's life when he's given a choice: do the right thing, you know, follow the rainbow, discover the pot of gold and shit it out to the poor.

Or you do bad.

In my case?

Very, very bad.

Nixon ended the phone call. My thoughts swarmed, thoughts of her, thoughts of him, thoughts of them together which really, really made me want to lose my mind and run my fist through the steering wheel or maybe a brick building.

My phone lit up again.

Phoenix, of course.

"You better be dead..." I cursed into the phone as I pulled onto the freeway. "...or at least bleeding from a fatal wound."

I hadn't heard from the bastard in days. I knew he was pissed about all the drama that had gone down with Nixon, but I also knew it was only a matter of time before Nixon forgave him, and we welcomed him back in the fold. He was one of us, after all.

"Sorry to shit on your sunshine," Phoenix hissed. "But we have a problem."

"We or you?"

"We." He drew the word out. "Us, the guys, we have a problem."

"Call Nixon."

"He's not answering, the bastard. Not that I blame him, all things considered."

Right. Which meant that had Phoenix called me... because I was second, second in command, second to find Trace, second to want her. When really, really if you look back, I was first, damn it, first. I clenched my fingers and counted to ten.

"Does this problem involve violence?"

"Lots."

"Address?"

Phoenix fired off an address a few miles away from where I was located. And hung up immediately.

One of our men had gone AWOL.

It happened.

Not often, but it did happen. They thought they could handle the life and then, after a few kills, they just stopped doing their jobs. They got nervous. I called it shaky-shit syndrome. Unable to keep a grasp on reality, they just bailed. I sighed and took the next exit.

You didn't bail when it came to the Mafia.

Bailing was code word for *Let me run away and hope they don't catch me.*

Word to the wise. We will always, and I do mean always, catch you, and when we find you, we don't give warnings. We simply shoot.

The guy Phoenix called me about had taken one look at Trace and Frank Alfero and had literally lost his mind, mumbling about Mafia wars and families invading from Sicily. Bullshit. We were fine.

But when people panicked, they did stupid things.

And this man, let's call him Joe. He was doing something so mind-numbingly stupid that I had no choice but to pull the trigger.

My car screeched to a halt in front of the restaurant. I turned off the ignition, made sure the safety was off of my gun, and made my way slowly into the Chinese place.

Tex was sitting at the bar, flirting with one of the waitresses. The place was pretty packed for a Monday night, but whatever. The room was soundproof.

"Sunshine." Tex wiggled his eyebrows at me.

"Asshole," I greeted in response then jerked the drink out of his hands and downed the whole thing.

"Riddle me this." He twisted the straw in his hands. "Is our boss not answering because he's playing house with the enemy?"

"Enemy…" I rolled my eyes. "Alright, pot, you do realize the kettle's black? Like, all of it?"

His eyes narrowed and, for a brief moment, I panicked. I never talked shit to Tex like that, at least about stuff that was real, stuff that mattered. And his situation? Very real and, hell yes, it mattered. He stood to his full height.

I cursed and looked away. "Phoenix?"

"Guarding the back, looks like hell too." He dropped the straw onto the bar and shrugged. "He figured it would be best for only one of us to go in, cleaner that way."

"Awesome. I kill. You do the paperwork?"

"Just call me secretary, bitch." He slapped me on the back and sauntered off.

Shaking my head, I made my way into the back room.

The click of the door must have notified Joe to my presence. Hell, I wasn't even sure if Joe was his real name, but I was going to go with it because I honestly didn't care if

ENFORCE

Bambi was his name, or if he had two cats and a dog, or even if he had a wife and kids. I wasn't paid to care.

And he wasn't paid to snitch.

He wasn't paid to go to the feds.

He let out a pitiful whimper.

"Joe." I pulled out my gun and scratched my head with it.

He lifted his head as if it weighed a thousand pounds. His hands were tied behind his back, and he was sitting in a metal chair from the bar.

"How's life, Joe?"

Sweat poured from his temples. "Can't complain."

"Good, good." I nodded, tapping my chin with the barrel of the gun, pacing in front of him. "You know I have to ask."

He hung his head.

"Did you give them any information, Joe?"

"No!" He shook his head violently. "I would never betray family. I would never---"

"But..." I held up my free hand and leaned in real close to his head. "...you kind of did... you ran, didn't finish a job, left two loose ends, and then went to the cops who then ran a background check on you and called the feds. Tell me what you told them."

"Nothing!" Joe yelled. "I said nothing. You have to believe me."

"Does it matter though?" I asked in cold voice. "Say I believe you. Now you're a target, you're dirty. So I'm going to ask nicely, Joe, how do you want it?"

"No!" Tears poured down his face. "No, you can't, Chase! You can't! If you just let me talk to Nixon—" I slapped him hard with the gun. Blood spilled out of his mouth.

"Nixon isn't here." I clenched my teeth into a fierce snap. "I am. Now I'm going to ask again... how do you want it?"

His body convulsed, and then he threw up all over the ground.

Cursing, I stepped back. "Dirty it is."

"NO! Wait! Clean! Make it clean!"

"Your wish is my command," I whispered then pulled the trigger, aiming directly between his eyes.

One shot.

I walked calmly out of the room, though my hands were shaking so aggressively it looked like I was a druggie in need of his next hit.

"Any games on tonight?" Tex asked, taking the gun from my hands and giving me two shots of whiskey in a glass.

I tipped it back. "We should ask Phoenix."

"Cool. Looks like the guy could use a friend. I know Nixon's pissed about what happened, but I'm pretty sure he's looking at it through breast-colored glasses, you know? Home?"

"Yeah," I croaked, refusing to touch that comment with a ten-foot pole, because if he was looking at her that way, then what the hell was I doing? The same damn thing, that's what. "Home."

I walked back through the restaurant after having killed a man.

I'd talked about football like it was normal to have blood on my hands.

And the sickest part of my night?

I felt no guilt over what I'd just done... because even after all that violence, after all that horror... my brain only had space for one thing.

Trace Rooks.

And I knew — I was going to have her if it was the last thing I did.

CHAPTER FORTY-FIVE
Cold hearts still break.

Nixon

Trace, my Bella: *Where are you?*

It was the second text she'd sent me that Monday. The second text I'd refused to answer. I wasn't sure what to say, how to handle the situation in a way that wouldn't break her heart. I hated being the reason for her tears, and it seemed that's all I did, bring her to tears, promise not to do it again, then repeat the process.

Letting out a loud groan, I stuffed my phone back in my pocket.

Chase elbowed me. "You good?"

"Fantastic," I lied. "Why wouldn't I be?"

His eyebrows arched. "Oh, you know, can't touch the girl you like? Or maybe the idea that you're forcing her presence on your more attractive cousin?"

"Asshole." I snorted out a laugh.

"You know it's true... the school's divided. Yesterday I saw a girl wearing a Team Nixon shirt... you've been hashtagged, brother."

I rolled my eyes. "Are you trying to make me feel better?"

"Team Chase, way better, those Chasers are hot. Seriously, for some reason, I tend to draw the exotic..." He let out a chuckle. "I don't discriminate."

Finally laughter gave way. "Thanks."

"For?" He shrugged, pulling his gaze away from me to the sidewalk.

"Being an ass just when I need it."

"I'll always be an ass for you."

"You guys need a moment?" Tex said coming up from behind us, wrapping his giant arms around both our bodies and trying to bring us together in a Campisi sandwich. "Because I got a little love to spread around too..."

"Get. Off." I pushed him away.

Laughing, he stumbled after us. "So, Phoenix lost his shit in class again... got kicked out. Dude's not well, Nixon. You should talk to him."

"And say what exactly?" I swore. "We're done with him."

"He's our best friend," Chase defended. "And you know how his dad is... Just... talk to him, throw him a bone. We all make mistakes. I participated in that one too, and you aren't putting a gun to my head."

"Yet." I glared. "Yet."

"I bet you'll tell the best bedtime stories to your kids." Tex nodded approvingly. "There once was a boy and girl in love... and then the boy bullied the girl and got shot. The end."

"Dude..." Chase rolled his eyes. "...just, no."

"Class." I nodded to them., "And yeah, I'll talk to Phoenix. I need to find out who they did business with last. The movement of cash into their account came from Sicily. It was a hell of a sum."

"Sicily?" Tex's eyebrows shot up. "You don't think—"

"No," I interrupted. "And you shouldn't either. Your father wouldn't do business with De Lange. Even to mess with you, he wouldn't do that."

Tex didn't look convinced.

And actually I wasn't totally convinced myself, but I wasn't going to say anything — yet.

"Later." I waved them off and went in search of Phoenix. Normally, he'd be in the business building, so I started there.

As soon as I opened the doors, I saw him leaning against one of the walls, cell phone pressed against his ear, face white as a ghost.

With trembling hands he ended the call and ran his fingers through his bleached blond hair. Never could figure out why he had to set himself apart from us by looking like a surfer from California, but part of me wondered if it was because he hated how much he resembled his own father.

Welcome to the club.

"Phoenix," I barked.

He glanced up and scowled. "What the hell do you want?"

I rolled my eyes as I approached him. He looked horrible. His uniform was rumpled like he'd slept in it, and dark circles marred his face. I didn't realize in that moment that it would be a scary glance into his future, one of unimaginable pain, one of horrors even I couldn't stomach.

"We should talk."

"I have nothing to say to you..." His voice was hollow, detached, as if he was a puppet, and someone else was speaking through him. "...or your whore."

My fists clenched. "Say it again, Phoenix. I dare you."

"She's ruining everything."

"This isn't about her, not anymore," I said, carefully gauging his reaction.

Scowling, he kicked at the ground. "It's always about women. They make the world go round, right? Can't do

business without 'em. It's always about them, either them or
him. Ever feel like you're living your own nightmare and can't
wake up?"

"Phoenix…" My eyes narrowed as they focused in on his
neck where bruises brushed against his collar. "…did
something happen with your father?"

"What do you care?" He pushed at my chest, but there
was no strength behind it. Even his muscles were giving up
like the rest of him. "He uses me, you use me. They use me!"
The last was said with such rage I backed up, worried he was
going to pull a weapon. "I hate everyone."

Things just went from bad to worse.

"But most of all, I hate her." His eyes flashed. "Things
were fine until she came here. Now look at me." His laugh
was without humor. "Hell, look at you. One girl and a
dynasty's brought to its knees." His hands shook as he
reached into his pockets. "That bitch should have stayed in
Wyoming."

Anger pounded through me. I barely restrained myself
from pulling my gun. "You were wounded before she came,
so don't go blaming your issues on a girl who didn't even
know who she was until yesterday."

I'd said too much.

Phoenix's smile was cruel. "Imagine my surprise…
Alfero…" He barked out a laugh. "And everything comes full
circle? My family still gets crapped on, I get nothing, and I lose
all my friends. Well, nobody ever said I deserved better."

He pushed away from me just in time for a body to run
directly into my chest.

I pulled the girl away and let out a little moan.

Trace.

With quite possibly the worst timing in the world,
because I wasn't sure if Phoenix was still watching, but I
couldn't take the chance that he was. It was time to put a plan
into action.

A plan to save her.

A plan to save him.

To keep them away from one another.

To keep her away from the gunfire.

I locked eyes with her and apologized for all for the things I was about to do. In my mind I held her close and whispered in her ear, I asked for forgiveness, and I slowly, reluctantly gave her heart back to her so she was free to give it to someone else, someone more deserving.

Goodbye, Trace.

I could have loved you.

I did love you.

Damn, but I do love you.

I gripped her arms and pushed her away from me. "What the hell do you think you're doing?"

"Huh?" Her face fell.

"Why are you touching me?" I sneered in my cruelest voice as students passed by.

"Because..." Her eyes flickered to the people around us and then back to me.

"Because?" I took a menacing step forward and tilted my head, damn-near losing my mind over the rejection in her eyes. "What, cat got your tongue? Or I guess in your case it would be a... cow?"

"A cow?" she repeated. "Nixon, what the hell is wrong with you? Last night..."

Gasps resounded around the hallway. Shit, Trace. Wrong thing to say, but I played into it perfectly because she made it so easy, and in that moment, I really was angry, angry that after pouring out my heart and soul to her, she'd so easily believed the lie, that I didn't want her.

"Was clearly a mistake if you still think I want more from you." I steeled myself against her sudden intake of breath, refusing to reach for her.

"But you said..."

"Are you deaf?" I shouted, my voice cracking. "I don't want you, Farm Girl. Not now, not last night... never." I laughed. "Let me put it into a way you understand, I will never want you. I mean, look at you. You're nothing like us, and you won't ever be. So do yourself a favor. Leave me the hell alone." My hands shook furiously as I looked away.

Tears streamed down her face as she stared.

"Get the hell away from me." I was almost chest to chest with her when I leaned in and whispered, "Leave. Now."

She finally pushed past me.

Under my breath, I hit the final nail into my own coffin and mumbled, "Moo."

Sobs wracked her body. I could hear them. Hell, the entire student body could hear them.

When I turned around, it was to see Trace run smack-dab into Phoenix. I quickly ducked into the closest classroom and listened in, all the while sending a Mayday text to Chase.

"Nice show. Good to know he's finally put you in your place. Maybe now that the whore's out of the picture, we can go back to the way things were before you polluted this school," Phoenix said.

The bastard.

But he believed it. Thank God, he believed it.

"Screw you!" she yelled.

I wanted to laugh, but my heart hurt too bad.

Chase: *WTF, Nixon?*

Me: *She's heading toward the west hall., Grab her, comfort her. Hell, I don't care. I'm out. I'm just... out.*

CHAPTER FORTY-SIX

Damn Mafia… damn hearts for being so freaking fragile.

Chase

I SHOVED MY PHONE back into my pocket then slammed my hand onto the wall nearest me.

A few students jumped at the noise. I rolled my eyes and was just about to leave the classroom to find Trace when she came barreling in, her eyes wild, tears streaming down her cheeks.

I would kill him for hurting her — again.

And for having to be the one to pick up all the broken pieces. Damn if I would put her back together just so he could steal her once she was healed. Trace crumpled to the floor, sobs escaping between her lips like she couldn't catch her breath.

I nodded to the students around us.

They shuffled out.

With a sigh, I knelt in front of her and brushed some of the wet hair away from her face. I'd kiss her if I knew where it hurt.

But you can't kiss away this type of pain.

Just like you can't be the stand-in for the guy her heart cries for.

Without a word, I picked her up into my arms and carried her out of the classroom and out of the building, not bothering to even curse in Italian as I'd used up my repertoire of horrible words concerning the Mafia.

I took her to our little hangout on campus and prayed to God that Nixon wasn't already there, stewing over whatever the hell he'd just done.

After I opened the door and placed Trace on the couch, I paced in front of her for a good five minutes, firing questions at her to make sure she was actually coherent.

What I got?

Silence.

"Damn it, Trace, listen to me!" I gripped her face between my hands. Her head bobbed a little forward. Damn it, had he sent her over the edge? Seriously? Swear words poured out of my mouth. I had absolutely no control over what I was saying, lots of F-bombs, lots of Nixons. Yeah, lots of those two combined.

"What?" she finally said, licking her lips and averting her eyes like I was worse than him.

I grabbed her chin, forcing her to look at me. "Do you need to go to the hospital? Lie down? Need a drink of water? Want a sedative? These are all the things I asked you on the way over, and again when I plopped you on the couch. Shit." I released her chin and ran my fingers through my hair. "What the hell was that? Are out of your freaking mind? You can't just..." I pushed away from her and started pacing for the second time in five minutes.

"You can't just break down at school like that. Can't let people see weakness. You're better than that. I don't care if the freaking president of the United States waltzed in here and told everyone you were a terrorist. You're an Alfero, for shit's sake. Start acting like one!" I was yelling. Why the hell was I yelling? Because I was angry, but it was more than that. I was yelling because I was terrified of losing her.

Losing her to him.

Losing her to some sort of Mafia war.

Even losing her to some of the pricks that graced Elite.

Her mouth dropped open.

Shit, I'd taken tough love way too far, crossed the bridge, pounced on the other side and then laughed in her face. Great. Asshole-of-the-Year award has just been passed down from Nixon to Chase.

Rather than cry more, she flipped me off.

Had to admit it was a bit of a proud moment for me, rubbing off on her like that. Bringing out the Alfero tiger.

I smiled. "Better, Trace. You can do better than flipping me off and telling me to go screw myself. I know this blows. Believe me, I know. But it's the only way."

"The only way?" she repeated with confusion.

I nodded. "You and Nixon. You can't happen. There's too much history — too much drama, and with Phoenix lurking around campus, you can't be the catalyst that brings this entire operation down. Believe me, you don't want that, and you don't want Nixon to be tempted to do that."

"Nixon," she spat, "He can do whatever the hell he wants."

"Good to know," Nixon said from behind me.

Oh look, shit. Meet fan.

I turned and leveled him with a glare, which he naturally ignored, because it was Nixon and he owned the world.

Nixon's eyes were wide with worry as he approached Trace. "Are you okay?" Oh, hell no.

I was ready to attack, but instead, a brown head of hair pushed past me and tackled Nixon, pushing him against the wall. Trace banged her fists against his chest. My mouth dropped open in shock. Glued to my spot, I could only watch in horror as she hit him repeatedly with her tiny fists, all the while sobbing out his name. I jumped from the couch so I could grab her before she hurt herself. Nixon finally pried her away just as I was able to get over my shock and peel her from his body.

"I—" Nixon's voice cracked.

"You're making it worse, man," I whispered. Trace trembled in my arms. "Just go. She doesn't want to see you. Hell, I don't even know if I want to see you. I know why... I just think this can't be fixed by your badass Mafia mojo."

"But—" Nixon cleared his throat. "Trace?" It was a question.

"Just go to hell." Her words vibrated against my chest as she tucked her head against me.

I swore. "Nixon, you had to choose. And I think you made it pretty clear to everyone within a fifty-mile radius who you chose."

"I just don't know if I want to live with the consequences," Nixon said, his face getting paler by the minute. Never had I seen him so upset, so... wrecked.

"I guess we'll see what this family really is made of." I whispered.

"Chase." Nixon's voice was hoarse. "Take care of her, please. Just—"

"Go!" Trace yelled, interrupting us.

I gave Nixon a firm nod.

He pointed to his phone.

Yeah, yeah, bastard. I'd wipe her tears then report to you.

Like I always did.

It was getting old.

This whole scene? Old.

Trace slumped against me. I was forced to pick her up again and carry her to the couch. Once she was settled, I went over to the lights, flicked them off, and lay down next to her.

ENFORCE

I sighed, pulling a blanket over us.

"Chase?" She sniffled.

"Hmm?"

"Why are you helping me?"

"Because you're hot." I rubbed her arm with my fingertips and let out a laugh at her tensing body. "Trace, I'm kidding. Don't get your panties in a bunch. I'm here because there's nowhere else I'd rather be. Because I hate to see chicks cry, and although popular opinion states I don't possess a heart, I actually do. So color me weird, but when I see a friend— And don't scowl. I can hear it from here. When I see a friend, a good friend, upset, I would freaking bleed myself out before letting her go through shit alone."

"That was a nice speech. Did you practice it?"

"Very funny." I pulled her tighter. Damn, but we fit perfectly. I really could have gone without that knowledge.

"Chase?"

"Yeah?"

"Why can you help me, but Nixon can't?"

Well shit. I licked my lips to give myself a second to think. "Loaded question, Farm Girl." I moved my hand up and down her arm in slow movements. "He's the mob boss. I'm the cousin. It's different. I'm not even next in line. I've always done my own thing. I mean, yeah, I work for the family. I guess you could say I'm lower on the totem pole, so I don't really matter as much. If anything, you're better off with me than Nixon anyway. At least with me you won't be a target for murder."

"How... reassuring."

I chuckled. "Hey, you asked. Now, please try to get some sleep."

"Will you be here when I wake up?"

"Always." I swore in that moment I would never let that girl go to sleep without the knowledge that I would be there for her when she woke up. Nixon or no Nixon, I would never

311

abandon her. Ever.

It must have been enough, because her body relaxed, and soon her breathing was deep and heavy.

I, however, didn't sleep at all.

Not for lack of trying — hell, I was exhausted. Always exhausted.

But I was too buzzed with emotion to do anything except hold her and wonder what it meant for us in the future. She had no idea I had feelings for her; only the guys did. And I wasn't so sure I wanted her to know. I wasn't really keen on girls pointing and laughing at me while I poured out my feelings, but damn, I could feel myself falling for her.

At first it had been so slow I hadn't realized it.

And now? Now I was halfway down the rabbit hole and propelling my arms so that I could fall faster, land on my feet harder.

Shit.

Nixon wasn't just asking me to protect her... he was trusting me with her.

And he really shouldn't.

Finally, I was able to close my eyes and drift off to sleep.

"What the hell, Trace?" I cursed, my swollen eyes opening, trying to make sense of how I'd gone from couch to the floor. "You could have at least told me before you tried to kill me!"

"Kill you?" She arched her eyebrows. "Right. Because if the one-foot fall wouldn't have done it, what? Your tiny heart would have burst?"

My eyes narrowed. Hilarious. "Look, I know you're heartbroken, and you're upset, blah, blah, blah, but do you have to be mean to the guy who helped you when you were having a nervous breakdown in front of most of the entire student body?"

"Valid point," she said through clenched teeth.

I grinned. "Knew you'd see it my way. Now, no attacking. I'm going to get off of you, help you to your feet, and attempt not to stare at your ass as you bend over to grab your bag."

"Such a gentleman," she grumbled, taking my hand as I helped her to her feet.

She tugged down her shirt and walked over to grab her book bag. I stared like a man starved. Her ass was fine in that skirt. "Sorry, Trace. I lied. No wonder Nixon was—"

"Can we just... *not* talk about him?" She tossed her bag over her shoulder and crossed her arms. So much for humor helping the situation.

With a nod, I held my hands up in surrender. "Good deal. Let me just grab my keycard, and I'll walk you to your dorm."

Her face immediately flushed, like the idea of me helping her was abhorrent. "You don't have to do that. You already let me hide out in here for most of the morning and—"

"I insist. Besides, it's kind of my job." I shrugged.

"Your job?"

"Chase Winter at your service. Get used to it, babe. I'm your official bodyguard."

"Says who?" she shrieked.

Yeah, funny. I had the same reaction but was given time to let it sink in; she, however, had two seconds.

"Um, Nixon? Your grandfather? Mo? Just about everyone who loves you..." I shrugged. When the Mafia says jump, you say how high and where.

"Nixon doesn't love me."

I exhaled the breath I'd been holding. "I refuse to get into that with you right now. Believe what you want, but that boy would flipping cut his own arm off before he let someone harm a hair on your head."

Her eyes filled with tears, "Sometimes, Chase... it's the emotional wounds that hurt the most." I pushed back the anger and sighed. "I'd rather he beat me. Cuts heal, bruises fade — but broken hearts? They carry scars for a lifetime."

Well said, damn it. I shoved my keycard back into my pocket and pulled her into my arms. I kissed her forehead. "I don't think any guy can promise not to break your heart. But I do promise that the next jackass who tries it will be on the other end of my fist."

She nodded.

"Come on, Trace..." I nudged her., "One smile. Give me one smile before we walk the plank."

She rolled her eyes.

"Please?" I jutted out my lower lip.

Her smile was pathetic, — looked more like a wince, like I smelled bad, and she was trying to reassure me it wasn't so horrible she couldn't breathe. Awesome.

Hopeless case, that Trace.

I led her outside. At least the sun was shining; that was something.

"See?" I whispered against her ear. "Smooth sailing."

Famous last words. Swear, the minute they left my mouth, people around us started whispering and pointing. Someone yelled, "Skank." Another yelled, "Whore." And somehow they turned into chants.

I made a mental note to kill them all.

And then I made another mental note that if I was to keep my sorry ass out of prison, I couldn't commit unnecessary murder. But was it really unnecessary when they were hurting her feelings? I ignored them as much as I could, told everyone to F off, and managed to get her to her dorm.

Cara came barreling out of the door the minute I swiped my card. Fantastic. Just the girl I wanted to see, the same one I'd rejected the week previous on account that I didn't feel like whoring myself out anymore, because my heart had kind of decided it didn't like it as much as it used to.

"Told you." Cara smirked at Trace then her eyes fell to me. "Nice of you to take over Nixon's sloppy seconds."

Oh, this was going to be too fun.

I always loved it when people momentarily forgot who I was, what I could do, what I was capable of.

Trace tried to tug me into the dorm, but I didn't budge.

"Sloppy seconds?" I repeated.

I released Trace's hand and began to circle Cara.

"Cara..." I threw my head back and laughed. "...I forgot how entertaining that little mouth of yours was, which is crazy because I could have sworn it was wrapped around Phoenix's junk last week."

Trace's face paled while Cara's mouth dropped open.

"Aw, baby, was that an invitation?" I chuckled. "I wonder how your boyfriend, Deacon, would feel about you screwing Phoenix behind his back? Hmm? I wonder what he would do. No, actually..." I snapped my fingers. "...I know exactly what he'd do. He'd drop your fat ass and move on to the next skank ready to spread her legs for him. Then again, maybe he likes that you're easy. Hey, why don't I call him right now and see if he wants to join us for a threesome? Hell, make that a foursome, since you clearly like what you see. I'll play."

Cara's lower lip began to tremble. Do it. Cry. I was just getting started. I would destroy her for making Trace feel small, freaking laugh when she cried for me to stop.

"Don't tell him. Please, just..." Cara looked at Trace for help.

Really? The girl you just insulted? Bullshit.

"You know what girls like you are worth?" I sneered, drawing her attention again, "Nothing. Absolutely nothing. You're a dime a dozen. I won't call Deacon because I truly believe he's your free ride to hell. Your future is clear as day to me. You'll be his perfect Stepford wife, stand back and smile politely while he screws every prostitute available to a man of his tastes, and you'll do Phoenix and whoever will give you the time of day on the side."

Tears streamed down Cara's face.

"Wake up." I stopped directly in front of her, my mouth inches from her face. "You will never be as good as Tracey. You will never be good enough to freaking lick the pavement where her shoes have been. Now listen, and listen very closely."

She nodded.

"You will never look at her in the eyes again. If I hear that you do. I'll ruin your perfectly caked-up face. If you breathe the same air as Tracey without my permission, I'll show you what it feels like to suffocate to death. And if you spread anymore rumors about her or the Elect…" I chuckled. "…you won't make it to Christmas break, without at least one of your pretty manicured fingers missing from your hand. Do we understand each other?"

Cara started to sob and then with a nod ran off, covering her face with her hands. At that rate, she was going to run into a tree and ruin that horrible nose job, but whatever. Not my problem.

"Have a good day!" I called after her, feeling a hell of a lot better after releasing some of that pent-up tension.

I whistled and sent a text of warning to Nixon that the student body was revolting. He'd do his usual scare act to get them to stop talking so I could focus on Trace.

"What the—"

"What?" I shrugged and looked up at Trace's horrified expression. "Hey, let's go inside. I'm cold."

"Right." She followed after me.

"So, you can be scary." Trace finally broke the silence.

Ha, girl had no idea the type of scary I could wreak into this world. "It's a family thing."

"Great." She was watching me closely, probably scared

shitless, but hey, better she see me how I really was then be thrown off later. That's what I did. I was the intimidator, the shit talker. It's what I was good at. I'd like to think it's what I exceled at.

The elevator doors opened, and I followed her in. I continued my awesome mood down her hall while girls whispered and pointed. I glared at each girl and gave them a nonverbal warning.

Pretty sure they were going to be locking their doors that night.

"Thanks for walking me home." Trace opened the door.

I followed her right in. May as well make myself comfortable.

"Um, what are you doing?"

"My job." I grinned and lay down on her bed, "Now get your homework done so we can watch a movie."

"We?"

"Yeah. As in you and I. What? You have a cow hidden in here somewhere?" I joked.

She blinked innocently.

"Holy crap, *do* you have a cow? That would be awesome." I'd never seen a cow up close in real life, so yeah, it really would be awesome. Impossible, but awesome.

"Yeah, Chase. I have a cow under my bed. It's invisible though, so you can't see it. But sometimes at night it comes out to play. What the hell is wrong with your brain?"

I winked and pulled out a creepy looking vampire novel off her nightstand. "Homework," I ordered with a bored voice. "Now."

"Okay, *Dad*."

My body came to life. I loved her teasing. "Oooh, say it again. Only this time call me daddy while you're—"

"CHASE!" Her face flushed bright red.

I cackled. I licked my lips and blew her a kiss, then opened the book.

CHAPTER FORTY-SEVEN
Stalker alert

Nixon

I CHECKED MY PHONE religiously.

It was getting ridiculous. Every damn time the thing went off, my breath caught in my throat, my heart pounded, I started to sweat — I needed a vacation or maybe just her.

What I got?

Tex.

The worst type of punishment, hearing him talk about Mo like she wasn't my sister and being forced to block out every single noise that came from her room at the house when she said she was doing homework.

Yeah, poly-sci homework didn't get me that worked up.

It shouldn't her either, damn it. I was just itching to end Tex's life on account that he knew his story wouldn't end pretty and her heart? Just another broken one I'd have to deal with.

I'd been staying at my house more and more, not because I wanted to Every damn inch of the place reminded me of my father. But staying on campus meant that I would possibly run into Trace, and I didn't trust myself enough not to charge toward her and apologize for being such an ass.

Chase updated both me and Frank on a daily basis.

And with every update, I got sicker and sicker. One week he sent me pictures of them eating ice cream at her dorm, and I almost lost it. I threw my phone against eh wall, shattering it on contact.

Over ice cream.

She was happy, so I should be happy.

But she was happy with him. Not me. Therefore, I was pissed. Always pissed.

Phoenix hadn't made things better. After our little falling out in the hallway, he'd refused to answer any of my phone calls or texts. Finally, he agreed to meet with me and hand over any information he could glean from his father about the shady deposit into their account.

What we both discovered wasn't pretty.

It linked them to some unknown family in Sicily.

Which meant it had to be a well-known family, who was pulling a lot of strings and paying De Lange a lot.

But why?

Phoenix had no idea.

And it seemed like the deeper we dug, the worse it became.

Not to mention that Phoenix had more bruises on his neck. He looked like hell. When I offered him a place to stay, he flipped me off and left the same way he'd come... broken.

I couldn't help but feel like a storm was brewing, like my entire life had led up to this moment, and I was somehow missing something huge.

Things were calm.

Too calm.

And in my line of work, calm could only mean one thing. A storm was coming... fast.

CHAPTER FORTY-EIGHT
Keep your girl.

Chase

SHE YELLED HIS NAME in her sleep.

And I hated her for it.

I hated both of them.

Yet I held her close.

Because it was all I could do — hold her and kiss away the tears, hope and pray that one day the tears would turn into smiles, and that she'd see me as more than just her protector, but her friend.

Weeks were spent by her side, weeks where I fell a little more in love with her each time she managed to laugh. Hell, she was beautiful, even when she cried.

I hadn't gotten it before — what had made Nixon so obsessed. But now I knew; it wasn't just one thing. You couldn't just say, *"Oh, it's because Trace is a really cool chick."*

It was everything about her.

The way she looked at life; the way she responded to the bad stuff just made you want to give her more good.

It was addicting, being with her. I felt better just walking by her side, knowing that I was going to wake up and spend my day with her. Then the moments of joy would get freaking stolen when Nixon would send me another ridiculous text about making sure she wore a sweater because it was cold out.

Really, dude?

Like I couldn't look at my iPhone app and figure out how cold it was.

The bastard was a constant pain in my ass, a constant reminder that I was guarding treasure — but not mine.

His.

I wondered, if things were different, would I stand a chance? Little moments caused me to believe she could fall for me. She was blushing more, holding my hand more, like it was completely normal for us to be walking around campus holding hands.

The real problem was I held her hand because I couldn't help it.

She held my hand because it made her feel safe.

Two very different reasons. Mine was obsession, plain and simple.

Hers was comfort.

Damn if that didn't make me want to jump out her stupid window.

"Chase?" Trace kicked the leaves with her booted feet. "Did you hear what I said?"

"Sure did."

"No, you didn't!" She laughed, elbowing me in the ribs. "Why aren't you dating as much anymore?"

Oh, you know, because I'm in love with a girl who doesn't know I exist. "Just not into it, not anymore."

She nodded, seemingly satisfied with my answer.

"You okay to go to class?"

Rolling her eyes, she leaned in and kissed me on the cheek. "Yes, I'm okay, just like yesterday I was okay, and this morning I was okay when you heard me yell from the shower."

I burst out laughing. "One can never be sure."

"Yeah well, you're lucky you didn't see me naked."

"I think you mean *unlucky*."

Blushing, she pulled her bag tighter across her body. "I'll see you after, alright? Then you can wrap me in bubble tape and push me toward my final class of the day."

"I love it when you talk dirty." I smirked.

"Go away."

"Say bubble tape again."

"Bye, Chase."

"Bye, muffin!" I called after her and sent my usual text to Nixon. This time it was a picture of cow going into the barn, my way of saying Trace was safe. It entertained me but pissed him off because I didn't use words, but whatever.

I watched her walk into the building, making sure she really was safely inside, then went over to the bench to wait. Outside. In the cold. For her to get done with class.

My own grades were suffering for her safety.

But I really wouldn't want it any other way.

I checked my phone. Another text from Nixon.

When I looked up, it was to see Phoenix glaring in my direction. He'd been pissing me off a lot lately, making my life a living hell since I'd had to actually protect Trace from him.

I despised him for it.

He knew it too. I could see it in his eyes. With a sneer, Phoenix grinned in my direction as he turned and walked away.

When did he go from being one of my best friends to my enemy? Was it when I'd caught him staring at Trace?

Was that really enough to throw away over a decade of friendship? I sighed and leaned against the wall.

The air crackled with excitement around me — but all I was focused on—was her scent. It was still on me.

Don't ask me how the hell that happened. It may have to

do with the fact that I'd spent the night with her, not slept with her the way I wanted to — the way I'm sure Nixon wanted too as well, the bastard.

But in her bed.

With her head tucked underneath mine — where it belonged. I'd gotten use to her breathing, the way the air blew out of her nose in a slow lazy rhythm, letting me know she was in a deep sleep, or the short gasps that sometimes escaped from her pretty lips, telling me she was having a bad dream.

I was there for it all.

The Good. The Bad.

And where was Nixon?

Doing his job.

She moaned in her sleep, not that I'd ever share that with Nixon. Last night she'd been scared, so I'd stayed. I always stayed until she fell asleep, but last night was different because Mo had been gone.

And I'd broken every damn rule I'd put into place — every damn rule that Nixon had said he'd enforce.

Touching her, being near her, was like getting a hit of adrenaline or doing drugs for the first time. You tell yourself that it's just one touch, but your body demands you take more.

My lips had grazed her head, and then my nose burrowed into her thick mop of brown air.

Moaning, she'd hit me across the face on accident — it had been enough to get me to pull back, to actually shake the insanity from my body.

I checked my watch; she'd be in class for at least an hour. I had just enough time to go across campus, grab a coffee, then meet her back at the bench. I took off, a smile crossing my face as I imagined her own excitement that I'd thought of her and grabbed an almond hot chocolate.

Damn, I wasn't just falling.

I was on the ground.

Looking up at the sky with a dumbfounded expression,

wondering how the hell I'd gone from being a trained assassin.

To a man in full-blown love.

Buying a girl who had no clue of his feelings a damn hot chocolate.

CHAPTER FORTY-NINE
I should have killed him.

Nixon

"DR. STEVENS IS OUT sick today, so I'll be filling in." My eyes scanned the room, finally landing on Trace. Without breaking eye contact, I instructed everyone to take notes on the movie assignment. Papers were passed out, and then the lights went out.

Trace closed her eyes. I watched her, waiting for her to acknowledge me. Instead, a lone tear ran down her cheek. With a curse, I moved to the back of the room and took the desk behind her.

"Trace," I whispered in her ear. Her entire body stiffened. She didn't turn around.

"Trace, don't be like that. I miss you..." My lips grazed her ear. She was driving me insane — I couldn't take it anymore. "...so damn much, and I wish... I wish I could tell you... Damn it, I wish I hadn't promised, but I did. I have to protect you. Being with you. It isn't safe. You have to understand that now."

She was as still as a statue.

RACHEL VAN DYKEN

"Please, sweetheart. Just please remember what I said."
My lip ring connected with her ear, and she shivered. "I
always keep my promises. If I don't — people die. Do you
understand? I can't have innocent blood on my hands,
especially when it could be yours."
I let out a heavy sigh. How could I make her understand?
"I had no choice, Trace."
In an instant she flipped around.
I jerked back, cursing.
"No, you listen." She pointed her finger at me and
whispered so nobody else could hear us. "There is always a
choice. I refuse to allow you to justify your actions by saying
your hands were tied. You're Nixon Abandonato. You had a
choice, and you made it. Screw your excuses. I'm so tired of it,
Nixon. All of it. I'm done. I'm..." She swallowed her eyes
darting back and forth. "...I'm not coming back next semester.
You're right. I can't do this. It's not my world. I don't belong
here."
I reached for her hand, but she jerked it away.
"You do, though, Trace. You belong here just as much as
anybody else and—"
"No." She shook her head. "I don't. I can't tell them who I
am, and even if I did, what would happen? I'd earn respect
because of my family, but it would all be fake. Meanwhile,
you'd come up with another excuse to break my heart into a
million pieces, saying you had no choice. Go to hell, Nixon.
Actually..." She laughed. "...don't. Because I've been living
there for the past three weeks. Just stay away from me."
She grabbed her books and charged out of class. I pressed
my hands against my forehead. I'd lost her. I'd lost her, and
for what? Nothing. Absolutely nothing.
I loved her.
And she was walking away.
Just like I'd told her to do.
Just like I'd done.

CHAPTER FIFTY
Broken

Phoenix

MY DAD HAD OFFICIALLY disowned me.

He'd told me to my face, slapped me, then laughed as the rest of the associates had watched — and done nothing.

I was humiliated.

And the worst part. I'd probably deserved it, because I'd said no to him. I'd finally stood up for myself, and he'd damn-near killed me for it.

He'd asked me to take another virgin.

Another one he'd been putting on the market for one of his special clients. I'd declined, telling him to go to hell.

Instead, he'd put me there.

I had no money.

No home.

No friends.

No family.

I was better off dead.

Just as I was about to go put a gun on my mouth and pull the trigger — because really what was the point anymore? —

Trace had barreled out of a classroom and whispered under her breath.

"Grandma, I wish you were here."

"Grandma?" I repeated. My voice unrecognizable— Who the hell was that talking? It was like I was present but not in control of my own actions— No, rage had long ago taken over; the monster inside had broken free.

Because I'd fed it.

Over and over again.

With sex.

With darkness.

With killing.

I'd fed it, and now it was hungry, angry, and needing more food. She was the reason I had nothing. She was the reason I was going to kill myself. And she deserved to be shamed, just like I felt shame.

Her eyes were afraid.

Something else snapped, maybe it was my conscience, because in that moment I didn't see her as a person but an object that needed to be destroyed, a problem that only I could fix.

"Grandma?" I repeated. "Would that be Grandma Alfero?"

She laughed and tried to walk past me. "I have no idea what you're talking about." She started texting, dismissing me as if I was nothing. Confirming my suspicions all along.

I was nothing.

A waste of air.

A waste of freaking humanity.

Just like my father said.

"Where do you think you're going?" I moved to stand in front of her.

She turned around and started walking in the other direction, but I jogged in front of her. My arms shot out to brace her shoulders. My fingers dug into her shoulders as I slammed her into the wall.

My enemy.

Who should have been my friend.

What the hell was I doing?

My body screamed for vengeance.

My mind was a jumbled mess of insults and darkness, and then her face became like every other face I'd screwed. Every girl I'd taken from...

Was found in her innocence.

I moved forward. Maybe if I kissed her, maybe she would fix it, make it better, suck the darkness from my soul. "Talk." I brushed my lips against hers.

She pushed against me.

Unwanted by her.

Of course. Because I wasn't him.

"Or not." I grinned, though I wasn't happy, just really, really sad and confused. "We could always do some other things. Word around the school is that you're used goods. Once I'm done with you, you'll forget all about Nixon and be screaming my name instead."

She kicked me, and I snapped, dragging her down the hall with me. She started screaming for help, but I knew nobody would help her.

"She likes it rough." I laughed.

People joined in.

I was living my own nightmare.

This wasn't me.

But I kept pulling her.

I kept choosing to let the anger control me, pound through my soul. Maybe I'd just kill her and shoot myself next.

Maybe I'd take from him like he'd stolen from me.

"No, No! Please! Please help me!" Her voice was frantic.

I ignored her plea and continued pulling her toward our campus hangout.

"Stop! Phoenix! STOP!"

She dug her heels into the ground, but it only made me laugh harder as I threw her over my shoulder.

"That's more like it," I said gruffly. "You think you're so perfect just because of who your family is? Do you even know who I am?" I jerked her head close to my mouth and yelled it into her ear. "And all because of you I've lost the chance to be with Nixon's family! My connections? Gone. My money? GONE! Wanna know why?"

She tried to shake her head.

The anger boiled inside, pushing out of my chest, making it twist with pain, pain she'd caused, pain she'd suffer from.

"Because the De Langes aren't a for-sure thing. Our money isn't good enough. But Nixon's? His name? It's freaking gold, and you went and ruined everything by batting your damn eyelashes. You're a freaking whore just like your mom…"

I slapped her across the face before I pushed her into the room, my own hands trembling.

What was I doing?

I hesitated for a moment.

But hesitation had never gotten me any more. It had left me unloved. It had left me with nothing. The monster needed to be fed.

I needed vengeance.

In order to die in peace, I needed something, didn't I? I deserved something! A son abused, a friend ignored, I just wanted purpose.

And she'd taken it from me. Stolen it from my hands.

Trace started frantically pushing the screen of her cell.

"What are you doing?" I grabbed her phone just as it rang. "Answer it. Tell him you're fine."

She shook her head. I pulled out a knife. "Answer it, or I'm going to make a permanent mark on your face."

With shaking hands, she took the phone and answered, "Hello?"

"Trace?" a loud male voice said from the other end. "Are you okay? Nixon said you left class and— Trace are you crying?"

"No." Her voice was strained.

I couldn't place the voice on the other end, but I assumed it was one of the guys.

"Um, Chase, I gotta run. I'm going to go back to my room to take a nap." She glanced at me, still talking on the phone. "Yeah?" Her eyes snapped shut, and she whispered. "Scorching."

When she handed me back the phone, I threw it against the wall. It shattered it on contact.

"Think you know all our little secrets just because you're an Alfero?" I pushed her against the same wall and laughed. "Where's Nixon now? Is he going to save you? Where was he when your parents died? Oh right. He was too young, unable to do anything. Just like he won't be able to do anything now."

"Why?" she choked out.

"Why?" I licked my lips then spit on her, just like my father had spit on me. How's it feel, princess? To be nothing. Treated like you don't matter. Like your existence was a mistake. "Because you're a dirty whore. Because you've ruined everything I've worked for years to build. Because the minute Nixon broke me away from the Elect, nobody in town would do business with us. I've been ordered by my father to take care of things in any way possible. This is my way of doing that. Can't have family secrets rearing their ugly heads, just because Nixon decided he had a heart, now can we?"

"Nixon will kill you." Her voice shook with rage.

I punched the wall above her head, knowing it was true and hoping the bastard would stop me, save me from myself, save me from doing something I didn't want to do, but had no control over. My hands shook, my body convulsed. This wasn't me. It wasn't me.

But the real me had died long ago.

He had been forced into submission.

"Not if I kill him first." I ripped the sweater from her body. "A thousand bucks says you're a virgin..." I slowly undid the buttons to her shirt. My hands still shaking, I gagged. This was what he had turned me into; my father had made sex an act of violence.

Even with someone like Trace.

It was violent.

It would be violent.

Because I wasn't a person anymore.

Her fist caught my jaw.

I staggered and then whispered, "I like a girl who's rough." The words coming from my mouth didn't match my actions, didn't match my feelings, but rage controlled everything.

She fought harder.

And again I saw those girls' faces.

And when I looked up, I imagined my face, the face of my father, as I ripped the skirt off her body.

He would pay.

They would all pay.

For turning me into the one thing I never wanted to be. When I'd been a little boy, it hadn't been monsters that had scared me.

It had been him.

Dean De Lange.

He'd terrified me.

I'd prayed to God, wished on every shooting star to just save me from his fate.

But God hadn't listened.

And the stars had chosen to shine on good little boys and girls, but not Phoenix De Lange, never Phoenix. My vision blurred as her skirt fell in pieces next to her.

What. The. Hell.

She tried to buck me off her.

I slapped her.

It made me feel better.

So I slapped her harder.

When a tear streamed down her face, and her expression was familiar, that of Trace and not one of the girls I'd used before, I blinked, my hands reaching toward her underwear, as if I couldn't stop myself.

But I wanted to.

So I prayed one more time.

One final time in my life.

I prayed for God to answer me. Just once.

Save me from what I've become.

Just save me from this.

Something pounded the door, and in a blur, Nixon and Chase charged in. Fists landed against my face.

And I smiled, not because I was getting the shit beat out of me.

But because... when it had mattered...

God had heard my prayer.

And saved me from myself.

CHAPTER FIFTY-ONE
My life flashed...

Nixon

TRACE HAD LEFT CLASS in tears, and I knew that I'd yet again been the cause of them. If only she knew that being mean to her was ripping me to shreds from the inside out. Not only had I made a promise to Frank to leave her the hell alone, but Phoenix had been sniffing around too closely.

He'd asked me about Trace. Again. And this time when he asked, he'd mentioned the necklace, her grandfather, and our relationship with the Alferos. It worried me to no end, because if he was smart, he'd use her as bait to draw us out. He'd use her to get to me. It would be easy to bend me to his will to get what he wanted, what his father wanted: more money and freedom. And he was angry enough to do just that.

So telling the girl I loved that I hated her? Mooing at her in the hall? All it had done was prove to Phoenix that she was just like everyone else — a dead end. Normal.

Not a freaking Alfero.

Not the daughter of two slain parents.

Granddaughter to the one Mafia boss who had a chip on

his shoulder bigger than mine.

Shit. I wiped my face with my hands.

Class dismissed.

I heard yelling in the hall but didn't pay attention. Instead, I picked up my phone and sent Chase quick text.

Me: *Trace left class. Check on her?*

Chase: *I'll call her — but for the record, I'd just leave her alone.*

The phone almost fell out of my hands. The last thing I needed was for Chase, of all people, to tell me to back off. The last time he'd threatened me I'd given him two black eyes and chipped his tooth.

With a sigh, I sat on the desk and waited for him to text me the okay.

Five minutes later, my alert went off.

And that time I really did drop the phone onto the floor.

Chase: *911 — Batcave — Phoenix has Trace.*

I forwarded the text to Frank as fast as my fingers let me, and then I yelled, panicked. For the first time in my life — I hesitated. Not because I wasn't going to go after her, but because my feet refused to move. Breathing had suddenly become a huge chore, as if my lungs had forgotten how to function.

I hit my own chest, sucking in the air greedily as I made my way to the door, legs like lead.

Her face. That's what I saw.

Her skin. That's what I felt.

Her lips.

Every damn part of her.

And he had her.

Alone.

If he touched her, if he laid one finger on her, touched a hair on her head, I was going to murder him, and I would do it slowly. I'd extend it days, maybe even weeks, and I'd smile as his body sank to the bottom of Lake Michigan.

People stared as I ran through the halls. I didn't even blink as I reached for the gun hidden in the back of my pants.

Five minutes.

It took me five damn minutes to run across campus to where Phoenix had her.

I was going to puke.

I'd seen some terrible things in my lifetime — but fear had been beaten out of me at a young age.

Or so I thought.

Chase reached the door just as I did. I swiped my card over it, but it didn't budge.

"Shit!" I kicked it with my foot then grabbed the knife from my leg. I shoved it between the metal plates of the scanner and shorted the wires.

The door opened.

My breath caught in my chest as my eyes fell on Phoenix's hands as they slid up her thighs.

A war-cry from hell erupted from my mouth.

I went for Phoenix's throat, while Chase went for Trace.

I didn't have time to think about what that meant. All I saw was blood — his blood — the blood I'd happily spill all over the floor.

My hands reached for his shirt. It tore as I ripped him away from the floor and threw him against the wall with so much force that a few pictures fell to the ground and shattered.

"I'll kill you for touching her," I spat, landing a blow to his stomach. "You low life..." I hit him again. "...piece of shit!"

With my left hand, I punched him in the jaw. Blood spewed from his mouth as he leaned into me. My knee met his face again and again. Bones cracked. I both felt and heard them.

Even if his body was found, they wouldn't be able to identify him. I'd make him unrecognizable then remove his teeth, fingernails, and every damn follicle of hair so they couldn't find his name — so he wouldn't have a burial. I'd send him to hell with bells on.

I reared back and pulled the dagger from my back pocket and jammed it into Phoenix's hand as he leaned against his own knees.

He screamed in pain.

Pain? I almost laughed. He had no idea the pain I was going to rain down on him.

I pulled the knife out just as Frank walked up beside me. Licking his lips, Frank nodded twice then mumbled, "Get a place ready."

The man who'd accompanied Frank ran out the door, phone pressed against his ear.

Phoenix slumped to the floor with a groan. I wiped the knife on my jeans and waited for Frank to assess the situation. After all, it wasn't just my honor at stake. It was his. Trace wasn't mine — as much as I wanted her to be. She was her grandfather's, so in the end, it was as much his call as it was Trace's.

"Your decision," Frank said in a cold voice.

"Hammer." I didn't even blink.

Frank looked behind me, disappeared for a few seconds, then returned with a hammer.

"You should close your eyes." I heard Chase whisper as Trace whimpered behind me.

Frank grabbed Phoenix's hands and tied his wrists together with zip ties I'm assuming he had snagged from the cupboard where we kept... toys.

"You look at her without asking? You lose an eye. You touch her with your dirty hands?" His accent came through thick in that moment, as if he was reverting to his roots.

"You lose your hands," I finished for him, noticing that Frank's entire body was shaking. That's why he'd said it was my call. Nobody carried out torture when they were that close to the situation. Which meant only one thing.

He still had no idea how deep my love was for Trace.

If there was anyone who shouldn't be carrying out the punishment, it would be me. Because Phoenix had touched mine. He'd attacked a girl who held a piece of my freaking soul.

And for that? I wouldn't offer forgiveness. I wouldn't allow him to repent. I'd destroy him.

I slammed the hammer down onto his right hand then his left, shattering his knuckles on contact.

I only stopped when Frank pushed me away from Phoenix. He'd passed out from the pain. And Trace, the love of my life...

Had passed out in Chase's arms.

CHAPTER FIFTY-TWO
Hammers are our friends.

Chase

"HELLO?" HER VOICE SOUNDED off.

"Trace?" I said her name slowly. "Are you okay? Nixon said you left class and— Are you crying?"

She hesitated. She never hesitated.

"No."

"But you texted 911. Usually that means you're either upset or someone called you a whore again..."

Her breathing was heavy.

"Trace?"

"Yeah?"

He was with her. He had to be.

"How hot is it in Arizona?" Arizona was our nickname for Phoenix.

"Scorching," she answered quickly.

"Shit." I hung up the phone and quickly traced her number. I'd put *Find a Friend* on both our phones so I could track her like the stalker bodyguard I was.

She was at the Batcave.

I sent the fastest text I could to Nixon and started to run.

My mind wouldn't stop replaying images of her eyes. Would Phoenix actually hurt her? Would he try anything? Would he dare touch a girl under my protection? Under Nixon's authority?

An eternity passed between the time Nixon and I met and when we tried to break down the door.

It had probably only been five minutes, but it felt like five years — five years of not knowing if she was breathing, if she had a gun pointed to her head, if she was afraid.

The door pushed open.

Phoenix was on her. His body pressed against hers in a way that made me want to cut off his balls, let him suffer for a day or two, and then shoot him in the foot, only to let him suffer longer, get a staph infection, and die.

Nixon yelled and charged toward him, but all I could see was Trace. I'd lusted after her for weeks, and now her shirt was ripped almost completely off, her skirt nearly gone. My stomach was sick. I could barely take a few steps toward her before I wanted to collapse onto the ground and sob against her chest.

No girl deserved that.

No girl asked for it.

And most girls never recovered.

I'd wanted to protect her from the ugly, but instead it seemed I was too late. I'd failed to protect her — I'd failed to do my duty. When it mattered the most. I. Had. Failed.

"Trace—" I whispered and pulled her into my arms, covering her with my jacket.

Her soft body trembled against me; her skin was freezing. I clutched her so tight my arms hurt. As Nixon beat the hell out of Phoenix, she sank harder and harder against me, like I was her everything.

Like I didn't just fail her.

"Hammer." Nixon's eyes met mine.

I nodded toward the cupboard. Frank went over and grabbed the hammer as well as a few zip ties.

The threats continued, but they were muffled to my ears — everything was. All I could focus on was her, and the fact that I never, ever wanted to see her hurt again.

I'd kill for her.

I'd die for her.

I'd go to prison for her.

Hell, if she told me she wanted to go to the moon, I'd find a way to take her there. I would do it. I wouldn't fail.

"You should close your eyes," I whispered.

Trace nodded and leaned her cheek against my chest. It was wet with tears. My entire body shook with anger.

If Nixon didn't kill Phoenix, I would.

And I'd enjoy every damn minute of it.

I rested my chin on her head and then, briefly, when everyone was focused on Phoenix's bloody mess, my lips touched her forehead.

I made a vow then and there.

Never again would she suffer or be afraid. I was going to take care of her. I was going to be the one to catch her tears. Even if that meant watching her be with Nixon. Even if it meant being on the outside desperately wanting to get in.

Failure wasn't an option.

Because — I protected those I loved.

And I loved her.

A sharp pain pierced my chest, and it's funny because all I could think was…. so that's what fear actually feels like.

CHAPTER FIFTY-THREE
Fixing the broken pieces

Nixon

"TRACE, LOOK AT ME."

She moaned and shook her head.

"Trace!" My voice took on a frantic note.

Her eyes finally fluttered open. "Trace, I need to…" Panic rose in my chest. "…I need to know if anything happened if he—" I swore, biting down on my lips to keep the sob in. This shouldn't have happened. I should have been there.

"No." Her voice was scratchy. "You guys came just in time." Her entire body started convulsing.

I snapped at Chase in Sicilian to let her go, that I was going to take over.

He shook his head no.

Frank stood next to me, speaking in the same language. "We shall take care of this now."

"Trace, baby girl, I—" Frank's eyes welled with tears. "I should have done better. I don't know what I would have done if Nixon and Chase—" He swallowed. "I can't lose you. Do you understand? I can't, Trace. You're my life."

Her smile was brave, shaky, but brave. "I'm not going anywhere, Grandpa."

He sighed in relief and stood. "Nixon, would you please stay with her?"

I couldn't hide my shock. What happened to him wanting to kill me?

Frank glanced over at Phoenix. He'd passed out from pain. "I'll have everything ready for your arrival... sir."

He called me *sir*.

All it had taken was his reason for living — almost dying.

I tried to hide my shock.

"Family sticks together," Frank said, shaking my hand.

"I'll protect this family until I breathe my last breath, to that I swear." My voice shook with meaning.

"I know that now." Frank's nostrils flared. "Tracey, I love you, sweet girl. Please listen to Nixon in my absence. I'll be only a phone call away, but as you can imagine, I have something to take care of."

Two men came into the room and lifted Phoenix into their arms.

"When you're ready." Frank slapped me on the back and walked off.

"Ready?" Trace asked, voice still hoarse from exertion.

I swallowed. "Ready to rub him out." I gave a dark chuckle. "Kill him, when I'm ready to end his life, Trace."

"Oh." Her eyes narrowed, like she was unsure that was the best course of action, but I'd never been more sure of anything in my life.

Trace struggled to her feet. I caught her and motioned for Chase to leave.

He hesitated, damn him.

I tried to remain calm. "Chase, you can go."

"But..." Chase licked his lips, his hands reaching for Trace.

Hell no.

RACHEL VAN DYKEN

Trace sighed and stepped into Chase's arms. Confused, I could only watch as the girl I loved thanked Chase and said she loved him.

Said the actual words, *"I love you."*

To my cousin.

My best friend.

With her back turned to me.

Unable to control my emotions, I closed my eyes, pulling from every ounce of strength I had.

"Love you too, Farm Girl." He pulled away and held her chin in his hand. "You call me if you need me, okay?"

She nodded as he walked out of the room.

The minute the door closed, Trace wobbled on her feet.

I picked her up and carried her to the bathroom

"No, please, no I just—" She fought against me.

I gently sat her on one of the wooden benches used for decoration in the bathroom and cupped her face. "Trace, look at me."

She squeezed her eyes shut.

My hurt felt like all the blood was getting drained out of me with a dull knife.

With tears streaming down her face, she opened one eye, then the other.

My eyes pooled with tears as I wiped her cheeks with my thumbs. "Thank God, I don't have experience in this sort of thing, but I figured you'd want to take a bath or shower or something."

She nodded and broke down into more sobs.

"You're beautiful, Trace," I murmured kissing her forehead. "And Phoenix is a monster. You know that, right? What he did — it's unforgiveable, and I promise you, I will make it right."

"By killing him?" she asked in a small voice.

Hell yes. I shook my head. Comfort, she needed comfort, not scary. "It's your call, sweetheart. I don't want to upset you more, but believe me when I say your family and mine won't let this slide without a severe punishment. We don't typically turn people over to the authorities, but if you want him to rot in a hell hole all his life, just say the word. I'll link his accounts to prostitution and a drug ring in five seconds. Hell, I'll frame him for murdering a politician. Just say the word."

She chewed her lower lip. Then, as if deciding that answer was good enough, lifted her arms into the air like she wanted me to help her undress, her facial expression fearful.

I'd die before I let her be afraid of my touch.

Her arms snaked around my neck. "Will you help me?"

I sighed. "Whatever you need. I'm here, Trace."

"You aren't going anywhere?"

"No."

"You aren't going to pretend to like me today and hate me tomorrow?"

"Hell no." My heart shattered. I'd made her doubt; that was all on me, but never again. Never again would she doubt my love. I'd end my own life before I ever made her doubt how much I loved her.

"You aren't going to say you love me and then take it back?" Her voice was thick with tears.

I jerked away from her. "Listen to me, because I don't want you to ever forget this."

Her body swayed a bit in my arms. "Remember what I said about making promises?"

She nodded.

"I promised, Trace. As a man, I promised your grandfather that nothing would happen to you. He believed the longer I was with you the sooner Phoenix would put the pieces together. He already blamed you for everything. If he saw us together..." I swore and looked down for a brief second before meeting her gaze again. "I had to make you believed me. I didn't know what else to do. I thought the day before, when we'd talked— Damn, Tracey, I thought you knew me better than that. I'll protect you until the day I die, even if it means I have to protect you from myself. Because in protecting you from me, I was protecting you from them."

"But you weren't."

"I know that now. And I'm not leaving, but Chase—"

"I love him too." She shrugged as if it really was that simple when I knew— Hell, Chase knew it wasn't. "He was there for me when you weren't."

"Do you love him like you love me?" I asked.

"Who said I loved you?" she fired back.

"You did."

"When?"

"That night when—"

She smirked.

"Glad to see you still have your sense of humor." I rolled my eyes and tried to shrug it off even when my heart was still going, *Holy shit, she doesn't love me?* "I'll understand if you're not ready. Shit, I don't even know if I'm ready, but Trace, I really want to kiss you."

She nodded. "First a bath. I don't want any part of him on me when you touch me."

I nodded and backed away as she stood in front of me. I gently helped her take off the jacket Chase had covered her up with. The minute the jacket was removed I saw bruising.

First on her stomach.

Then her neck.

Fingerprints.

"Son of a bitch!"

I closed my eyes and pinched the bridge of my nose. "Breaking his hands wasn't enough. Not by a long shot. I'm going to cut out his tongue and—"

"Can we not talk about him?"

"Sorry," I muttered, reaching for the spigot. I turned on the water then dumped some of Chase's girly bath-stuff into it.

Suddenly nervous, I rubbed the back of my neck. I slowly

turned her away from me, unzipped her skirt and watched it fall to the floor.

I examined her from head to toe, kissing every bruise, vowing to every scar that I'd end Phoenix's life.

When I was finished, I was so upset it was hard to speak. "I'll turn around while you get in. There should be enough bubbles too cover you up."

"And if there aren't?"

"Then I'll pretend like I can't see," I said through clenched teeth.

She peeled off the rest of her clothes and stepped into the tub. Her foot slid, causing a shriek to erupt from her lips.

I caught her before she collided with the tile.

Her breasts were pressed against my chest.

Worst timing in the world.

I wanted her.

But not after all that trauma. It wouldn't be right.

But I was still a man.

"You okay?" I asked, voice rough.

"Yeah, sorry. It was slippery." Her voice wavered.

I let out a groan and released her into the water, my eyes refusing to leave hers as she sunk beneath the bubbles. "Damn bubbles," I mumbled, taking a seat on the wood bench and running my fingers through my hair.

"You got something against bubbles?"

"Yeah. I do." I pointed at the tub. "They're practically kissing every naked part of your skin while I sit here and watch." I let out a dark laugh. "I had someone rip a nail from my finger once. This..." I swallowed and looked away. "...is so much worse."

"Because of the bubbles?" A smile formed across her lips.

"Yes, because of the damn bubbles. Are you done yet?" I twitched in my seat, damn-near needing to sit on my hands.

"I just got in."

I swore. "Right. Well, can't you... just... be faster?"

"I thought you wanted me to relax? I was just attacked."

I moved so fast I almost tripped and fell into the water. Within seconds, my hands were touching her skin. I dipped the loofa into the water and ran it over her broken body, my breathing so slow I felt like I was going to stop inhaling altogether and just pass out on the spot.

I washed her clean.

Washed him away.

"That feels good." She closed her eyes as my warm hands replaced the loofa and began massaging her neck and shoulders.

"Just so you know," I croaked, my hands still kneading into her flesh. "I've never had to practice so much restraint in all my life."

"It builds character," she mumbled, her eyes flickering open.

My hands froze as my gaze went to her chest. The same bubbles I'd been cursing minutes before had all but disappeared, giving me a perfect view of her breasts, her tight stomach. Shit. I was going to lose my mind. I pressed my lips together to keep from saying something I'd regret and managed not to kiss her.

"Sorry." She moved to cover herself.

"Don't be." I swallowed slowly so I wouldn't choke on the dryness. "Don't you ever apologize for being beautiful — for being perfect. You are..." I moved my hands to tilt her chin. "...exquisite."

She nodded and then burst into sobs.

"Trace." I wrapped my arms around her and lifted her out of the tub. Without speaking, I set her down then grabbed a towel and covered her body. She felt almost weightless as I carried her into one of the bedrooms.

I located a pair of sweats and a t-shirt and handed them to her. When she dropped the towel, I closed my eyes, unable to handle seeing her naked three times in the span of fifteen minutes without doing something.

Wet lips met my cheek.

I opened my eyes and scooped her into my arms. With a grunt, I tucked her into my body, pulled her onto the bed and held her while she cried.

"I won't let anything happen to you. I swear on my life, I'll protect you until the day I die," I whispered hoarsely.

"That's a pretty big promise."

"Well, you're a pretty important person. Important people deserve big promises, and you, Trace? You deserve the world."

She shook her head as if she didn't believe me.

With a curse I tugged her closer. "You deserve the white dress, Trace. And the flowers and the music. You deserve that first dance with your husband. The stars in his eyes when he sees you walking down the aisle. You deserve the castle and the prince. A man who adores you, a family who sacrifices for you, friends who take care of you. Trace — you deserve it, but you have to believe it."

She sniffled. "What if I just want you? What if I just want that one thing?"

"Damn it, Trace, I'm the one that doesn't deserve you. The messed-up part is I know it, but I want you anyway."

"Want?"

"Need," I croaked. "I need you like I need my heart to pump blood through my body, like I need air to breathe, like we need gravity. Hell, Trace, you are my gravity. Being with you makes me feel centered and whole, and I'm too screwed up to convince you to want any different. I'm too selfish to push you into someone else's arms when I know mine may be the worst ones for you to be in."

"But I want..." Her lower lip trembled. She bit down so hard it turned white. "I want you."

My breath hitched, and then my lips found her my neck. She leaned into me. I swore in Sicilian then gently pushed her onto her back. I didn't get on top of her; instead, I stayed by her side and continued raining kisses down her neck.

"Where did he touch you?" I asked.

"Huh?"

"Where?"

She pointed to a spot on her neck.

I kissed it whole again.

She pointed to another area on her arm.

I followed the same tedious process of making sure my kisses healed what his hands had destroyed. I was out to fuse the pieces he'd tried to break up and destroy.

"And here." She pointed to her mouth.

I smiled and then devoured — not kissed — her lips. My mouth covered hers as my tongue slipped past her lips and touched her own.

Her hands circled my neck, pulling me firmer against her.

Damn, but she felt so good, so right. After hesitating, I slowly moved so that I was hovering over her. My hands dove into her hair as I deepened the kiss, tasting her, drinking from her, reassuring myself that she was here, and she was all right. Her tongue flicked my lip ring. With a moan, I forced myself to stay in check.

My hands gripped her face as she arched beneath me.

I knew I needed to stop.

But I didn't want to.

I just wanted her to feel whole.

But I didn't have the right to give that back to her, and she didn't have the right to ask me to.

It wasn't something a person could take from you or something you could willingly give.

"You're killing me, Trace," I groaned against her neck. With another sigh, I pulled back. "And I'm probably going to hate myself later tonight for saying this, but after everything…" I shook my head. "…I can't… I can't—"

Ignoring me, she licked her lips and leaned forward.

"Ah, hell." My mouth crushed hers, our lips molding against one another, eager, hot. My body was on fire for her. With each nip and kiss, I fell a little harder, taking her with me.

Her hands moved to my shirt. I was just about to help her pull it off when a throat cleared.

I jerked away and snapped, "This better be good, Chase, or I'm going to strangle you."

Chase's eyes weren't even on me, but Trace. He looked hurt, disappointed, upset.

He blinked at her as if trying to figure out why she'd be with me and not him then clenched the sides of the doorframe until his knuckles went white.

"I just thought you should know that Mr. Alfero has everything set up and ready. Seems he was a bit over zealous about getting some of the men together. I didn't think you would want Phoenix to die without letting Trace have a crack."

"A crack?" Trace repeated.

"At Phoenix." Chase's smile didn't reach his eyes. "You do want to slap him, don't you? Because if you don't, I sure as hell will. Shit. I'll break both his legs for you."

"How are you?" Chase walked into the room.

I held up my hand for him to stop.

"She's fine," I answered for her. Teeth clenched as I narrowed my gaze on Chase.

"She can answer for herself," Chase argued. "Trace, I—"

I leapt off the bed. "I said she's fine. You aren't needed anymore. Alright? Text me the address, and we'll be there in a few. I've gotta get her some clothes to put on."

Chase's nostrils flared. "Maybe you should have been thinking about that before you started taking her clothes off."

Bastard! I lunged for Chase's body.

Trace scrambled off the bed. "Guys, stop!"

Chase reached for Trace, but I intervened, tucking her

into my arm.

"Sorry, Trace. I'm just… shit. I'm just a little messed up after seeing everything go down today." Chase looked at Trace, his eyes full of questions.

Trace suddenly pulled away from me, not enough for Chase to notice, but enough for me to know. She didn't want Chase to feel bad.

But she wasn't really choosing me.

Not yet.

Fresh raw pain sliced through me.

"Now what?" Trace asked.

"Now…" I sighed. "You decide if he lives or dies. Just know my vote is death."

"And if I want him to get punished but live?"

I didn't respond; instead, I released her and walked toward the door, finally giving her the answer she probably needed, but not one I was sure I could keep. "I'll try to listen."

CHAPTER FIFTY-FOUR
Endings aren't all fairytales.

Chase

I CLENCHED AND UNCLENCHED my fists as I made my way into the back room of the restaurant where we were meeting. Blood pounded through every vein, every vessel in my body, demanding vengeance. Almost as much as it demanded I rip Trace from Nixon's hands and run away with her.

I loved her.

And she didn't even know it.

I loved her.

And I'd almost lost her, yet I wasn't allowed to comfort her. I couldn't kiss away the pain, the tears, the shame — no, that was all my best friend. I hated him for it, almost as much as I hated myself for not being there when she'd needed me the most.

I sighed and leaned against the wall. Phoenix was sitting in the middle of the room, his ass strapped to a metal chair and zip ties keeping his hands firmly in front of him. We'd called a small commission. I say *small* because we hadn't had a big commission in over thirty years. Shit always went down at those, and we didn't want the drama.

A rep from each family was present, making their interest known. After all, we couldn't just wipe out his line — as much as I wanted to.

When Trace and Nixon walked in, Phoenix smirked, but it wasn't one of those smirks that said, *"Ha ha, fooled you all."* It was fake, forced, like he knew he was screwed and wanted me to shoot him in the face and ask questions later.

I was about to say something when Trace lunged for him and smacked him hard across the cheek.

He cursed and fell to the cement ground.

Well, that's a fun way to quiet up the room. The men sitting around immediately stopped drinking wine and stared.

"Is that it?" Phoenix taunted from the ground.

Trace lunged again, but Nixon grabbed her before her toe collide with the bastard's front tooth.

Frank cleared his throat. "Will all members of the commission please stand?"

"Commission?" Trace asked quietly.

Nixon pulled her close.

I had to look away.

"Each family is represented by one person. It's kind of how we hold court. Each person has a representative, and each representative gets a vote."

"Are you one?" Her voice quivered with fear.

"Unfortunately, no. Since I'm one of the bosses, I elected someone else from my family."

"Who?"

It was me. I heard him say my name, and I looked up to make eye contact with her. I would do right by her; it was the only thing I could do in this situation, other than kill him.

"Chase."

"Oh." She nodded, sagging against him. "That's good then."

"Great," Nixon said dryly as he glanced at me.

I'd been standing at the door for the past few minutes, observing.

"Everyone's present," Frank announced. "Each representative of the commission is allowed to speak on behalf of their family. I'll go last, considering the subject matter."

Several men nodded.

"I'll go first." Faust stepped forward. I'd hated that kid ever since he'd stole my toy truck when I was five. He was a made man for Nicolasi. "Trace, is it?"

Faust was a coldhearted bastard. Swear, when God created him, He'd forgotten to add a soul. He had dark coloring and brown hair. I'd always thought his eyes were soulless holes of nothingness, like he was possessed.

Nixon tensed next to Trace as the guy approached.

"Faust Assante, at your service." He gave a wide smile and bent over her hand.

Nixon grunted.

"Now." Faust stood to his full height and nodded to Trace. "Your side of the story, if you don't mind." He nodded. "When you're ready... Trace."

"My side?" she squeaked. "Does that mean even he gets to have a say?" She pointed a shaky finger at Phoenix. "After what he did to me? Well, Faust..." She damn-near hissed his name. "...my side is pretty much summed up in one word. Rape. That guy sitting over there beat me, bruised me, and then tried to rip my clothes off. When I said no, he said yes, when I pushed, he pushed back, so yeah, that's basically my side. He would have killed me had Chase and Nixon not intervened."

"You don't know that." Faust's eyes flashed. "After all, if what you're wearing now is any indication of what you wear on a day-to-day basis, I'd say you were a tease."

Holy shit! I was going to rip that prick's head from his body and use it as a kickball.

Nixon pushed Trace behind him and stood in front of

Faust. "You've got to be kidding me. Who the hell do you think you are?"

Faust smirked. "I am merely stating a fact. If a woman is asking for something and not careful, well, she will get exactly what she deserves."

Nixon swung hard and hit Faust across the jaw, sending him sailing to the ground.

Good thing he did because I was just about to.

"Anyone else care to tell Trace what she deserves? Be my guest." Nixon's breathing was ragged as he stood there and waited for someone to speak.

Frank and I moved to stand next to him. The rest of the men in the room shifted on their feet and looked at Trace.

Her hands started to shake. Damn it.

I moved behind her and put my arms around her body, much to Nixon's irritation, but he was busy. And I was done standing on the outside looking in. My girl needed me, and I sure as hell wasn't going to be silent about it. She relaxed in my arms immediately.

"I have something to say," I said slowly.

Every eye in the room was on me.

"I should have killed that bastard the minute I saw him on top of Trace. To be honest, the only reason I didn't was because I was saving the honor for her. So if anyone else has anything to say, say it now. We're just wasting time, and every breath that asshole breathes offends me so much that I want to crush his windpipe."

The rest of the commission whispered to one another and nodded their vote.

A man stepped forward. "We do not need to hear anything else. Mr. Alfero?"

Frank moved to stand in front of Phoenix. "You've hurt this family for the last time."

Phoenix smirked. "I seriously doubt that. After all, it's only a matter of time before they figure out who she is. And when they do, there won't be anything that can save you. Not your power, not your money, and not your name. They will come for you all. And I'll be smiling from hell."

Nixon handed Frank a bat.

Trace tensed beneath my arms.

He swung hard and hit Phoenix in the head, sending him to the ground with a grunt.

Frank turned, his eyes calm. "Your choice, Trace. Make the call."

Slowly, she pried herself free and approached Phoenix's limp form. Her booted foot connected between his legs. The bastard was already passed out, but he'd have a hell of a fun time when he woke up, if he woke up.

"He lives," she whispered, turning to Nixon. "Remember what you said about the whole setting him up thing?"

Nixon nodded once at her then at me. "Done."

Great. So basically I was going to have to set up Phoenix. Awesome. Just what I'd been wanting to do.

I held open my arms. Trace walked in to them and laid her head against my chest. I couldn't control my racing heart. I felt better just knowing she was in my arms, knowing right then I was doing my best to protect her from the world. "You should have let me kill him," I whispered.

"Sorry to ruin your fun," she mumbled.

I sighed. "Not fun. Just pleasure."

I put in a call to Dean De Lange. He needed to get his ass to the restaurant and fast. We chose to wait to call him until everyone had said what they needed to say.

I hated the man.

Hell, I think he hated himself. What made it worse was that I knew the shit he'd pulled with Phoenix. He deserved to be shot for what he'd put him through. He'd created a monster.

Dean De Lange walked in and swore. "Phoenix, what have you done?"

"Yes," Nixon sneered. "What have you done?"

Phoenix smirked, having woken up only minutes before his father's arrival. Blood stained his teeth where he had been punched repeatedly. "You think you can silence me?" He laughed. "Father, guess who our little Tracey is? You should know. After all, you killed her parents."

"What?" De Lange paled and gaped at his son. "What the hell are you talking about?"

"It's over. And I'm not stupid," Phoenix spat. "You set them up. I know everything, and now they do too."

"I didn't—" his father repeated, but his words were silenced, by the crack of a gun.

I ran toward him, my mind going a hundred miles a minute. Who pulled the trigger? When I turned around, I saw Frank with a gun in the air. Oh shit.

"It is over," Frank said hoarsely.

Phoenix laughed from his position on the ground, blood trailing down his chin. "Oh, it's far from over. You have any idea what you've just done?"

"Killed the man who murdered my son!" Frank yelled.

"I lied." Phoenix grinned. "And now you'll never know. By the way, congratulations on killing the one man standing in the way of making me the boss. You just bought me my freedom."

"Like hell he did!" Nixon stepped forward, but Frank held out his hand to stop him.

"War is coming," Faust said from the corner. He knew it, I knew it, we all knew it, and we were all witnesses to it.

My blood ran cold. We had fought so hard to protect Trace from the De Langes — hell, even from her own family.

I never once thought we'd have to protect her from them.

From the originals.

The ones who kept order.

I had a vision of Tex's father. Oh hell, that would be bad.

But what would be worse? If the Nicolasi family caught wind of our downfall, our involvement, because they'd been itching to rule the world ever since our family kicked them out of the country? Shit.

"The Sicilians are coming." Phoenix laughed from the ground.

"God help us all." I swore and pulled Trace from the room. I couldn't think, couldn't react, couldn't feel.

We were screwed.

And there was no way, no chance in hell we were all going to make it out alive.

Trace and I didn't speak the entire way back to campus.

Nixon was the boss, so he'd have to stay and help clean up... which probably meant putting her grandfather into hiding and begging the rest of the men to keep silent.

Which sure as hell wasn't going to happen with Phoenix as the new boss.

Because of what Frank had done, we could no longer control Phoenix; his birthright was to be head of that family, and he'd just freaking handed it over to him.

Trace finally spoke when we were safely in her room. "War? And the Sicilians?"

I swore and tried to think of a way to explain it to her that made it sound less scary than it actually was. "Our family — we've been in charge of keeping the peace for over a hundred years, Trace. Your grandfather just shot the De Lange mob boss in cold blood. Who the hell knows what's going to happen to Phoenix? We either have to kill him or buy his silence. You can't just go around shooting people."

"Yeah, got that part. But aren't you the Mafia? I mean—"

I said a few choice words and ran my hands through my hair, gripping the ends and giving a little tug. "Trace, listen, you clearly don't understand. You don't want the Sicilians here. Hell, I don't even want them in Sicily. If they come, and if they find out everything that's been happening. Shit!" I kicked the bed out of frustration, would have shot it too if I could get away with it.

"But they won't find out. I mean who's going to tell?"

Was she serious? "Trace, did you see all the men in there? Do you realize how desperate some of them are for money or to get on the good side of one of the originals? You can't control people, and you sure as hell can't keep them from looking out for themselves."

"What does this mean, for... for all of us?" she asked, collapsing onto the bed in a huff.

"It means we face them. Together," Nixon said from the door. One eye was turning black and blue, and blood ran down his chin.

"What happened?"

Nixon shook his head and winced. "Don't worry about it. Pack your stuff. You're leaving."

"Leaving?"

He ignored Trace and looked directly at me. "Get a bag?"

"Hold on one second!" Trace threw her hands into the air. "You can't just make me leave!"

"Trace..." Nixon pinched the bridge of his nose. "...your grandfather and I decided it's safer for you to be with me at all times. I can't exactly shimmy into your dorm at all hours without people finding out. It's just not safe."

"So I'm going to be a prisoner in my grandfather's home?"

"Of course not." Nixon smiled. "You're going to be a prisoner in mine."

A snort escaped before I could stop it.

"What was that?" Nixon snapped at me.

Bastard. Was this really the time to play house, asshole?

"Air." I coughed. "Found a bag." I handed Nixon the small duffel and saluted Trace. "Love ya, Trace. I'll be waiting at Nixon's. I think it's best if we all pow-wow together."

"Okay." She waved goodbye, dismissing me.

Just like that.

CHAPTER FIFTY-FIVE

Let me fight them for you.

Nixon

TRACE SAID GOODBYE TO Chase and turned toward me, inspecting my bloody lip. "You've lost your mind."

"Probably." I pulled her into my arms and sighed. "I can't lose you again."

She pressed her face against my chest and started crying softly. "I'm scared."

"I'll be scared with you," I murmured, repeating the words she'd told me when I was a little kid. "I'll be scared until you aren't scared anymore, okay?"

"Okay."

"And I'll save you from all of it, Trace. I promise."

"That's stupid." She laughed into my chest. "Boys can't save girls."

"You're right." I kissed her temple. "It's the other way around, because you saved me, Trace. You saved me when you were six, and you're saving me now."

"By doing what?"

"Staying alive... and allowing me to rescue you."

"Stupid girls. We always need rescuing."

"Stupid boys, we always jump at the chance to do it." I fought back tears of rage, tears of vengeance, tears of anger that my precious girl would have to endure the fires of hell at my hands. It was never supposed to be this way — never.

"I love you." She kissed my lips.

"I love you too." I kissed her back softly. "Now, let's pack. It looks like we'll have plenty of time to slumber-party in the next few months."

"Yay." She rolled her eyes.

"And..." I flashed a shameless grin. "...maybe we'll find some time to work on that whole goal you have before you die."

"What goal?" Her eyebrows puckered together in confusion.

"The goal." I eyed her up and down. "You know, about not dying a virgin."

"Ass." She tossed a pillow at my head and let out a breathless laugh.

"Hey, I'm just offering to help with the bucket list!"

Mo burst into the room. "Is it true?" She looked between me and Trace and back at me again, waiting for me to confirm the ugly truth.

I nodded.

She closed her eyes and let out a heavy sigh. "They're going to come for all of us."

"I know." I walked over to Mo and pulled her in for a hug. "But we'll be ready."

"Promise?"

"I promise." I held out my hand to Trace.

She wrapped it around mine and joined in on the hug.

Funny, on the first day of school the only thing I'd been able to think of was how the hell I was going to get the new girl out of my life.

And now?

Now, I was fighting like hell to keep her in it.

To keep her alive.

To keep my sister alive.

And to keep my best friend from taking away the one girl who had the power to change it all.

CHAPTER FIFTY-SIX
The final countdown

Chase

EVERY PERSON HAS A moment where time stands still.

I'd just experienced mine. The funny part? I'd almost missed it. It had been such a foreign feeling that I'd passed it off as having low blood sugar — being lethargic.

Legs heavy, breathing labored, I walked across campus toward my car.

The wind picked up, and a few leaves danced around the grass, swirling at my feet. I looked up.

She was walking toward me.

My heart slammed in my chest.

How was it possible that a person's mere presence could render me speechless?

Trace was wearing the boots I'd gotten her. She pulled her black leather jacket tight around her body and continued walking.

Where the hell was her security? I'd left her in Nixon's very capable hands for the past hour. And now she was alone.

"Hey," I called out, my voice low, hoarse.

"Hey."

Her smile lit up my world, just like everything else she did. I felt calm around her — like a cloud of peace had descended on the war raging inside of me.

Visions of betrayal danced in my head as I watched her breathe in and out, having no idea that just the fact that she was breathing in the same air I was... was pushing me over the edge, making me want to choose. Making me want to force her to choose.

Not that she had any idea there was a choice in the first place.

That was the part that sucked. She didn't know. She had no freaking idea that I was a man obsessed, deranged, sick for her.

"Where's Nixon?" I asked calmly.

"Oh he's picking me up in a few minutes." She rolled her eyes. "I had to go grab more comfortable shoes anyway."

"Are you saying my boots suck?" I pretended to be offended and offered her my arm.

Rolling her eyes, she looped her arm within mine and laughed. "No. Your boots rock. Come on, they're original Wyns!"

"Are you mocking me?"

"Depends. You in a teasing mood, or did you just get done shooting someone?"

I laughed. "Yes... and yes."

"Yes and yes?"

"I'm in a teasing mood." I tilted my head toward her and winked. "And I didn't just get done shooting someone, but it's entirely possible a knife was involved, lots of blood, boy violence, making a grown man cry — you know, a typical day in the life of Chase."

"Well..." She sighed. "...at least you aren't making girls cry."

"Aw, honey, if they're crying, I can guarantee it's not

because they're sad."

"Fear?" she guessed.

"Pleasure," I whispered, overstepping my boundaries. Scratch that — freaking jumping over the boundary and pulling her closer to my body so that we shared the same heat.

Her eyebrows shot up. "If Nixon see's you, he's going to threaten you again."

"Let me handle Nixon." All teasing had left my voice.

The smile fell from Trace's face. "Are you okay?"

No. I wasn't okay. I was in pain. My heart cracked against my chest, hurting like hell. "I'm always okay," I lied.

"Chase..." Trace reached out and cupped my cheek.

Her fingers scalded me — changed me from the inside out.

"...is it getting too hard for you? To be my personal bodyguard? Nixon said something about —"

Her voice died off.

"What did the boss say?" I wrapped my arm around her and forced a smile.

"That you..." She shook her head. "You know what? Never mind. We're friends, right?"

"The best of..." Another lie.

"Good." She let out a sigh. "Promise me something?"

"Anything."

"Don't ever leave without saying goodbye."

"Who says I'm leaving?" I stopped walking again and pulled her closer to me.

"It's just..." Her eyes focused on the ground as she shrugged. "I'm not sure. I just get this weird feeling when I'm around you, like you're five seconds away from losing it or just... leaving."

I loved her.

I loved her.

I loved her.

I wondered how long I could hold it back before I ruined

everything — before she was finally able to put the pieces of my giant-ass puzzle together.

"I'm not a jackass, Trace. I would never leave you defenseless, let alone without saying goodbye."

She exhaled. "Good."

"So what are you and Nixon gonna do?"

"It's a surprise." Her face lit up. "But I have a sneaking suspicion it has to do with self-defense, especially after the whole fiasco last week."

The fiasco, meaning her grandfather going into hiding and she having to move into Nixon's house of horrors.

"Ah, I see." Because, I really did.

"Anyway, it will be good to have some time alone."

"Yeah." I sighed.

Trace twirled a piece of hair around her finger, and that's when the second part of the moment happened, where I let my imagination run rampant with hope.

I spent more time with her than he did.

I loved her more. She just didn't know it.

I could protect her.

I could save her.

And in return — she'd save me.

Right? Isn't that how love worked?

She bit down on her bottom lip as she looked up at the dorm and put her hands on her hips.

I wondered if Nixon knew that was the stance she took when she was feeling lazy and not wanting to go up the stairs.

I wondered if he knew that every time she nibbled her lower lip it meant she was thinking.

I wondered if he was aware that Trace hated chipmunks but loved squirrels, or that she thought the color yellow was irritating, or that rain made her happy.

These were the things I knew — I knew them by heart just like I knew her scent, her favorite things. And I hated that, even though he knew less, he owned her in a way I probably never would.

"Well, I better go change." Trace interrupted my thoughts. "Thanks, Chase."

The slow-motion thing happened again — the moment I didn't pull back as she stood on her tiptoes and placed a kiss on my cheek.

A half inch. And our lips would have been touching.

I closed my eyes as her mouth lingered on my hot skin.

When she pulled back, I almost cursed Nixon to hell and pushed her up against the brick wall.

Instead, I let the moment pass.

The second moment.

The second moment in my time with Trace that I should have done something different.

As I walked away I realized that was all I'd been doing with her, walking in the opposite direction.

But things were about to change.

Because next time. I'd take full advantage, and Nixon would just have to fight. I'd make him fight, because I was tired of allowing him to win on default.

No more moments would pass — I wouldn't let them.

If he wanted her, he was going to have to prove he loved her more than life itself — because I already knew I did.

PREVIEW

EMBER
Eagle Elite Book 5

Ember: A small piece of burning coal. **Origin:** Old English, Germanic. Example: All it takes is a one tiny piece of Ember to start a flame, one small flame to burst forth into a fire. One spark, and a man's world may implode from the inside out.

PROLOGUE

Phoenix

"DO IT," MY FATHER spat. "Or I will."

I looked at the girl at my feet and back at my father. "No."

He lifted his hand above my head, I knew what was coming, knew it would hurt like hell but had no way to fight back—he'd already starved me of my food for the past three days for arguing, for trying to save the girl.

His fist hit my temple so hard that I fell to the ground with a cry. The click of his boots against the cement gave me the only warning I'd have as he reared back and kicked me in the ribs; over and over again he kicked. The girl screamed, but I stayed silent. Screaming didn't help, nothing did.

I waited until he was done—I prayed that he would kill me this time. I prayed so hard that I was convinced God was finally going to hear me and take me away from my hell. Anything was better than living, anything.

"You worthless—" Another kick to the head. "Piece of shit!" A kick to my gut. "You will never be boss, not if you cry every time you must do the hard thing!" Finally blessed darkness enveloped my line of vision.

I woke up from the nightmare screaming, not even realizing that I was safe, in my own bed. With a curse I checked the clock.

Three a.m.

Well, at least I'd only had one nightmare—that I'd remembered. I'd been living with Sergio for the past week, his house was so big that I basically took the East Wing and he took the West, said he'd hated living alone anyways. I wasn't stupid, I knew the guy wasn't exactly a big fan, but it worked, I needed to stay in the States while I figured shit out.

And I wasn't ready to leave. Not when I needed to learn all I could from Nixon. Not when I had responsibility.

"Hey!" Bee barged into my room.

"Damn it!" I pulled the blankets over my naked body, my heart picking up speed at her tousled hair and bedroom eyes. Tex's sister, Tex's sister. My body wasn't accepting that— physically it wasn't accepting any information other than she was beautiful.

And it was dark.

I looked away scowling.

"I heard screaming." Bee took a step forward, her perfume floating off of her body like an aphrodisiac or drug, making me calm, making me want something I had no business wanting.

"Yeah well." I gave her a cold glance. "Clearly I'm fine, so you should go. Actually, why are you here? You know you live with Tex right?"

She shrugged and sat on my bed. I clenched my fists around the blankets to keep from reaching out to her.

"He's with Mo, and they need privacy, I'm not stupid, so I asked Sergio if I could move in for a while."

"You did what?" I asked in a deadly tone.

She grinned. "I'm your new roomie!" Bee bounced on the bed and gave me a shy look beneath her dark lashes. "Admit it, you miss our slumber parties."

Forget the nightmare—I was looking at it.

CHAPTER ONE

Phoenix

IF THAT GIRL TEXTED me another picture of herself one more time I was going to lose my damn mind.

I drove like an insane asylum escapee back to Sergio's then speeded to a stop right in front of the gate, waiting impatiently for it to open, tapping my fingers harshly against the leather steering wheel of my Mercedes C class coupe. Another gift from Luca... I would have rather had his life, than the new car every guy on the planet was salivating over.

I wanted a lot of things.

But want didn't really belong in my vocabulary anymore.

The gate opened, slower than I would have liked since I was pissed off. I sped through the minute I saw an opening, not caring that I could possibly scratch the ridiculously expensive car and pulled to a stop right before hitting Bee.

"Damn it!" I threw open the door and slammed it as hard as I could. "What the hell are you doing?"

"You curse more now." Bee's eyebrows furrowed. "You know that?"

Yeah I was picking up bad habits where she was

concerned, really, freaking awful bad habits. "What do you want, Bee? And didn't we talk about the pictures? I don't have time to respond to pictures of goats and sheep and ugly dogs. I have a business to run, a family to protect..." My voice trailed as her face scrunched up with hurt.

"I just..." She shrugged. "Thought they would cheer you up."

"How is a turtle making it through traffic then causing a ten car pileup cheerful?" I challenged.

She smiled wide, hitting me square in the chest. "Because the turtle made it!" She danced around in front of me and clapped, then paused and arched her eyebrows in my direction.

"I'm not clapping."

"It's worth clapping for."

"Turtle power," I said through clenched teeth. "Now, was there anything else? You said something about an emergency?"

"Oh." She waved me off. "I need help picking out my first day of school outfit."

"Call a girl," I snapped, walking past her.

I felt warm fingers on my arm, and before I could jerk away, I was rendered completely paralyzed by her tender grasp. Shaking, I swallowed the terror and gave her a pointed look.

Her face fell but she didn't remove her hand. "I just... I heard they wear uniforms at Elite I just don't want to look stupid, I only have a few choices, I mean it's not a big deal, I just..."

Well, damn me to Hell. I sighed and hung my head. "Fine." I'll just try to ignore the way that the clothes hugged her body then when she was done twirling in front of me, I'd go puke in the bathroom and run ten miles to get the image out of my head. Sounded like the time of my life. Bring it on. After all, I deserved that type of torture, didn't I?

"Yay!" She clapped again then looped her arm in mine. "Thanks, Phoenix, I knew I could count on you."

Funny she should say that... after all, I wasn't that guy. The trustworthy one, the accountable one, the mature one. I may as well be a body without a soul. It's what I felt like most days and she did nothing but remind me... that I'd once had it all and lost it.

"Hey." Bee nudged me. "You look like you've seen a ghost."

"Every day in the mirror, Bee, every day."

"What?" Her smile fell.

I forced my own. "Nothing, let's go pick out shoes."

"Awesome!"

ACKNOWLEDGEMENTS

God is so good. Seriously. I get to wake up every day and do something I love… I get to jump into a world of organized crime and stay there for hours on end… I love my job and I know it's only because of Him that I'm able to do it.

I seriously have the best readers in the universe. You guys make this a fun and rewarding experience. I'm so blessed to have such a supportive group online!

My agent Erica, who saves me daily from losing my mind, thanks for encouraging me and ALWAYS being on my team!

I have two amazing publishers right now who are pretty incredible to be okay with me self publishing while I do other projects, Skyscape and Forever Romance, thank you for taking a chance on me and thanks for letting me be creative and write other series simultaneously! I know it's rare to be able to do that and I so appreciate it!

Inkslinger PR: Danielle, oh my gosh..seriously? You keep my head screwed on straight when it comes to book releases, Im pretty sure if we compiled all our emails into one giant book it would be hilarious, lots of exclamation points and all caps lol, mostly me freaking out, you being like it's okay it's okay!

Bloggers: I say this every time, but you guys rock my world. You're constantly supporting and encouraging indie authors and you don't get paid to do what you do. Its b/c you LOVE books and for that reason alone I'm forever in your debt. Thank you so much for posting, s haring, tweeting, reviewing, AH! You're amazing.

My editing and admin team: Laura, Kay, Jill, Becca, Jennifer, Liza, Kristin, Paula… um yeah you guys are simply irreplaceable… wait, that's a song right? :)

My ROCKING readers: you guys make me smile, every day.

I know I'm forgetting people. Just know that I love and appreciate all of you who help me on a daily basis!

HUGS,

RVD

OTHER BOOKS BY RACHEL VAN DYKEN

The Bet Series
The Bet (Forever Romance)
The Wager (Forever Romance)
The Dare

Eagle Elite
Elite (Forever Romance)
Elect (Forever Romance)
Entice
Elicit
Enforce
Ember

Seaside Series
Tear
Pull
Shatter
Forever
Fall
Strung
Eternal

Wallflower Trilogy
Waltzing with the Wallflower
Beguiling Bridget
Taming Wilde

London Fairy Tales
Upon a Midnight Dream
Whispered Music
The Wolf's Pursuit
When Ash Falls

Renwick House

The Ugly Duckling Debutante
The Seduction of Sebastian St. James
The Redemption of Lord Rawlings
An Unlikely Alliance
The Devil Duke Takes a Bride

Ruin Series

Ruin
Toxic
Fearless
Shame

Other Titles

The Parting Gift
Compromising Kessen
Savage Winter
Divine Uprising
Every Girl Does It

About the Author

Rachel Van Dyken is the *New York Times, Wall Street Journal,* and *USA Today* bestselling author of over 29 books. She is obsessed with all things Starbucks and makes her home in Idaho with her husband and two snoring boxers.